The Acquisitor

By Gene Stern

The Acquisitor

A Novel by Gene Stern

The Acquisitor

A Novel by Gene Stern

Chapter One

It was a typical mild sunny mid November day, not like the blustery cold weather that this region had experienced the past few days, quite unexpectedly. However, this day turned out to be a unique day of brilliant sunshine after that horrendous cold spell that seemed to have finally passed through the region. The sun was beating down on the light covering of fresh snow, which was on top of an already few inches that had fallen a few days ago, that had dropped just not twenty four hours ago, but even though the sun was piercing through the once troubled sky, it still had little effect on the white frozen tundra. Albeit, the welcomed sunshine was still not yet having an affect on the stubborn winter wonderland, but it did give some respite for the people who were milling around the scene this very day. Even though it was a brilliant but cold mid November day, it was the bleakest and most horrific known day in this county, in all of its 400 plus years since the fateful day of its inception and establishment. Detective Tom Royce had walked out of the old half dilapidated barn, walking nowhere in particular, as he was lingering without purpose, when he suddenly stopped dead cold in his tracks. He stopped not because someone stopped him, but because his rubbery legs would take him no further then where he stopped. His heavy footprints that were left in the hard packed snow, by him, were deep and lumbersome, as if he was walking with the weight of the world on his shoulders. He looked down at his hands, his weathered and tired hands, and then suddenly and unexpectedly, he fell down to his knees. He retched and heaved, immediately vomiting up the undigested portions from today's earlier meal, which at that time he had enjoyed with gusto. That was not the case at this time. He could observe the bits of bacon and eggs that he had devoured earlier, but now that very enjoyment had become his undoing. He retched until his stomach could bring nothing else up, and still he dry heaved another minute or so, but nothing more came out of his belly. He just couldn't believe it! He raised his hands in the air, hoping to make some type of sense of this entire ordeal, but his mind was swirling in so many directions that he had nothing he could unload into the realm of making any type of sense. Where did he go wrong? Could he truly have prevented this? Why hadn't he prevented this? As with anyone in this type of situation, he blamed himself for not finding out earlier, for not seeing the now obvious signs, no matter how opaque and vague they were before him. It was his job, his duty, to protect and serve, and he had utterly failed this community. He heard someone else behind him retching as well from the horrific sight that they had stumbled upon, and sadly enough he had no words of encouragement for that distressed officer either, so he let that fresh recruit suffer on their own. He remained, steadfast, on his cold knees as his mind continued to try to make sense of it all, of anything, and yet still of nothing, as ideas and thoughts were stretched throughout his burdened mind. His knees were cold, his hands were cold, his face was chilly, but his heart was consumed with emotion, and his mind was a chaotic storm of unprocessed thoughts and fears. Were there more than what they had just found? God, I hope not, he hoped silently to himself! He finally stood up and slowly walked over to his patrol car, and he sat right on the hood of the car, not caring what marks or even how cold it was. He needed only to get off his still wobbly legs and support his full weight as everything pressed down on him more and more, so that he could try to make some semblance of sensibility to himself, or at least that was what he wished for. He heard retching from the other officer and maybe more officers as well, and that was when he realized that even one of the EMT's that were close by also had a weak stomach. One of his fellow officers, Linda, was pale faced and looked as if she were going to pass out, and that was when he suddenly realized that she was holding her breath, to not take in the smell that seemed to barrage their olfactory senses, since finding the discovery. He mentioned with a stern and still empathetic voice;

"Linda…….. breathe, sweetie, please take a breath….!" Instantly, Linda looked over as if she hadn't even realized that she was holding her breath, and she finally exhaled fully and then took a deep inhale, nearly choking on all the air she was taking in, but at least her color came back to her face and she presented better than just a minute ago. She needed something to do, something that she could do from her vehicle and get away from what they both just saw. So, he asked her, kindly, to contact the coroner, and to go have a seat while doing this. She shook her head in both acknowledgement and also to thank him for asking her to do such a mundane request. Still, she first pulled out a cigarette, and with visibly tremoring hands, she brought the pack to bare, tapped on the back of the pack, dropping one cig out. She, unfortunately, missed the catch in her distraught state and so the first one fell lazily to the ground. She tapped the back of the pack a little lighter this time and one came out far enough for her trembling hands to grasp. She then slowly placed the cig up to her lips, as her hands continued to tremor, nearly uncontrollably. She fumbled with her lighter, trying to get the stupid plastic piece of crap to light, but she just couldn't. Tom walked over toward her, and gently grasped her hand with the lighter, slowly took possession of the lighter and he was able to obtain a flame for her. She leaned into the flame so as the cigarette touched flame, becoming lit, it was then that she took a few deep inhales, which ignited the parchment paper even more. Then she was full on smoking her cig with fervent vigor, trying to forget what she had seen. She tipped her head at him, acknowledging and thanking him for his gentle and kind assistance. Tom hadn't touched a cigarette, himself, in over a month, but he looked at her and without saying a word, she tapped the pack once more for him. Out dropped a slim cigarette, but this time it wasn't for her, but for her coworker. He took the cig and put it to his own lips, and he ignited his smoke as well, with ease, and took a long drag from an old welcome friend at this point. It felt like a guilty sinful pleasure to him as he took it in, and then he exhaled to the side a long exhale, forcing out the cloud of smoke in a quasi ring pattern. He looked at Linda and gave her a gentle reassuring smile and a warm embrace, and she responded likewise from his kindness, and then she turned to do what he had asked of her. Tom called out to her, in a quiet voice, as a reminder;

"Linda, I am …..sorry….. this……. happened……. Well…… the way we found….it…, but we will get through this." She nodded her head solemnly, but she did not believe the reassuring words that he had just spoken to her. Still even though his words were meant to be positive and supportive, nothing he, nor anyone could say could make this day any less bleak. Tom continued to puff away on his cigarette, now standing all alone, between the police vehicles, looking for guidance from anyone or anything as to what he should do now. Did he really make a difference, he thought with a grave conviction? Did anything really matter anymore, especially after something like this? Nothing he could do or say could ever take away from the severity of this horrific tragedy. Nothing at all! No matter what, sadly, he still had a job to do, and for the first time in his life, he didn't know where to start or what to do to make this any better or to even try to start wrapping this up. There were too many questions! The

5

heinous deeds were done, and he couldn't turn back time. People had died, grotesque crimes were committed, and innocence was not just lost but completely obliterated from this gentle earth! Yet still, he had no explainable answers, nothing that could help him or even his officers, process any of this. He might even have to call in some grief counselors for anyone who will be permanently affected by this ordeal, which meant not only the responders, but the families as well. Any normal person would experience grief, disbelief, and sympathy toward the victims, and even the victim's families, once recognition were obtained from the remnants that they had. So many bodies, so much carnage, and also so much blatant hatred......... The images would not leave his mind, those dreadful images! It was as if this place, not that he was a devout religious person, just had a wickedness or a dank heaviness about it, almost as if this place was just pure evil, if that was even possible. And yet, he remained standing there until his cig was down to a mere nub, enjoying every inhale of his borrowed cancerous stick. Once done, he dropped the nub in the snow, and the discarded ember extinguished quickly, leaving a slight hole in the frozen tundra. He then placed his cold hands in his pockets and thought it might be a good time to grab a few pairs of gloves. This was going to be a long day and a long night, that was for sure. They were going to need extra lights, heaters, probably a tent, maybe a canopy or two, and maybe even some food brought in, if people could stomach it. He knew that he needed to start calling other people to get things rolling, but as of now, no one besides his crew knew anything. That was all going to change and it was going to change very soon. He started making plans as he went to his vehicle to grab his gloves for his already cold hands. Why did this have to happen, he thought once more, as he retrieved his warm gloves out of his still running vehicle. This had to be the worst day of his life, no question about it........ The worst day of his life!

Chapter Two

It was a beautiful late spring day as summer was right around the corner, some five months prior, and the community of Glen Fork was bustling with activity and visitors from all over the country. They came to enjoy nature and what the area had to offer. Glen Fork was a larger community just north of the Blue Ridge mountains of northern Georgia and southwestern North Carolina. Most of the community was in North Carolina, but there were many that lived in Georgia. The town name remained the same for both states, just different addresses and different zip codes. There were so many towns from different states with the same names, just none that were side by side and with both their own entity in a way. It was a true split town between two states, something not seen before. Each town had its own council, its own state budget, but they also combined their monies at times to help pay for projects and needs that each needed. It seemed to be the best of both worlds, that was for sure. It hadn't always been that way, because in the past this town had been divided and of course politicians had divided it before also. Still over time they were able to disperse the quarrels and start living as a joint and not as two separate communities. The internal revenue service of the government hated this town for this reason, but in the end and after four hundred some years, it came together. The recent mayors and councils had a good hand in that as they worked together to make it better for the people, instead of being divided by imposition. It was working, and best of all it was possible.

The summer heat hadn't set in yet, so the mornings were still a perfect brisk temperature and the evenings were mildly cooler, while the midday was a tolerable temperature to be outside in. Any day now, that would change though as the summer was pressing in so very close now. The song birds were singing their usual songs with melodious harmony as they flew to and fro collecting berries, seeds, and whatever else struck their fancy for their meals. They also found the occasional debris for making their nests for upcoming hatchlings, which would be soon considered that mating season was already starting to occur. Winged insects of all known orders hastily buzzed around the flowers and newly blooming plants to catch any nectar that they could to feed off of, to sustain their daily activity and expenditure of energy. It was the type of day where one could get lost in the forest and not regret it, because all that mother nature had to offer was alive and thriving, starting the cyclic circle of life as happens every spring. And so it was, just as nature came alive once more, so did the town and the people who live amongst the community as well. It had been an unusually and particularly cold winter, with many days of frigid weather and many inches of snow, which were welcomed by some and frowned upon by others. Happily those wintery mix days were gone, and those who remained indoors most of the colder months were finally able to be sprung from their household tombs. The day was grand indeed as children ran around frolicking through the green grasses playing their games, and even the local canines were out in numbers, leading their owners to their favorite spots to leave their marks and interact by sniffing one another intently. The smell of freshly cut grass and backyard barbecues also lingered in the air, enticing passerbyers as they felt led by their olfactory senses, which in turn produced the salivary glands to work overtime at the thought of securing a tasty bite of grilled food. It was a lovely time and one that was beheld by all in the community, both residents and visitors alike. Loaded up trucks with their boats and trailers could be seen clogging the roadways and local gas stations as they tried to get their vessels into the water, to enjoy every ounce of this spring weather. Fishing was a large part of the direct and indirect income for this area as well, as both local and not so local fishermen flocked to catch the wild and stocked farm raised trout and bass. Bait stores were booming with business as they stocked all the fishermen who had to have the latest and greatest reels, rods, and bait to stock their personal supply. The local restaurants also brought in good money as those who were hungry, whether it be locals or non residents flocked for the good southern cooking that was known to this area. All these activities were well within a two hour drive of the nice size community. The busy season had officially started and now was a welcome influx of money to the area. Spring had sprung which would lead into the busy summer as well.

Detective Tom Royce was tired of doing paperwork and therefore decided to go out and enjoy the pleasing weather, just as so many of the officers have done thus far in their precinct. He passed Officer Pine on his way out, and he stopped and chatted some with Jeremy to see how his family was doing. He had known Jeremy for some time, and had even met his wife and children, so he was well acquainted with the Pine family. He also asked him how his ailing grandfather was doing with the ongoing breathing problems, as what comes with fifty plus years of smoking. Eventually it all catches up with you, he thought grimly, thinking about his own weakness to the guilty pleasure of puffing a cigarette once in a while(or moreso which was the case for the most part). After chatting for some time, Tom finished his walk out of the building, stepped outside, and stopped immediately, looking straight up into the radiant sunlight basking in the glory of the outdoors(which he loved so dearly since he was a child). The sunshine warmed his face and he gushed with exuberance at the feeling, never forgetting it from his younger years. He had always been into sports and just being outside, being one with nature and enjoying what he could, and he continued that to this day, well at least what he could given his work schedule. Suddenly, he heard his cell phone give an alert and he immediately reached for it in his back pocket. He pulled it out with the phone making the alert noise, as there was an amber alert from the neighboring county of a missing teenager. He cut the noise off first and then looked at the message and it read that a child the age of sixteen years old named Jade Freely, went missing over four plus weeks ago from a neighboring town. It states that she was last seen wearing cutoff jean shorts, cowboy boots, a plaid button down shirt, and a white tank top. She was last seen in the Dade County area (one of the adjacent counties), but to be on the lookout. He took a look at the photo of the young girl and also took a screenshot of it, for him to remember better. What a shame he thought, another young girl probably upset with her parents running off with a girlfriend or a boyfriend, and not wanting her parents to know or find out about it. He had seen it happen so many times, and sadly this wasn't the first one that went missing and they had never found or had a cold trail as to the child's whereabouts. Most assumed they found their way to the larger city, such as Atlanta or even further away in all directions and all over the country, but those were only his assumptions and not definitive proof. Yet, teens disappear every year by the droves, and as sad as it was, it seemed like they were always fighting an uphill battle as to finding them again, returning them to their families, or not just finding them but also finding them alive. It was a sad and dim reality to an ongoing problem, which no one seemed to have an answer to.

He was so caught up in his thoughts that he hadn't even realized that he was half way down the street, heading in a direction he had no idea and to what destination, he had no clue. He laughed at his spaciness and his ability to be present, but not present at the same time......it was truly a gift. He walked a few more steps and then entered a deli shop, to maybe pick up a small meal and see what struck his fancy. He looked straight up at the menu, without even looking at the workers behind the counter. He found what he wanted as the counter clerk waited for his attention to be drawn away from the menu. He had been here many times before, but today...yes today...he wanted something different than his usual lunchtime snack. Finally he looked down and saw a familiar face glaring back at him, and then he sheepishly was about to chat to the older man, who stood there with a furrowed brow looking at him and a puzzled expression. The old man piped up first however, by saying;

"Well Tommy boy, what will it be today? The usual?"

"I dunno Frank, I am thinking of trying something new today, whatcha think my friend?"

"Well you already seem to be somewhat offset by something, as you came in and didn't even acknowledge me like you normally do. Something got your griddle cooking uneven?" Tom smiled at the odd reference, because it was quite common for Frank to come up with the quirkiest, funniest, and most unusual lines, metaphors, or statements than anyone he had ever known. It was quite a gift that Frank possessed, as Tom was not quite that fast with the wit as Frank had always been.

"Well, my friend, you are right, I reckon I just have some things on my mind and therefore I am sorry for ignoring you. It wasn't intentional at all. Thank you for calling me out on it."

"Well sure, that's what friends are for.....you know that....anyway, so what would you like to try today?" Tom looked back up and suddenly he came up with the brilliant idea of this monster of a sandwich. He answered with;

"You know what, Frank, I think I will try the dagwood sandwich, a small bag of the barbeque potato chips, and a small sweet tea..... To go please, by the way!"

"As you wish, and off he scuttled around the back, now with his back turned to Tom, busily trying to prepare the sandwich for his old friend. Frank started slicing the bread from one of the huge loaves that he had made earlier that day, and then slowly started building up the sandwich to his liking. He stopped once to grab a glass, fill up the sweet tea from the large vat of freshly made tea and then handed it to him. Tom thanked him and took a long drink from the plastic cup that had been filled to the brim with the delicious handmade teas. So delightfully sweet, refreshing, and satisfying this succulent drink was to him, that he barely stopped to take a breath as he nearly downed half the drink in one large pull. He smacked his lips with exuberance and then placed the cup back down to take a breather, as he continued to watch Fred working on his meal preparation. Fred had just got done stacking the sandwich to his specifications, and then he used a large knife, cutting through the sandwich with ease and perfection, making two perfectly stacked sandwiches. He used the sandwich covering paper available to him, wrapped the sandwich up carefully, and paper bagged the scrumptious looking meal with delicate precision. He then turned back to his awaiting customer and then gently placed the bagged sandwich down on the counter. He turned somewhat to his side and grabbed the requested bag of chips as per his friend's request and also placed them in the bag also. He gently grabbed the partially drunk drink cup once more, refilling it and placing a lid on the cup so that Tom could take it with him. Frank then nodded at his friend, as Tom spoke up asking the stout man behind the counter;

"So what's the damage, buddy?"

"That will be $12.50." Was the response by Frank. Tom pulled out a $10 and a $5 dollar bill and instructed his friend to keep the change. Then he collected his food and went outside back into the gorgeous weather. He walked a little further until he found an empty park bench in the downtown area called Veteran's Park. He selectively sat down on a clean looking bench with his delightful eats and his refreshing drink. He made himself a little nook to enjoy his lunch, just the way he wanted to and set up everything, while listening to the sounds of nature, even here in the middle of the town, where there was this small reprieve.

He pulled up his bag, pulled out the chips first and opened them up. A strong wind blew by and tried to remove the chips from his bench, but he adeptly caught them and saved most of them from an untimely loss. He then secured them with the edge of his cup as he pulled out the sandwich to check it out. He had never tried the dagwood and he was rather interested in seeing if it was as good as it looked to him. He unraveled the paper from his sandwich, and slowly inspected the deliciously stacked deli meal. After a close inspection and then a sniff of the delightfully pleasing delicatessen, he finally opened his maw and sank his teeth into the hopefully tasty morsel. Biting down, he tasted every different meat and texture in the sandwich with one large mouthful. 'Oh my goodness', he thought as he started masticating his meal, this was orgasmic, in relation to the taste of this well made and satiable food. This was wonderful, he thought, as he continued trying to chew his meal. He stopped, took a sip of sweet tea, and then resumed devouring his first large bite. He continued bite after bite until the sandwich was gone, except for a few wayward crumbs and a loose pickel, which he snatched up quickly and ate that as well with gusto. He took another long pull of his sweet tea, till he was nearly halfway through it. He turned back to the bag of chips, but only after securing the already nearly empty bag as the wind had picked up once more. He stuck his hand inside the bag of chips and eagerly ate this delicious version of his favorite chips, enjoying each crunchy nibble and broken pieces. It wasn't long before all that was left were simply crumbs, in the bottom of the bag. He gave up on trying to get them, and that was when his meal had gained the attention of some local songbirds who were scrounging around for food near him. He turned, stood up, and walked a few steps to a spot to dump out the remnants of the chips, so that the birds may enjoy a little meal. It didn't take long for the feathered friends to swoop down and start pecking at the ground where he had released the crumbs to them. The feathered friends finished up the pieces in no time, with some flying away to enjoy their snack on their own terms. So he went back over and sat back down on the bench and finished up his sweet tea, one lovely sip at a time. It was such a lovely day, and he couldn't ask for better weather, when all of a sudden his radio jumped to life with the voice of the daytime dispatcher.

"A.P.B.: Missing young adult, 16 year old female, named Teresa, Last seen 24 plus hours ago around the Middle School playground area, wearing jean shorts, white t-shirt, sneakers, and with her skateboard with her. Further information pending." Oh great, he thought, another young adult goes missing. He finished placing his trash in the bag, and started walking back toward the station, making sure to properly dispose of his trash at one of the park trash receptacles he passed along the way. He hurried back at a more rapid pace than the leisurely pace that he had come there with. He started going over where to start looking for the child, which would probably be checking in with the parents, then friends, and whomever had seen poor Teresa last. He was formulating a plan and what he needed to do. Twenty four hours wasn't a long time for a young adult, but he also knew how devastating and frustrating it can be for parents to not know where their little girl had gone. This sadly wasn't the first missing person in the past year, but it was not something he could ever get used to. He had a grown college-aged daughter, so he could empathize with the parents and what they must be going through at this time. He had to be both direct, tactful, but also compassionate if they were going to help him out and answer the questions he would have for them. His wife, when she had been alive, had always told him he could be more compassionate than what he was, but he never seemed to listen, that is until she had passed from this world. He had a brief moment of sadness as he thought of his late wife, Jeanine, and the struggle that she had been through, all those months of treatment for her affliction that she had persevered. Such an amazing woman she is....was he thought, no he corrected his mind, she still is. She will always live deep inside his heart, his mind, his soul, and he would never love another woman like he loved her! It just wasn't possible for that much luck, that he knew and always said, because very rarely one strikes gold twice in a lifetime, so he remained single and dedicated himself to his work since her passing. He will always love her, no matter what and with that thought he smiled genuinely at the remembrance of her facial features, her million dollar smile, her crazy gorgeous red hair, and her genuine and lovely demeanor. He was so happy for the time he had with her, even though it was never enough(from his perspective), but he was always grateful for even a minute of knowing and being able to love her. He had been so preoccupied with his thoughts of his darling late wife, that he didn't realize that he walked the entire way back and had even entered the building once again to grab some things before heading out. He stopped by to ask Darla a question, before heading out, and said;

"Hey Darla, anyone looking into the missing girl yet?"

"Nope, you are the first to inquire or respond at this time, Tom."

"Ok, well I'll check it out from here. Could you send me all the info that you have and I'll grab what I can from it!

"Already done, sweetie, so I'll mark you as the primary officer on this one(she said while typing and not even looking up at him). Then after a few seconds, she was done typing, and she started once more;

"Ok, you got it, love, your new assignment. Thank you."

"Thank you, too, kind Darla." and with that he went out her door and back out to the gorgeous outside weather again. Such a beautiful day, he thought to himself momentarily. Such a beautiful day, indeed, he thought again as the rays of sun beat down on him while he crossed the parking lot to his parked vehicle. He opened his door, just then officer Craig Foley drove up and parked his vehicle right beside him. He looked over and shot Craig a smile, and Craig gave him the middle finger. This was the game they played as coworkers and friends, antagonizing one another. He just laughed at his buddy getting one up on him and catching him off guard. He waved and yelled out to him;

"Some of us have to go work, unlike some slackers, I know......!" Craig rolled his eyes and went back to exiting his vehicle, grabbing his gear as he went. Tom pulled out in his vehicle and started slowly rolling in the direction of Craig, who had his hands full as he headed toward the building. Just as he had passed by, Tom slowly drove by and laid on the horn, causing Craig to jump unexpectedly and drop a few things that he had in his overly full hands. Craig looked over at his friend and shook his head at Tom as he rolled by, heading out of the parking lot. He heard Craig in the distance yell out;

"This is far from over, my friend, ….far from o…v…..!." The last word trailed off as Tom drove off down the road heading toward Teresa's parents' home address to hopefully have an informational chat with them about their daughter.

The drive was short as he made his way down a few streets, then a few side roads, and then down an older gravel road. He was driving beside a gorgeous stream, which was nice to view as he made his way closer to the parents' house.Finally he came upon a group of mailboxes and one by one, he saw the house number he was looking for. He turned and continued down the short paved road, toward the trailer park that this area encompassed. He drove until he found the house number on the siding of their domicile. He had driven nearly past it, so he had to check his mirrors and back up some to get back into the driveway area, which was just to the right of the home. He stopped , parked, and then checked over his information first before exiting his vehicle with a notebook to take notes with, for his full report. He looked around and saw a few places that seemed deserted as they were in a bad state of disrepair. It was as if the owner of the area didn't care anymore and just let things go, sadly, for those who still lived there. He turned his attention back to the mobile home in front of him, and this one seemed to be the nicest one in the small neighborhood. It has a fenced in yard, an entrance overhead trellis, which had a nice amount of a vine plant of some type, and that vine continued along the upper part of the fence for what looked like halfway around the home. He walked with purpose toward the front door, and that was when he made it to the small front porch of the mobile home. He climbed the stairs easily and stood in front of the closed door. He could hear the window air conditioning units (two within eyesight) running, trying to keep the home at a comfortable temperature for the occupants within. It wasn't that warm out, but he was sure the home became stifling once the full sun hit it everyday. He raised his hand and knocked on the front door, and then patiently waited for a response. He could hear a loud television playing also inside the home, so he knocked once more, this time a little firmer to see if someone would hear him now. The television then was either put on mute or turned down and he heard yelling from inside the home, which sounded like this;

"Hey, honey, are you expecting anyone?"

"No, dear, I am not…."

"Well better get my shotgun just in case.." It was at this time after hearing the last statement from the male voice that, he spoke up loudly saying;

"This is Detective Royce of the Glen Fork Police Department, trying to get a hold of the parents of Teresa Astel!" It was after the last statement that the door finally opened and before him stood a middle aged gruffy looking man, with the look of not sleeping much as he had dark circles under his eyes. Tom looked down at his notebook and then he looked back up, asking the man in front of him;

"Excuse me sir, but are you Blain Astel?"

"Yes, sir that be me, what can I do ya fer? Did ya find our little girl?"

"Well, I am here to take a statement and gather information regarding the disappearance of your daughter....... If that would be ok with you?" Blain easily relaxed somewhat, and then responded with;

"I am sorry, I work the night shift and haven't slept at all today, worrying about our girl. Thank you for coming and please, do come in." With that he opened the door and Tom walked inside the home, and just as he entered a petite female came around the corner and nervously walked over to the counter to put some laundry down, that she must have been folding just before he had arrived. Blain motioned for Tom to go over to the couch, but Tom instead motioned toward the kitchen table and wood chairs that were in sight, instead of the relaxing sofa. It was just easier to take notes when sitting someplace more appropriate, he thought to himself. Both Blain and Lorie sat down across from him at the table and waited for him to say something. He didn't at first as he tried to find his pen that he had brought with him, but alas he couldn't figure out which pocket he had placed it in. Just as he was about to give up and ask for a writing utensil, he finally felt the outline of his pen in his one chest pocket that he had missed when he first felt for it. He brought the pen out, opened his notebook again and looked at both Blain and Lorie. Blain, like he thought originally, just looked rough, not in the sense that he didn't take care of himself, but that the night shift was wearing on him, or that his missing daughter was wearing on him. He had a small amount of extra weight on him, but he appeared to keep himself in average shape for his age. Lorie, on the other hand, looked well presented and probably was about eight to ten years younger than Blain, and was a very attractive woman with a well maintained weight. She had a grace about her as she walked and sat down, like she floated across the floor with ease. She was peering at him with concerned eyes as she probably was doing some keep busy tasks and chores, just to

15

remain sane and not to stress herself out so much. He had seen this before, what people do when the unknown is going on around them and they have no control over the circumstances whatsoever. After making a quick assessment of whom he was going to converse with, that he started asking them;

"Well, I am here to get any type of information I can get from you that may help out in the investigation of your missing daughter. Have you called everyone you can think of to see if she was at someone's house?" The immediate look he got was like he was an idiot asking such a question, but then he resumed with;

"I realize you may have already done so, but I am just making sure, that is all." With that both Blain and Lorie looked at each other for a few seconds, as if they were telekinetically asking one another the same question he had asked, but then Lorie looked over at him and said;

"Yes sir, we called everyone we could think of, but no one seems to have an answer for us." Tom nodded his appreciation of her response and then continued asking questions;

"Ok when was the last time that either of you saw your daughter? I was told it was twenty four hours, is that correct?"

"Well", Blaine responded firstly, " I saw her last not yesterday afternoon, as my wife had last seen her, but I saw her last that morning, after I had come home from being at work. I just saw her leaving for the day, as I tried to get some sleep." He looked over at his wife, waiting for her to answer then. She looked over at Tom with some tears streaking down her face, and she started to say with a shaken and distressed voice;

"Well….I …saw….um…… Her… last, yesterday afternoon, say ….around…….. 2 pm …..in ….the…. afternoon." She said with a shaky voice and also while looking up at the clock on the wall, as if she was trying to get some kind of affirmation of her unsurity. Tom noted the guess-timation in his notes and continued to listen to what they had to say. They were definitely shaken by this development, and they seemed to be worried about their daughter, so he ruled out, pretty quickly, foul play by the parents, but still he had to get something more to go on. The dad continued talking about what a good girl she is and how she loved being outside and on her skateboard. She mostly went by herself, but occasionally she would meet up with a small group of skaters, but she never brought them back home for the parents to meet her friends, he confessed to Tom. The parents continued talking for a few more minutes and then they were finished.

Tom then had to ask a few hard questions, which always hurt to hear but they were ones that had to be answered in some form. He started off with the least threatening;

"So have there been any troubles at home?" He asked plainly.

"What do you mean?" Blain responded with a puzzling look. Ok, this was it, thought Tom to himself.

"Has there or is there any history of abuse?" There was a look of shock at first, then which triggered some angry looks, but then just before Blain blew up with something that he would wish he hadn't said, Lori piped in to save her husband from getting in trouble, by saying;

"No, sir, she was well loved with no history of physical or mental abuse, by anyone in the family. That is the honest to God's truth." Tom was happy for that and Blain seemed to still be perturbed but he kept his tongue about him, for now. Tom spoke frankly before continuing with any more questions;

"Sorry these questions have to be asked, but I have to know everything to better find your child. I mean no disrespect whatsoever to either of you, just so you know." He paused for a few seconds to let those words sink in, and then he continued;

"So she was well loved and therefore doesn't seem to have a need to run away, so has she ever done this before?"

"No, sir." Lori once more responded instead of her husband.

"Ok, well did she have a boyfriend?"

"Not that we were well aware of, or at least we never met him?"

"Was your daughter sexually active?" He paused for a brief moment………. "Again I am sorry but this could be related to a motive, so that is why I am asking." He said that just as Blain looked about to blow his top once again. Lori placed her hand on her husband's arm and asked him something and so he left the room to head outside, after grabbing a pack of his smokes. Lorie smiled and asked Tom to continue. Tom looked at her and mouthed 'I am sorry'. She nodded and waited for him to be ready to write.

"To be honest, she was active previously, she confessed to me before, but not as of recent." Lori confessed and clarified what she knew about the situation of her daughter's sexual activity. Tom wrote a couple notes and then he also asked;

"So do you know where she skated?"

"Yes, she went to the skate park, over in town at times, but she also mentioned about an older run down factory or somethen' of the sort, where some of her friends and her set up ramps or half to pipes or whatever you call what they do, to skate on and over."

"So, they had vert ramps and half pipes set up somewhere in town, but you aren't sure where?"

"No, sorry, she never confessed that to me. I wish I knew more.... I .. am ...sorry... I guess ...we ...are .. bad ..parents...." she said with a shameful down-cast look. He quickly spoke up saying;

"No, please no, you both seem like kind and loving parents. I am trying not to rock the boat of your life, I just have to see what, if anything, can lead me to where she could possibly be. Don't call yourselves bad parents, because kids run away for all types of reasons, not that she did, but it seems the highest likelihood, at this point." He said that with the calmest and most sincere voice he could muster up. He didn't just say those words to blow smoke either, but he was truthful and candid at the same time. He knew he had struck a bad chord with those questions, but he already grabbed many ideas and what he thought may have happened. Lori had started crying some, so she grabbed a tissue and wiped her face, trying to recollect herself for anything else the detective had to ask. Tom waited patiently for her to gather herself, and then he asked one more question;

"Do you have a recent photo of your daughter, like real recent?" Lori choked back her tears and grabbed her phone looking through the photo storage section to try to find the most current picture of her beloved daughter. Finally she found one and showed him her phone to see it. He acknowledged that it seemed to be recent and he asked her to send it to his phone, so he gave her his number and she sent it promptly. He checked his phone, acknowledging the pic to have come through and he stood up and said to her;

"Thank you for your time, both of your time, during this difficult situation. I would appreciate that if anything else comes up at a later time, please contact me. At any time, you can get a hold of me, especially if she comes back home. We will find your little girl, just try to hang in there, and this will all work itself out." With those final words, he showed himself out the front door, leaving the parents behind as he made his way to his vehicle. He sat there, in his vehicle, a few minutes as he regretted having to do this part of the job. Even though he never meant to insinuate anything, no matter how he worded it, it always sounded harsh. Therefore, in the long run he just said it plainly and matter of factly, just to get it out there and see the response from the family as well. He was sure it stung to be asked those questions, but he had a job to do as well and to do his job he had to know everything. He wanted to find Teresa and he wanted to make sure he found her before something happened to her. So his next plan of action was to check out the skate park area to see if he could talk with some kids who knew her, or at least some who knew where else to skate. This could be interesting, because not all kids wanted to chat with him or give up someone's whereabouts, especially a friend of theirs, but at least he was in plain clothes. Still he had to give it a try, it's the least he could do.

      Not thirty-six hours earlier, it was another beautifully gorgeous day with hardly a cloud in the sky and Teresa was jonesing for some time on her board. She had saved up some money and replaced her trucks recently with one of the brand name companies in the top five, but she couldn't afford the top brand at this time. Still with her nostalgic board and her newer trucks, she definitely wanted to try some new tricks out. She had been working on the crooked grind, the indy grab, and of course the Five-O. She wasn't as much of an am as she used to be, her buddies now considered her a thrasher. Yet, all she cared about was landing some gnarly seshes to elevate her game even more. So she grabbed her brain bucket, a bottle of water, and of course her board, by the deck, and ran out of her parent's trailer. She just needed to be free and sk8 like nothing else mattered, and to her nothing else did really matter. She started walking down the road, but her step had some gallop in it as well. She skated when the road surface allowed it, then all of a sudden she cut off the road and into the dense brush. She knew this way and she would always take this way as it was way quicker than using the main road. She skirted some rusty old cars that were littering a vacant field, jumped over a few fences, and then finally in the distance she could see the large warehouse building. She was already sweating some on her forehead from the sweltering heat and the areas she was circumventing to get to her destination. Still she lived for this and her sk8'ing is what made her truly happy. She often dreamed about being a pro and going around doing comps for a living. That would be a dream come true in so many ways. She could get out of this ridiculous town, the crappy home she lived in, and change her life for the better. She hurried past the spot where she had lost her innocence to some older boy who more or less treated her like shit after she let him go all the way with her, still she could care less at this point. She learned her lesson and wouldn't let any boy near her again, at least not in that sense. She was leaning more toward the older men nowadays, like those in their 30's. Those that were technically much too older for her, but one who would actually enjoy being with her and not use her just for her body as so many younger boys do. She would never make that mistake again! There was a man she had seen a few times in/around town that caught her eye. She wasn't sure of his name, but he was always kind to her. He would ask her questions about boarding and also about living here. He said he was from out of town, separated but not yet divorced, and had a young girl that was really interested in trying out this cool sport as well. That sparked her interest and she spent some time chatting with him the last few times that she had come in contact with him. They talked about getting together, a time when he could bring his little girl along and she could teach her to skate. She was enthralled with the idea, because secretly she always wanted a younger sister when she was younger herself, however now that she was older she was thinking about maybe even having a child, and she would love a little girl the best. So just with that thought in her head, she promised to meet the attractive slightly older man and his adorable daughter, who had already shown her a picture of his delightful daughter. She was hooked from that point on, and now she was on her way to meet up with them both. He even promised to pay her some and she at first said no, but he insisted and then she thought how she could use that to buy her new trucks. So she had a friend at the local shop and she put them on store credit for now, however he let her have them instead of waiting till she paid them off. She had first mentioned the skate park to be the best spot to meet up at, but then he balked and suggested someplace easier for his daughter to learn at. He didn't want his little girl to be intimidated by the older kids who were better than her, and so she suggested the old mill as a good place to board some. She could use some of the pieces of debris around there to make a little obstacle course for the little girl, with her guiding her of course.

She was nearly there when she started thinking about her parents then. She figured that her parents would not approve, so she never told them so she wouldn't have to deal with the questions or even chance of being grounded. She didn't like telling her mom things, who was her real confidant, but she thought it best to be prudent in this case. She smiled as she thought of the little girl, just as she broke out of the vegetation and into the clearing which was a large parking lot for the old mill. She immediately hopped on her board and started warming up by doing some kick flips, a few heel flips, and she even threw in an ollie, for good measure. After that she just did some fakeys and even a goofy foot for fun. She stopped a few times and looked around but didn't see or hear anything, so then she started riding more toward the factory to set up an obstacle course for the little girl. She was in heaven, enjoying the sunshine and all the day had to offer. She hopped off her board and kicked her board up into her hand, and then she laid it down on a platform. She then started working on collecting duller edged items to make a little obstacle course that she could run the little girl through. She was trying to think of everything she could teach her, if the girl was willing, and all the fun they could have. She even wondered what it would be like to have this little girl as her daughter. It was possible, if he and her got together, it would be magical, that was for sure. She would be the best mom to that little girl, ever! So she started setting up the course, but in the meantime she didn't hear a vehicle on the other side of the building drive slowly and then cut off its engine. Little did she know that just on the other side of the building, just out of sight was the man she had befriended trying to find her. The car door opened and the man got out of the vehicle, gently closing the door behind him to prevent an echo. He walked around the outside of the factory, and then found an open door, continuing his walk through the factory instead to get to the other side. He slowly came closer to the wall that separated him from Teresa, unbeknownst to her as she was diligently getting ready. Just as she finished up her little course, she backed up toward the wall and looked at what she had meticulously made for the little girl. Shoot, what was her name she thought, Kate?....no Jasmin?. .... Oh crap she completely forgot, she chided herself for her short-sightedness. She can still figure it out without him knowing that she forgot. This will work, she thought, proud of herself and of her work. Just as she leaned against the metal building, she felt something touch her shoulder, and so she freaked out and swatted at what had just come in contact with her. She blushed however when she saw it was none other than Todd who had grabbed her. She stifled her scream and instead laughed at what he did to put fear into her. She breathed a sigh of relief and he came out from behind the wall, laughing at her response. He then walked over and hugged her, which surprised her at first since this was the first time he had actually made physical contact with her, such as this. She welcomed it and hugged him back, but she was also looking for his little girl, over his shoulder.

"Where is your daughter?" She asked him inquisitively, but still trusting him fully.

"Oh, since I didn't know where you were, I asked her to wait in the car, which is just around the other side of the building. She is so excited to meet you, he said as he started walking back through the doorway to cut through the factory again. All of sudden she stopped and said;

"Shit, wait! I forgot my board!" Then she ran back over and collected her board from the place she had placed it, and ran back to him. She followed him into the building, where he stopped suddenly and turned toward her, placing his one hand up to her cheek, as if drawing her to him. She wasn't sure at first so she hesitated, but then she gave in and leaned into him and she welcomed whatever he would do to her. He leaned in kissing her squarely on the lips, and then he kissed her a little more, placing his hands behind her head. She felt the warm taste of his lips as she pressed back with her lips, slowly opening her mouth giving him a little tongue with her responsive kiss. She felt a sting on her neck, like a bee had just stung her, but she let it slide because she was in romantic heaven. Todd broke from her suddenly and backed away slowly from her. She was wearing a sweet grin and he said to her;

"You are my special girl, Teresa......" She smiled longingly at him and then she looked down at his hand and saw something in it. It didn't register at first, but then she looked again and it looked like a syringe. Suddenly, her vision started to become hazy and blurry and she started to lose her strength. What had he done to her, she silently screamed at him, internally, and yet nothing came out of her mouth. She lost control of her body and she started to fall, but he moved in, caught her mid fall, and held her close. He then repeated to her in a whisper;

"You..... are..... my special girl.....I will.... take ...good... care of you........", He said as he kissed her on her forehead. She felt the wetness of his lips, momentarily, but it was only fleeting, and then she slowly passed into an oblivion of numbness as she could no longer remain awake. She had made her last mistake, and the world was black.

Chapter Three

      Tom drove down the road heading toward the skatepark, to hopefully find someone who would divulge some more information regarding possible whereabouts of the recently missing Teresa. He didn't have much to go on so far, but any little bit of assistance would be better than where he is at present. He drove down the road, moving slowly as he was in no hurry, enjoying the drive and the day. He wasn't sure what he would find with some of these local kids or even if they would say anything at all. He could only hope they would, but nothing was definite especially when asking questions to younger teens. He drove in a large upside down u shape because of where the skate park was positioned, and eventually he made it there, but not until after a few wrong turns. It was surprisingly empty as he got out of his vehicle and walked around some, looking to see if anyone was out here to ask questions too. He walked around a few minutes and still saw not a single soul, so he sat down on one of the ramps and waited patiently. While he waited, he watched the road in the distance, since the park was visible from the road somewhat. He looked over some of the obstacles and he remembered when he used to skateboard as a young boy. He was not good and therefore he gave that up for bmx biking instead. He thought he was better at that and even did a few smaller races, but sadly no matter how good he was, he would usually get smoked at the races. So eventually he gave that up for more varsity type sports in high school, and a jock is what he became, over time, spanning a few different sports. He was getting bored quickly even though he enjoyed being outside, he knew he was just wasting time at this point. So unfortunately he gave up for right now and started heading back toward his vehicle. Then out of nowhere, a younger teen skater came out and started performing his repertoire of tricks. Tom was amazed at how good the youngster was on his colorfully decorated board. He lost his board while trying an ollie which led into a railslide. Sadly the youngster had to bail and catch himself from face planting on the concrete. He rolled out of the dangerous miscue and came to a stop rubbing the back of his head as he tapped it a little harder than he had wanted to. Still he was safe and sound and free of major injury. He popped back and this is when Tom made his move and walked over to the youngster. Tom started with;

"Great try on the rail slide… you nearly had it." The boy looked over at him, surprised that this old man(or at least by his thought process) knew any names of the tricks of skaters. He didn't seem the type, but one never knows. Still the first thing to the boy thought was this guy was a cop, and what was he doing here.Eventually the teen responded with;

"Yeah, thanks brau, I made it more than half the time, but that run wasn't my best."

"Practice makes perfect, so no worries." The board had made a solo run right over in front of Tom and he tapped the back of the board with his foot, kicking up the front end and catching it before it fell down again. This move surprised the teenager, that this man was able to do that. Tom turned the board over and mentioned haphazardly;

"Nice trucks too." With that comment, the teen smiled and seemed to be more at ease, and he walked over after Tom offered his board back to him, and said;

"Thanks." The teen said with a smile. This was my chance, Tom thought as he started asking questions, now that the ice was broken.

"What's your name, son?"

"My name is Jacob or J-dog as my friends know me."

"Well J-dog, can I show you a picture of someone to see if you recognize that person at all?"

"Sure, mister… I …am…game!" Tom pulled out the photo of Teresa and showed it to the teen.

"So have you seen or ….do you know her?" The teen looked up at him and smartly responded first by asking;

"She's not in trouble, is she?"

"No, not at all, ……..not at all. Her parents are looking for her, she has been missing well over twenty four hours now. So I'm helping them, in an attempt to find or at least be able to converse with her, to make sure she is safe and not in any major trouble." He explained completely to remain on the teen's good side. The teen looked at him and then back at the photo, and then piped up with;

"Yup, I seen her here before."

"Recently?" Tom asked quickly.

"No not in a few weeks, but she is a decent rider and a really cool girl.She ain't done never talked much with me, she's older, but still I seen her!"

"Thank you for that acknowledgement." He paused for a few seconds and then asked;

"Was she with anyone?"

"Not anyone out of the ordinary, just some of the guys and girls. And no, I never saw her with anyone of interest."

"Thanks, that takes care of that question..... Well if she hasn't been here, is there somewhere else y'all can skate?" The teen looked at him up and down, not sure if he wished to relate something or not, so Tom took that as if there was somewhere else to skate. He continued with;

"Listen, son, I am not and I promise you this, trying to get anyone in trouble or spy on you kids. I am here just looking for Teresa. That's it! I just need help finding her is all. So what do ya say?" The teen looked at him again, but then he relaxed some after hearing those words and he pointed directly behind Tom's left shoulder. Tom spun around and looked still within the skate park, but didn't see anything of interest. He turned back and the teen had actually pointed once more but higher this time, like into the distance. Tom looked at where the boy may have been pointing, and it was well past the park and into the distance. He seemed to be pointing directly at the old mill further down the road. He looked back around and the teen was already skating away from him, like he had done his duty and was now gone like the wind. He watched the teen disappear and then he turned back toward the old mill. Yes, that makes sense because it is a perfect place to escape and have someone not find you, especially if you didn't wish to be found. A perfect place, indeed, he thought.

He got into his vehicle and drove the less traveled and poorly maintained road over to the old mill. There were overgrown foliage all over the cracks in the road, which he had to swerve some to go around them, but he was going slow enough that it wasn't a bother. He drove until he came up on the right side of the building, but found nothing on that side, and so he turned around and started to drive around to the other side. He stopped once he got close, because there were concrete barriers preventing him from reaching that side, so he parked his vehicle and decided to do it by foot. He looked around first before heading out, looking in all directions and getting a feel for the defunct building and failed business. He hadn't been out here in quite some time, if ever as he tried to recollect. He started walking slowly, going up to one of the doors that was partially open. He looked inside the building at first but then decided to actually go inside and investigate better. There was some dust on the left behind machinery, but there wasn't much dust on the floors, as probably all kinds of kids came traipsing through this old building just to play and mess around (just like he did when he was a teenager). He would not get much out of this building he assumed, but he still continued to walk around just in case he might come across something. Finally after some time, he left the building and headed back out into the early evening light. He walked around outside and even found what looked like some type of course that the skateboard would travel through and around. There were no wheel marks though of someone trying the course out, and so it seems that the course was possibly set up without ever being used. Still no matter how long he searched, he found no evidence of Teresa being there, which discouraged him. He was truly hoping he would find something, but alas, to him, it seemed as if she hadn't been here at all. Still he lingered for another half hour or so, until he truly had to call it a day. He started walking back to his vehicle in quiet disappointment, and then he was about to start the vehicle back up but stopped, momentarily. The evening sky had turned a vibrant orange/red color and was just a simply gorgeous sight to behold. He watched the amazing array of colors in the sky for a few minutes longer, before finally entering, turning on, and slowly driving his vehicle away. This was not as a productive day as he would have hoped for, but then again he still held hope that Teresa may show up on her own and surprise everyone, and especially even him. He found nothing of significance to believe that Teresa had even been there that day as she had told her parents before leaving the house, but then again he may have to come back another day to see if there were some different skaters there. Maybe someone else knew or had seen her earlier that day, or at least he could only hope for such.

Tom drove slowly back to the office, not in a rush to get home, because there was no one waiting at home for him. He had a feline at home, but even she was moody as ever and he felt like he just existed in her world to feed and take care of her. He did that but that was about the extent of their relationship. Ever since his wife died of ovarian cancer, he hadn't had the stomach to date again. He figured there was no chance he could ever be that lucky again, so therefore he resigned himself to the single life. He spent some time with friends and still talked to his daughter when he had the chance. Karly (his daughter in college) often worried about him, and she voiced her displeasure at him not seeking out companionship, but he just had never found anyone that he wished to pursue since his wife Jeanine (Jean for short) had left this earth. He still loved his wife immensely, even now after all this time. Just thinking of being with another woman, no matter how innocent it may be, sickened him almost as if he were cheating on his wife. So until he could come to terms with such feelings, then and only then would he try to date again, but at this time it was out of the question. He drove leisurely back to town, not in any hurry, since all he had to do was more work in his cubicle. The ride was pleasing, as the sun was dipping ever so quickly from the sky, and he could even see the moon rising as well. He loved the sunset here in the mountains and yes the beach was amazing because he had seen it many times with his wife in years past, but he still would choose the mountains over the beach anytime. He thought back to one particular time with his wife, that one time they went on a trip down to the Virgin Islands. The sun, the sand, and the surf was just spectacularly out of this world as they happily frolicked in the warm grainy sand, splashing the crisp clear light blue ocean water, and shared many kisses, embraces, and lover's look of desire. They were both in love and even with all the pain and discomfort that he went through the last few years with her, he would not change a thing. Every moment that he had with her was a blessing, a moment not to regret, and something he would never change, not for anything in this world. He dearly loved his wife and she would always have his heart until his last breath on this earth. He thought of the happy times, but he also lamented over the sad times, those last few months as he saw her wither away to a person that hardly resembled his wife. He had taken a leave of absence and had never left her side through it all, and even after her last breath came out of her frail body, he was there holding her hand. There were no visiting hours when she had been hospitalized, because no one would dare tell him he had to go home. It was unthinkable to him to have to leave her side and have her wake up and be alone. It was not easy though, seeing his beloved in pain and he could only sit there helpless and limited in what he could do for her. She seemed to handle the pain well, but she could not not in her eyes, because he knew her that well. She blew off how much pain she had and she even gladly accepted it, because it was one thing that led her to realize that she was still alive, yet. It wasn't until the pain took its toll and visibly wrecked her entire body that she could not hide the pain anymore, and that was when he made the decision to add a pain medication via an infusion pump that she would constantly get a continuous dose to ease her obvious discomfort. She didn't seem to be akin to the idea of it at first, that is until she started getting some relief and then she finally rested some. Sleep had been one aspect of life that had eluded her for so long, because of the pain issues and the constant uncomfortableness. Once the direct and constant flow of pain medication continued to ease her pain, she actually tried to smile once in a while. It was a welcome sight, even though her gaunt face didn't have the twinkle of a smile that he knew from years before, she still nevertheless was able to force a smirkish kind of smile out.

He remembered how her smile, that devilish and adorable smile melted his heart the first time he had met her, those many years ago. He had attended a wedding, an old friend's wedding, and sure enough he saw her there. She was wearing a gorgeous flowy dress as it was a lake wedding, as it was occurring on the beach aspect of the lake, and she had that look….that look, that smile, and he knew this was a woman he had to meet. The funny aspect of her being there was the fact that she and a friend had made a bet that they could crash a wedding and not get caught. So, here were these two gorgeous young ladies dancing, drinking, and having a great time that no one actually knew. There wasn't a problem until the father of the bride confronted them, personally, and asked them what side of the family they were on. The women had no response at first, which was not smart on their part. That or maybe they had a little too much to drink, and therefore that caused their slight hesitation, but either way they were condemning themselves with their uncertain silence. He had purposefully moved closer to the action to see what would become of these two ladies when confronted with such irrefutable facts. Just as the father of the bride was about to escort them out, he stepped in and grabbed his future wife's hand and asked her;

"Darling, are you ready to dance now?" With that question she openly said yes and kissed him on his cheek, all the while smiling at the father of the bride(FOB). With that the FOB became a little sheepish and apologized for accusing them of crashing their wedding. Jean, being both graceful and eloquent, brushed it off and kissed the FOB on his cheek as well, saying;

"Is ok, love, you are stressed and so much here to take care of. By the way, it is a beautiful wedding and I am so happy to have been able to attend it. Thank you for everything….now I must dance with my man if you don't mind excusing me……"

With that and the wink of an eye, she twirled and kissed her new savior, Tom, directly on his lips, and then whispered in his ear;

"Thank you so much for saving me and my friend from getting kicked out of this shindig." He smiled at her and she turned to look for her friend, and here he had one of his single buddies come over and whisked her friend away to a dance as well, so they were both saved from event banishment and embarrassing ridicule. They danced the night away and as funny as it seems, the entire world became non-existent as they melded into each other. They talked extensively, laughed more times than either of them could remember, and still they danced. They danced even when there wasn't any music playing, as the music of the waves was the only tunes they needed as love filled each of their hearts. After that fateful day, they were inseparable in all aspects of life. Within a year of their first interaction, they themselves were married at a small ceremony with just friends and a few family members. Then shortly after that they had their first child who was a young boy, but sadly within two years, the poor child was killed due to complications from a severe motor vehicle accident. That took quite a toll on the both of them, draining them both emotionally and testing their marriage quite extensively. However, within a year they tried once more for another child, and within six months they were able to conceive their daughter, Karly. She had been the joy that they needed in their lives, and the precious gem that helped them overcome the sorrow from the loss of their deceased son. They had tried a few more times to have another child, but it just wasn't meant to be so they stopped worrying, fretting, and trying for another one and just enjoyed the one healthy child that they had made together in love.

He was smiling profusely now as he was just arriving at the station and he parked his vehicle in the appointed parking space for him. Those were wonderful days, he thought to himself, such wonderful days of their lives. In retrospect, he wished that they did have one more child, just so he could have another part of his late wife's presence still today. The unexpected but pleasant aspect of his daughter growing up was how insanely much she looked like her mother. So it is always good to see her, when they do get a chance to see one another at holidays, but it is also a reminder of his wife not being around anymore, sadly. He wrapped up these thoughts and reflections as he finally exited his vehicle, so that he could head inside to get some work done before going home tonight. Still those thoughts and memories were happy ones and ones that he didn't mind recollecting, and so as he walked he still had a permanent grin on his face. He used his badge and the door unlocked, so he entered the building and he heard the click of the locking door behind him. He went to the first room on his right and he entered the coffee room, to grab a cup of joe. Sadly the pots were empty, therefore he took a few minutes to prepare, make, and brew another pot for himself, and anyone else who remained here this evening. After a few minutes there was enough for him to pour a cup, and so he poured himself a cup full, adding nothing to it, and took a sip of the hot delicious caffeinated liquid. Hmmm….., so delicious he appreciated the strong flavor and robust aroma. He took a few more sips, refilled what he had just drunk, and then headed down the hallway to his cubicle. Immediately he figured out he was the only one in the building at the time, well, besides the dispatcher also, but they had their own little office upstairs. On this level there were minimal lights on and so he had the place to himself at this point. A patrol officer would probably be stopping later, but that all depended on what issues or trouble he ran into while out doing rounds. He went over to his cubicle, adjusted the light after turning it on, and then sat down in his comfortable desk chair. He typed in his password on his laptop and went to the appropriate portal to type in his notes from Teresa's parents to start. He pulled out his small notebook and looked at his scribblings as he typed proficiently the notes he had taken. Within ten minutes, he had finished that report, but then he made an addendum regarding the direction he was led at the skatepark. He finished up the reports and filed them for now, but then he pulled up the missing and exploited children portal to check to see how many young women have gone missing in the past year. He wanted to see if there was a trend at this point, or anything else he could go on that would assist him in any way feasible. He started perusing through the online pages of missing children. There were always too many which always bothered him and that very fact was scary also, as the state of times that we live in, to see this many displaced, abducted, or missing children. It saddened him to see all these children's files that went missing all over the nation. He narrowed the search to just to within the state and then by county to make it easy to see how many were from their specific region. There was only one from their town, but there were a few in the outlying areas also, and some just south in the state of Georgia also. Those communities were all close enough to make even smaller communities easy prey areas for those predators who did such unthinkable and deplorable acts. It was demoralizing seeing all the young faces, such innocent faces, either missing or taken. He knew she was in there,

Teresa, and after a few more young girls and boys, she was there. He looked over the information that had been placed in the computer earlier. Everything seemed to be accurate and straight forward. There was nothing he could add that would enhance or make things better, and so he left it as it was for now. He looked at the one picture that was on her profile and he could only hope that he would be able to do what he could do to find her.

He finished up the work he had to do, tidied up his desk some, and then he called it a night and proceeded to leave the station. He drove home to his simple and small home, unlocked the door, and walked inside. As soon as he got inside he could hear his cat meowing at him for not feeding her yet, and so he walked over, got some partially full canned cat food out of the fridge, took off the aluminum foil that he covered it up with, and then using a spoon he dished food into the cat's bowl. The cat purred as it rubbed against his leg until he placed the food on the floor, and then the cat had nothing to do with him again. He went into the partial bathroom and saw the litter pan was overflowing from use, with even some outside remnants on the floor also. He grabbed some paper towels, the pooper scooper, and then a plastic grocery bag and scooped up the kitty clumped pieces out of the pan. He then added some litter to refill it, some, and then he wiped up the floor afterwards. After he was done, he disposed of the waste in the garbage can, making sure to tie it tight and double bag it, and then he washed his hands thoroughly. He opened up his fridge to see if there was any food worth eating, but as usual he hadn't replenished his stock recently. With the dismal results he opened up the freezer and sadly that was even worse. So he walked over to the tiny pantry he had and he found a box of ramen noodles and some hot sauce, so he cooked up the noodles in the microwave and then doused it with the hot sauce, making a somewhat appetizing concoction. He grabbed a beer, turned on the television, and then found some old movie suitable to watch, and delved into his food while sipping his beer, alone. The cat came close to him, laid down on the floor, but didn't actually come in contact with him as is the usual, and did its normal job of cleaning itself after its evening meal. Tom finished up consuming his meal, drank another two beers, and then promptly fell asleep on the recliner chair he was sitting in for his evening meal. He woke up the next morning around 5 am, took a long shower, made some coffee, and then started getting ready for the day ahead. He noticed his cat sleeping on his bed, something he never ended up sleeping in half the time anymore, so he left the resting feline behind, and exited the home to head off to work. Firstly, though, he wanted to stop and get a bacon, egg, and cheese bagel sandwich for his morning breakfast. He drove the short distance to the station, parked his vehicle, and then started walking toward the small sandwich shoppe, right there on main street in downtown. The shoppe he was looking for was not as far as his friend Frank's shoppe, and in minutes he was there at the front door. He looked inside and as usual the little place was hopping with activity, as the normal breakfast rush was on. He walked inside, the little bell overtop of his head rang to allow the counter workers to acknowledge another customer had arrived. A red headed, cheery, and slightly plump woman behind the counter waved with excited exuberance as he found his way in line, waiting for his turn to order. After about four people and ten minutes later, he made it to the front of the line and met the owner of this lovely cozy feeding hole, called Bev's Breakfast Nook. Bev, the owner greeted him with a large smile and asked him directly;

"So what will it be this morning, Tommy boy?" Bev knew that Tom didn't entirely like the whole 'Tommy' name, but he didn't dissuade her to be able to say it, since it made her happy. He answered with;

"Well, let me see there darlin', ..." Just that response made her grin even larger as he paused a moment before finishing what he was saying;

".....I think I'll have the sausage, bacon, egg, and cheese bagel please...... and the bagel toasted lightly. Thank you."

"That'll be just fine..... But I know what you need my dear....." And then she yelled out profoundly;

"I need a skinny heart attack on a bun, lightly bruised, and buckled for the departure!" All that meant to him was that she was making one of her ultimate sandwiches for him that consisted of a small portion of sausage, a few pieces of bacon, egg, cheese, hash brown and hot sauce. It was considered skinny as compared to the more robust version as his version skipped the pork roll, less bacon, and only two slices of cheese compared to four which was on the normal version. It was a good sandwich and he had tasted it once before, and even standing waiting there for his order, his mouth started to water. He watched it being made and was ready to delve into that succulent morsel as soon as it was delivered to him. As expected the sandwich was wrapped for him to take it on the go and Miss Bev already had a large poured cup of coffee to go for him as well. He smiled at her and he placed his money on the counter, giving her a tip as well as he said to her;

"Thank you so much as always, Bev. Have a great day." Bev smiled and responded likewise as he started to leave, by saying;

"My pleasure, darlin', anything for my de-tec-tive man!" She said as she winked at him and watched him go out the door. Then she turned and was busy back at her duties of receiving, making and preparing the orders for the morning crowd. It was going to be a good day, a good day, she thought to herself.

He walked back to the department building carrying his meal with him and sipping on his deliciously made and brimming hot coffee. He made it back in a short time span and just as he arrived at the side door that he commonly used to enter the station, he ran into none other than Officer Ryan Scott, a young and energetic officer who brought youth and eagerness into their department. They stopped and chatted for a few minutes, talking about some old cases and also about the new missing child case, and then Tom excused himself to go eat his still warm sandwich. Ryan stated he would stop by later to continue their chat, of which he accepted the invite, well, that is if he wasn't busy with other matters, of course. Off he went to his office space to consume his delicious breakfast. He pulled out his chair, sat down, moved a few things to make room for his sandwich/meal and then he took one scrumptious bite. Sadly, his meal was interrupted as often happens, by a phone call. He looked at his sandwich, looked at the land line phone screen (which he could tell was an outside line), placed his sandwich down after a few more rings, and then picked up his phone to answer the call. He picked it up and didn't immediately notice the female sounding voice on the other end asking for him, so he responded appropriately;

"Yes, ma'am this is Tom Royce, Glen Fork's PD detective..: How may I assist you?"

"Yes, is this the detective?....I ...have....... some...thing ....to ....report...."

"Yes ma'am, I am the detective. What is it that I may do for you? What do you have to report?"

"It is my sister! I think.... she..... may..... be..... missing...... or something had happened to her." The woman responded with an upset and saddened voice.

"Ok, ma'am: first tell me your name please, and then everything you know.." He heard the woman trying to settle herself some, and then she finally spoke up after some sniffles, blowing of her nose, and some throat clearing, by saying;

"My name is Jessie Brant and I live just outside the Glen Fork city limits, ...but I am calling regarding my sister, Suzie.....Suzie Barker. She came to see me about a week and a half to two weeks ago, and then after she spent a few days with me she decided to head out and do some back trail hiking and camping. I haven't heard from her in nearly four days. I have called her number repeatedly, but it just goes to voicemail every time. I tried to ping her phone, but it seems to be completely dead or destroyed, because I get no signal from it. So I am afraid something happened to her...." she started lightly sobbing again for a few seconds and then she finished with... "What should I do?" There was a moment of silence as he thought of what to tell her, and then finally he spoke up, responding with;

"Well ma'am, just per.. chance did you contact the forest service also to let them know?"

"Yes....... I ...did.. but... they said they can't promise anything at this point." She said with sadness in her voice.

"Ok, I was just making sure we went through all avenues. Do you have a few recent photos of her and I will start putting it into the computer so that we can get an A.P.B. out for her. Do you also know where she put in at, and where her vehicle was parked?"

"No, sir I don't because she told me a friend was dropping her off at a spot, so that she didn't leave her car there unattended for days. Her vehicle is at my house, awaiting her return. I wasn't worried at first because she has done such things before, but she had previously called me or gave me updates to her status and some of the sights she observed. So her not getting back to me scares me deeply, for her life. Can you please help me?"

"Yes, Jessie, I /we will help locate her. What about the friend? Have you checked with them or do you know that person's name or vehicle? Anything additional you can think of would be assistance for us in trying to do our job. You don't have to know everything now, I just need you to really think, and get back to me as soon as possible, is all. If there is anything else you can think of please contact me at this cell phone number or the landline number you called me on. Do you have a pen and paper, ma'am? Ok my number is....." He recited his number to her and she read it back to confirm the correctness of the number. She was concerned and he thought it was right for her to be so, since we don't have a specific timeline as to when her sister actually went missing. This one would even be tougher to locate then the missing Teresa, who was probably still just a runaway type issue. Just a coincidence, he wondered, but then again too early to tell if foul play, if something just happened to her, accident wise or she just went off the beaten path type of hiker, which was not uncommon either. They would have to get the local mountain rescue team together, if the forest service didn't already contact them, and go searching for the possible missing hiker/backpacker. She thanked him for his time and she stated that she would try to find out more information about the friend, if she could. He thanked her for her patience and her reaching out for help. So many things can happen up in the mountains, so it was never easy trying to locate someone that may be missing without a definitive area to start the search. Hopefully her sister was just laid up somewhere and couldn't be reached, but now that it had been so long, her concern was just that, sheer reaching at this point.

Just eight days earlier, a woman in her late thirties was dropped off at a hiking trailhead called Passion Point. The trailhead was named that many moons ago, by the early younger townsfolk who frequented this area, and by their actions which led them to name it thusly. The area was gorgeous with many small cascades, a few bigger waterfalls, and a small pool of water where people are often found swimming, sometimes clothed and sometimes ceremoniously unclothed also. This woman unloaded her pack from the vehicle that dropped her off, gave the driver a quick hug, and then collected herself and her belongings to start down the trail. This trail was part of the Appalachian Trail, and therefore even had a sign-in book for those braving this part of the trail. She opened the small water resistant pedestal that this book was stored in and she opened up the book carefully, making sure not to drop the pen that was in it as well. She rifled through the pages, enjoyed the drawings that other hikers put in there, and she even found some pictures as well. She thumbed through the pages until she found an empty spot to sign on, and she even wrote a small saying in there as well. It read:

'To abide in this life and not find the peace that dwells deep in nature is not only to miss out on life, but also to miss out on what this great earth had given to us to enjoy, revel in, and appreciate. Hike smart my fellow travelers.'

Suzie 'The Sparkler' Barker

Happy with what she wrote, she smiled, closed the book, and placed it back in the location she had found it. Perfect she thought, as she cinched up her pack on her toned shoulders and started her hike down the well traveled trail. There were many day hikers and sometimes through hikers seen, but on this particular day, the trails actually appeared to be somewhat empty. As luck would have it, as soon as she started hiking, it started to drizzle some, and so she grabbed her packable lightweight weather jacket and started to put it on, but she had to stop and take off her pack to properly put on the jacket to keep her from getting too wet. After getting her jacket on, but only partially zipping it up just enough to keep her dry but not too much to make her sweat from overheating. She reslung her pack up on her shoulders, snapped the buckles together, and started off once again. She wasn't using a hiking pole yet, but most likely later in the day she would need it and so it was attached to her pack. The gorgeous light drizzle animated the flowers and petals of the local plant life as everything glistened from the unexpected moisture. She couldn't help but enjoy the moisture on her smiling face and on her bare hands as she let them down by her side, touching some of the damp plant life with her delicate fingers. She lumbered some up a small hill as she was just trying to get her pace down. Just as she crested the short knoll, she was ultimately startled as there was another hiker in the path with their pack off. She had had her head turned so she nearly ran into him initially. So she immediately stopped as she nearly walked into him, saying apologetically;

"Excuse me, I am so sorry, so...sorry..." She continued to repeat as the other hiker, a man probably in his early forties blushed and also apologized for being in the way. He started off with;

"No, please I am sorry. I am the one who was in your way. I couldn't help it though as my one strap malfunctioned and I am trying to rig it up so I can continue my hike." He immediately went back to working on the strap, as she continued to watch him try to fix the issue at hand. Then she asked him;

"Are you sure you have this?"

"Yes...yes...I am fine. I will figure it out."

"Ok but I will head out if you don't need my assistance..."

"Yes, yes...that is fine... I think I have it...." Just as she started to walk away, he fumbled more with the damaged strap, and then just as she looked back, he had kicked his bag. So she turned around and went back down the trail to try to help him out. As she came close, she could hear him swearing profanities at the bag and it looked as if he might even pick it up and toss it off the trail for good. She stopped him by mentioned kindly;

"How about I give you a hand and we fix this minor issue…" She dropped her pack and unzipped one pocket and pulled something out. She had some plastic zip ties and so she used the zip ties to makeshift a new buckle and after lacing the strap back through it, it actually seemed to work. She lifted the pack up by that strap and it held up. He smiled at her and once more started saying;

"Oh dear, thank you so much…. Wow you are amazing! I can never repay you or thank you enough for this quick fix!"

"It is ok, we all have a need of assistance at times and today was your day, tomorrow may be my day. Just happy that I came along and had what you needed."

"Again thank you, …….do you mind if I hike with you awhile?…. As it is lonely out here."

"Yes, that should be fine", she piped up as she wouldn't mind the company as well. She had hiked many times with people she met on the trail, and maybe chatting with someone will make the miles pass more quickly, especially with this steady drizzle as it is now.

So they started hiking, after both of them reslung their packs on their backs and off they walked together, like old friends. The conversation was mostly light and consisted of small talk and how much hiking they had done in the past. It was light and just pleasant, and then it ultimately went to how far each one was going, how long they would be out on the trail, and then why each one hikes solo as they were today. Suzie felt no worries with this man, as he seemed to present no issues. He told her that he was married and had two children, whose names were Jan and Brock. He talked about them for some time and then stopped as he realized he was monopolizing the conversation, and Suzie snickered at how proud he must be of his kids, since he couldn't stop talking about them. They both had a light laugh, and then they came across an old gravel road with overgrown weeds and grasses, but still in fair driving condition. They both looked both ways, and Suzie saw a vehicle down the road a little distance, parked there. She wondered what that was about, but soon they both started walking again across the gravel trail and back into the woods. She took one last look at the vehicle, but it didn't seem to be running, so she didn't pay it too much mind once they passed the sight of it. She thought that it could be a hunter in the area, or maybe even a trapper, just trying to get some viable game to live off of. They had gone another 50 feet when suddenly her trail companion slipped and fell forward, nearly flat on his face. Suzie stopped and knelt down to check on her trail mate, saying to him;

"Are you alright? You didn't hurt yourself did you?"

"No, No, I think I am ok. What a dolt!" He said with a slight bit of laughter as he tried to stand up. He didn't make it and slid back some on the mud underneath him. Suzie smiled at him and asked;

"Do you think that you need a little hand?"

"I think I actually might, I must confess, and thank you once again...." And so she reached down to assist him by giving him one of her arms to pull himself up with. She had pulled up both sleeves to just about the elbow area as she had gotten warm already, but really didn't wish to take the jacket completely off, as of yet. As soon as she reached out her arm, something in his hand came up to bay just as he grabbed her helping arm. He jerked her somewhat with a pull of his own arm, unexpectedly. She immediately felt a tinge of pain, and then a weird woozy feeling as if something had been pushed onto or had been injected into her. She looked down at her arm that she had extended to assist the troubled man, and that was when she saw it. There was a spot of blood right in her antecubital vein, and he had hit it just dead on. She looked with a horrified expression first down at her arm and then squarely in his face as if to say, 'How could you?' Within milli-seconds, she felt the unusually warm feeling and then felt an uncontrollable numbness come over her entire body. She tried in vain to fight it, but she couldn't muster her strength as her muscles relaxed nearly instantaneously and she started to lose her physical strength and the world around her spun. She saw the needle that he had violated her with and jabbed into her, but she had no idea what or why he had done such a heinous deed. Her eyes started to water some as the man grasped her as she started to slowly fall to the ground. She wanted to run but that was a luxury she couldn't manage to do at this point. She had lost all control of her basic physical functions. Then, suddenly, her world went dark and she fell uncontrollably to the ground. What had just happened, she thought, as she barely maintained consciousness. Next thing she knew she was cuddled by the man that she had just met and somehow had insanely trusted, and now look what happened. She was being abducted by some crazed man for some inexplicable reason, the rat bastard. He looked into her fixed staring eyes, but she couldn't move her own body now. She wanted to scream, but she couldn't. 'What have you done to me?' She wanted to yell at him but nothing came out. He looked gently into her tearful eyes, brushed back her lovely hair, and then he whispered to her secretly, with such desire and adoration;

"Don't worry sweet love, you are a dear gem. Thank you for your sacrifice and your desire to be mine. I promise to always care for and love you in so many ways, til death do you part!" She internally screamed again, but again not a single sound or peep came out of her throat and mouth in any way. He finally stood up, with ease as his ploy had worked, not like previously where he had had issues with getting to his feet. He picked up her body and moved her right off the trail and covered her with some loose brush and tree limbs, so that she wouldn't be seen. Then he grabbed her pack and his pack and off he went down the trail from which they had come. She couldn't move, she couldn't do anything, but watch and wait. She heard something in the distance and it sounded like a vehicle, but there was nothing she could do to flag it down or even yell for it. Random raindrops fell into her eyes, but she couldn't wipe them and clear them. She just had to suffer through as it stung her eyes and made her vision extremely blurry. The vehicle sounded like it drove some, then came to a stop, but it seemed to remain in its running state. It was then that she heard the pounding of someone moving fast down the trail, like toward a destination. She waited, prayed, and hoped that it wasn't the man who betrayed her and left her there right off the trail to her untimely demise. Then before long she had her answer, and to her great dismay, just as soon as the footsteps stopped, there was some heavy breathing. Unfortunately, the breathing stopped just right of her peripheral view, but it did stop right in front of her and then some foliage was removed to reveal the person. Immediately, the regret sunk in as she saw that it was indeed him that had come back to get her, for whatever reason. She again wanted and tried to scream, but alas she couldn't and then she gave up, resigning her fate to whatever may come. She was absolutely helpless in every conceivable way and she knew it. He gently pulled her back out from under the area he had stashed her body and made sure to gently lift the brush that had covered her. To him she was perfect and he didn't wish to taint her perfection. He brought her close to him, as he was about to heft her up onto his shoulder like a rag doll. But before he did that, he looked at her, looked longingly into her eyes and he whispered a few words;

"It is fate that brought you to me on this dreary day. You are definitely a catch for my collection, that is true!" He kissed her on her forehead and then he hefted her onto his one shoulder and carried her down the trail and back into the trailhead clearing, where he had his waiting car stashed. He, cautiously, looked both ways prior to exposing them out into the gravel trail road, and once he saw it was clear, he went over to the back of the vacant car and lifted up the already unlocked trunk door and placed Suzie inside the open area in a careful and loving manner. There she lay nestled in blankets as if she were posing for some photo shoot, awaiting the shutter noise. He looked warmly at her, smiled, and then said one more additional sentence;

"Don't worry, darling,........I will take care of you!" With that he closed the trunk and she was in total darkness, as she was left with an unsure fate to become of her. The car drove slowly and unnoticed down the gravel trail toward its destination.

Chapter Four

The following day, after getting home late, hardly sleeping and then waking up to the normal routine, Detective Royce found his way to his vehicle. He was groggy, didn't feel like working today, and quite honestly was just plain tired of it all. He wished he could retire and just live off the land, not a care in the world, and just disappear into the woods. He was going to drive to the office, but then instead he stopped his vehicle and sat there on the side of the road for a few minutes, rethinking his current train of thought. He should go down the most known drop off spots and see if there is any sign of the young lady. Then again, look how many days it has been, any good leads would have been washed away, since it had rained a few times since the lady went missing. That and she probably just went off the beaten trail, which so many experienced hikers do, oftentimes. Why should he worry about one hiker who just decided to get away from it all, which was a very likely aspect. He contemplated a little longer, as he took another sip of his lackluster coffee. He should go into town and get some good genuine coffee to wake him up better, but he would be further away and he would never check out some of the trails as he probably should, at least not on this particular day. The longer he waited, the more he thought, until finally he took another sip of coffee, looked both ways, and pulled out to go in the direction he needed to go. He thought himself stupid for doing this but he wanted to see with his own eyes, if he would find anything that would say where she had been dropped off at. He sped down the road to check on some trailheads that he knew of that were some of the most common spots to hike in at. It took him about thirty five minutes to get there, but he finally made it one of the four most common spots to start to hike from.He first went to Lackey Cove trailhead to see if he could see or talk with anyone that may have come in contact with the young lady. He still had a picture of her on his phone, at least that was a plus. He parked in an appropriate spot and then he slowly got out of his vehicle and surveyed the area. He didn't see anything, but then again it was a trailhead, as he wasn't sure exactly what he would find anyway. He started walking down the trail some twenty five feet at first, and then after another twenty five feet, he came around a blind corner and nearly ran into two hikers. They had their backpacks full and were determined, especially at the pace they were moving along at. He stumbled out of the way, but not before apologizing first for interfering with their rhythm. They also apologized and as soon as they passed him, he all of sudden dawned on him as to why he was here. He called out to them just before they made another corner, by saying;

"Hey guys! Hey, I am Detective Tom Royce, and I need to ask you questions about a possible missing person. Could you give me five minutes of your time?" Both young men stopped, although disgruntled, and then turned around waiting for him, not wishing to go back down the trail. Tom walked over to them and pulled out his phone, showing a picture of Suzie to the duo.

"Sorry to bother you gents, but I am looking for this woman, who went missing some three days ago. Have any of you seen her on the trail?" Both men looked at the photo and then at him and then back down at the photo once more. Eventually they looked up, responding as such;

"Nope, I ain't seen her." The first said to Tom.

"Neither haves I." Said the second man.

Are we done now?", asked the first young man, so they could go on their way. Tom interrupted them though and offered them one of his cards, and finished off with;

""Well I appreciate your time, and sorry to bother you again, fellows. But if you do see her or hear of anyone seeing a lone female, please contact me. Her family is really concerned. Take care and enjoy your hike" The men were gone with those words, and so he turned around and continued a little further down the trail, but there was nothing to see, so he turned around. He walked back to his vehicle and waited around a little longer, but no one else walked by. He gave up at this spot and started up his vehicle once more and headed off down the road, toward the next location. He honestly hoped the next spot would have better luck than he had at this one.

He drove a little further down the road and then had to drive in a more westerly fashion to reach the next common spot for day hikers and/or drop in spots. The next location was aptly called Creekside trailhead, as it was at the intersection of two creeks and also included a gorgeous cascade just a little ways down the trail. He drove up and encountered two other vehicles in the parking area, so he pulled up behind them and took their license plates down, just in case. One never knows when opportunity will knock, so don't look a gift horse in the mouth, or so to speak. He checked them on his computer in his vehicle, but both drivers had no priors, so the chance was pretty remote, but he still held onto them in case one would be a sleeper. He exited his car after he parked it alongside the other vehicles and he looked all around. This was a remarkably gorgeous entrance to a trail, that was for sure he thought, as the sun had come out a little basking on the mid morning leaves with delightful energy. It was a picture perfect scene as he continued surveying the area. He even remembered coming down here with his wife a few times, before she was sick, and he smiled as he remembered how much she loved nature and being amongst the trees, water, and the animals. He remembered her silhouette against the water as she frolicked it, not caring what she got wet or what she wore. She was such a darling person and someone who truly was one with nature. They joked often about her being a gypsy or a guardian of nature because of how she responded to nature and how it responded to her. Every animal she came across seemed to come up to her gentle spirit and her loving demeanor and just feel at ease. Corny as it sounds, it was almost like out of a movie, but he had experienced it firsthand and he knew it to be true. She had rescued animals before, and for a while he used to gripe about it, saying that she couldn't keep doing that without his knowledge, but in the end he surrendered to her wishes and she did what she wanted to. He smiled now as he thought about her and how lovely she was, no matter what she did or said to him. His attention was brought back immediately, as he heard people talking coming down the trail. 'A-ha', he thought to himself, my first person to bug. So then he decided to head toward the direction of the voices as he got his phone ready to show the picture off to the next few people. Hopefully, one of these folks had seen Suzie, in the last week. Hope was a word he seemed to be scarce of recently.

He walked down the trail some, until he saw two people coming his direction. It was a couple coming toward him and he was within normal earshot, when he put up his hand to pause the couple coming his direction. The couple paused, unsure what to think at first, and then eased when they saw him hold up his badge to them. He started by saying;

"Hey Folks, sorry to bug you, but my name is Detective Royce from the Glen Fork P.D. Do you mind looking at this picture of this hiker that may have gone missing to see if you recognize her, or have seen her in your travels?" The two people edged forward crooning to look at the picture on the phone, and then Tom handed them the phone for them to see it better. The female and male hiker looked, conversed, and then looked back at the photo once more. They handed the phone back to him and then said;

"Well mister dude........we did see someone that looked like her ...at least ...once before... but not in a long time.Least we think so..." The male said to him, but then the female piped in with;

"I dunno, Luke, it may not be the one we saw.... I dunno it had been too long,....like maybe a year or so. Sorry that's all I remember at this time, mister." Tom thanked them for at least looking at the photo, and he retrieved his phone back from them. He gave them his card anyway, just in case they thought of something else along the way, and then he let them continue on their hike. He continued walking down the trail then to see if he would come across anything else. As soon as he was probably ten feet down the trail, he smelled the smoke, the distinct aroma of weed being smoked. That makes sense as their answers were both cryptic and non committed ones at that. Just another bunch of tokers, he thought, as he continued traveling down the trail to hopefully a much better lead. He truly enjoyed this trail he was walking on, taking in the scents of nature, the glorious colors of the mountains, and the off and on sunlight blazing through the canopy tops. Once again he was completely immersed in his thoughts and his enjoyment of such, that he nearly tripped over himself as he came upon a younger black bear walking down toward him. They both surprised one another with Tom falling backwards into a growth of ferns and the bear, being just as startled, careening into a small batch of thistle bushes. The black bear made a noise of displeasure from being startled and then ran away quickly into the thick brush to the opposite side of the babbling stream, and out of his life. Tom recovered from the startling effect and took a few deep breaths as he had never been this close to a bear before, well , except for the times he used to take his daughter to the zoo. Still, not a wild bear at that, but thankfully it was just a young black bear and not a mother who can be testy and angry at times with any type of human interaction near her beloved cub(s). Either way that was such a possible close call, by his standards. After he recouped enough, he continued down the trail but didn't see anything. He stopped, looked around and thought that this was nearly impossible. If they don't know the trail, it would be like looking for a microscopic needle in a haystack. So he made the choice to turn around and head back out toward his vehicle. He just hoped for a break in this missing person sooner than later.

It was a long slow drive to wherever she was being taken too, but it distressed Suzie immensely, as she still couldn't move any of her appendages, nor did she have any feeling in them. It was like she didn't have arms and legs at all, which was so awkward and fearful for her. She could do nothing that could change her situation, at this point so she just remained still and tried to remain calm as well. The later part was the most difficult by far. She was completely freaking out inside, as she was afraid she had seen her last day on this good earth. Why had this man done this to her? What was his reasoning and why did he choose her? Had he been following her? These and so many more questions riddled her mind as her body remained defunct. She was completely helpless and that was what she hated most. She was a fighter, that was for sure, because she had survived breast cancer at an early age, ran a few marathons after that, and even had hiked most of the Appalachian Trail, although not a through hike, but intermittently. Still she had been on every aspect of the trail and she kept coming back for more. She would fight well when her body allowed her to, but at this point she would fight in spirit and hope for some way to get out of this predicament. There is always a way out, she thought with positive intentions, always a way out! One just has to wait for the perfect opportunity and not be afraid to take that chance. Her thoughts were interrupted as the road suddenly became bumpier as if they were going down a gravel road to some horrible destination, she surmised. She still wanted to keep all options open as the drive continued. Maybe a half hour had passed since she left the trail area where she had been abducted, but that was just an estimated guess. When she got her strength back from whatever drug that devious man had given her, she needed to be ready to skedaddle, and with extreme haste. Eventually the vehicle slowed some, nearly coming to a stop, but then it turned hard to the right and her body shifted without her permission from the movement. About another twenty minutes and a few more bumpy roads, the vehicle finally slowed to a crawl, and then finally jerked to a ceasing of forward movement. The car shook some as if the driver was moving around in the front of the vehicle, as if to grab something hard to reach. Finally she heard the door open and she heard steps on the gravel coming around the vehicle. She waited for the trunk to open, but it never did. It was getting warm in there also and she was sweating profusely, for the typical reasons. She waited for what seemed like a long time but nothing ever occurred, and eventually she fell asleep from lack of activity. Suddenly she was awoken by a flurry of activity as the man opened up the trunk, grabbed her and put her on an old pull type of cart. She was strapped down, a blanket pulled overtop of her, and was being pulled into an old building, maybe it was an old barn and then she was inside the building. She still couldn't move her head, but her eyes caught glimpses of movements with her peripheral vision. She then heard some noises, moans, and soft voices. Then she heard a gentle whimpering voice as the pull cart stopped right next to the now pleading soft feminine voice. Then after hearing the pleading voice asking for something, there was a harsh admonishment from the man who took her. Then a little crackle of something electric and the voice immediately whimpered once more and then went quiet, but only after a soft cry of anguish. What the hell was that man doing to that girl(as she seemed to tell the voice was a younger feminine voice). The man said a few words of apology, but he also mentioned;

"See my love, if you are good, you won't get reprimanded. So, please don't make me use this on you again! I will take care of you, dear. Supper will be coming soon after I am done here." There was no response to the man's voice, so she assumed it was a nodded silent approval.The cart jolted again and she noticed she felt her fingers again. The medication was wearing off, so she had to be ready. There was a metal cage door creak as it was opened and then the man's voice was heard grumbling. The sounds of things being moved around was prevalent as she continued to wait. Now she could move her hand some, so this was definitely hope for her. It was a weird feeling, but she started feeling all her extremities once more, and she finally was moving her hands that were bound. This may be her only chance, she thought to herself. She just needed a little more time and for the man to be distracted enough. Eventually she heard his heavy footsteps again on what sounded like old creaky wooden boards, and then she heard his breathing as he was right in front of her. Her arms were weak but she could move them, so just when he pulled the blanket back, it gave her the only chance she had. The man bent down and reached for her, and just when he did she moved her weak and heavy arms upward, catching him directly on his nose. He groaned and staggered back, cursing as he did so. She quickly tried to move her bound legs but they weren't quite there, so she used her momentum and rolled out of the pull cart, falling heavily onto the uneven wooden floor. It smelled musty and old, but she didn't care as she had struck back in the only way she could. The only problem with her plan of action is that she couldn't run away, sadly, and therefore she was still stuck where she was. The man moved on her quickly and he jerked her hard up by her ponytail, and she could see the man again. He had an oozing bloody nose from where she had struck him, but in his eyes was complete unadulterated fury. His bloody nose dripped on her cheek as he put his face that close to hers, in a very uncomfortable moment. He slowly exclaimed with angst in his voice to her;

"Now, look at what you've done! That was just stupid! There is no action that doesn't yield a reaction, so let this be a lesson for you, my dear." With that she felt him grab her one hand and he bent her finger back until it snapped, breaking the bone inside. She screamed in painful agony, but that was stifled by a dirty old rag shoved in her mouth. Her eyes immediately teared up from the incredible pain, and she nearly passed out. She felt another injection, a much rougher one jabbed into her this time and she was immediately helpless once more. Her one opportunity wasn't a complete loss, as she did at least inflict some type of discomfort on him, but the cost was high as her one finger was now dangling useless. Not that she could move it or truly tell at this point as her entire body went numb again. But for that one moment, she had the upper hand, and she knew that she would try again given the opportunity.

The man picked her up after attending to his nose immediately after the strike, and with rough hands he tossed her into what seemed like a metal cage. She could only look around with her line of sight and peripheral vision, since she couldn't move her head but all she could see were heavy metal bars. It seemed like some kind of wild animal cage, and it didn't seem that big either. She was shoved and pushed inside, and once again she heard the man speak up, saying;

"Now if you are good, you will get a bigger home, but until then you deserve to be caged like a wild animal, just the way you acted out at me. If you are good, you get rewarded, but if you are bad, don't listen, cry out, or act stupid, then you will get rewarded with pain and suffering! What I did to your finger is nothing, as next time I will chop off your entire hand. So be a good girl, and maybe I will feed you tomorrow. Then again maybe I won't! Either way don't think I won't snatch your life from you at any moment. I care about you and want you, but I will not be made a fool! Do you hear me?" With that he closed the door, and she heard a lock being put on the door. Right before he left, he shocked her with an electric rod type of prodder, which even though she couldn't move, made her body shake a little. It was the searing pain that she felt and immediately she peed on herself, soiling her clothes. She couldn't stop it and she had no way to control much of anything. She was totally at his mercy, which irked her to all get out. She closed her eyes and tried to think of being at a better place, as his footsteps walked away toward the door that she had been brought into, or so she imagined. 'Shit, you got yourself in a pickle now', she thought grimly to herself. She was happy that she got the asshole of a man, even though it cost her dearly in discomfort and considerable pain. Still she knew she could at least get to him. She figured her chances of getting out of here were slim, but at least she wouldn't go down without a fight. Incapacitated or not, she would go down with a fight, that was for sure. There is always an opportunity, one just has to seize control and do what one must do to fight, overcome, and even survive another day. He had no idea who he was messing with, but before it was all said and done, she would let him know, by god even if it meant forgoing her life!

A few hours had passed and Suzie woke up to someone trying to speak with her. It was nearly pitch black in the area she was in, with only one red dim light up in the one corner. It gave off odd and creepy shadows as she turned her head to look around at her settings. At least she could turn her head, finally! That in itself was a blessing to her. She turned her head, but it was definitely stiff from something; whether it was the drug itself, her position that she found herself in her cage, or maybe a little bit of both. Either way, she was stiff, sore, and miserable. Her clothes were still wet from the water and from soiling herself, but she couldn't help that at this point so she didn't give another thought to that. She slowly attempted to move her hands what she could, but being that she was still bound the movement was limited. She stopped as she immediately felt the mangled finger that her captor had bent back in retaliation for her attack on him. Her toned arms were still heavy from the drugs, so her movement was minimal at best, at this point. Her legs were also bound and her ankles were sore from the pressure and tightness of the heavy bands that kept her from moving. There it was again, she thought, as she was so concentrated on what she was doing, she nearly forgot about the voice that was trying to reach out to her. She tried to speak a few words, but her mouth was as dry as a dehydrated cactus in a scorched and barren desert. So the words that came out sounded like a sick frog croaking, which came out louder than she expected and then she heard the little voice quiveringly say;

"Pleassseeee……. Keeeeppp…… your…….voice…..low…….so….. he …..doe..sn'..t …….hear……you……"

"Ok," she whispered much quieter than she previously was a minute ago. "I can barely see, where are we?"

"In…. hell….." The other voice said in a stern voice.

"Ok….. How long have you been here, then? Do you know?" Suzie asked the other female.

"Ummm….. Maybe …….a week ….or two…..honestly ……..I am not……. even sure. I really…. am….. scared and…. I …am….afraid…" The trembling voice responded to her.

"I am sorry you have been here….. that ….long, …that must be so very…scary." Suzie empathized with the distressed woman in her torment.

"I ….was …..not… the….. first… and…..now….that ….you… are …here……I'm….not…..the…. Last! …There were…..many…at …one……time…here…" The voice trailed off with a melancholy and hopeless tone. Hearing that news scared Suzie immensely as it meant that they were just being used for whatever he wanted them for, and then discarding the others one at a time, or so she imagined. She couldn't imagine that type of person actually exists, as such, in this day in age. Still she knew that wasn't true, but she had never come face to face with such evil, such a devious and diabolical mindset. How will she, or even both of them get out of here? Was there even a chance? No matter what she had to try and stay focused and be ready for anything, any chance to escape and then even if she couldn't take the other female with her, she should be able to reach help and bring the thunder down on this man and his games. But then she knew if she left (escaped), the other woman was most likely doomed, and probably in an even more heinous way than originally was planned for her. She couldn't do that to someone, to another human. It just was not in her nature. Then she heard the voice pipe up again;

"Are….you….still… there..?"

"Yes, my dear, I am. I can't tell you we will make it out of here alive. I don't dare tell you that we will die here either, because no matter what there is always hope......."

"No, ...we will die here just like the.. .others." The voice said in a blank and matter of fact voice and without much hesitation. She had already given up hope and if she, herself, did escape this woman may not go with her, sadly. She didn't want to leave her, but they would not escape if one or the other was not in it wholeheartedly. This would be an all or nothing effort, that was the only thing that was feasible. Only time will tell, and hopefully something will happen so that she could seize the opportunity, or else she may be in the same position as this poor disheartened girl.

Suzie was restless and lightly sleeping in the best position she could move around in when all of a sudden an ultra bright light came on, waking her up and blinding her as soon as she opened her eyes. It was so blinding, she saw circles and she couldn't avoid it as then another light came on. It was then that she heard the generator running in the background, although it was quiet she was able to realize the noise it made. She wanted to stick her hand up to shield her eyes, but she was still bound, so all she could do was shut her eyes and then try to turn away. She heard a man's voice, that same man's voice who had grabbed her, say something;

"So, you wish to be all chatty, do you? A little girl talk between the two of you? Well, you know what I told you about that.....Never again!" Then she heard the girl's voice whimper and cry as something was being done to her, but she couldn't see as the blinding light was preventing her from seeing the surrounding area and what was going on. That infuriated her immensely, and she knew she had to say something, to not let this dirtbag get the upper hand, and so she tried to provoke him, by saying;

"Sure, what a big man you are. Can only pick on those that are restrained or drugged up. What a piece of colossal shit you are! Stay away from her and bring your ass over here where I can see you, you disgusting sewer rat!" With those words, the girl's whimpering stopped, and therefore whatever he was doing to her had ceased, for now. She heard footsteps but still couldn't see the man who had abducted her. She waited to see if he would once again reveal himself, but alas he did not. What she did hear was what sounded like water, and then all hell broke loose as a solid jet stream of water shot through the cage and directly at her. The harsh stream of pressurized water came at her with such force that it actually hurt, as it stung her exposed skin, from where it came in contact. It felt like it was being shot out of a

49

water cannon, and then all of a sudden it hit her in her face. She tried to duck her head, but it went straight into her left ear, and she fought desperately to hide deep within herself. Just as she felt that she was going to tragically drown from the water, it suddenly ceased. She breathed heavily as she honestly thought that he was trying to drown her with that forced high pressure water. She gasped, spat, and sputtered with the water that her body had been doused with. She tried to shake the water out of her ears and to stop the dull ringing, but sadly it wouldn't stop. She was not as truly miserable as she was soaking wet and also sitting in the pool of water that had collected, covering the bottom part of the cage she was stuck in. The bright lights were still on her, so even if she could open her eyes, she still wouldn't be able to see anything. She was also afraid that if she did, he would just douse her again, therefore she remained in as much of a ball as she could get in and kept her eyes firmly closed. Her feet and her butt were completely immersed in water, and it was cold water too. Also oddly enough it didn't taste good either. The water smelled of a disgusting sulfur odor and tasted like it hadn't been checked in some time, so she knew it was an old well that was being used. She sat there, but nothing more happened and so she slowly opened her eyes and then it happened. A jolt of conductive electricity ran through the water that she was sitting in, and therefore ran through her body as well. She spasmed uncontrollably as the electricity took over, causing her to urinate, defecate, and wretch on herself as she shuddered beyond anything she had ever experienced before or could ever imagine. It was like a taser on steroids, the amount of electricity that was coursing through her. She bit her tongue, she started bleeding out her nose, and she was right on the verge of passing out. Then it suddenly stopped. She couldn't move, breathe, or even think! She just laid there in utter misery, like a dead log. She had never suffered through anything like this, ever before. Then she felt a heavy hand pulling her hair and her head twisted to the side. The pain coursed through her as he turned her head more, and then she felt his warm foul breath from his mouth that was right near her still ringing ear and he said;

"Listen, you ever come between me and my prizes again. I will end your life, snuff it out of existence with my bare hands! Do you hear me? Do you hear me…….you ungrateful bitch!" Then he banged her head hard against the cage railing and the world quickly disappeared into darkness, as she lost consciousness.

A few days later and back at the task of checking the trailheads, Tom had driven to the last one he knew that was popular to jump on the AT at. This trailhead was called Passion Point, and it was called that from the many times young boys had brought and defiled their female companions over the years. The name stuck and now it is officially called that. This trailhead was also another very beautiful spot to jump in as it was also beside a fast running stream and a small cascade a little further up the trail. It did cross a gravel road as well, but the road was often used by dirt bike riders and even some ATV riders. He didn't expect to find anything worth his while, but he would do his duty and do all he can to look for clues. He came to the parking area, and there were a few vehicles there, which was good as he could stop people, but it also meant that with this much activity, the chances of finding a clue were slim to none. He checked his phone as the battery was nearly dead, so he plugged it in to charge it a little before heading out. He checked all the license plates of the vehicles in the lot, but nothing came up on any of them besides some speeding tickets that were dutifully paid off. Nothing that stood out as someone who would be a criminal, and so he started doing a little bit of the paperwork trail while he waited for his phone to charge. Unbeknownst to him, a couple came out of the trailhead, got into their vehicle, and had started their car. It wasn't till they had backed up and started forward momentum that he finally looked up from what he was doing, that he saw them. He was about to get out of his vehicle, but by that time they were moving with forward momentum and had just turned onto the main road. 'Well', he thought brazenly, as he had their plate in case he needed to investigate them or question them further. He finished up his follow up computer work, logging in all that he had done, seen, and not come up with, unfortunately. He gently pushed his computer away, grabbed his partially charged phone, took a swig of some old cold coffee, and got out of his vehicle for good now. He locked his door and started walking around this area some more and even took some pictures of the entrance area, just in case. He started walking down the trail, not hearing or seeing anyone at this point, so he figured that they must be further down the trail. This trail was just a nicer hiking trail, as it had more flowers, more close knit brush and trees, a nicer parking area, and well it seemed to have more sounds of nature also. He hiked until he came to a gravel and dirt road that the trail crossed. He stopped, looked up and down the minimally used trail and then decided to walk down the makeshift road a little distance. He walked all the while looking down at tread marks, but it looks like some atvers and motocrossers had been down here recently as there were ruts and torn up parts of the road. He would get nothing from this section of road, and so he turned around and walked the opposite direction. Again he found nothing, so he turned back toward the trail again. He stopped at the intersection and looked both ways, but it honestly looked like there was nothing here. He bowed his head in defeat and started back down the trail and towards his vehicle. He walked with his head down, looking just at the trail and lost in his thoughts, when he ran straight into someone. He walked right into the back of a heavy and well stocked backpack. His gait fumbled some but neither the person he ran into nor himself fell, and so a little off balance correction was in order. He heard a voice say, before he could even speak;

"Whoa there nelly!" As the person who said it fumbled with something in his hands and dropped whatever it was. Tom quickly and apologetically responded with;

"I am so sorry, mate. So, sorry for that!"

"Is ok, it happens." As the hiker was about to bend over and grab what Tom had made him drop. Tom stopped him though and said;

"Oh, I'll get that for you, please it is the least I can do." So he bent over and picked up the compass that the hiker had lost with the impact of their collision. After grabbing it, he handed it back to the hiker and that's when he saw the other hiker with him, an attractive young female. He apologized to her too, but it was too late he was staring in her direction. It wasn't that he was even staring at her, but where she had come from that stopped him. The young man cleared his throat, thinking that Tom was looking at his gal friend for way too long, and that was when Tom broke free from the trance and spoke up, clarifying his actions with;

"I am so sorry, I wasn't staring inappropriately at your friend, but what was she doing there?"

"Whatever bud, but what she was doing was autographing the sign-in book, right over there!" The man pointed behind his girl and watched and waited for Tom's reaction. Tom moved swiftly toward the female and she moved to the side and immediately into a self defense position that she had learned years ago at a class, thinking that he was going after her. In mere seconds, he rushed up on her and then he went right by her and started frantically paging through the book. The pair looked at each other, and then back at Tom's back (which was facing them now) and wondered what a freakin weirdo he was. Not wasting any time, they left there in haste and down the trail for their three day overnight hike excursion, leaving the strange oddity far behind them. Tom couldn't believe that he had missed the sign in the book, as he had totally walked by it previously. Tom flipped hastily through the book until he came to one passage and then he stopped dead in his tracks. He pulled out his phone and took a few photos of what was written, then he thought the hell with it, and ripped the page out as well. There on that page in plain sight was the quote written by Suzie, the missing hiker. So she did use this trail, and now at least they can search down this trail to see if they can find her. This was the first real clue they had and he was so happy he ran into the bloke, as he turned to see where they went, but they were gone. This was a good sign, indeed, he thought happily. He went back to his vehicle directly and looked over the page many times. She had been here and there it was in plain sight. He would verify it was her writing with her family just to be sure, and then they would start searching with more fervor now. They had a clue, they finally had a clue of where she had last been. Something was better than nothing to go on, he thought, thankful for anything at this juncture.

Tom called Jessie, Suzie's sister, and asked her rather bluntly;

"Are you available to meet now? It is important."

"Well, I am at work right now, but I should be able to wrap things up in say thirty minutes. Is that feasible?"

"Yes, ma'am, that would be fine with me. How about you come by the station, I have something for you to verify."

"Oh...m y...god,,..... Is my sister dead?"

"No, no, we didn't find her yet, but we found something that may be her handwriting. Nothing major, but for us, it gives up an idea which direction and what trail she used. I will tell you more when you arrive."

"Ok, I understand, and I will be there as soon as I can...!" Than the conversation ended and Tom continued driving back to the station to start on the paperwork and computer trail. He also called the forest service and let them know that he found the trail that she had been on , and to see if they could send a few volunteers down the trail to check to see if anything came up. He also texted his captain, Craig Foley, to let him know the new lead as well, which was not actually finding her, but then again beggars can't be choosers. He made it back and immediately started working on the accountability aspects of his job. Well, he started as soon as he got himself a new cup of hot flavorful coffee to quench his parched mouth. He took a few long sips and then one of the officers, Gus Lapard, came over to ask him a few questions, as he was trying to help out with the missing youngster, Teresa. Not much was going on on that end, but still they had to make sure everything was looked into also with that case. Before he knew it, Officer Linda Phillips had been looking for and found him, to tell him that he had someone there to see him. Tom saved his progress, got up, and went to the front desk to see who was there to see him. As a matter of fact it was Jessie (Suzie's sister), as she had finally made it as he requested her to. He walked over, extended his hand and said to her;

"Greetings Jessie, it is good to see you again. Follow me back to my desk, please." He said to her as he buzzed her in through the front desk area, and held the door for her. She walked by and then waited for him to lead her to where they needed to go. She did respond softly;

"Thank you Detective Tom, happy you called me about some progress. Sorry, I am running behind but something came up at work, last minute go figure."

"No worries, I just wanted to keep you informed, and thank you for taking time out of your day." Tom led her to his office and then he offered her a chair, held it for her, to allow her to sit down, and then he went around his desk and sat at his chair. He smiled at Jessie, and she tried to smile back but it was definitely feigned as she had no idea what the news was that he had for her. He looked over at Jessie and noticed that she was an attractive woman in her late thirties or early forties. She seemed to be in fairly good shape as he could see her toned arms as she nervously waited for him to start. She had auburn tight curly hair that she had put up into a partial bun, but the curls were slowly falling out from working all day and with it up. Her eyes definitely looked tired, albeit hopeful for some good news from his mouth. She fidgeted some as she moved in the chair, as he pulled out the paper he had torn from the trail sign-in book. He started off saying to her;

"So on this paper looks to be Suzie's name, and I need you to verify that this is her writing, or at least her signature..." He pushed the paper over and she eagerly looked at it, and then asked him;

"May I hold it, please?" She inquired of him and he gladly handed it over to her. She looked long and hard and then looked up at him and said;

"Yes, I can confirm that it is her writing and her signature, that is for sure." she said calmly.

"Great, that is good news, for sure."

Where did you find this entry?" she asked while looking at the paper and a few of the other signatures on the page. He continued with;

"Well, oddly enough, I stumbled into it accidentally, but it was found at the last trail system I checked out, which was the Passion Point trailhead, down the road. It was in the sign-in book, so she was there at one point, which is good news. The forest service, our team, and our local rescue team will start searching for her shortly to see if anything turns up. But I just needed to make sure that this was her signature to verify the prospect of being down the trail. So now we can officially search the area." She smiled visibly at his words and she breathed a big sigh of relief at the same time. He smiled knowing that they found something to establish her last location was better than not knowing anything at all. Hope was a good thing but also a strange aspect, because without hope a person can be devoid of vigor and robust of life. However, having excessive misplaced hope can also alienate and crush someone as well, sucking the very life out of that person. It was a fine line that one had to constantly dance around. Still she was happy to have some news and he continued with;

"I will keep you informed of continued progress with the search, and of course when we find her. Just be patient and we will continue to do our job and bring her home to you." He stood up and went over to her. She started lightly tearing up and she immediately also arose onto her feet and then she gave him a firm embrace. She cried on his sleeve some as he let her play out her emotions and her fears, in the aspect of releasing them in the tears streaming down her face. He lightly embraced her, to give her positive support and to know that he was here for her. She broke away, finally, and she gave a sheepish smile and a look of, 'I'm sorry for that'. He waved his hand and said to her;

"Please, you are allowed to express your emotions at any time. Hang in there and I will be in contact. Thank you for stopping by, again." She smiled weakly and turned to leave, letting herself out, so that he could get back to work. He sat back down at his desk and just wished that he could find her sister for her, but still it is yet to be seen. Nothing is absolute, and so at this point it still didn't look obvious that there was any real foul play, but there was always that chance. There was always a chance, no matter how normal everything looked.

He continued to work at his desk, trying to follow up with the paper trail of what he had done the last few days, that is until the captain came into his office, closing the door behind him. He sat across from Captain Foley and he looked at his boss to see what he needed. The captain spoke up first by asking;

"So, Tommy boy, how does it look?"

"To which case are you referring, Craig?"

"The missing woman or was there more than one?"

"Well there was a missing girl and a missing female hiker, so far. Neither of them have much to go on at this point, but the missing hiker at least, we know of her last position, as of a few days ago. The girl is tough ,as she hasn't been missing that long yet, but she could have run off with a boy too for some parentless joy riding or other activities. Regarding the girl, I put some feelers out to the surrounding big cities to see if they could keep an eye out for her, and I also put her on the national registry for missing children. So far, no foul play is in evidence at this time, and that even goes with the parents, who seem to be not to blame.

"Well keep on it, and keep me updated, okay, Tommy?"

"Yes sir, will do that. Anything else I can get ya?"

"Nope, that's it. Remain with what you are doing, I will see myself out." With those last words, Craig had opened up the door and headed back down the hallway. No telling what that was all about, Tom thought to himself. Someone must be putting the heat on him, he thought amusingly. Probably the mayor, as soon as he got wind of missing people. They were doing their best, that was for sure. He swiveled in his chair and looked outside, through his one small window, and started thinking. He wondered when they would start the search of the trail, but for all he knew the forest service may have some volunteers check down the trail, just to start somewhere. He thought about calling his daughter, but that passed rather quickly as she was probably too busy for him. After about thirty minutes he finished his little respite and went back to work, trying to finish up what he needed to do. About that time he was wrapping up most of his work, Jeremy popped into his office, but not before knocking first. Jeremy knocked hard enough to get his friend's attention and then strolled right on in, saying to his friend;

"What's up, buddy?"

"Uhhh, it's this missing woman case. Something just doesn't smell right with it, but I can't put my finger on it either. I mean, she hasn't been missing that long, but there are too many unknowns in this equation, and that bugs me to no end. You know what I mean?"

"Yes, I do, my friend......Is there anything I can do for you, to help you out?" Jeremy said with heartfelt sentiment to his buddy.

"No", Tom responded. "Not at this point, but I can't guarantee I won't ask for your help in the future. I really do appreciate it, that is for sure." He hesitated but then continued on with, "Just keep your ears and eyes open for me, if you don't mind!"

"Always do, my friend, always do......... How about I go get you a good coffee? What-da-think?"

"That sounds nice, I could use it for sure." Tom said with a smile. So Jeremy left his friend to his thoughts and went and retrieved him a coffee from the local coffee shop. Tom was trying to figure something out, when he suddenly got a phone call on his office landline. It was Lorie Astel, mother of the missing teen Teresa.

"Hello, is this Detective Tom Royce's number? This is Mrs. Astel, Teresa's mom."He didn't know what to say to her as he hadn't found anything that would lead to any foul play yet, so he was at a loss for words as he hesitated for a few moments before answering, with;

"Yes, ma'am..... I am sorry, you caught me in the middle of something, but what can I do for you?"

"Yes, I am sorry to interrupt you, but I was just wondering if there was anything we could be doing on our end? I mean, we feel helpless here and we don't know what to do with ourselves. Does that make sense? "

"I am sorry, but at this point there is nothing you can do, other than keep an eye out for her. She may turn up, yet, but I am sure you are concerned and somewhat afraid of the worst case scenario, but all we can do is one day at a time and continue our efforts of trying to locate her. However, if there is anything more that I need from you, or you can participate in, I will call you personally and let you know. I am sorry though, as there is nothing new to report to you at this time. I did go check out the areas which I was told where she hung out, but sadly nothing materialized from it." There was a hesitation from the other end of the line this time, then a little gasp of inhaled air, a sigh of sadness, and then she responded with;

"Thank you, ... good day...." She said as her emotions got the best of her and she started sobbing before she finished hanging up the phone. This was tough indeed, he thought and so with that he stood up from his chair, and started to head outside to track down some more teenagers to see if they had seen Teresa, or knew her. He couldn't get completely sidetracked by the missing hiker search, as his first priority had to be the first one that went missing. Just as he left his office and started heading out the door to the building, Jeremy had come back inside and just caught his friend heading out now. He handed Tom a hot cup of joe and he asked, inquisitively;

"So where are we off to now?"

"We? Well I just got a call from Teresa's mom..the missing skater girl... and she is not in a good place, so before I spend all my time looking for the hiker I must first do my part with the search for the skater."

"I hear ya, but hopefully she just didn't get upset at her parents and run off for a few days, which will make us all look stupid, you know?"

"Yes, I get what you are saying, but what if something did happen to her and we overlook something? That will haunt me forever, and I don't want that on my conscience!"

"I get it my friend, I get it. Well either way I am going with you!" Tom smiled at his friend's desire to help him out, even though it was his job, technically. It was the willingness that mattered to him, and so he took a sip of tasty coffee and the two of them headed out the door to hopefully get some questions answered.

Chapter Five

Suzie awoke from her forced slumber, head throbbing, and feeling like complete crap. She was stiff all over, hungry, miserable, and just plain annoyed. The funny thing about her situation is that she wasn't even truly scared of what could or may happen. She licked her dry lips with her cotton mouthed tongue, and then she looked down at the water that she was partially lying in, and said 'what the hell' to herself, and was about to lick some of the water. Yes, it may have some of her urine in it, but at this point, she didn't have any other choice, and just when she was about to lap a drink, she saw a bottle hanging from the cage. It looked like a water bottle but set up like hamsters, gerbils, or rabbits have in their cages to allow them to drink water. Primitive as it was, she was at least able to get a small lukewarm drink, once she figured out how to work it and get some drops. Her dignity gone, she lapped up the small trickle of refreshing water coming out of the hanging container. The trickle of water was so refreshing as little as it was and she continued drinking for some time, just trying to quench her insatiable thirst. She ached all over like someone had pulled hard on all her joints, but then again that was most likely partially to the fact that she had been electrocuted for her stated crimes of annoying her captor. She smiled at that thought as she stopped for a moment and tried to take in her surroundings again. The bright lights were off now and the entire place was in near darkness, save for a very dim red light in the far corner of the area they were staged in. It took about another thirty minutes until her night vision truly kicked in and she was able to see other cages spaced sporadically throughout this floor. There didn't seem to be any movement in the cages, but she kept looking in the hopes that someone else was here in this living hell, besides herself. Then she finally saw some movement in the closest cage. She cleared her throat with just enough noise that the person in there moved more and sat up. The woman in there said rather bluntly and with utter disdain;

"She told you to be quiet…. And now she is gone also."

"What do you mean…. Gone where…?"

"She is probably in the nether world, now, …….never to see or be seen again."

"I thought there were only two of us in here before, before the prick …….assaulted me?…."

"There may have been, but he seems to move us around whenever he wants to. I was brought in just earlier, then he took her out, all the while that you were still unconscious. I actually had thought that you were dead, since you hadn't moved in such a long time. Lucky you, I was envious at first …….I guess." That last statement made her think some, as the words were spoken and with such sharp conviction. These girls obviously know their captor, but even though it cost her, she was happy to be able to control some aspect of this entire ordeal. That was something that jack-hole never expected, and so, by God, it was well worth it. She had to find out as much as she could from this newer person. She continued asking questions, hoping that the girl would continue answering her.

"So, what has he…. done….to you?" There was a sigh, and then silence as if the girl was wondering whether or not she wanted to divulge anything more to her. Then after a few minutes of silence, she responded with;

"Well at first he was gentle and kind, as long as I did what he wanted. But recently, he has been more ….should I say different. Like he was preoccupied. That or maybe it was because of ……..you." Immediately, Suzie now had some regret on how she acted as it seems like her actions may have had a lasting negative effect on the other girls as well. Maybe it wasn't fair, but she didn't think she should be shamed for standing up for herself. Still it bugged her that this girl was blaming her for their captor's change in demeanor or attitude. Then again she did get him a little, but she definitely paid the price for it, in the long run. Still she had to know more and so she kept with the questions.

"So, has, he sexually assaulted you, at all?" Again, there was silence and then finally the girl spoke up.

"No."

"Is that it? There must be something……."

"No, he hasn't but he will get you naked, tied up and take pictures of your nakedness. A few of the girls in the past, or so I have heard, have been assaulted or penetrated with certain …..objects, but never he himself."

"Does he do anything else that you know of?"

"Shhhh. …..Enough with the questions. I don't feel like talking anymore." Suzie heard the girl move as the cage creaked and then there was nothing but silence again. She was frustrated that obviously this girl had given up as well, but there was nothing else she could do. These abused and defeated women and girls, however many there were, had obviously fought their demons and have now resigned themselves to whatever fate was in store for them. She was different though and she knew that she would not give up. She thought and day dreamed for a long period of time, about being somewhere else, anywhere else besides here. She brought back memories of one of her hikes that she had done previously, and how much she missed the smells of the outdoors, the buzzing insects, and yes even the rain on her face and body as she delved deeper into the woods and forests. She so longed for that now more than ever, to be 'lost' out in the woods, enjoying nature and all it has to offer. Eventually she fell asleep, in an awkward position, but she could hardly change her position as she was still bound of sorts to the cage and her extremities as well. She hoped that she would dream of better days, and then she was fast asleep.

The slumbering and drugged Suzie was abruptly awoken by something metal banging against her cage. She groggily woke up, and saw that her bounds had been cut and she was free in the cage, well except the heavy leather prong collar that chained her to the cage yet. But at least she could finally move her legs and arms again. They were severely stiff, sore, and weak since they were bound for so long.

She looked up, but the bright lights were in her eyes again, so she couldn't see her captor that well, to see if she had left lasting damage when she assaulted him. He ordered her to strip naked as he had other clothes for her. She wanted to get these crusty clothes off her body, but she surely wasn't going to be nude in front of this man either, so she shook her head no and remained where she was. He told her to do it again, or there would be consequences, but she held firm and didn't budge. Then she heard the taser-like prodder that zookeepers or old circus workers would/could use on animals if they are violent. It was supposed to be used for protection and not as a weapon, but here this man was using it as a weapon against her. She curled up more into a ball, half expecting him to use it once again, but he did not this time. She breathed a sigh of relief and then he said to her;

"Well, Miss attitude, since you still wish to play these games and act like an animal, you will get fed not what you could get, but you will receive what you deserve." Seconds later he tossed in a plate full of what looked to be cheap wet canned dog food. He had no utensils of course, but just a paper plate full of disgusting looking and horrible smelling dog food. Then the lights went out and it was quiet again. She sat there in silence, not sure what to do. How dare he give her this horrific meal! Why not just starve her, she would appreciate it better. She grabbed the sagging plate full of dog food and tossed it outside her cage and onto the wooden floor. She would not eat that shit, ever! She called out for the girl again, but she heard nothing, no movement or any noise at all. Crap, was she gone already? Was she all alone again? Not that it mattered much, but still it was nice to know that someone else was in the same room with her. She used her hands, minus the broken finger which was flopping around, so she was unable to use it properly, to grab the heavy collar to check if she could get it off, but it was locked behind her neck and it was solid too. Dang, she thought, if only she could pick locks, but not like she had anything to pick the lock with. She stopped messing with the collar as it was there and she had no way to get it off. The chain was a heavy grade chain too, that secured her to the cage. She pulled on that for some time trying and pleading for the links to give, but they were obviously cold hardened steel and they would not break that easily. There was nothing else to do, so she tore off a piece of her shirt, and brought her broken finger back in place, but not without excruciating pain, and secured it to one of her good fingers. That was the best she could do for now, she surmised. Hopefully eventually she will have a plastic spoon that she could use to splint it better, but who knows if that will ever happen. Then she started singing a song, an old classic rock song to make the time pass by. It did help but again she was parched so she took another drink from the gerbil feeder, and it tasted stale, but it was refreshing. About an hour or so passed and then she heard squeaking noises, and it seemed that some mice were enjoying the plate of food she threw on the floor. There were many squeaking noises as it seemed that a few were vying for the food, but after a while it became quiet again and so she stretched her limbs some by abducting and adducting her joints to keep them limber and help deter the stiffness. She kept herself busy by singing more songs, looking around the poorly lit inside of the building , and then she also relieved herself, which she hadn't done in some time. She arched her butt somewhat against the cage, so that she could try to aim her liquid waste outside the cage. She did a decent job considering her status. At least she hadn't gone on herself again, like she had earlier when she had been shocked. She continued trying to bide her time, and then she fell asleep because she had nothing better to do at this time. She napped off and on, awaking for short periods of time and then falling back asleep, but not till changing bodily positions. This really sucked she thought, for she would rather be dead than contained and controlled as she is now! This was not living but only slowly dying, and she would rather end her life somehow and go out kicking than be this man's pet for however long he decided to keep her. It was just wrong.

She was once again awoken out of a dead sleep, but not because of the bright lights or the irritating voice of their captor, but because she felt as if someone was watching her. She looked up one direction but she had to adjust her vision to the hazy darkness again, but saw no one. She turned her head the opposite direction and she jumped, nearly out of her own skin. There before her, was standing a ghastly looking woman standing there with two eye patches and a tight head wrap on. She had no idea how or when this woman showed up, but she could see that the woman was like a ghost (a mere shell) and not acting like a human any longer. It was as if her spirit was gone from her body/broken and she accepted whatever fate may bring her. Suzie didn't know what to do, so she slowly and with unsure hesitation reached her hand to the edge of her cage, right near the woman's one outstretched hand. She didn't dare touch her, but the woman was just standing there not moving at all, almost like in a trance or maybe this woman was truly an apparition or figment of her own imagination. She truly didn't know, but she had to find out. So, against her better judgment, she reached for the woman's hand and finally barely touched the woman. For a split second, there was no response but in the next few seconds, the woman started groaning and then screaming, which unfortunately turned into a high pitched shrieking. Suzie covered her ears with her hands and closed her eyes as the shrieking continued for what seemed like a minute, and then it stopped. She looked up where the woman had once been standing, but she was no longer there. Had she been dreaming? No, it wasn't possible as her ears were still ringing from the horrific and deafening noise. Either way she assumed that someone else was in here and pulled the woman away, without her seeing it. There had to be someone else in here then, that wasn't caged up. She called out, saying;

"I know someone else is in here with me.......please let me know that I am not crazy!" There was no response, and so she continued her plea;

"Please, just answer me! I promise I won't ask any questions! I just need to know that someone is here!?.....please!" Then finally after a few more minutes, a calm and sorrowful voice spoke up, saying;

"I am here."

"Ok....thank you....." She decided to press her luck and press on with a question or two. She continued with;

"So, what happened to that girl?"

"You said no questions, so no questions."

"Ok, I am sorry. I am just trying to make sense of everything, that is all. Do you understand that?"

"There is no sense, so don't bother. We do what we must to survive, as you must, as she must, and as I must. That is the hand we are dealt." There was a slight hesitation, and then she said a few more words;

"That girl chose her path and now she must live with the consequences....... We must do what we must to survive............" Then the voice was gone as it sounded like she left through a door. She was alone with her thoughts again, which after that last interaction, had her wondering even more. She was so hungry, but at least she had her drink, and she used her bottle once more, licking and drinking for quite some time. She wondered if what that girl said is the reason why she could come and go as she pleases, to a point. She must have sold her soul to the devil or so to speak as she seemed to assist the captor out in some way, or so it seems. She wasn't judging her, because she had no idea what the girl could have endured or how long she had been here, but there was no way she would ever help that defiler out in any way. She didn't know if there was an afterlife or not, because most of her life she hadn't cared about such celestial issues, but if that girl did truly sell her soul to help herself out, she hoped there was some punishment or penitence for her wrong doing. It only seemed fair, but not that life was fair. Then after a long period of quiet solitude, she fell back asleep again. Hopefully this time she would wake up at a different place, another life, or anywhere but this hell hole which she has been confined to. She drifted off to sleep once again.

Suzie was awoken from her slumber once more, abruptly as she felt something sting her shoulder and once she realized it she jolted awake. She saw her captor back away from her cage again, as she swung at it, at him, as an afterthought. He snickered at her 'playfulness' and 'spirit', but he also sneered as he watched her. She felt the drugs in her taking effect, and there was nothing she could do as her body became helpless once more. In the next minute she was out, and he jolted her some before opening up the cage and going inside and doing what he was there to do. She remained helpless and out, thankfully as he did what he wished and wanted to do to her, without her consent, knowledge or even her choice. After about an hour or so, his alarm on his watch went off and he hurried out of the cage with some of the objects he had entered with, and an extra object as well. He had finished up with her and he closed the door. He handed the items to his apprentice helper that was always with him when he performed such deeds. She didn't smile, but just remained stoic as he handed the items to her, which she stowed on the small wheeled cart that they brought with them. There were medical instruments, a few jars, and some bloody bandages left. She honestly didn't like what he did to the girls, but if she didn't help out, he would have done the same to her a long time ago, and she would be gone off this earth by now. She had regrets, regrets every single day for her part in the heinous crimes done to these girls and women, but she was a survivor and she would do whatever she must to remain alive. She didn't know these girls, she didn't owe them any allegiance, and even though she felt sorry for them, she still did what she must do. This world is a harsh place and sometimes we must make decisions we don't wish to make in life, however that may be. The battered wife continues to live with the abusing husband because even though she knows it is wrong, she almost needs that to retain her own identity. What is the difference between them and her? None by her standards, and so she continued to assist this dark man with

64

his doings, so that hopefully one day she would have the chance to live and be free. She begged and prayed every day for her captor to be caught by the police and this living hell to fade away. Yet everyday, she still did what she had to do until such time should come about. She made the decision long ago to just play the game and continue to live whatever existence she could until her death or until her freedom. That was the only reason to keep going on, a little sliver of hope. Sadly though every day, every week, and every month that goes by, that hope was slowly fading away, fading into the darkness of reality and what she is helping this man do. Still, she reasoned, choices were made and at least she was not dead.

Sometime later on, Suzie awoke once more from a drug induced slumber, but this time was different. There was something not right as she tried to open her eyes and realized that she could only open one eye. She panicked and started banging her one arm against the cage. She then raised her hand up and felt a bandage and just playing with it, the pain shot through her body and she immediately vomited on her floor. She panicked and she felt something in her arm and she was about to rip it out, as it was an IV site. She stopped and then she looked up with her one blurry but uncovered eye and saw that it was some medication. Maybe it was pain medication, not that she wanted to be doped up, but she felt horrible pain when she messed with her eye, whatever had happened to it. What had he done to her eye? Did he injure it, play God with it, or did he remove it? She had no clue and just when she was about to claw the dressing open, she was stopped by the same female voice that she had talked to last. The girl who she didn't know the name of, but she decided to call her evil weasel, because of what she did to help out their captor. The girl said to her;

"Don't remove the bandages."

"Why? Why should I listen to you?"

"Because, I am the only one you can trust!"

"Whatever, I don't believe you! You weasel, you evil weasel! Helping that prick out and do his bidding. It's just wrong!"

"It may be, but I am still alive, not in a cage, and whole." The girl said rather bluntly and with some disdain, probably at being called a weasel.

"What did and why did he do that to me, and what, exactly, is going in my arm? ....Tell me!......Tell me now!!!"

"What you have going into your arm is IV pain medication to alleviate the pain from the surgery. He removed your right eye. Please don't pull the IV out or it will be much more painful, then it is currently, that's for sure. Trust me with that, but do what you think is right. Be happy you are alive."

"Alive?.......Alive?" Suzie screamed out loud! "What the hell do you mean alive? I am in a cage, chained to a cage, have been electrocuted, drugged up, and now am missing an eye. Why the hell should I be happy? You ....tell....me....!"

"Anger is a typical defense mechanism when this happens. But he could have killed you or even worse made you a living zombie, like that other poor soul you saw. That girl had fought him all the way and now look at her pitiful existence. If you continue to fight, that outcome will happen to you also. It is not a threat, but a grim reality to what your actions are, and how they are received. Still, you do what you must, for it is your life after all." With that she turned and left Suzie to her thoughts. Suzie was so pissed off, she was fuming at what she had just been told. She wanted to throttle that girl. If she couldn't get her captor, then maybe she could at least end that girl's life, as it was one that deserved to be ended. If she had the chance and she could make it happen , she would do this. Not that her captor would care, as he would just get someone else to do his bidding, so in the end it would do nothing. But damn if it wouldn't make her feel good! She smiled at that thought, the one of her with her hands around the woman's throat and crushing her windpipe. Her anger was definitely getting the best of her, as she looked at her arm and almost pulled the IV out of her arm, just in spite. It was only now that she realized that she was completely naked also. She was so caught up in her eye, the IV, the girl, and her pain that she hadn't even realized that she was stark naked. She looked around and found some type of paper clothes, like something psych wards or hospitals have, and she immediately put it on the best she could so that she was covered up at least. She had to tear the back to fit it over her neck harness , so her back was open but at least her chest was covered. She wanted to pull out the IV, but then again she was worried about how much pain she would have. She slowly and gently felt the dressing to her right eye and she wanted to cry. She had broken a bone or two before , but she had never lost a body part before. Then she noticed that her pelvic and vaginal area had some discomfort, so she guessed that she had been violated in some way by her nasty creepy captor, while she was asleep. Once again something was taken from her, by force! She wanted to just weep, and her left eye started tearing up, but she didn't know what that would do with her empty socket, or she guessed that was what was left of her orbital socket. She had no clue, nor did she really wish to see it either. She couldn't believe what her life had become. All she saw in her mind was the girl that shrieked that awful noise when she had touched her hand. That was insane, but obviously that girl had lost both eyes and also probably had some type of head surgery as well, maybe like a lobotomy or something of the sort. So this captor was obviously a medically derived person as how would he have the capability to do such surgeries, have medications, or even the knowledge of such. Or maybe he was just some sadistic idiot who looked all this up and somehow had an inside way of getting such drugs or medical devices for such procedures. Still he would have to have some schooling, that only made sense. She surmised for quite some time, as she continued lightly touching the dressing over her removed eye. She stretched out her legs and arms as much as she could. Her stomach was growling so loudly as she hadn't eaten in who knows how long as her concept of time was completely gone. Time didn't mean anything to her at this point, and since she couldn't see the outside, she had no idea what time of day it was. All she had was the dim red light and darkness, that was all that her world existed of at this time, much to her dismay. She lamented in her misery and she went to a darker place than she ever had before in her life. She nearly let the situation get the best of her, and she could see why so many of the girls have given up at this point. She was slowly starting to see the truth, and that was that she had no control anymore. She wasn't giving up, not by any stretch at all, but she really had no control over her life anymore. She was completely at her captor's whims and will. This was one hard pill to swallow as she was the most independent woman in her circle of friends and family. She always did things when she wanted to and never had to worry about checking in with anyone. She had always been a loner, which made her family worry, but she always blew it off as she can take care of herself, no matter what. Now and just now, she had come to terms with the fact that they were right all along. No matter how many good and kind people there were in this world, there were always ones on the opposite end of the spectrum or equation. She had never come across that other end, until now. She just wished she had a pencil and paper so she could write her last thoughts, her wishes, and her heartfelt sentiment to her family, who she loved so much. She just didn't want to be erased off this earth without saying her heart words to those she loves. Maybe she could get something from the weasel girl, not that she wanted to befriend her, but she would be more amicable if she could do that for her. Sometimes one must do what they must to survive........Dang that sounded exactly like weasels words. Maybe there was some truth in those words after all, but still not to the degree that she had taken it. Still some truth was still evident. Slowly, she curled up the best she could and fell back asleep, because there wasn't anything else to do at this point.

Some unknown amount of time later, Suzie woke up to someone touching her. She cringed away from the touch, as she opened her one good eye, and that's when she saw that it was the weasel girl again. She had something with her and she tried to strain her left eye to see what it was, which was a plate of food. This time there wasn't any dog food, but actual real edible human food. The bowl (which was only lightweight plastic) was handed to her (between the larger diameter poles of the lower aspects of the cage) and she eagerly ate with her hands and shoved the food inside her mouth. She had eaten half the bowl, before the girl spoke up to her;

"Don't eat too fast or you will possibly vomit and not retain any of the nutrition from the food." Once the girl she called Weasel said those words, Suzie realized that made sense and she stopped some after she swallowed the last glob of food she took. It was some type of oatmeal with fruit in it, sugar, and milk as well. It was delicious as she hadn't eaten in who knows how long. It tasted like the best surf and turf that she had ever eaten in her life: it tasted that good! She continued eating the food, while the girl watched her. She enjoyed every tasty bit and she even licked the bowl clean. She looked up and asked;

"Any chance for more?"

"No, sorry, that is it for now." The girl said with a bleak look. We all get fed very minimal food, but it is still nutritionally balanced. I have lost some weight since I have been here, as you will too."

"I could stand to lose some anyway, but I don't think the dog food was nutritional, by human standards!" Suzie suddenly joked out of nowhere as she smiled and left out a slight chuckle. The girl just looked at her and didn't say a word or even crack a smile. Obviously a tough crowd, Suzie thought to herself, as she handed the empty bowl back. Oh well, such is life. She curled back up, and the girl just sat there watching her. Finally the girl spoke up again, saying;

"You sure are a pretty looking woman", she said as she lowered her eyes down to the floor and her feet.

"Why, thank you, I guess, but I am not so pretty any longer." she said as she pointed at her eye. The girl just looked down at the floor again. There was an awkward silence for a few minutes, as both had nothing really to say to one another. Suzie had to empty her bladder again, so she looked at the girl and asked her;

"Do you mind, I have to pee."

"No, I don't mind at all...." The girl said as she continued staring at Suzie. Suzie shrugged her shoulders and did what she had to do to relieve herself. This time though, the peeing burned some, so she knew that she definitely had been violated in some way. She knew she couldn't change that now, so she pulled up her pants and said rather bluntly to the girl;

"You are an odd one, to say the least." The girl stood silently, turned to walk away but stopped, looked down again, and then walked away without saying another audible word. It became deathly quiet inside her area of the building again, and so she tried to fall back asleep as there was nothing else to do. The intravenous pain medication, whatever it was, was working well to keep her comfortable enough, thankfully. She couldn't imagine the amount of pain she would be having without it, so she made the smart choice of not suffering any more than she had to and by keeping the IV in place and not tampering with it. She started humming a song and then started to look around to see if she could see any cameras, but if there were any she couldn't ascertain their location. They might be hi-tec infrared or some other fancy type of dark viewing cameras. She did see a small red light up in one corner, when she squinted with her left eye, but that caused pain in her right side, so she ceased that action immediately. This just sucks, she remorsed at the thought of living with only one eye, but then again she didn't wish to lose both either. She sort of regretted doing what she did to provoke her captor, but then again he might have done what he did regardless. There was no telling at this point but she had definitely pissed him off, that was for sure. Eventually she may know if that was a good decision or not, but either way she couldn't change anything at this point. She curled up again after humming some more tunes, some classic rock from the late 70's and early 80's, and closed her one eye. There were a lot of small regrets in her life that she wished she could change, but none more than going solo on that last hike. She missed her sister, she missed her friends, but most of all she missed her freedom. Sadly though that was another life now, and this was the life she had to dwell and exist in, for now. She didn't want any more drugs, but she didn't wish to be in excruciating pain either, so she would have to just exist as now, and see what more games her buffoon captor could come up with.

Her captor watched her on the scope of cameras, the well placed and nearly difficult to see lot of cameras that he had posted in each area. He flipped back and forth between them all, checking on all his girls and seeing who was doing what and how they were all doing. He kept a close eye on each girl, switching camera angles and zooming in when he wanted to, to get a much better view. He remained looking at a few choice girls and then he lastly zoomed in on Suzie. Was he mad at her for doing what she did and rebelling? Yet, he was overwhelmingly happy he chose her, Yes indeed! She was spirited in so many ways, and he actually liked that immensely about her. She was his favorite, of this lot, that was the truth. He rubbed the bridge of his nose, as it was still sore from where she landed the blow on him. Even though it wasn't full strength, he still took a solid blow and she was strong beyond her initial looks. He would not make that same mistake again. He had to teach her a lesson so that none of the others would get any ideas about giving him grief, and so in honesty, he had to set a precedent for poorly thought out actions. So he had to do what he did with her surgically and also physically when he violated her, because she deserved it, for lack of better words. He glanced over at the cooler and figured he must stow his goods that he was able to extrapolate from his girls. He was proud of his girls and even of his hench lady, because she helped keep the women in line, and help them see that there was no escape, that there was no hope, and that there was nothing they could do about it. Without her, he would have to do so much more to control these ladies and girls, but with her being such an asset that he could enjoy times like these. She would be coming back and checking in with him soon to see if he had anything else for her to do for the night. He laughed when he heard Suzie call his assistant a weasel. Funny thing is, she truly looked like one, and that is why he might just have to start calling her that. He would ponder on it, that was for sure.

He looked at the notebook beside him, and opened it up once more. He rummaged through the meticulously placed pictures and he stopped on occasion to inspect and enjoy the scenes that they displayed. Before him, the pictures were all pictures of his girls, mostly nude and mostly in some seductive pose that he had stuck them in. There were also some before and after pics of his procedures as well. With each procedure he was becoming more adept at his handiwork and his expertise in such surgical matters. He took pride in his work, whether it be the surgeries themselves or even with the photos. He smiled at every picture, every detail, and every perfection of his girls. They were all beautiful in their own right. Such perfection should always be shared, but at this point he dare not, lest he get jealous of someone else's thoughts on his girls. He was very protective of them and that was that. He closed the book after some five minutes of reflection and set about doing his daily chores again. He had to keep things tidy as his obsessive compulsive disorder would take over, and he would be offset and infuriated by his slackfulness. He started getting irritated just thinking about it, and so he started doing his tasks in a fury or activity before the unsettling thoughts sunk in. He had to keep things tidy and remain in control! He finished up and stopped momentarily to grasp his inner equilibrium, to bring his inner demons back under control. He sat down in his little circle behind the desk, lit some candles, and started chanting to recapture his chi, his balance. When he was younger his parents had put him on medication, but once he realized that the meds were taking his very soul from him, he stopped them. He did use drugs for long periods of time, which helped momentarily, but it wasn't till he found meditation that he found true happiness with his inner self (and the voices within).

He had to be careful as he truly watched how many women/girls he picked up from each area. The further he went out from his home base, the better chance it was for him to get caught. He had come here to this old abandoned homestead some time ago. He wasn't even sure when it had been abandoned, but it had been empty a long time. This house had a huge barn which was unattached but very close to the house. There were no neighbors within miles and he was able to stay undetected for this long. Still he knew his limitations, so he would try to find one more prize girl and call it for a little while. She would have to be special and not someone who would truly be missed that much. Maybe a teenager thinking about running away, yes that would be the perfect find. He thought of where to start looking, like what hang-outs would be best. He knew that there was a skatepark just outside of town and maybe he could find a rebellious teen there that was in desperate need of a father figure or longing for the older man to pamper her. He grabbed his camera, checked his film, and yes he still used film cameras because he developed the film himself, obviously. He loved the nostalgia of the film and he could control it better. Easier to burn a book then erase digital pictures. That reason alone but also digital pictures leave a trace somewhere, like in your storage areas, such as a cloud or zip drive. That was harder to deal with and more complicated, and so he kept it as simple and easy as he could. Also he enjoyed the task of a dark room and making his own film. Yes, it was retro and old fashioned but there was something simple, something pure about it and that is why he did thus. His Obsessive compulsive disorder was also perfect when he did the dark room work and produced such perfect memories of his times with his girls. He loved all his girls so much. He would touch them at times, shower them, get them naked, but he never had sex with any of them. He used other things and objects to defile them, but not his own body. As a matter of fact he hadn't had sex in like, never. He was still a virgin, sexually, but not in spiritualality or mentation. He had performed countless sexual related acts with numerous women, but only in his complex mind and in his vivid imagination. He just never actually had in his real life. Still, he was fine with that, because to him it heightened his senses and his ability to love better without performing true acts of the flesh. So in respect, he remained pure in that aspect, and he knew that made him appreciate his girls, their bodies, and the wondrous traits each one of his girls contributes to his collection. He loved his different life and what he has accomplished thus far, and yet he had more plans for many additional years of collecting to come, many more years!

Chapter Six

It was a long day, a long day indeed for both Officer Pine and Detective Royce. They had been all over town, showing Teresa's photo around. Some people have recognized her, as in seeing her around, but never truly chatted with her. Others had previously had some minor interactions with the girl, but no long exchanges or anything withstanding, so more or less they had casual interactions only. They happened upon one other boy who truly seemed to have more than just one interaction with the young missing girl. Tom showed Eli the photo of Teresa, and after Eli moved his overgrown curly locks away from his face, he stared at the photo for a few minutes. Tom asked him;

"So, you know this girl or have seen her?"

"Uh-huh." The boy said lazily and with little interest. Then Tom continued pressing, saying;

"Well, boy, which one is it?"

"Both brah."

"Well, have you conversed with her at all?"

"Yup."

"Listen here boy, I am trying to be nice, but you are pissing me off, now." Tom said bluntly and with no emotion. The boy looked at the detective, cocked his head and then the officer next to him, who was giving a dirty look. He figured these guys weren't playing and so he just wanted to leave, but he figured they would bother him until he gave them a better answer. Against his better judgment he said;

"Ok, listen now. I had talked to her a few times b-fore, but then she started hanging out with some older guy, so she stopped talking to me. Wasn't any of my business, so I let it be." Finally, Tom thought they were getting somewhere.

"Do you see this older man around town?"

"No, not much and not in sum time."

"Ok, well do you think you would recognize him if you saw him again?"

"Maybe, dunno, I guess."

"Could you pick him out of a picture or photo or describe him in any way?"

"Nor sure, you got a pic?" Tom looked at the boy and wondered for a second. If I had one, I wouldn't need him he thought, as he placed his hand to his head in utter bewilderment. He looked back at Jeremy and the look on his face was utter dumbfoundment also. This boy obviously wouldn't be able to pick the guy out, as his brain is fried from too many shrooms, drugs, or something.

"Are we dun?" the boy asked calmly just as he placed his board down again.

"Yes, we are done, thank you for your time." With that the boy left and Tom and Jeremy looked at each other and then laughed at how much that boy seemed to be lacking something along the way. Still he saw an older man, but no other description, sadly. Now, they could ask about an older man hanging around the teens in town, that could possibly be a lead. Either way this wasn't looking good at all. Maybe someone else would be able to better describe the man, so they would go looking around some more for other skaters. Well, maybe after a fresh cup of coffee that is, thought Tom. He looked over at Jeremy and asked him;

"Ready for a refill on a fresh cup of joe?"

"Hell, yes!" Responded Jeremy with ecstatic resonance.

After a stroll to the Frank's Deli to grab another drink, and, well, a small bite to eat as well, the two of them set out looking for more skaters. The snack and the coffee were both a delicious welcome as they set out on their never-ending task of trying to find more kids that might know Teresa. They made their way to the skate park again, where this evening it was a flurry of activity as skaters were trying their darndest to pull off their stunts and tricks with ease and purpose. Some of the kid's acrobatics and skills were amazing as both Tom and Jeremy watched the kids. Tom stood mesmerized at how good some of them were, but also the budding ones who were out there giving it their all and trying as hard as they could. Eventually some of the kids took some breaks and that was when Tom and Jeremy started showing pictures around again. Most of the kids said no that they didn't know her, however they seemed to only see her off and on. They were told that she skated by herself mostly, so she was sort of an outcast or loner by choice, but either way hard to say. No one shunned her, she just tended to keep to herself was all. They also found out that she was a decent skater overall, too, or at least by most of the comments from some of the well known locals. They watched the kids for a little longer and waited to see if anyone else would show up, but before long darkness was setting in as the sun went down for the evening. They called it a night and Jeremy went home for the night and Tom went back to the office for a little while longer. He looked at the two separate boards that he had set up for both women to see the progress of their disappearance. Each board had a picture at the top of it, one with Teresa and one with Suzie on it. Both of them were within the same week and probably only a few days apart at best. Two different locations, well they didn't know exactly where Teresa had been taken from. At this point he had to assume that Teresa had been taken and not run away, at least until something else said otherwise. It is best to go on the worst case scenario and then improve from there, hopefully. Teresa was last checked in on the trail and then she disappeared from existence. The local rescue squad and some volunteers were starting their search, tomorrow, to see if she could be found somewhere along the trail, which hopefully she will be. Still it didn't seem the most probable as he had been told she had all kinds of wilderness survival training and wilderness first aid. She was in decent toned shape and it was not uncommon to see her hiking many miles daily. So unless something unusual happened to her, it was a guess that she had been taken somewhere along the way. She could have disappeared 2-4 days ago was the problem with her case. And Teresa could have been taken anytime between the last 36-40 hours. They were very close in comparison, timeline wise, but not too close that it couldn't be done. He pondered on what he didn't know, which was practically everything about both cases. He stood thinking to himself, 'this freaking sucks!'. He honestly didn't know where else to begin or what to do the next day concerning either of these women. Everyday that they were missing meant one day closer to not being found alive, but what else could he be doing to help find both or even either of them. If they were both taken, and by the same person, he probably wasn't going to be looking for someone new anytime soon, since he has two in the bag at this time. They dearly needed a break, but at this point, any break in either of these cases would be purely luck or coincidental. He honestly felt like a failure to these girls, because he had no idea what he was going to do.

He called it a night and left the office around ten o'clock at night. He was tired, perplexed, unsure of himself, and just plain weary from the millions of questions that he had for the cases. He stopped by the local convenience store and picked up a pack of cigarettes and a small bottle of whiskey. He hadn't smoked in quite some time, but he felt the need and the urge tonight and so he stood outside the store and smoked at least two times in succession and even had a small drink of whiskey. He then got into his vehicle and drove the short distance to his place. So, he sat down on his balcony and smoked a few cigs and drank half the bottle of tasteful whiskey, and completely enjoyed his indulgence. He sorely missed his wife. It was at times like these that he thought of her, when he was down and enjoying such sinful pleasures. He missed her smell, her smile, her everything...... he just missed.... his sweet Jeanine ....so crazy much. He slumped over the chair on the balcony and slowly fell asleep with a lit cigarette in his hand. It wasn't until one in the morning that he fell asleep, and then he awoke at five, just four hours later with a sore back and a tight neck from the way he fell asleep in the uncomfortable sleeping chair. He had to desperately sober up, and so he went over and started a fresh pot of strong coffee to start his ritualistic waking up process. Thankfully, the cigarette that he had fallen asleep with in his hand had simply fallen into a pot of soil that used to have a live plant in it, but has since been dead for months now. So the burning cancer stick fizzled out with the soil and he didn't accidentally burn the place down to ashes. After starting the pot of coffee and feeding the cat, he turned on the shower and the hot water to full dial. Before long, the bathroom was full of steam and the shower was ready for him to jump into it. He finally took off yesterday's clothes, discarding them in the dirty laundry bin, which was sadly overflowing by now with clothes that needed attending too. He clambered into the shower, but not before bumping his head on the door of the shower. He rubbed his head and stood underneath the stream of water, enjoying every little bead of water that ran over his body. With his hands pressed up against the wall of the shower, he just enjoyed the washing away of the crustiness of yesterday. He thought of the days when he used to take a shower with his wife. He closed his eyes and envisioned seeing her lovely and shapely body as she rubbed soap all over herself, cleansing her body. It was a simple act, but even those simple and meaningless aspects of people that many forget, he chose to remember. He could see her tight butt and her toned legs(long before she was sick), meet and make the cutest little dimple that turned him on the first time he had seen that aspect of her. She would laugh and say that he was being silly, but he could still see that aspect of her body that he remembered even more than the obvious aspects of it. He had been underneath the shower so long that his skin tone had turned red from the barrage of hot water on it for so long. He shut the water off, after a quick refreshing hit of cold water to ease his skin and counteract the hot water redness. He toweled himself off, mostly drying himself, and then he wrapped the towel around himself and headed for the kitchen. Opening up a cupboard, he grabbed a clean cup, poured a nice cup of hot coffee into the waiting cup and then took a sip. Hmmm, it was perfect and he didn't have to add anything, even though sometimes he did just to add some more flavor. It all depended on his mood at the time. There was a dirty pan in the sink that he grabbed, and so he mildly cleaned it off first before placing it on the stove and turning on the burner. He sprayed the pan with non-stick spray, put a little pad of butter in it, and then grabbed what was left of the eggs. Cracking each egg, he dropped them one by one into the pan and they started to cook almost immediately. The spatula was just nearby and he wiped it off first and then started to mix up the eggs some, going for more of a scramble today. There was a loaf of bread nearby that he grabbed and put two pieces into the toaster oven to toast them for a sandwich. Once toasted, he buttered the pieces and prepared them for the eggs to finish. He even put a thin slice of provolone cheese on the toast, and then he grabbed the pan and brushed the scrambled eggs onto the awaiting slices. Then he placed the slices together and took a nice bite of toasted egg sandwich. He dearly wanted bacon, but he was out of such luxuries at the moment. So he enjoyed what he had available with gusto. After breakfast and his first cup of coffee, he went back into the bedroom to change his clothes for the day. He decided that it was a casual day today, and so he wore blue jeans, a nice button down shirt, and a more leisurely sports jacket, this very day. He left his place and headed back out to the office, but changed his mind and headed back over to where Teresa may have been skating last. The old factory on the outskirts of town, near where Teresa resided with her parents. He figured that he might as well check it once more, if even for no more than shits and giggles.

   The drive was short, albeit it was still dark out yet. He had to be more careful driving at night in that direction or he could hit something inadvertently and then he would have an issue. He used his spotlight on his car also once he got closer. He was sure someone might see his light and report him as a poacher spotting deer, but oh well such as it was. He searched with his light at first and then he parked his vehicle, leaving the lights on and walked around with just his high powered flashlight beam leading the way. He rechecked every aspect of that building, hoping and praying for something to turn up, but alas after spending more than three hours there, he gave up. Dawn had come and since then good with the early morning being evident now. He was done and he headed out with his tail between his legs, as again he hadn't found anything which would get him any closer to finding poor, possibly missing, Teresa. He headed back toward the skate park and parked about a half block away, just to see if he would see anyone that looked out of place at a skatepark mostly frequented by kids. He sat there bored but checking his phone for messages and he had another delinquent notice on some old medical bills from his late wife. They were blood suckers and would try to squeeze blood out of turnips if they could, he thought as he laughed about it and put those in the trash bin of his email. There were a few small businesses around the park, yet nothing of substance, however there was a rinky dink pawn shop just at the one corner, which meant they at least had a security camera inside, if not one outside also. 'Shit', he thought, why didn't he think of that previously? He tried to remember the owner of the shop......Brian.....Brent...no. no.....Ben! That's it he thought, Ben...Ben ..dang, he always had trouble with the nice man's last name.....Ben ...Koschek! A really nice man who moved to their local area about 10 years ago from the big apple, New York City. He knew he had a family but didn't know how many children or how old they were. He

77

met Ben's wife before, but he definitely didn't remember her name, at this point, but either way, he stepped out of his vehicle and headed in the direction of the shop which was only about a block walk away from where he parked. The day was overcast, but still nice outside as he took the little walk. He watched all the vehicles as he crossed the street to see if anyone looked suspicious, but he didn't notice anything out of the ordinary. He yawned widely as he took the last few steps, hopping back on the sidewalk. He was so tired, as he hadn't gotten a good night's rest in who knew how long. Still he was grateful he could at least sleep some, because he remembered after his wife passed away, he went nearly a week with only sleeping about an hour a night and that was unsafe in so many ways, that was for sure. He was snapped out of his little reverie as he automatically knocked on the door, as the closed sign was still in the window. Yes it was early, but he figured Ben would be there and in seconds he was rewarded with Ben's smiling bearded face. He waved immediately at him, but then held up a finger to say, 'give me a minute'. He waited outside looking around, enjoying this section of town, which he always didn't visit very often, at least not till now. Just as his thoughts were going in another direction, he heard the click of a door lock and then another heavy slide of a deadbolt lock. The door opened behind him, the bell chimed as when a new customer opens up the door, and he stepped forward, since the door swung out, and then he turned to greet Ben. The interaction started between the two with Ben talking first, saying;

"Hey Tom! How are ya? I haven't seen you in a long time." Ben said with a pleasantly greeting smile.

"I know, sorry Ben. I just thought about how I haven't been on this side of town in quite some time, which can be good, because my services haven't been needed, but it doesn't excuse myself for not stepping in to say hello."

"Is all good my friend, is all good. Anyway, why don't you come in and maybe you can tell me what I can do for you, or even better yet, what can I sell you?" Tom chuckled at Ben's desire to get a sale no matter what.

"Sounds fair, and do you mind if I use your restroom first? Long night and too much coffee already this morning."

"Sure go ahead, just go back through the corridor there, and it is the second door on the left. Matter of fact, I think I will put a pot of coffee on as well." Ben said, winking at Tom as he went by, and Tom chuckled at the thought of him drinking even more coffee before relieving himself.

A few minutes later, Tom was back out in the corridor and heading toward the desk where Ben was. Ben had since gone back and relocked the door, placed a pot of coffee on, and then was perched in a high stool behind his counter now. Tom smiled at the delightful aroma of the brewing coffee, and he walked on over standing before Ben, ready to ask him a few questions. Ben looked at him and so he started with;

"Hey Ben, Do you happen to have any outside cameras on this building?"

"Well, I used to, as in meaning it is still up, but it hasn't worked in some time. Don't tell anyone that though, because I am sure it still keeps burglars away. I do have two inside that work, one pointed at the door, and one back in the corridor looking out. I also have a hidden one behind me, right there." He said, pointing behind himself at the wall, where Tom could barely make out a small hole. Smart of him, thought Tom, as who knows what kind of riffraff that his business could attract. He knew of a few times over the years, especially after Ben first opened up, that they were called to deal with an attempted burglary. That camera had helped him many times and unless you were looking for it, one wouldn't see it, so it was well planned. The quietness after his last remark led Ben to think what Tom was asking him, so Ben continued with one more question;

"Why do you ask? Something amiss?" Tom thought another second before answering, but then replied with;

"Yes, actually, something is amiss. There is a young, well a teenager, girl that went missing from her home around two days ago. We are still unsure whether she ran away or something worse happened to her. The leads are slim pickings right now, but she is a skater that seemed to frequent this area often, so I was wondering if I could check out some of your footage. Just to see if there is anything that would give us a clue about the people she was with."

"So one of the skate punks went missing, sorry if I don't shed a tear for that prospect." Ben said with obvious disdain and sarcasm at first, but then he finished with; "Yes, you can check out the footage. It is back in the office area, if that is ok? I have to open up soon, so if you don't mind checking it out yourself after I show you how to work it, then I have to get to my business."

"Sure Ben, that would be great! I want to stay out of your way so you can do your daily duties." And so, Ben took Tom back to his office, showed him the program, and how it worked , giving him a quick tutorial and then he went back out front, as it was time for him to open. Tom sat down in the comfy chair and started the program. This was going to be another long day. Just as he got started, Ben came back to the office with a large cup of fresh coffee for him. Ben smiled and said;

"I figured you might need this." And then he was gone again. Tom started scrolling through the recorded footage, and sadly he had to bypass a few days to get to the days he hoped would be helpful. He started truly watching when he got the notice that she was missing. He definitely didn't wish to miss anything, so he started to scroll slowly through the footage of the camera facing the front door, with dim hopes of finding something worthwhile. He spent the next hour or so seeing way too much on these recordings, such as: people in the store picking their noses, grabbing their crotches, itching their butts, with their hands inside their pants, and even someone making off with something that Ben must have missed. He snapshotted the man's face and printed it out so that he could follow up with that and charge this man for the theft of property. Now, Tom wondered how many times this had happened in the past and it went unseen, sadly. He would have to remind Ben to update his system if he could afford to, so that he didn't get cheated out of too much money. It was always a vicious cycle to see people turn into criminals just for a few bucks here and there. People are always dealt hard times in their lives, at certain stages, but staying true to discern between right and wrong at those times was always a tricky issue. He had to unfortunately charge many a felony for stealing what wasn't theirs, but he also had let a few people go, as long as they turned over the stolen property to him. So even though he was just, he always considered himself to be somewhat fair as well. Lost in his thoughts and with the mundane aspect of watching the footage, he had missed some, so he had to back it up and watch it over again. So far he found nothing of importance or anything out of the ordinary that was anything resembling a lead.

He stopped his viewing for a little, as his eyelids were starting to close occasionally, and he decided to walk out to the main area of the store to see how Ben was doing with his customers today. The shop was pretty busy today as no less than six people were in his store at one time. Ben was swamped and Tom didn't see Ben's wife, so he figured he would make himself useful and went over to see if he could assist the first customer. He walked over and there was a middle-aged female customer looking at some musical instruments, especially the guitars. He walked up to her and asked her;

"Can I assist you, miss?" She looked up at him, smiled and then pointed at the guitar in front of her and asked;

"Yes, sir, I was wondering what the history of this acoustic guitar was and what type of wood it is."

"Well I am not the store owner, and I am unsure of the history per say, but I imagine it to have been pawned off by a musician as you tell by the heavy and worn leather strap with this one", he said as he picked it up and looked it over. Then he continued saying, "And these strings and bridge are not the normal cheap strings or standard bridge, as you can see these are heavy aftermarket ones and the bridge appears to be made of titanium, if I am correct." She looked at the guitar with more intensity as he handed it over to her, and then he also said;

"I believe this body of the guitar to be made of Swamp ash wood"(he said looking it over), "and the neck seems to be made of mahogany, so this is a really nice acoustic guitar for the listed price." He saw a pick on the shelf beside him, so he asked for the guitar back from the lady, and then he strummed the guitar with ease and the strings came alive with a melodious sound. He stopped and tuned it just a little, to make it sound even better, as he went to truly play something now. Everyone in the store stopped for a moment and listened to the little well known riff being played by the strange man in the corner. The tune went on for about three minutes which consisted of his rusty but melodious playing. The woman before him smiled with the sound of the resonating guitar, as he continued strumming the strings, with unexpected agility and obvious experience. Just when he became aware he was being watched by everyone, he hit one slightly off chord, to add to his embarrassment. But to the ones watching in the store, that didn't matter as everyone was quite impressed by his musical adeptness and ability to play such a lovely string instrument. He had gotten so enthralled at what he was doing, he hadn't even paid attention to anyone else and what attention he had commanded in his effort to sell this nice instrument. He finally looked up after handing the guitar to the woman, and then he absently said;

"Sorry everyone, I didn't mean to distract you..."

"Oh, it was just wonderful! Thank you for making up my mind!" The woman before him said as she gently handled the played guitar with renewed interest, and she promptly went up to the sales desk to buy the instrument. He turned and went back toward the corridor and headed back to the office. He hadn't remembered the last time he played or even touched a guitar, but it had not been since his wife had passed. He was mildly amused at how much fun it was and the ease at which he played, and it had honestly caught him by surprise. He truly thought he had forgotten how to play, but then again he just hadn't strummed in so long, that he nearly forgot what it had felt like. So he hadn't truly forgotten, he had just merely repressed it. Sometimes time can heal wounds, but not always. He was lost in his musical related thoughts when he heard the door chime ring as someone had most likely left. Maybe it was the middle-aged woman who he helped sell the guitar to, after making her purchase. Hopefully she will enjoy it, he thought, as he once more started the camera footage rolling. Another lifetime, he thought....maybe ..... another lifetime..... he might have tried to be a musician. Not that he regretted any of his decisions in life, but he would have enjoyed trying to go that route, even if for a little while. Still he loved his life and he would not change anything for the life that he had enjoyed and was able to experience with his wife and of course his child as well. He went back to the mundane task of what he was doing, hopefully, tracking down something that would help him with his investigation.

Chapter Seven

Suzie woke up some time later, unaware how long she had been asleep, drugged, or passed out. She heard some squeaking and then she felt something on her arm and it was then that she threw whatever was on her, off her immediately. The small rat flew up, and hit one of the bars that crossed over her head. The rat thunked hard, but landed back near her feet and then she reached over and grabbed it, choking it into its timely demise. She then threw the corpse of the dead rodent out of her cage and onto the floor. She put her hand directly up to her face and felt the dressing to her missing eye, and thankfully it was still present. It had been chewed on some, as some of it unraveled, but at least the nasty rodent hadn't devoured through the dressing. She spat in disgust at her current living conditions. She looked around and she didn't know what to look for as it was still dark, and then she thought she saw a figure in a cage. Was this a new person/prisoner? She wondered quietly to herself? She wasn't even sure if she truly wanted to know at this point as the last girl she had talked to, took the steam right out of her ideas and thought process. She just sat there and watched and waited to see if there was someone else there. She didn't need to piss her captor off again and cause further injury to herself, not yet at least. Eventually, she settled back in and then she heard it, a little whimpering coming from that general direction, so in fact there was another girl here. She cleared her throat ever so slightly, and suddenly the whimpering ceased. A few minutes later, she heard a young voice sat something;

"Hello?"

"Yes, dear, but keep your voice low…" Oh God, that sounded oddly familiar even as she said it, like the first time she spoke up and the other girl responded to her likewise.

"Are we alone, …here?"

"Yes, for now. But there is our captor and a henchwoman who helps him. I call her weasel by the way.Just be careful who you trust….only saying…"

"Can….you….be ….trusted…..?" Suzie sat there a moment and thought about what had happened to her so far and what trust really meant in the situation they were in. She then spoke up, answering the obviously scared girl, by saying;

"Yes…..I am about the only one…. You can trust."

"Thank you. What is your name?"

"My name is Suzie, and what is yours, young lady?"

"My name is Teresa…" Once they knew each other's names, they left the conversation drop at that, for now. Some more quiet time had passed, until a heavy slide door opened up (at least that was what Suzie thought considering the noise of the rusty wheels of the door slide). She heard the scampering footsteps of their weasel coming to visit again. She waited for the odd helper to come to her cage, but instead she stopped by the new girl's cage and started whispering something to her. She was sure it was probably misplaced words of encouragement and acceptance so that the girl didn't try to escape, but either way the whispers were too quiet for her to truly hear them. She crooned her neck a little more and was as quiet as she could be, but she figured that the weasel was also trying to be quiet for some reason. Eventually Weasel came walking over to her and she had some stew type food for her in a moderate sized bowl. Weasel did her usual awkward stare as she handed Suzie her meal for the day. Suzie took a few bites as Weasel continued to watch her, and at this point she didn't give a shit if this strange girl wanted to watch her eat. It was what it was. But then she stopped eating and looked up at weasel, and asked her a question;

"So when did the new girl get here?"

"Just earlier to.........." She stopped immediately for saying something that could get her in trouble. Weasel looked Suzie over with an intense stare, like she figured out what game this one-eyed woman was trying to play suddenly. Suzie didn't pay her any mind whatsoever and started eating again, acting like what she asked was a nonchalant question with no underlying meaning whatsoever. It wasn't until Suzie was done that weasel spoke up again, with a quick question;

"So what is your game here?"

"My game?....... My game, weasel..... Is only staying alive, make no ifs and/or butts about it.... You daft protege." Weasel stepped back with those words as if those words stung her deeply and like a knife to the heart. Weasel spoke up, stuttering somewhat, and saying;

"I thought..... we...... were...... friends?" Suzie looked right into weasel's eyes with her one good eye, and said, bluntly;

"Listen to me.....NO!....We are not friends!!! I am currently imprisoned by your mentor, so..... no, we cannot be friends and until you realize that, the very fact is that I am going to probably die here. Meanwhile, you continue to live your shoddy and worthless existence, being a puppet to that life-robbing creep!" With that being said, Weasel stumbled back and the tears that formed in her eyes started streaming down her face. She has been betrayed, belittled, and besmirched by her only friend here, or at least she thought that. How could Suzie do that to her, after all the time they had spent together. Suzie had no idea how many times she had snuck in here and caressed Suzie's hair when she was unconscious to the world. Or how many times she spoke up to save her when her master wanted to find her a better home than in this living world. She felt betrayed, hurt, angry, and ....wanting to strike back at the woman who now despised her. She turned abruptly around and walked back from where she had come, and through the crack from the heavy door she had pushed aside. Now after closing it behind her, she walked away from that strange and spiteful woman. Never again would she trust another girl brought in, never again.

Suzie wasn't sure if what she did was the smartest thing, but she had to tell it like it was and not think that this woman was important. She had put Weasel in her place and that was that. She didn't worry about repercussions, because she will probably end up being dead in the end as well, so why not go out with a bang then, she thought quite happily. She had been beaten, electrocuted, drugged, molested, and had been surgically preyed on, and so at this point; what did she honestly have to lose? She was tired, malnourished, hungry, angry, and tired of the bullshit. So whatever happens after this, happens, but at least she will be able to stand tall with her convictions and her integrity intact. She would bow to no man, nor woman in this lifetime. She remembered suddenly the other girl in the cage across the room from her, so she started conversation once more, saying;

"Did you hear what I said to that woman, weasel of a woman?"

"Yes…. I did….. and it was harsh……. Just saying…"

"Yes it was but believe me, that woman is not your friend. She is just trying to save her own hide and she doesn't give a rat's ass about what happens to us. That's the honest to god's truth!"

"Why are you telling me this….. I am so confused…."

"Listen to me, they may have got my body but they don't have my spirit or my dignity. They have violated me, hurt me, abused me, made fun of me, and have taken my one eye from me….. All for standing up for myself. Don't let them take away your very meaning, because you have meaning and you deserve to get out of here. Find a way, fight your way out, do what you must, but don't give in just for the sake of convenience. It is not worth it. They drug you with the water, they give you shitty food, and they don't care whether we live or die, so by my standards I choose death over living this way for the rest of my pitiful existence. Do you understand me, child?"

"Yes…. I ….do……. I am sorry you had all those things done to you, but she told me I would be safe if I just listened."

"Bullshit!!! That is not true and deep down you know it to be thus as well, so don't give them the pleasure of knowing that they have you defeated. Live to fight another day and always be free in your heart and mind, then you will always be who you are, even in the end.Listen I have only been here a short time, but I have seen girls be led out never to be seen or heard of again. Don't be foolish and disregard my statements, but, please, heed my words in case these are the last words I speak on this earth."

"Ok……. I hear you. But why help me, who am I?"

"I dunno who you are, but I know one thing, I wish you to be the last one to go through this ordeal. No one else should have to pay the ultimate price. So, always be ready for anything."

"Suzie....."

"Yes, Teresa......"

"Who .....are..... You?"

"I am their worst nightmare! Now get some rest, as you will need it, because they will come for you soon enough."

"Ok, goodnight.... And thank you....for ....for your concern."

Meanwhile in the adjoining room, the girl aptly named "Weasel" was crying uncontrollably, sobbing to no end at what had just transpired. Why had she been treated this way? She didn't deserve to be treated this harshly, she surmised to herself! There was no excuse for Suzie to be that incredibly mean, for if only she knew how she dearly fought for her, practically on a daily basis for the girl's rights, and for all of them to have their own personal caretaker. She had absolutely nothing to be ashamed of, because she did what she had to do to stay alive and not be another victim like so many of the other girls who had passed through. They should all feel lucky for her, tending to them, caring for them, loving them all to the point of being there for them. She had sat and listened to many a girl venting their feelings to her. She knew that all the girls needed her, well maybe not Suzie, as she was the most defiant that her master had ever selected. She had brushed so many of the girl's hair over time, even embraced an occasional one, but whatever she did, she always did it for their sake, and for their well being and not her own pleasure. She did remember the one girl (Amber) one time, so many moons ago, that she had become almost to love deeply. She had sat with her for many hours and even held her hand when she passed away from this earth. That was the only one that she had ever kissed before. She remembered how lovely Amber's lips were, even when she was dehydrated and her lips cracked they still tasted as sweet as the finest moscato or zinfandel bottle of wine. She had held her close and even broke the rules by actually sitting in beloved Amber's cell while she took her last agonizing breaths. She was there, not her master, not any of the other girls; no one but her! Yes she was heartbroken when Amber had died, and yes, Amber was a name she will never ever forget! Yes, she remembered the kisses, the embraces and yes even the one time that she played with Amber's body, when she was asleep. It was innocent, but it was a few weeks after she had first arrived, when Amber was more than a shell of a girl at that time. Amber had a curvy body and that appealed to her tastes, since her body was thin, frail, and not shapely at all. It was after her master had drugged her up some, and before he put so many cameras all around. She had first sat outside the cell watching Amber sleep from the drug induced sedation, and then she started to play with her hair. Then minutes went by that she even unbuttoned Amber's shirt, the same type of shirt all the girls wore, that way they could put them on and take them off with their neck collar and chain on. She had placed her hand gently inside Amber's shirt and had fondled her supple breasts. The feeling of touching another female drove her, no...compelled her she thought, to make even further advances. She had spent many moments playing with Amber's body, while she had been asleep. It did become her favorite pastime and something she looked forward to everyday. Amber never knew how much she dearly needed and , well ...loved her, but sometimes it was best not to know. She showed her girl compassion, desire, love, and yes dedication. It didn't however last because her master had placed more cameras and he had been watching her for some time. Because she had gotten too close, he made Amber suffer a long and ugly death. He stopped feeding her and only gave her minimal water also. She had to watch as her dear love became weaker and weaker, until she could barely lift her head. She could do nothing, because she knew her master would kill her too if she tried to save her beloved Amber. So instead, she had a front row seat to watch her slowly die. It was so sad and it took her months to recover from that harsh reality. Luckily when she was passing, her master went out of town to get groceries and resupply, as he never liked to shop in the same town that he found his 'prizes' in. He would take one of his vehicles and travel to at least one or two towns over to buy his supplies and food stores. Always using a couple stores and always using cash of course. He would usually lock her in a room while he was gone, but the time that Amber was slowly dying, he let her spend time , the last moments with her dying beloved. So even though her master seemed mean and abducted these women, he truly cared for her and for them. The most important aspect was that she was his favorite and she adored that.

Yet, of course, she had some repercussions done to her before as well. He had cut both her pinky fingers off with shears, without meds, and then used a torch to cauterize it and stem the flow of blood. She had cried when he did thus, but she did not scream, because screaming would have resulted in more affliction. So she took her wounds, her punishment, in stoic silence and just tears streaming down her face. She had deserved it though, so she understood how much he cared for her, and just like a belligerent child, she had to be taught right from wrong. Still, she dearly missed Amber and she had never thought about another woman, that is until Suzie came along. Suzie was strong, defiant, beautiful, sexy, and smart. Suzie did what she wanted to no matter what the consequences were, and so really she envied her immensely. Suzie was everything that she wanted to be, that was for sure. She was caught up with Suzie the first time she saw her, and then the way she acted solidified the desire to get to know her and share with her, maybe in the hopes that she would like her back. That came to a slamming halt though as the last words from Suzie stung still as they rang through her mind, those cold words of hatred. Still she didn't hate Suzie for her words, her harsh, mean and spiteful words, but it did sadden her that she felt that way toward her. Even just as a battered spouse stays with those who continue to use them as a punching bag or use derogatory remarks on them, she knows that she will stay true to her new love, Suzie. So no matter what she says, she will still show devotion, caring, and be the kind soul that she is to her, and that will not change. She will do what she must to make her happy and to ensure that Suzie remains intact. She even liked the fact that she had only one eye, because as a child she always loved pirates, and so now she loves her own gruff and tough pirate, she thought as she smiled at the memory. Her childhood seemed like so many lifetimes ago, but still the memories remain locked in her vault of her fragile mind. She remembered being abused by her alcoholic father and her drugged-up mother died early in her childhood, and left her to deal with the aftermath, which was her father. He would come into her room and brush her hair, stroke her hair, and then have her undress in front of him to do a fashion show. She fancied that because it made her feel pretty and loved, something she didn't get much of. It started off innocent enough, and then one day he touched her where she knew he probably shouldn't touch her, but she trusted him as he was her protector. So after that time, she became his sexual release, but sadly he would leave as soon as he got what he wanted. Sadly though she never got what she wanted which was to be held, told everything will be ok, and to feel like someone in her life still cares for her. Then one day he came home really drunk and didn't lie with her, but instead beat her and made her feel less than she should be made to feel. She remained a few weeks after that, but eventually she ran away for good. She left that horrendous childhood behind her and went off in search of someone to love her. She had been in and out of relationships, mostly unhealthy ones at that, until she was abducted by her master, her savior. He loved her in ways that she never felt loved before. He fed her, kept her safe, let her experiment with others, and was there to listen when she needed to talk. That was one reason why she thinks that he disposed of Amber, because he was jealous of her, of how she felt for Amber. So once that was stripped from her life, he became the number one again, which was what she wanted. She needed that to survive, because she didn't know how she would survive without him in her life. She just wanted to be desired is all. Isn't that what we all desire as humans, she thought to herself. We wish to be accepted, loved, cared for, and desired for who we are. Life is not perfect and neither is any human, so why fight the reality of it all. Just find someone, your particular type of weirdness and accept them for who they are and give them your all. That is all we can do in life, she surmised finally as the tears had long since dried up from being upset. No she wasn't mad at Suzie, a little hurt, but not mad. She still loved her, no matter how she treated her or what she said. That is what unconditional love is all about.

Little did shel know, but her master, her captor, was watching and listening to the entire interaction between his assistant and the two alive women. He watched Suzie and her interaction and how little Weasel responded to those harsh words said. He then zoomed in and watched his helper cry and start contemplating life, of sorts, as she cried until the tears dried up. It was eye opening to see and genuinely sad, but he didn't feel sad for her, but for the decision he would have to make about Suzie. That woman was a spitfire and one he knew would cause trouble to no end, if he kept her around. He already knew what he had to do, but he would not do it yet, as he was still going to watch, learn and listen to the conversations between his weasel and his girls. He could think of nothing better than to sit back and watch his cameras like they were a soap opera. He remembered as a boy the times that he was made to watch all the old soap opera shows that were on television back in the day. He would watch as his grandmother made him and she also would make him play with barbies and those types of dolls/toys related to being a girl more than he really wanted to. He wasn't embarrassed by it, to say the least, but he also wanted to play with cars, trucks, and building blocks. However, he wasn't allowed to, so he played with what he was allowed to and that probably was the precursor to his developing the fondness of the female body. It may have also pointed him down the path of collecting and those imaginable thoughts also led him to do what he does now today. He admired, adored, and was just simply captivated by the female body. He grew up an awkward kid and was picked on and laughed at way too often by the other children his age and even older. He had a history of being beaten up, stripped naked, and robbed of nearly everything he wore at one time or the other, but still he came back everyday hoping that the next day would be better than the last. It never was, sadly, but he still hoped for the best. He used to secretly take pictures of the young girls in the showers, in the locker rooms, up their skirts during sporting events, and anywhere else he could nab a good photo of the young beauties. He ended up amassing quite a collection of instant pictures of young girl's bodies in different forms of undress and clothed, depending on where he was able to snap the photo. Since his grandmother could never go into the basement because of her arthritic knees and joints, that is where he stored his hundreds of photos. They were mostly out of sight and he even made a little cubie area in the old cold cellar in his grandmother's old house. It was safe there because no one had gone down there (except him) in years. His late grandfather had passed many years prior and he never really got to know him, therefore it was just his grandmother and him for most of his young life. There were some of her odd and old friends that stopped by quite often, but for the most part it was only the two of them. His birth dad resided in the state penitentiary right after he was born, and then his mom (a few years later) took off to California to become an actress and /or a singer. Sadly, though, she never made it in that line of work but, instead, ended up living in and around the Las Vegas area and becoming a prostitute and porn film actress. Either way, he never saw her again and that is when his grandmother raised him from when he was a toddler(since no one else would take him in). In the end, he both hated and loved his grandmother, as odd as that sounds. He mourned some when she passed from this world, but he also celebrated because he was free from her reins of mental bondage.

He fondly remembered his large hidden stash of girl's and women's risque and body pictures. Then he glanced over at his wall in his present office that he was sitting in, and there on that far wall was his new wall of fame of his girls from over the years that he had and was collecting. Just like when he was younger, he enjoyed the art of passive collecting, and then eventually he went from collecting pictures (passively) to actually collecting the actual girls and women themselves(actively). Even though this type of collecting, active collecting, was so much more dangerous, yet that didn't matter that much to him, because it was also extremely thrilling and fulfilling as well. He likened his collecting to be like those that collect vintage cars, or action figures, or any other truly desirable collection. He just collected people, and more specifically girls and women. Because he loved what he did, in the long run it was more to what he desired to do and more of a true form of what he wanted to do over the many years of his life or as long as he could. He was ecstatic that he could be doing what he dearly wanted to do, and he often called it 'his calling' in life. He couldn't imagine living day to day in a mundane and normal tedious job, because that was not him at all. Luckily, he was able to do this also without actually working too much, because the only thing his grandmother left him was at least some money. So he could maintain his lifestyle that he placed himself in, as long as he kept his spending in check. Then he did what he had to do, which was to sell his grandmother's house/ land and he went on the road from then on. He had bounced around medium-sized towns and communities all over the country, just to see if there was some place that he would wish to live in, permanently. He still opted to do the occasional freelance odd type of jobs just to get a little in with the locals of the area. None of the jobs were lasting and were mostly just computer type of work for people, so he didn't actually have to meet too many of them in person. That was helpful because he definitely wasn't a people person, as his social skills never truly developed that well over the years of growing up in those conditions. Yet, if the time would come up, he was able to maintain his cool in crowded situations. It wasn't easy for him, but he started getting better at it over time. That and he would blend in with the rest, so someone couldn't actually be able to pick him out that well. He looked like every other normal bloke, which allowed him to pass through crowds and not truly be observed. He enjoyed reminiscing about his past and his direction in life that he had catapulted toward. He sat back in his deluxe reclining desk chair and smiled at how life had brought him such happiness and has enriched it not only with monetary rewards, but with trophy rewards as well. The gods smiled down on him on a daily basis.

He went about some of his daily tasks and checks after he was done taking in all that he had been given. He checked on the cameras, by doing an system check of his computer drive and from this terminal he was able to run a camera check on each individual camera, which took about thirty minutes in total. The cameras included those inside the cell areas, the adjacent rooms and the common areas (where Weasel often went), and then the outer perimeter cameras which looked out toward the approaching roads and towards the outer aspects of the buildings. He also had a camera near the gate, but high up in a tree so as not to be seen or noticed by passerbyers. He also had a drone to use, if need be, for even better observation. He cleaned up his area, shredding any papers that he had that could lead anyone in his direction if something would ever happen. He wiped down all the consoles he touched and removed all the fingerprints by checking the cleaned areas with an ultraviolet light, and making sure that his tracks were covered. He wore vinyl gloves often and surgical style gloves as well, so that he didn't have to clean everything over and over again. But this area, his area, he made sure he cleaned at least every day or two, but never any longer than that. That was his routine and if he didn't plan and stick to his routine, then he would commonly have a melt down. Now, that didn't happen that often, but when it did, look out because no one was safe, not even his prizes/trophies. He would almost go into a manic state at first and then that would lead into a frenzy. He one time had even disposed of three of his prized girls because of the severity of his angst at the time. He regretted it afterwards, but by that time the damage had been done and he had to live with the consequences. That was the last time he had gotten on such a horrific tangent, and he definitely didn't want that to happen again, at least not to that degree. After he was done cleaning up his desk, he opened up the cabinet behind him and he rifled through some of the gear that he had in there. He pulled out a covered tray and placed it down with ease. After placing it down, he flipped off the catches that kept the lid tight on the container and then removed the lid. He inspected the contents of the hard plastic box and then was content with what he saw, so he placed the lid back on and replaced the clasps. He marked it with a sharpie and dated it as being checked for today, noting that the instruments inside were ready for use and inspected on this very day. There, the thought, his tasks being done for now, he might make a round of his girls before taking a nap. He looked around, content that things are as they should be and then he headed out the door to his office, locking the door behind him. He didn't trust his weasely helper, so he made sure he kept things secured.

He walked down the dimly lit corridor with barrels lining the entire walls and an older 1950's style and a few others older style refrigerators. He was moving slowly to let his eyes adjust to the poor lighting, and after about 30 seconds he could differentiate the shadows and the outlines better. He made it to the first door to his right, unlocked it, slid the door open, and then went through it. There inside this padded room for soundproofing was a row of three quiet generators and a large tank. He had gas cans lined up and he checked the levels of the fuel gauges of each generator and his large fuel tank. He grabbed one can at a time and filled up the tank more, since it was only about half full. Once he dumped all the cans he could put into it, he placed the cans out in the hallway from whence he came, so that he could refill them soon. Luckily, he didn't use a lot of power, but he had the generators rigged so that they alternated usage and time running. Being an electrician at one time in his life had come in handy as well, so he had then rigged in parallel and they all fed off the main tank. If one did shut down, there would be a slight milli- second lapse and then the next one would take over and take the lead. He even had a switch in his office to show if there was a problem, thankfully. One of his earlier times, he didn't have that and there was a logistical mess, so he made sure that that wouldn't happen again as well. He primarily used the generators so as not to pull much power from the grid, since he was not paying for it. Once done here, he checked everything again and it looked to be well. He checked the ventilation fan as well and it was working properly as well. He didn't need any fumes building up in this room. After relocking the door, he was walking down the remaining few feet to the door he was planning on going through. He opened this locked door with his key ring, but not until fumbling some with his gloves and his keys. He needs to switch gloves again, as these were starting to wear after messing with the gas cans. He opened the sliding door very slowly and as quietly as he could. Then he put the sliding door back where it belonged and then relocked it behind him. He then slowly crept around the outskirts of the small room, stopping just in front of a marked area on the wall. Slowly he slid the latch back very quietly (or as quietly as he could), and then he peered through the peephole that was there.His vision didn't adjust yet therefore he could see very little. Looking down, he reached and grabbed a pair of odd looking goggles. After placing the goggles on, he turned them on, and then adjusted the focus ever so slightly and then he could see clearly the outline of his two prisoners. His night vision goggles worked well for this application, which was to secretly spy on his girls at a closer distance, instead of just using the cameras on the wall. He watched intently as Suzie appeared to be sleeping and then he looked over toward his new favorite, the young girl named Teresa. She was awake, cowering with her arms over her legs, which were curled up into her chest. She appeared to be sobbing, as her body was gently shaking steadily. He frowned some at how unhappy she seemed to be, and he swore to do what he could to make her feel at home. She was a lovely young girl and one he definitely wanted to protect and keep as his own. She looked to be in good shape overall, so he would feed her better than Suzie, who was fast becoming a pain in his ass. Still even though she was a thorn, he still liked her in many ways. Did he trust her, No! But she is serving a purpose, for now.....for now, he thought as he continued to watch her, ...for now......

Suzie suddenly awoke with a start, feeling like someone was watching her. It was an eerie feeling, but it was unmistakable and so she remained deathly still. She looked over and barely made out the girl named Teresa in the far cell. She remained deathly quiet and it was also just as quiet in the room. Then she heard a whirl sound, like something with batteries adjusting, like a camera. She heard it again, but it didn't seem like the ones that were mostly hidden up on the ceiling, but this one almost sounded like it came from her left and behind her. It almost seemed as if someone was watching them, but who would it be, if not for their captor, the bane of her existence. She knew now that he in fact was keeping all kinds of tabs on them. She stirred slightly and she didn't hear the noise any more. She settled in and tried to go back to sleep, but she was trying to brew up a plan, and she was going to try to use Weasel to enact it as well. It may be her only chance.

Chapter Eight

Tom watched for hours and only saw one time where someone passed in front of a vehicle, but the feed was so grainy and at the angle it was, there was nothing to be able to tell what vehicle or who the person was. So he left the pawn shop unsettled and unsure where to look next. Both of these cases seemed like they hit dead ends already, which was both sad and discouraging at the same time to him. He called his buddy Andy, a member of the rescue squad and also a forest service hotshot. He luckily got a hold of him in a few rings and asked;

"Hey Andy, this is Tom. Was wondering, did you happen to find anything with the missing hiker regarding the trailhead?"

"Hey Tom, how are you, friend? Well, it is funny you ask because we just came off the trail. Some of us started at one spot miles up the trail and the remainder of us started back at the original entrance. After an intensive search, both on and off the trail, we honestly found nothing of the missing hiker, Suzie. We did also ask a few folks on the trail, but with the same results. Sadly, we found nothing, no sign of her, and no sign of any type of abduction or what may have happened to her, at this point. I am sorry, but that's all we can attest to. Wish we had more. We will continue to search as much as we can, but I don't know what else to tell you, boss." Tom sighed a heavy sigh of frustration at the endless nothing results, thus far. Then he responded as such;

"Thank you Andy, and thank your team too. I appreciate it. Just keep your eyes and ears open for me, if you would, and hopefully this will all make sense soon."

"Will do, bud. Catch up with you later!"

"Thanks again , Andy." And with that they both hung up the phone. Tom furrowed his eyebrows with utter unsurity. He honestly didn't know what to do next. He was completely devoid of any idea what to do next. He sat down in his vehicle and just sat there, thinking and rethinking everything he could. The time went by in a slow painstaking clueless mind crunch on what to do and where to look next. Before long ten minutes turned into twenty minutes, and then into 60 minutes, and still he had absolutely no answers. He desperately needed some more coffee, so he drove across town and parked close to a local organic eatery that had different coffees and other hot drinks. He wanted to go where he could think and not be deterred by idle conversation with someone he knew or even a passer-byer. He just wasn't in that kind of mood, and this organic bar actually had a lot of younger people in it too, so maybe he would just listen into the local conversation and eavesdrop on some.He walked the short distance from his vehicle to the door, and opened the door for a young lady heading out, who didn't even reciprocate a 'thank you'. He thought about the rudeness of the younger generation, nowadays, as they seem to forget about common courtesy half of the time. He went inside and saw a wealth of younger gens and some older hippy types hanging out, most never looked his way or didn't even give him a thought. He went up to the barista and before he could say what he wanted the young man behind the counter asked him;

"Yeah, what will it be?" The youth said that without even looking up and seeing who his customer was. Tom responded with;

"Well, give me the Fearsome organic coffee, in a large cup, please."

"Want any extras, any additives to it?"

"No, just black, please, and thank you." It was then that he noticed that the theme seemed to be scary or horror movies as most were listed under famous horror flick villains or horror movies. He snickered at the names as the barista worked on his brew. He scooted down the line to the register area and the girl at the register had the same attitude as she never looked up, but still asked him what he had ordered. He told her and she flatly and devoid of emotion or even a smile, listed the price for the coffee. It was slightly overpriced, but he pulled out his wallet and paid with cash. The change he received back, he placed in a half empty tip jar that was directly beside the register.He smiled at a young hippie looking lady with a tie dye shirt on and a mix-matched tie dye skirt. She had clumpy shoes on that didn't look comfortable whatsoever, but then again the style today wasn't about comfort, but coolness and being a certain style or even non-style so as not to conform to society ways. Either way he nodded and smiled at the young lady, who just smirked back at him and then went about typing on her laptop computer some more. Once his coffee was ready, they called it out and he went over and picked it up. He then went over to a table, near a few people talking, and started to slowly drink his coffee as he listened to what was being said.

At first it was nothing important, like upcoming concerts around the area and even a few festivals that are coming up in a few months, were being talked about, but either way it was just idle talk to him. Still he maintained his impudence and listened to make sure that nothing being said by others was missed by him. He remained there drinking his coffee painstakingly slowly and rather methodically to keep listening in. A few of the people left, but other ones came in to replace their spots at the tables. The last group to come in was a small bunch of skaters, and these were some he never saw before. He pretended to be looking at his phone and perusing the internet, but in all honesty, he was listening intently to the conversation taking place. The skaters were conversing about some of their friends and the tricks they were trying out, sometimes bragging, and sometimes just over elaborating it with their 'dudes' and 'brahs' being spoken with every other word. He nearly gave up on listening to the idle conversation, and was about to stand up to leave, but he stopped in his tracks when he heard one of the young skaters, say;

"Brah, I'm telling ya, dude, that the girl from the trailer park has gone missen' some time."

"No way, brah?"

"Way, brah. Jakey told me so yesterday. Some old cop dude asked him about her the other day. He didn't know much, cuz that's Jake, he always be stoned...... but any-who, so what he said, was the girl disappeared."

"Wait brah, which girl?" The one said with a stupefied look on his face.

"Dude, the hot younger one, that does some gnarly tricks. The one that used to be able to outskate me, you daft punk ass!" Tom nearly snickered at the way the one talking treated his friend. It was rather comical, but he held it back since he wasn't supposed to be listening. He continued to act like he was surfing his phone while he mocked drinking out of his now empty cup of coffee.

"Oh that one, brah, I got it now. She is a hottie, that is for sure."

"Yeah, I don't remember seeing her recently, but she was cool with her skills." Then one who was just listening and hadn't said a word until now, piped in suddenly with;

"Yeah I was trying to get with her, but she was cold to me, so I wasn't playing that game. She told me that she was a daddy's girl and liked her men, you know, older, so I scoffed at her and bolted the bitch."

"It wasn't that weird guy that hung around the park at times was it?" The other one asked, innocently enough.

"Yeah, he.....was odd, that's for sure. I saw him walking around but I didn't go near the weirdo. I figured some fucked up old man who likes little girls and boys, you know the pervy type."

"Yeah, brah, gotcha." It was then that Tom leaned over and introduced himself, more properly, saying;

"Sorry, boys for listening in, but I have to ask you about the girl and the old man that was around the park."

"Who the hell are you, you freak."

"Well, I am Detective Tom, and I talked to your friend Jake the other day. I heard what you are saying, and do you think you could point the man out in a book of perps?" He asked the boy who said he saw the man from a distance. The boy looked at him, seemingly not trusting him at his word and so then Tom showed them his badge. The boy stared it up and down and then to him to check if it was really him, and then Tom nodded, seemingly saying, 'yes it is me'. The boy calmed some, sat back again, and then said to him;

"The man was too far away so I really didn't get that good a look at him, and I didn't hang around to be propositioned by the perv, so I won't be able to help you, brah."

"How about any type of description or even of his vehicle, or any defining marks, haircut, clothes, or anything that could help?" The boy sat back and thought long and hard, as his friends watched the interaction between Tom and the boy. Finally after about a minute of quietness and Tom waiting patiently, the boy then said;

"Yeah, brah, he was probably about your height, but a little thinner than you, maybe a little lankier, but he did have a sleeve tattoo on his right arm, that was for sure. Don't know what of, but it was there and looked cool . That's about it, sorry we gotta bolt now."

"Yes, thank you for your information, and sorry to eavesdrop on your conversation again." The boys nodded and they dropped their boards and skated out of the building as someone held the door open for them when they left. So, Tom thought, he had a little more information, even if it was only a tidbit, it was better than nothing.

He was happy he came into this establishment that day, and with that he tossed his cup into the paper recycle bin, there at the front of the store, and he exited the building. It was nearly dark now as he stretched his back and decided to not head back to the office, but to walk around town some. You never know what you will find if you just walk and interact somewhat with people, as he just found out with those boys. Sometimes it pays off to be friendly, he thought, snickering as he walked down the sidewalk, passing closing stores and also some as their lights came on out front, inviting those evening customers into their businesses so they could earn money and to stay afloat. He liked this town as he continued walking down the street, watching the people come out to enjoy an evening 'on the town' or so to speak. He stopped and did some window shopping, but he also had flashbacks of when his wife, him and their daughter walked downtown many times when she was younger, looking at the store fronts and just enjoying an evening out together. He honestly didn't remember when he last did something like this, just walk downtown to enjoy the sights and sounds of the busy area. 'I guess', he thought to himself it was before his wife was sick, and to him that seemed really sad and improper, the more he thought of it. He had practically stopped living, in a sort of way, after his wife had passed, as he just lived to work and that was about it, anymore . He really hadn't kept in contact with his (their) old friends that they had known as a couple, because he had sold the house they had lived in(because of outstanding medical bills) and moved into where he lives now. He did feel empty at times, his heart was devoid of emotion, care, and concern like it had used to be. He had hardened his heart to love, friendship(except a few), and companionship in his life. His only friends, now, were really just his coworkers. There were a few old shop owners that he had known for years that he sort of remained friends with, but other than seeing them from time to time, he didn't interact with them much more than that. He just couldn't continue being close friends with those his wife and him used to be friends with. It was nothing they did or said, but it was just the daily reminder of his wife whenever he saw them. It was the flooding of memories back to his mind whenever he interacted with them, so he did what he had to do to protect himself and he decided to distance himself from those kind and once highly regarded people he used to call friends. Occasionally, one more distant one would text him, and he would respond at times, but it was only platonic chat and that was all. He figured and hoped that they understood his dilemma, but even if they didn't he wasn't too concerned about that. He couldn't live in the past (for he had suffered enough with the loss of his wife), and so he was forced to move on. He ended up dropping as much of the past as he could to escape the memories that always seemed to haunt him on a daily basis.

Before he knew it, he had walked for something like two and a half to nearly three hours, as his thoughts swarmed in his head. He couldn't believe that time had gone that fast. He must have looked like a zombie walking the street, someone devoid of purpose and surroundings, lumbering past people without acknowledging them. Hopefully he didn't offend anybody, he thought as he looked around to see who was near him. He had gone down a more dimly lit alley and stopped to get his bearings about him. Suddenly out of nowhere, someone came up behind him and held something to his back. This person almost whispered silently in a gruff voice, obviously trying to conceal their real voice. It was a man, by the sound of the voice and then he felt a sharp point in his back, right around his kidney area. This guy obviously knew where to stab, so he listened as the guy said to him;

"Listen, I don't wanna hurt you, but I will if you make me. Just give me all your money, your watch, and whatever else you have of value! Move slowly or I will stab you dead and slit your throat. You hear me?"

"Listen, buddy, you don't want to do this. You are fucking with the wrong person." Tom said calmly and with a distinct voice. Still his words didn't deter the man, and he pushed the blade into his back a little, most likely drawing a little blood. Alright, Tom thought enough of this, and in one swift motion he turned and side stepped at the same time, causing the knife wielding man to lunge forward slightly as his target had moved so unexpectedly and with precision. Tom swung his arm around pushing the knife hand out further away from the area that the attacker could use it, and he pulled his gun with his left hand and stuck the barrel of the loaded weapon right in the man's forehead. The slightly unbalanced man stopped moving instantly as he saw what his dilemma was and he dropped the knife immediately, even before Tom said a single word. The knife rattled against the pavement and Tom kicked it away from them instinctively, and it made a distinctive metallic sound as it shuttered across the pavement and hit an older metal garbage can.

"I told you that you made a mistake messing with me!" Tom said with a cold and direct voice. The man looked at him, expecting to either be dead or locked up in handcuffs at any moment. Tom thought otherwise, as putting this dolt in jail would probably do nothing for him. So he decided to let him go, but right before he let him go, he would teach him a lesson. Tom had inexplicable rage deep in him as he had the gun pointed at the man's forehead, but he couldn't let the rage take over. Thankfully, he kept it in check and decided to do something more memorable. So he took the barrel of his gun and he popped the guy on the temple with it, hard enough to drop the attacker and probably leave a nice mark also. The injured man verbally exclaimed his feelings toward the instant pain, by saying;

"Ouch, dammit!"

"Listen, you are lucky I didn't shoot your stupid ass, so be thankful that is all you get. I don't have time to lock you up so get the hell out of here, and if I ever see or hear of you doing something like this again, you will be locked up for a very long time. Do you hear me!" The man was cowering at his feet now, and he didn't say any words, but just shook his head. Tom finished up with;

"Get out of here, you vermin scum and think about getting a real job, and changing your life. Now, beat it!! Scram!!" The man stumbled once over his own feet and then fell to the ground, but got up quickly and took off down the alley, trying to distance himself from that crazy cop. Tom watched the man scamper away and then he went over and picked the knife up, which actually wasn't a cheap knife, but one that actually cost a little money. But who knows, maybe the dirt bag stole it from someone. He grabbed a plastic grocery type bag that was there lying on the side of the garbage can, and he deftly grabbed the knife with the inside of the bag, so that he could keep the man's finger prints intact and check up on him later to see who he was. He probably shouldn't have let him go, but he wasn't in the mood at all for this type of crap tonight. Carefully placing the knife in the pocket of his jacket, he continued his walk but this time heading home after he got his vehicle. He would log the weapon in tomorrow, as he didn't feel like going to the office again tonight.

After about another thirty minute walk, he walked up to his front door and grabbed the overflowing mail that was in his assigned slot, not getting it for a few days of delivery. His place just felt lonely and he fed and watered his cat. He looked at his few house plants and they were all dead except for the cactus, which somehow remained alive yet. He dropped a few drops of water in that pot, and then unclothed to go take a shower. He let the water run for a few minutes to get warm, as he looked at his somewhat unkempt self. He did some basic hair trimming, clipped his visible nose and ear hairs, and did a little shaving, deciding on keeping a goatee for some reason, for the time being. He might change his mind later, but for now he trimmed it and kept it. He hopped in the shower and remained, just standing there, under the water for a few minutes. He felt his back where the man had stabbed him slightly, it had scabbed already, so he left it alone. It only felt superficial anyway, which was good. He remained under the hot water for what seemed like an eternity, but in all actuality it was about twenty minutes. He felt hot now, so he turned the handle more to the cold water side and cooled down quickly with a quick refreshing splash of the colder water. He got out and toweled himself off, walking into his bedroom as such in the meantime. Opening a dresser drawer and pulling out an old oversized sleep shirt and a pair of shorts, he stopped and looked at his bed. He turned off the light switch and left the bedroom. Going over to the freezer to see what he had to eat, he opened it up and found an old frozen meal that looked somewhat edible. He read the instructions on the box, discarded the box, cut a slit in the protective film, and then stuck it in the microwave. Sadly, he couldn't remember what the instructions said, so he walked over to the garbage and pulled the box out of the can and looked once more at the instructions. Punching in the correct cooking time into the microwave, he then went over and pulled out a beer to enjoy until his food was ready. He downed that beer in a matter of minutes and grabbed one more cold brewsky. About the time he was halfway through that drink, the microwave sounded off, so he prepared his plate for underneath the hot food, removed the film, and grabbed some utensils to eat with and walked around toward his sofa. He grabbed the remote and turned on the television to some movie that was already on and playing on one of his regularly watched channels. He waited a few minutes for the meal to cool down and then he ate the lackluster looking meal with hungry gusto. After the meal was consumed, he continued sipping on his beer as he laid down on the couch. Within minutes his cat had crawled up onto his chest, walked around until it found a spot it liked, circling many times first, and then rested there. It had just started to purr continuously as he took the last sip of beer. With the cat purring nonstop, after him drinking two beers, and consuming his hot meal, he was ready to fall asleep. He fell asleep right there on the sofa, but already it was after one in the morning, so within a few hours he would have to get up again and start the day again. But for now, he was content and so was his feline friend as they both slept for the remainder of the morning. He didn't dream at all, which was not unusual, or maybe he just didn't remember his dreams anymore, but he was restless. His legs twitched often and he moved at times, dislodging the cat from her position, but she just moved around and found another spot close to his head then, up on the back of the sofa, away from harm's way. This continued until the waking hours of the new day came to be. Until then Tom actually slept a few hours, the first continuous hours he had slept in a few days or that he remembered..

That morning waking hours came way too early for him and Tom's internal alarm clock went off around 5:30 in the early morning. He awoke with his legs half off the sofa, and the cat nowhere to be seen. His back ached some from the position he had slept in, and his arm was half asleep most likely from lying on it. He sat up, shook off the cobwebs from his sleepiness and then stood up, but remained a little hunched over at best. He hobbled to his bathroom and applied some muscle tightness cream liberally on his lower back. He washed his hands and then stretched out in his bedroom, on the floor, to try to work the kinks out of his old and slightly out of shape body. He really needed to start working out again, even if just a little, to remain in better shape so every day isn't like this, a deliberate difficult start. Once he

102

was done, he grabbed a pair of fairly worn jeans and a somewhat unwrinkled button down shirt, so at least he didn't look like he just crawled out of bed. He grabbed another sport jacket and brushed his teeth, before making some coffee for the day. He looked in the cupboard and the fridge and only had enough for about two cups, oh well, it is what it is, he thought. He scribbled coffee on the piece of paper on the fridge that was his grocery list, but by all the items on there, he knew he would not remember anytime soon. After waiting a few minutes, the coffee was done and he grabbed one of his to-go cups and poured the hot liquid inside. Just when he was replacing the lid, he saw 'Kat', his feline, come walking into the kitchen. He reached up and grabbed a few kitty treats out of the cupboard and dropped them in his sleeping buddy's bowl to nibble on. He petted the back of his cat and then he turned off most of the lights, except the one overtop of the oven, and headed out the door for the day. Another day, another dollar, he thought as he got into his vehicle, and pulled out into the street. The roads were pretty empty this early and he headed right to the station. He was there in no time at all, and as he exited the vehicle he grabbed the knife that he had taken from the would-be thief the night before. He walked into the building, after unlocking the door, and headed right to the break room to start another pot of coffee. The one good thing is that the chief kept the place filled with coffee for all of them. Sometimes they each brought some extra in, but it was taken care of, being fully stocked for the most part. After starting the coffee, he immediately went to the evidence room and logged in the knife, placing it in an appropriate heavy log-in bag for future reference. He placed the item on the correct shelf and position per the paperwork, and then that was that. He would finger print it if he wished to, but at least he had the perps prints for possible future reference. After leaving the evidence room, he decided to turn on a few more lights, one of which was his office area. His tired eyes averted from the brightness of the lights, but he had to wake up so he could start doing some work for the day. He walked into the restroom and immediately started running the cold water. Bending down, he splashed some refreshing frigid water on his face as he tried to wake up some more. Hopefully this will help since the coffee didn't even seem to touch him yet. After relieving himself, he washed his hands and left the bathroom, to head toward his office. As soon as he entered the hallway, he practically ran right into Officer Linda Phillips. She squeaked in surprise as she wasn't quite awake as well and was startled by him being there. He immediately said;

"Oh my goodness, Linda, I am so sorry to startle you." He said with a sincere apologetic tone. Linda had stopped and took a few seconds to recover before responding with;

"Oh dear Jesus, Tom, you completely surprised me. Dadnabit, you got me on that one." She said smiling to him as he placed his hand on her arm to give an apologetic reassurance that he hadn't meant to frighten her, as such. Linda was a very nice woman and she was one of their better police officers, not that he would tell his buddy, Jeremy, that, but in all honesty she was a very dutiful coworker and public servant. He always enjoyed shooting the shit with her, and she was a kind and compassionate soul. Not that he ever thought about it, at least not that he remembered, but when she smiled, her dimples came on display and really resonated with her attractiveness. He never thought of her that way, previously, but for some reason today, he absolutely noticed her natural beauty. He was so caught up in his thoughts and gazing upon her that he hadn't even noticed her speaking to him. It wasn't until he actually saw her lips moving, that she was addressing him. Finally, he transitioned out of his little 'zoning out' moment and he looked at her, as if for her to ask her question to him once more. She looked at him with a concerned look on her face, as the dark green orbs, her eyes, softened somewhat and she repeated her question for the third time, in just over a minute. She asked him;

"Tom, I asked you if you were getting enough sleep? Obviously, by your phasing out, you are not. You must take care of yourself, we need you running on all pistons. I am concerned about you...... ......you probably just need a vacation, is what you may need......" She had hesitated as if she wanted to say something else, but she said those last words as a little cover to what she had dismissed previously. Tom smiled back at her, a true smile, not just a mock one that he flashed to appease people. He thought about what she said to him and a few words echoed through his mind, which were: "I am concerned about you....". He didn't ever remember her saying anything of the such, previously. That was nice he thought, for her to be concerned with him, but then again she had been very supportive and had been there for him, when he needed someone to talk to of the feminine gender (meaning someone with a different perspective on life than his male officer friends). He had always appreciated her for that kindness, because he had experienced many difficult moments during that melancholy time period. Before making it extremely awkward, he answered her with;

"Sorry, Linda, yes I am not sleeping great, but it is ok. Too much going on with the two missing people, living alone, and no desire to actually be home, sort of reverberates through my brain. Sometimes my brain just doesn't want to shut down, which doesn't help at all. Thank you for your concern, and I'll try to do better……. at least hide it from you better. Sorry I don't know why I just told you all of that. I really sound pitiful, don't I?" He quipped at the end, which immediately raised a smile on Linda's face as she even smirked at his light humor, while trying to ease her concerned mind somewhat. She nodded and then placed her hand on his arm and as she walked away down the hallway, she slowly removed her hand and mentioned while walking away;

"No you don't, just overworked and stressed is all I see." she said with a smile. "Ok, crazy man, I'll catch up with you later, so get your ass back to work, now!." And with that she waved him adieu, and went down the hallway and into a changing room to do what she had to do.

He watched her go, and wondered exactly what those words of hers, her concern, and her lingering touch meant. He wasn't sure, but one thing was for sure and that his eyes were now a little open to her in a totally different way. How weird life is, he thought as he went back to what it was he was doing. Then again he didn't remember what he was doing, and so he just headed back to his office, in the hopes that he would remember eventually what task he was before startling Linda. Of course he stopped by the small kitchen area first to grab another hot cup of coffee and made sure there was enough for the other officers coming in before too long. So he decided to put on the second pot of coffee for the crew coming in. After finishing that, he then headed back to his office to officially start his day. He had to catch up on some paperwork and fax some papers to another police station regarding someone that they had arrested. It was a repeat offender and just some finishing up of paperwork prior to the man being sentenced for his larceny crimes. Where most districts and stations use a digital record, they were still a little behind the times and only about a quarter of their information and records were digitized. They were working on it, but it was a slow transition. Either way he was old school, because he grew up doing paperwork, so it didn't bother him much at all. He walked over to his desk, stopped but didn't sit down. He went over to the tack board that he had made for the current missing persons. There he had a map of the region and a red tack in the spot each girl went missing from (or approximately since he didn't truly know exactly at this point in time). He stared at it for over five minutes, recalling what was said to him from everyone he had questioned, encountered or been informed by. He still had way too many time gaps and not enough validity to timelines from either of the missing women. All he really knew was an approximate time when each woman was not seen from again, but other than that, he honestly had nothing worthwhile. He shook his head at the complexity of this scenario. What was the motive if they were taken or was it mere coincidence that both women are missing somewhere between two to five days apart from one another. If it was someone who snatched these gals, then two to five days would be an appropriate timeline to pick up another girl. Yet, taking another that soon would be foolish and would raise too much suspicion, so that didn't make much sense either. He went over to his desk and pulled his chair aside, sitting down in a frustrated way, and pulled his computer over in front of him. He looked back up at the board and then he checked the database of missing persons within the last month, anywhere from a one to six hour drive from their county. He had to start looking out more to see if there was an approximate relation to all those missing. The only way was to start searching outside the box and see what he could dig up. There was a definitive chance that he was completely wasting his time, and more importantly the timeline of the missing women, but then again, he had to start looking where he might not have previously. It was well worth the effort. He then thought that when the captain comes in, he may ask for additional help with this matter, so that he doesn't expend all his time on something that may very well be frivolous. He started the search, and delved into what could or may be a link, possibly. And yet he was unsure of himself even as he started looking.

The more he started looking into it, the more he was wondering that maybe it was some crazy outsider that came into town and possibly took the women, which would make them even harder to locate in the long run. Still it was an option that he had to entertain, no matter what. He started writing down the possibilities as he waited for the missing person's databases to come up with his searches. He looked around his desk and rummaged through a few drawers until he found what he was looking for, which was a larger scale map of their community plus other outlying areas and towns. He decided to keep that map handy, as he may need it in the near future. Their internet connection was acting up as he had service and his search was progressing, but then the service would disconnect and he would have to start over again. He was getting annoyed and frustrated, as he had voiced his concerns regarding the crappy internet service numerous times to the captain. Again, as was quite common, nothing came about from it. The captain seemed to be only concerned with saving money and looking good to the townsfolk and the leaders of the town. He found it very irritating, to say the least, but he tried to keep his emotions in check, as he restarted the search, yet again. He kept chugging away at it, until a smiling face came back and poked her head into his office door, unexpectedly. He looked up and smiled as he saw Linda again. She smiled at him, and then asked him;

"Sorry, Tom, I didn't want to disturb you but I was just wondering something......" Tom looked at her with a questioning look and then he responded with;

"Yes, Linda, I am sorry I am lost in this case so far, that leads nowhere. Anyway, sorry you probably don't wish to hear this, so what can I do for you?"

"Well, I was just wondering, would you be willing to get something to eat, maybe tonight, if you aren't too busy?" She asked him sheepishly, while somewhat averting her eyes, somewhat, as if she expected him to say 'No' or come up with some excuse. "It's no big deal if you are, ..." She finished saying before turning to leave.

"Wait one minute, please!" He said with a kind but determined voice as he smiled at her. "I didn't even have the time to answer your question appropriately." She looked at him, smiled and mouthed the words, 'I'm sorry' to him. He smiled back and then said with a calm and interested tone of voice;

"I certainly would enjoy catching something to eat with you. Thank you so much for asking...!" She smiled and nodded her head appreciatively and then she asked him a follow up question, saying;

"What time should we meet..... and where?"

"How about the Steak and Bake Grill, ummm.....say 8:00 pm?"

"That sounds lovely and I look forward to seeing you there. Just let me know if anything changes, ok Tom."

"I will, Linda, but I will be there. Also, thank you for asking!" She smiled and waved a little good-bye before heading out the door. She couldn't believe that she just asked him, but she was hoping he would. After some time since he didn't she knew she may have to make the first move, which she happily did. No matter what, this is going to be such a marvelous day indeed, she thought as she walked away with a huge smile on her cheerful face.

Across town, Blain Astel (Teresa's father) hadn't slept much the last few days as he was worried for his daughter. His wife was more patient than he was and she waited for the detective, Detective Tom, to update them. Which of course he hadn't done much of that at this time, so in his lack of knowledge of what had occured, it was now his turn to take over and to find things out. He was sure he would do a better job than the police, so he grabbed his keys and told his wife he had some odd jobs to catch up on, and he left the house. He hopped into his five year old diesel pickup truck, and started it up. It roared alive with ease and darker smoke exited the tail pipe as it warmed up. He backed up and then slowly left the parking area and headed off toward town and hopefully some answers. He was getting more pissed off the longer he drove down the road. He got hung up in some funeral traffic as some older gent from the local nursing home had passed. He had read about it in the paper, and so the man had passed and today happened to be the day of the funeral, He had to wait some time for the procession to pass him by, which didn't help out his mind as it kept him believing that he would find his daughter long before anyone else would. 'This was a man's job', he said over and over again. He reached over to his glove compartment and opened it up. It was an unusually deep compartment and so it held quite a bit of paperwork and miscellaneous items. Yet, what he reached for as he stuck his hand in there was actually something in a shiny silver color. He reached for the item and he inadvertently swerved on the road with the distraction. He grabbed the gun and rescued it from its paper prison that his glove box had become, sadly. He checked the revolver's cylinders and it was filled with six bullets ready to use, his favorite gun, the 357 magnum caliber pistol. He will get answers one way or another, that was for sure. The more he drove the angrier he became, and the more he wanted revenge against whomever it was that took his girl away from him.

Blain drove down to the skatepark to lie in wait and see if something would come up. At least waiting here was better than waiting at home. He nervously looked around, but still tried to remain cool and calm so as not to look too out of place. He fidgeted quite a bit and drank some beer that he had brought along, it wasn't super cold, but it still tasted delicious to him and at this point in time. He continued to sip it as he watched every vehicle coming near and into the park. Most were just the skaters, but there were a few cars that dropped their kids off to skate, while the parents went and did something other than watch their children. The poor lambs were laid out to slaughter , for anyone to pick up without their parents there, he thought dismally. Then again, that was why he was there, to protect those that can't always protect themselves, he figured and reasoned for his actions of the day. He grabbed a bite of deer jerky that he had made from last year's deer meat, when he had taken down a nice ten point buck. It tasted so good to him and he loved going hunting. He had been doing it since his earlier years and it was something that he had hoped he could pass down to his children, but to his dismay he never had a boy and Teresa wanted nothing of the sort. So it was just his kin and himself that went every year. He started thinking about this year's hunt as well and where they were planning on going. It was a new property for them to use and he didn't like change, especially when it comes to hunting, but he was willing to accept it if it yielded favorable results. That was all that matters is what the rewards were with hunting, especially deer. There hadn't been a time that he hadn't come home with a deer though that he could remember in the last few years. So at least he had been protective in some way shape or form with his favorite endeavor. He continued watching from a distance for the next few hours and at the same time, he continued to drink more too which was not in his plan, but it came all too naturally for him when he was stressed out. He even stepped out of his truck and found some bushes off to the side and out of line of sight of anyone and he relieved himself, as the beer drinking had been catching up with him. As he went to get back in, a police SUV went by him, slowly and then the officer waved, as did Blain in return and then the officer drove off again. That was close he thought, as he got back into his truck and started it up to move it, just in case the officer came back, he wouldn't be at the same spot. There were some parked cars in a parking lot near the pawn shop so he drove over there and parked his truck there. The pawn shop had since closed and this looked like it could be overflow parking for some of the other mom and pop businesses along this stretch of road, so he imagined it to be a safe place to sit and watch. He could still see, but he was forced to use his binoculars at times to get a better view from his distance and angle of perspective. It would be dark soon and then he knew he would have to somehow move closer to keep a better eye on things. Whomever it was who took his girl would probably come back for more, and so he wanted to be sure to catch the evil predator in action. Now was his time, time for vigilante justice.

Chapter Nine

It was early evening and Tom left work a little early so he could go home and get freshened up before his dinner with Linda. He got home, but not right away, because of course he had a few errands to run. So in all actuality he was running a little behind by the time he made it home to his place. He rushed in like a small Texas tornado throwing his things down in a rush, trying to shave and clean up, and also starting his shower water. He rummaged through his closet and his drawers for something presentable. Unfortunately, everything he tried on was a little too small as he had gained enough weight to be the next size up, since last time he tried to look nice for anyone. He had his work shirts and that just wouldn't do, so he kept going through all he had until he finally found something half decent, in the form of a quasi cool Hawaiian style shirt. 'This will have to do', he said to no one there but his cat who was enjoying lying on all the clothes that now decorated his bed. She laid down, but not till after pacing around in circles a little, to soften her spot up, and then after she nestled into her groove, she proceeded to lick her paws as she whimsically watched him scurry about in some sort of rush. He showered, brushed his hair, threw on deodorant, and some light musky cologne, and then he worked on getting dressed. He pulled out the colorful shirt and almost tucked it in, but then decided that would show his little belly more, and so he decided to try to be casual and keep it cool. He pulled on a pair of nicer(his only pair) cotton shorts, and then pulled out his ever casual boat shoes and put those on also. After looking in the mirror, he immediately was second guessing his attire and his decisions, but he looked down at his watch, saw the time, and he knew he didn't have the minutes to switch it out. Therefore, he committed to what he wore and that was just going to be that. Just as he was about to leave, he tried to see if he forgot anything and he didn't remember anything that he may have forgotten. The cat lazily meowed, and that reminded him to feed his feline companion and he did so hurriedly. 'Shit!' he thought, and so he grabbed his keys, his phone, his wallet badge and gun(as was typical no matter what), and he flew out the door. The perturbed cat looked over at the door, not really sure what her human's problem was tonight but she purred as she walked over toward the food that he had plopped into her dish, hoping it was something good tonight. She took one bite of food, when her owner came flying back through the door and into the restroom. He brushed his teeth in record time, gargled mouthwash in a mere two seconds and spit it out, not even rinsing his sink afterwards, and then rushed out the door, whisking right by the eating cat. The cat never looked up at her owner, even as the door closed again, because she was eating some delicious tuna flavored meal and didn't have time for her human at this point. She finished her meal in quietness, just the way she liked it.

      Tom pulled into the Steak and Bake Grill about two minutes after eight in the evening. He had trouble finding a parking spot as it seemed to be excessively busy tonight. He parked on the grass and that was the only place he could find. He hurried out of his vehicle and hastily walked toward the front door, with his phone, his wallet, and his keys as he tried to find places for everything. He stopped in the middle of the parking lot and took a few breaths to calm himself down, and then he continued toward the entrance. He didn't think he looked like anything fabulous, but for now he hoped he looked good enough. He glanced up and saw Linda standing there, in a nice flowy summer dress. It was a perfect playful length, but not too long of one, just about mid calf length. She waved exuberantly at him with obvious excitement and she even checked herself, putting her hand down after she had first done such. So she was obviously nervous as well, he thought, happy for that at least. He smiled back and did a light wave, and she smiled back at him. She was a naturally beautiful woman, especially out of the typical uniform, which is usually only how he ever saw her. Her face was round, soft, and her smile was naturally genuine. Her eyes were well beyond her years, because she had been through so much, but they were still gentle and gave a kind heartfelt gaze. Her body was looking rather entertaining tonight as her dress cut across her chest nicely, revealing just a little touch of cleavage to tease, but not too much to give off like she only wanted a romp in the hay. She was a woman that didn't mind showing her body off, but still with respect for her body and he appreciated that immensely. She had some elevated flats on, but they weren't really heels, so it made her slightly taller than she normally is, but that was fine by him. They accentuated nicely with her dress and they matched nearly perfect in color. Her long full head of hair, as it is usually pulled back in a ponytail, was actually loose tonight, but he still her preferred straight look, and he was finally able to see how long her locks actually were outside of work. He could truly appreciate Linda for the beautiful woman she was, standing before him, just as he made it up into her space. He walked up to her and immediately started apologizing for being tardy, by saying;

"Oh, Linda. I am so sorry I am running behind tonight. I would say that it is not like me, but you know that would not be truthful, in the least." He smiled with the last comment, flashing his teeth and seeing how she responded. She looked up at him and responded with;

"Oh, please, I should have known and that is why I just got here." she teased, smiling back at him hopefully being playful at the same time. What she said didn't get lost on him either, and by that he understood by her comment that she forgave him already. At that moment, she had confessed that she had likely been running a little behind as well. He walked with her over to the door, and then with his chivalrous bone implanted in him by his mother, he held the door open and allowed her to walk in first. She smiled at him kindly for his gentlemanly gesture and walked inside the busy place. They surprisingly only had to wait a few minutes for a table, which was nice, and then they started to follow the hostess(named Brooke) to their assigned seating. In the main room it was very loud, but as they traveled back into the next room, it really was not too loud where they happened to be heading. They headed into a connecting room as this establishment was situated inside an old multi room one story house. The largest rooms, where the bar was, were back up front and used by ones not staying long or just desiring a drink or to even pick up food. The back rooms were for dining room patrons only, and so the restaurant owners did a great job of trying to keep people happy and seperate. It had worked for many years, and so it made no sense to change it now.

They were in one of the off rooms, which pleased both of them. He smiled at a few people that he knew and she did likewise, but they didn't start up a conversation as probably some of them wanted to. Instead, they continued to follow their hostess until they were led to their small table in the back corner. This was perfect, he thought, nervously but also he was happy with it at the same time. The hostess pulled out Linda's chair, so he didn't have to but he still waited until she was seated before he took his own seat. They were both given menus and the hostess said to them;

"Thank you for coming to Steak and Bake. Your server will be Cheyenne, and she should be with you shortly." Brooke said lastly before turning to leave.

"Thank you kindly, Brooke." Tom said, trying to acknowledge their appreciation of where she chose for their seating. Linda looked over at him and he smiled, but before another second went by he spoke up to make sure his manners were on par. He said, or more or less blurted out with short pauses, saying;

"Linda, …..you look ……. simply stunning… tonight……… with your dress and……….. your matching shoes." He felt like a horse's ass the way he delivered it, but it was out there and he can't take it back now. She was not expecting his sweet comments and so she didn't respond right away and then she reached over for his hand and placed her soft hand onto his, saying to him;

"Thank you so much, Tom. It's ok, we are both new at this so there are no rules, procedures , or guidelines to follow with this course of action. You look great too and thank you for wishing to spend time with me." She smiled evenly and squeezed his hand ever so gently. The way her words flowed out of her mouth, almost like she was reciting something that she had written long ago. She definitely knew him and knew what to say to make him feel more at ease. He smiled back at her and then he turned his hand over as they touched palms, gently, and even lingered there until the young waitress assigned to them walked up on them. The young waitress came away from another table and came over to their table with a decisive but still gentle way, and she pulled an empty chair from an adjoining table as she sat down , now eye level with her customers. She started off with;

"Hi Y'all! My name is Cheyenne and I will be your waitress tonight in this section. So what would you like to drink?"

"Nice to meet you, Cheyenne. My name is Tom and this is Linda, but we haven't decided yet on what to drink, so maybe just bring us a house red wine now, until we decide what we desire for consumption in the food sense."

"Sounds great, you two, so how about I bring a glass of Pinot Noir, to get you both started with our bread bowl?"

"That sounds lovely, Cheyenne, and thank you." Tom responded but then looked over at Linda, and said sweetly. "I guess we have to decide what to eat, now." Linda laughed and they both opened up their bountiful menus across from one another and started scanning what contents were within. There were so many delicious meals, so many possibilities that they both looked at each other, wondering if the other's mouth was watering as much as their own. Some prices were reasonable and others were a little up there, but they did have a nice spread and choice of food, that wax for sure. They did carry many different cuts of steak (makes sense because of their name), but they also had some chicken, pig and even some elk choices. They also had some local fishes, but most of those were small portions that enhanced an already meat main course. The 'bake' part of the restaurant's name was the interesting part, as they not only carried typical potatoes and sweet ones also, but they also carried such sides as baked ziti, small lasagnas, penne, and of course some standard veggies like asparagus and small corn on the cobs. It was overwhelmingly a lot to choose from, that was for sure, Tom thought. But within minutes he thought he had narrowed it down to two or three choices. He looked over at Linda, who looked like she was unsure as of yet also, so he respected her quandary in decision making at this time. Just as he looked up, Cheyenne was back at their table with the wine and bread.

"Here y'all are", She said as she smartly put down the wine glasses very gently, pouring each of them a quarter full glass, and then she placed the bread down just between them. "So, did y'all decide yet?" Tom looked over at Linda who still looked like she needed a lot more time yet to think, so Tom asked Cheyenne politely;

"Well, what do you recommend if you were eating here for the first time, Cheyenne?" Linda looked up from her quandry to listen to what the girl had to say, just as did Tom. Cheyenne sat down in the seat again, and looked at him then at her, not sure where to start off, but then she spouted off three steak dinners that were quite delicious, two chicken dinners, and the one elk dish. She wasn't keen on the pork, so she didn't know what to say there. All her ideas were great choices as Tom had already picked out two of the three choices she had mentioned. Linda looked visibly relieved, but she still didn't seem quite ready so he was about to tell the waitress another minute, but suddenly Linda piped in with;

"Ok, I think I know now...." Cheyenne turned to her first and Linda continued reciting her order..."I think...I'll...have the Porterhouse steak.... 8 oz....., medium rare, please. Then I'll have a smaller sized baked potato, if you could please find me a smaller one, Cheyenne, (looking over at the waitress with a smile) loaded with light butter and sour cream, and a side of the baked ziti as well. There, I believe I am done, now." She said lastly as she put her menu down on the table and looked at Tom. Now he wasn't sure because what she mentioned sounded delicious, but he went with his first gut feeling as he said aloud;

"And that means I'll have the filet mignon, cooked medium rare please, baked potato with sour cream and bacon pieces, and I'll try your asparagus, please."

Cheyenne smiled at both of them after taking the order and then was about to get up, when Tom added in;

"Oh, also if you could add a bottle of the Cabernet Sauvignon, please, with the food delivery. Thank you, darlen'." Cheyenne produced a smile at the good ole southern sayen' and she whisked away with their order, but not before stopping to help a coworker out with delivering their food to the customers. She seemed like a nice kid, Tom thought and a hard worker, which is not always common in this day in age. Such pretty eye color she had too as he had noticed that the girl had one green and one blue eye color, which is not that common, or at least that he knew of.

Linda nicely placed her oversized napkin across her lap to prevent crumbs from the bread from getting on her dress. Well, that and it was appropriate for a lady, as her mama taught her. Tom did likewise and then he cut up the bread for her and offered her a piece of the warm and slightly hard crusted bread. It looked and smelled delicious. He placed two pieces on her bread plate and then offered the butter knife to her so that she could butter up her bread firstly. He didn't want to do it for her, as some don't even prefer large slabs of butter on their bread, so in offering her the knife he was giving her the options. She thanked him and started buttering her slices with just a hint. She talked as she was buttering, saying;

"I am sorry it took me so long to figure out, but I forgot about how many choices they have here. Well, that and I am famished and have hardly eaten all day. And as my momma would say, 'I could eat corn through a picket fence'." She giggled after she said it and how absurd it sounded and she looked over at Tom, who had just taken a sip of wine and nearly spit it out because her comment had nearly made him burst out laughing. "However, she used to call my deadbeat uncle, 'Worthless as gum on a boot heel' also. With that Tom put his drink down as obviously he could not drink now and he burst out a hearty laugh, drawing attention of not only the table nearest to them, but a few others further away. One good thing about being in a place that was a little louder, was it could hide a good hearty laugh easily. He looked around and apologized for his outburst to the table closest to them, because they had looked over to see if he was ok. They nodded pleasantly, so all was well. He looked over at Linda and she had a huge smile on her face and was laughing inside, but keeping it in. She enjoyed seeing him laugh and always did enjoy his hearty laugh at the office. They looked at each other, smiled and then went back to eating the bread and he finally got to taste and enjoy the wine. It was a nice mixture and he could taste the flavors very well. He thought there to be a classic cherry, no it was raspberry flavor, with a forest floor, and even some vanilla, and a hint of mushroom, or so he thought. He looked over at Linda, who also now took a sip of the red colored alcoholic drink in her glass and her eyes went alive as well. So he asked her;

"Wow, that is a really good Pinot. So what do you think?"

"I totally agree, and the flavors are just spot on." She said as she swirled the glass, gently stuck her nose into the top of the glass, and took in the flavors of the dark fermented liquid she had already lightly tested. He continued with;

"No worries about the food indecisions, I get it, too much good food on the menu makes your brain mush when trying to make choices. I had narrowed it down to three top choices already, so my task was easier. Thank you again, this is something I haven't done in a long time."

"I know, Tom, and we both needed this....", she said as she lifted her glass up toward his glass for a toast. "To the days ahead, whatever may come, but just let the minutes flow by like a steady drone of dragonflies as we enjoy one another's company and time."

"Well said, sweet Linda, well said!" And they 'chinked' their glasses lightly together for the memorable toast. They chatted with first small talk and then some work talk, but they kept their voices low for that specific kind of talk. Then they talked of their past and what brought them to this place in their life. They had polished off their wine already without even truly paying attention that they had. They each listened intently to one another, and then their food had arrived. They made room on their table and they took in the feast that they had been presented with. Tom spoke up, just as Cheyenne started pouring their new chilled bottle of wine into their fresh respective glasses.

"Thank you so much, Cheyenne. Wow, it smells and looks perfect. My compliments to the chef and owner."

"Sure thing, sweetie. We aim to please. Are you good darlin' (asking Linda)?"

"Yes, I am miss, I am just so hungry I don't know where to start." With that being said Tom snickered again and even Cheyenne broke a wide grinned smile at the indecisive woman she was tending to. After that, Cheyenne took the used wine glasses, the bread plates, and left them to their meal.

It was a wonderfully shared meal together between the two, Tom and Linda. They shared food with one another, taking food samples off each other's forks, they smiled a lot, laughed when appropriate and the biggest thing is that they gave each other caring glances more than he could say. He hadn't looked at a woman in this fashion since his late wife, but for some reason the timing and the opportunity just seemed right. So he was going to tide it out and see what could happen. He had just lost taste in even trying, so he had stopped and he even confessed that to Linda, and she completely understood because of what she had gone through as well. They were going through the wine quickly as it was just the right one that complimented their meal perfectly. Many of the other guests were trickling out as the evening wore on, but not these two as their conversation continued to flow with ease. They talked about their children, he had one girl in college and she had a boy and a girl, who were both on their own by now, off to college as well. She was definitely missing not having them at home, but she was also happy to be on her own also and have a chance to live her own life now. He asked her about her divorce and how that affected her. She thought hard on his questions and answered them like someone who had done all their thinking previously (good and bad), been through the hell that follows those questions and the divorce, and came out a better person. He did slightly backstep after she went into a long narrative, and it wasn't that he didn't enjoy hearing about it, but he didn't wish to presume too much. He said to her;

"I am sorry, Linda, I didn't mean to bring up anything bad, such as memories or triggers. So I hope you accept my apologies for asking too much."

"Nonsense, you may ask me anything, and if I wish to tell you, I will. Thank you for your tender words, but I am a big girl and you don't have to apologize for anything, love, we are all adults. My demons are in my past and I have dealt with them. You, however, are just too kind of a person..." she said as they once again touched hands across the table from one another. Wow, he couldn't believe his luck, to meet two such amazing women in his life. Wait, hold it, he thought to himself, take it easy, it is just their first date. With his history, he never fell often but when he did, he would always fall hard, and fast. He must keep it in check though, as she may not be thinking that way, so he smiled but also continued touching her soft and lovely fingers. They even interlocked fingers a time or two, which was a desirable interest from both parties. It was well into the night now, and Cheyenne brought over the tab, as she would be leaving soon. He looked at his watch and it was already fifteen minutes after eleven at night. He had no idea that they had been there so long, as the

117

direction, context, and feeling of the conversation and company had taken him anyway from his normal mundane life and time didn't seem to exist at this moment. He decided to pay the bill with his card and left a generous tip for Cheyenne. Linda did offer to pay, but he declined, respectfully, and said to her;

"How about you get the next time, then, ok?" she smiled warmly and responded with;

"Definitely, oh most definitely!" Just then Cheyenne came back to their table and was about to leave, when Tom spoke up quickly, saying;

"Cheyenne, sweetie, do you live far away? You don't walk do you? Or do you have a ride home?"

"Um, I usually do walk, yes, as I don't have my license yet but hopefully, soon."

"Well, we could take you home, to make sure you get home safely..." Tom innocently asked Cheyenne.

"Uh, sir, you two are nice people, but I am not into that type of thing. Sorry you have to find another girl for that..." . Tom immediately realized the verbal quandary that he had just put them into. He didn't mean it that way, but I guess it may have sounded that way. He looked over and Linda looked horrified, and then he quickly put in, to make sure there was no more confusion;

No....No ...I didn't mean it that way at all. We are both police officers and it is just a safety thing. That is all it was, please. Don't look at that the wrong way." There was a sigh of relief on Cheyenne's face as she was happy that these nice folks weren't weirdo perverts or something of the sort, and then she leaned against the table behind her, saying;

"Thank gawd, you have me worried there for a second." Then all three of them laughed at the miscommunication of the mistaken verbal interaction between them. Cheyenne continued with, "I was thinking, Gawd, I like you people but not like that. I appreciate it, but one of the guys here lives out my way so I will get a ride with him. Hope you come back again, y'all!"

"Okay, and I again am sorry. Thank you for being such a great waitress and such a good person. Are you ready, Linda, dear?"

"Yes, indeed, my perverted friend...." And with that being said, all three laughed again at the misinterpretation of the interaction.

Tom and Linda walked out of the restaurant holding hands. It just felt natural and so they both went for it. Then once outside, she leaned in on his shoulder, snuggling close to him. It was a gorgeous night outside tonight, and the weather was still warm but not unbearable yet. He looked at her and she at him and they decided to take a little walk as the restaurant wasn't that far from a well lit and used walking and biking trail. They walked hand and hand, talking and she leaned in quite a few times, laughing at his little jokes or when he said something funny. She felt wonderful on his arm and he felt stirrings of desire and love that he had nearly forgotten had existed in him. She shook part way through the walk, getting a slight chill, and so he stopped and cradled her in his arms. She reached in and placed her arms around his body and together they shared a loving and gentle embrace. He surrounded her and she seemed to fit perfectly into his arms and the moment was just about perfect, as they continued to cuddle. Linda backed away just slightly as she looked up into Tom's eyes, and they both had the idea, but who would be the first to make the move. He was about to say something, but then he stopped just prior to blurting something stupid out, and instead, he dipped his head and face toward hers. She closed her eyes and also leaned into him, reaching toward the skies, towards his warm lips. All night he was wondering what her soft puffy supple lips tasted like pressed against his, and in a matter of milliseconds, he would find out. He kissed her on the lips, gently, caring and with desire and passion for someone, like he hadn't felt since his late wife. Not that he was thinking of his wife, as all he thought about was Linda. He brought his hands up and cupped her shoulders, then her neck, and then her face itself, as they continued to passionately share lips with one another. She was getting into it as well, as her tongue came out and was soon in his mouth adeptly and with the same amount of passion as he was giving her. The kiss seemed to last a blissful eternity as both didn't ever want it to end, as it was their first official kiss. After some time and a little light groping, their lips parted and they looked into each other's eyes. Tom whispered quietly to her;

"Wow, ...Linda...... Wow!"

"I agree, darling, Tom, I don't have the words......."

They kissed one more time but not as long, as nothing could compare to that first one, and so then they continued walking with her leaning on his arm and them having their fingers intertwined in a true lover's display of affection. Not that they saw as they were both preoccupied, but during their first passionate kiss, up in the star-filled sky, a shooting star traveled its path through space, displaying its illuminated path as it went. It was almost as if the heavens above looked down and were happy for the joy and love shared between these two once broken people. What this signified for them was lost in translation on the two happy lovebirds, as they continued to enjoy one another's company, while the rest of the world, just for a few minutes, didn't exist to them.

After a nice long walk together and realizing that it was nearly one in the morning, Tom walked Linda back to her vehicle, where they stood and chatted for a few minutes. She looked up at him, and was about to ask him something, but then she stopped, trying not to embarrass herself in any way. He started to say something as well, but she put her finger to his lip and then reached up and passionately kissed him again, like their first kiss. After another lovely and memorable kiss, she asked him, hesitantly;

"You can come over…. If you like to….. For…." She lowered her head but didn't finish, yet they both knew what she meant.

"Linda, sweet darling, Linda. You have no idea how much I wish to say yes and share more with you, but….."

"I get it, I understand. You are worried about complicating things and such forth. You are probably right…." she started to respond and say before he was finished as he had paused for a moment. He looked at her and there was a slight tear in her eye at the little bit of disappointment she must feel at her misinterpreting what he wanted to say to her. Then he spoke up, making sure she got what he meant, saying;

"No, sweet and darling Linda, that is not what I was thinking, at all. I had the best time of my life with you tonight, and I don't want to spoil that at all with something else, at this time! I want more time spent with you and if , no I mean, when our feelings go that direction, then we will take that step as it comes. But please know, I adore you and long to be held by you, kissed by you, and spend time with you. My intentions are true and meaningful for you, and we will have time for all else, but you have truly rocked my world." With those words, her tears dried and her eyes lit up again like a spark in a newly lit fire. She leaned in and hugged him with such intensity as him being a perfect gentleman, even at the end, when she had offered him her body with sex. He embraced her warmly, berating himself for being such a gentleman, because he dearly did wish to go home with her and explore areas with her that they both haven't explored in such a long time. Still, he knew they had time and he wanted to forge a foundation of a relationship before jumping into bed right away and giving in to their sexual desires. They broke away from kissing, and he corrected her dress some, as it had accidentally shifted some with their passionate kissing, and her cleavage was clearly showing more now, and that made him desire her even more as he desperately tried to avert his gaze. Her one strap was nearly off her shoulder, and if that happened he knew he would have a full glimpse of her most lovely shaped breasts and that would cause a dilemma in that he would want her even more. Before he had realized it, he slowly and gently scooped up the strap and placed it back in place on her shoulder because if it had dipped any lower, he would have freed her swollen and hard nipples from their light fabric prison. Once that would have occurred, it would have definitely been game over and they would have ravaged each other, for sure. Painfully, he reached over and opened up her door for her. She turned to get in her vehicle, but in doing so she also swept her arm and hand in a fashion that she grazed the front of his shorts at his crotch area, feeling the firmness being held back by his own fabric. Both sighed, a sigh of resigned acceptance, but also of sexual frustration at the same time. He kissed her again, and said to her;

"Can hardly wait till we can do this again, sweet Linda. You are an incredibly ravishing and perfect woman." She purred at his words and said to him;

"Hmmm, anytime, tiger, you know how to get a hold of me1" With that she dropped into her car and he closed her door. She started up her car, blew him a kiss, and then slowly pulled away. He walked over to his vehicle and was about to get in, when he stopped and cooled down a second. He would not overthink this, this was a perfect date and at the perfect moment. He looked up and asked the heavens, but in all actuality he asked his wife;

"So what do you think, hon?" There was no response of course, not that he honestly expected one, but still. Then about that time, he glanced up one more time and he experienced the first shooting star that he had seen in who knows how long. It shot across the sky, with its tail leaving a light trail and then it was gone. He couldn't believe his eyes, and suddenly he teared up some, saying aloud;

"Thank you sweetheart, thank you, I got your message." He dropped into the seat of his vehicle and he started the engine and drove off, not believing what had just occurred and how it all had transpired. What a crazy life this is, he thought, on his way home to his apartment and his cat. What a crazy life......as he went home to take a cold shower.

Chapter Ten

It was odd, but Suzie hadn't seen her captor since the time that she caught him looking in on them. An unknown amount of time had passed, but she had really had no idea how much or how long it had been, as time was meaningless to her, in her prison. All she knew was that she had about ten meals, no wait, or was it twelve? Shit, now she can't even remember, which was not what she wanted. She would see Weasel, maybe every other meal, not that she didn't deliver them both, but she just hadn't been awake when she had placed the food down. There was nothing else to do but sleep. She had pinched off her IV a few times, but then she just started aching with soreness all over, and that was just unacceptable, so she would always restart it in a short amount of time. Obviously, it wasn't enough pain meds to make her hallucinate, but it was enough to keep her in check with the pain and give her a light who gives a shit feeling. That explains also why so many girls had given up over time and just said 'to hell with it' and just existed in their state. Weasel did confess to her that she does not get too complacent, because if the master gets bored with her he would dispose of her, like so many before. That was something she wouldn't forget none too soon, as she shook her cobwebs out of her foggy mind. Gawd, she wished for a whipped cappuccino right now or some other delicious coffee drink. She had asked Weasel for one, but she was denied her request. Probably had something to do with the meds she was receiving, but then again that was just her thought process on it. Her eye socket was healing up nicely as the pain was minimal now and per Weasel, there didn't seem to be any infection. She had used a clear flashlight to check it since it was mostly the red light in this area., most of the time. She was given a washcloth and a plastic tub intermittently in her cell to wash off. It was better than someone doing it for...to her. At least she felt less violated. Her hair was slowly growing back on her legs, since she hadn't shaved in so long, well that and all the other normal areas hair grows back if not maintained in some type of way. She saw other girls here and there, but they didn't always seem to be the same one all the time. So it was good to know (well not in the sense that they were captured) that there were a few more that were there also, which still gave her the chance to plan her escape and take others with her. She found herself humming old classic songs that were her favorites, and occasionally she would sing aloud. Curse that bastard if he should penalize her for keeping hope alive and believing that there is a better place besides here, for her. Usually she wouldn't sing aloud too long, because her voice would croak or she would become too dry, and then she would need a drink. She drank just enough to keep herself going and not too much more. It kept her from wetting herself or having to alleviate herself all the time. She sadly had to admit that she was wetting herself at times while she slept. Maybe it was the meds, maybe it was the stress, or who knows why else, but either way she had trouble where she never had trouble with that before. It was degrading, in a way, but at this point who gave a shit: she was a captive to a freak, she lost her eye for her rebellion, and she was stuck in this cage 24/7. Shit, she thought, how much worse can it truly get? Being stuck inside and in a cage was significantly wearing down her spirit over time. She was a true outdoors chick, and not being able to see nature, take in all the smells, and see how glorious the world is, was honestly killing her inside, more than she would actually confess to. Minutes were not existent, hours could not be counted, days were lost, and maybe even weeks were stripped from her life forever. She always said that that was one thing in life that we can never recover, and that was time. Once it had passed, it was gone. People worry so much about money, love, and world possessions, but time is the ultimate gift given and taken, which could never, ever, be returned. So she did the best she could with what was given to her. This had to be her life, for now.....

Her captor was watching, but only from a distance. He kept all his 'gifts' in check, especially spirited Suzie. He still enjoyed her the best, but his newest girl, Teresa was a true gem as well, and she was second in running. He was slowly getting bored of some of the others, and therefore he was already making plans for his next move. His key was that he didn't just haphazardly go out and take someone! That would just not do at all, and that was actually cowardly. His entire aspect was to somehow get to know them in some way shape or form. He enjoyed the thrill of trying to somehow get into each girl's life, just enough to tip the scales in his favor. He would seek out or poach, so to speak, each girl carefully. Sometimes it would only take a week or less, but many times they were more difficult to obtain so he would take months, and even one time he took an entire year. It was a lot of planning and a lot of notes and he kept a notebook on each girl; how they met, how they interacted, notes on how he planned or was planning to take her away and sweep her off her feet to make her an easier target. To be able to find that certain thing that triggers a person is not something that is usually learned in a day. There were exceptions as always though too, just like Teresa, because she was so into skateboarding that it was such an easy thing for him, but that didn't happen most times. He thought back on everything he had done, as he opened up his second cabinet drawer in his desk. He had a small notebook of all the things that he had learned over the years. Each thing that he had done was a different girl, for the most part. He prided himself in not many doubles, which would just be boring and mundane in abductor standards. He had learned how to square dance, play the violin, the harp, the flute, and yes even the guitar. He also learned how to race cars and was a near expert level dirt track driver, he knew how to motocross, even though he was never that great at that, he still got the attention from the young cuties, when he did do well. He took classes in entrepreneurship, finance, restaurant owner, bartender, dog walker, cleaner, babysitter, and even other sports such as archery, shooting, tennis, pickleball, and ping pong. Still he always wished to learn more, to do more, as his mind was always yearning for the next rush, which would also include an abduction of course, too. He looked through his drawer, through all his fake IDs and credit cards. They were all rubber banded together per identity and he even had them in alphabetical order, which was a must for him. Once he must have mistakenly misplaced one and he found it out of order much later, and so who else had the opportunity to mess with such aspects of his life, only Weasel. So she had paid a price for that one, even though it wasn't her fault, he figured in the end, he still made her pay as the scapegoat. After that he locked everything, made sure all was secure, and that she couldn't get into certain places without him present. It was the price he had to pay, but it was well worth the comfort of knowing that no one could get him or undermine him. That was him. He had to be in control, no matter what, and he wouldn't have it any other way. Besides he was the one risking everything for his conquests, his girls.

. He was in his office, playing some Beethoven...no wait, some Chopin....he ridiculed himself for getting those two mixed up. It is like apples and oranges, he said to himself. Chopin played much smaller and intimate pieces, or so he thought of Beethoven's more grand and sometimes overwhelming compositions. Such a dolt he was that he almost caused himself pain to recompense for his daft musical comparison. He continued to sit there a little longer, trying to settle himself down, and he remained there until his angst had thus subsided. Now that his emotions were in check, he went back to what he was doing, and grabbed one of his clipboards and headed out of his office/control room. He walked down the corridor into the area where his refrigerators were. There he stopped, checked his watch to verify his time, and then he opened the first refrigerator door. He checked the temperature, opened up three heavy duty egg type containers that were placed inside this particular one, and ended up checking on the contents. He inspected to see how everything looked with them, pulling out the smaller heavy duty plastic bags which housed the contents and some clear liquid, and then he reclosed the containers and the fridge to maintain the coldness, since this was an older fridge. He went to the next one and saw that the inside contents in their plastic bags were looking ok and that the temps were good here as well. He checked each of the fridges to make sure all was well and that there were no malfunctions occurring which would damage his stock. The last one he came to was empty, but it was still working well and ready to use when he needed it. He then went along and checked the lids on his many heavy plastic barrels as well, and everything seemed to be holding up nicely with no signs of leaking or contamination. He checked it all off of his clipboard and then he was done with that. Once more he checked on his generators, but all was well and he added more fuel also. He would soon have to make a fuel run. In this case it was an all day ordeal, because he would go to different gas stations over the areas, to make sure that he wasn't overconsuming at one and something would look suspicious. He would also use his cash on hand and do such, since it would leave no electronic footprint. After checking everything, he decided not to check on his girls at the moment, as he had watched them all morning, so instead he used his key and unlocked a door, and then opened it, went outside and relocked the door. He was now outside and checking the perimeter of his area, his base, for now. He walked around thoroughly looking for anything that would be out of place or in question, of which he didn't find , thankfully. He visually checked out all the cameras and he even went to another small shed. There he unlocked that one and pulled out a drone. He walked over to a clearing, the same one he always used and then turned on everything and got it ready for flight. The drone started its whirring noise as it prepared for flight, and then he used his controller and slowly the fancy and expensive drone took off. The drone went high above the trees (straight up) to get a bird's eye view and that was when he turned and had it do a slow 360 degree panorama of the area. All looked good from that height, so he dropped it down closer to the trees and slowly started moving it above the treeline to check everything out. He did a nape of the earth (tree line) flight pattern as he checked the most distant areas of the property he was on. After about thirty minutes of checks and rechecks, he brought the drone back to his position. He lowered it down and landed it nicely in the small opening. Picking up the drone, he went back to the shed and stowed his new age observer. He set to recharge its batteries and then he neatly placed everything back where it should belong. Thankfully all looked peaceful and quiet. He had run into a group of kids on motorbikes before as they had ignored the purple paint and the numerous signs that were posted all over the fencing perimeter of the property. They rode their motocross type bikes all over the place and around the abandoned quarry, which borders the property that he had taken over. They even came a little onto his property, but he set his drone up and he buzzed them numerous times. They tried to throw rocks at the drone, but they missed horribly. In the end, he ran them off and nothing more had occurred since that day. He wanted to make sure it remained that way as well. Any issue, he would resolve immediately and as quietly as he could. He would kill some of the local animals, such as deer, wild pig, rabbits, and even squirrels at times and then he would clean off the skulls and set them on the fence posts to ward off anyone who might think of entering. He would use the meat as the source of food for his girls with the stews and the mush meals he made them. He tried to be resourceful and not wasteful in every way possible. He did what he must to maintain control and to maintain his elusiveness.

A few hours later, just as it was turning dusk, he had checked everything that he needed to check and so he reentered his building, the barn, and he went directly to his office. He had a bed in there that he often slept on, and tonight would be no different. He went to the small kitchen area and pulled a microwave meal out of the small freezer, and he nuked himself a meal. He relieved himself in the small bathroom that was next door that also had a mini shower. It was basic but it was what he used mostly. He had a trailer that he pulled and lived out of many a time, but he hadn't used it as of recently. After the microwave beeped loudly, making him aware that his meal was now ready, or at least he hoped for such. He went over, removed the plastic covering, and let the overly hot meal cool off some. In the meantime, he went over and hooked up his outside camera feeds to one monitor, inside camera feeds to another, and the last monitor he put on a classic TV show back from when he was a kid. He enjoyed watching the classic and not the dribble from today's societal constructs. Life was just more simple back then and so he reveled in the nostalgia of the classic humorous shows, where people could make fun of people and not get in trouble for doing so. He glanced over at his map on the wall, which was a US map of the states. He had different color thumbtacks adorning this map, with yellow being places that he had been , meaning he had done some collecting. Then there were blue ones for future moves to possible places that would accommodate him and his needs he had to fulfill. There were red tacks for danger zones, which were places he checked out or was in and had close calls with being caught. He steered clear of the red zones, that was for sure. He had been nearly all over the country, at one time or another, but he had collected only in ...one, two, three, four, five,....yeah six states, he thought. He walked over, collected his one fork and knife out of his utensil drawer, because one set was all he needed. Haste makes waste, he always said to himself , as this was one of the many things that had been taught to him by his grandmother. He sat down, put his feet up, looked around at the other monitors, and then he took his first bite of his cooked food. It wasn't too bad considering it was a microwave meal, but it was still really hot, yet. So he placed it down again, and he leaned over and poured himself a tall glass of red wine to cool down his palate. Hmmm, this year of wine was delicious, he thought as he turned and checked the label. Yes, just what he thought, it was a Petite Sirah red, so delicious and full of tannins. Lovely bold taste and one he had before. He must get more of this he thought, and then he placed it down and started to eat his meal once more. He laughed hardily, nearly choking on his food as the TV show made him burst out at the stupidity but silliness of what he was watching. After a few more minutes, he had polished off his meal and discarded the container in the trash can to his side. He continued to sip the wine and enjoy his show, stopping periodically to check in on things with the other cameras, but all looked well. He glanced over at his map and he started to figure out where he was going to go next. He had done a minor surveillance on a few of them, and he had narrowed it down to two candidates. Now looking, he zoned in on one, and he thought, why not, he hadn't been up north in some time. The area was in central Pennsylvania and he made it definitive. He would prepare, as the prep took a few months and even up to six months to depart this place and not leave any indicative signs behind. Still he wanted one more girl to collect before he did so and he knew who she was, the local waitress, that was for sure. He knew he had to have her for many reasons, but the most indicative one was that she had one green and one blue eye. That would be the ideal find!

        Meanwhile back in town, Tom went home after his lovely date with Linda, and he was still on a little high as he couldn't believe how easy it was to chat with her, interact with her, and share his life with her. Yes, he had known her for a while now, but this very night had shined an entirely different light on how he knew her. They were both consenting adults, but still this complicated so much their relationship, or at least he thought. He parked his vehicle, got out, and unlocked his door walking into his place shortly after. He sat down on the lounge chair and stared at the wall for a few minutes. Why was this so hard for him to comprehend? He felt like he was cheating on his late wife, but he knew he wasn't and he also imagined her trying to kick him in the ass and live again. They had talked about this before her passing, and she made him promise her that he would continue to live, no matter what befalls her, and not become a recluse. That was her dying wish that he would find happiness again, but for all this time he maintained his solidarity and he did not even look for anyone. So when Linda had asked him, it had totally taken him by surprise. They had shared life's stories and the traumatic events which led them to where they are today, previously, especially after his wife had passed, because he had leaned on her shoulder many times, since she was the strong but nurturing type. She had seen him at his lowest and she bided her time and waited for him to be ready, or maybe she just got tired of waiting, so then she made her move. This was all going through his mind at a million miles an hour, as he tried to make sense of everything. He finally got up, after petting the cat some, and he stripped off his clothes and turned on the water. He started off hot, but then he turned the dial back to lukewarm. He opened the curtain and stepped inside the shower, letting the water fall over his head and body. Using his right arm, he leaned against the shower wall and the water fell all over him. He stood there for some time just trying to process everything and for him to clear his mind. Eventually, he stopped thinking about everything and just remained in the moment and the shower. Of course the way his mind works, that didn't last long as he started to think about the case now, which is not something he really wanted to do right now either. He finished washing himself and then he exited and dried himself off. After donning a pair of shorts and a soft t-shirt for sleeping, he walked back out into the kitchen and paid attention to the kitty for a little bit, as the cat showed its appreciation by purring and 'making dough' on his leg. His mind left the case, as there would be enough thinking of that tomorrow, and so he went back to his new found feelings for Linda. That was the thing, he actually felt guilty, because he did truly have feelings for Linda! He admitted it, and out loud he said, 'I have feelings for you, Linda!' The cat turned and looked at him, as if saying, 'who cares loser, just pet me.' He snickered at the cat's reaction to his remark, and so he did the bidding of his feline master and continued to pet and stroke the cat in a way pleasing to continue its engine purring. His mind continued to wander and he finally settled it, after about another hour of being awake, that he indeed liked Linda, and that he wanted to pursue her romantically. This may not seem like a big deal to most people, but to him it was a big deal, and therefore even with the tell-tale signs, he still needed to think about it. That was another reason why he didn't want to sleep with her that night. That might have edged him slightly toward the idea that he was making a mistake, and he didn't want to feel that way or make her feel any other way. Did he wish to sleep with her, 'Hell yes', but he knew that he just couldn't. He had to think things through, and now that he did, he was ready to move on with his relationship with her, but still slowly. He just wanted to respect her and the process since they both have a long history of issues from their past. He believed that she would feel the same way too, or at least he hoped. Eventually he started to drift off in his chair as seems to be the norm for him these days.

      Just a little earlier and half way across town, Linda made it back to her home, with a large smile on her face. She couldn't believe how the evening had transpired as well, but she loved every minute of it. She wasn't second guessing things as Tom was doing at the same time(unbeknownst to her), but she was smiling and happy for how it all came about. She knew Tom's history well and she was not always forward when it came to dating someone, but she waited for some time for him to see if he would ask her. She thought she would never push someone into such a predicament, whether it be good or for bad, so she just bided her time and waited. Now it was her time, as she had waited long enough. Her biggest concern was that maybe he didn't feel anything toward her, which would have been devastatingly difficult for her to take. Yet, it was a very realistic possibility that crossed her mind many times previously, but she figured if you don't take that chance, one will never know. Rather than to have loved (tried) and lost, than to never have loved (or tried)at all. She took the chance and the results had been a milllion times better than what she had imagined. They had clicked like she hadn't clicked in years with someone, and it invigorated her, scared her, and also humbled her. The night had gone so well and they enjoyed each other's company so much that she never wished it to end. Still she couldn't believe her luck, because Tom was truly someone worth any woman's while, but here she was lucky enough to have found favor in his eyes. She blushed as she stood in front of her mirror and took off her light make-up, carefully. Once that was off, she stripped out of her dress and let it fall to the floor. She stood naked in front of the mirror for only a few seconds, before she grabbed her nightshirt and slipped it over her head. She brushed her teeth and then she used the restroom. Once done she went back out into the kitchen to have another small glass of wine. She poured a small glass of Zinfandel, and started slowly sipping from that. She enjoyed the sweeter and fruitier taste of this white wine closer to bed. She replayed the entire night in her head and how things just fell into line and she cuddled up with some blankets as she thought of their first shared kiss that very night. He was even a better kisser than she would have ever imagined and he had such passion just as she had, deep within her waiting to be released with the right person, and she knew now that it was with Tommy. She remembered the obvious turn on in the way he kissed her, held her, and touched her and her body shivered right there. Even with the blankets over her, she knew it was not from being cold, but it was from how he made her feel. She drank another few sips, remembering how if he had wanted to take her and sleep with her at that very instant, she would have gladly given in and accepted because she was that far gone. Much to her surprise, but then again not so much since he was such a gentleman, he had declined the invitation to delight in lovers' bliss and sleep together that night. Yes it was a little unexpected, but she also saw and welcomed it as a sign of respect to her as well. So, she silently thanked him for respecting her enough and to wish to leave it off where they did, which was an incredible and wonderful date, beautifully shared time together, and with a burning and wanting desire for one another. She respected his choices and he respected their relationship and her body enough to put the brakes on when it was needed. That was truly a good man, she said to herself. She got up, after she had drank much of her wine and she placed the glass inside the sink, and walked off and into her bedroom. She didn't even desire a smoke, and she was thankful for that since she was trying to quit that distasteful(as she saw it) habit. She curled up in bed as her little Bichon, Fritz, came over and curled up behind her legs, before she covered herself up, as he always does. He had been outside through the little doggy door of her back door, after what she figured was doing his business and now he was ready for bed with his mommy. She slowly fell off to sleep and she had desirable and wanton dreams of what her and Tom would do together. Her little puppy remained faithfully by her side even as she tossed and turned. The perfect end to a most perfect night.

Chapter Eleven

The next few days passed by quickly and up into the next two weeks were a whirlwind of activity as the police issues seemed to have doubled overnight, with a vehicle theft and consequential arrest and a few home and one business burglaries, all which ended in arrests of some sort. One perp had outstanding felonies in another state, so that person was transported to that state to get prosecuted to the full extent of the law there. Also there was an influx of visitors as well, so there was a lot more patrolling, parking tickets, and fender benders that occupied their time even more so than usual. Sadly because of this business, Tom hardly had any time to look into the disappearances of the two women that he had made a board for. He did continue to try to follow leads, ask questions, and patrol the possible areas where the women went missing, but still he had nothing, nothing more to go on. It was frustrating not only for him, but for the families as well, that was for sure. Still he did what he could and what time allowed him to. His blossoming romance with Linda continued to grow and even though they were much busier than the previous week, they found time to share with lunches and even a late dinner date, at her house. Still they didn't go any further in their relationship than kissing and some fondling, but that seemed to be quite alright for both of them. They knew that when the time was to come, it would occur naturally and not be forced in any sense of the matter. He was happy enough spending time with Linda, the happiest he had been in a long time and he began to accept her as the next best thing in his life. The other officers seemed to respond with happiness as well, well, after the initial shock that is, but they gave their blessings to both, hoping that it would last. Office romances can turn into a mess, if they don't work out so they actually laid down some odds and betted to see how long and if it would last, unbeknownst to both Tom and Linda. Tom seemed to be sleeping a little better as of recently also, which also lifted his spirits some, and both his coworkers and Linda noticed the difference. She was happy that he seemed to be happy with his life more and especially with her. They snuck kisses here and there in passing, touches of the hands, and reassuring glances. It was what they did, both acting like teenagers in love, but then again it had been so long for both of them that it was well deserved and cute as well. Her puppy even came over and met his cat at his place one time. It didn't go that well, as the cat thwacked her poor investigative puppy as soon as it came too close for comfort, but Fritz easily backed away and started barking at the oblivious and malcontent feline. Both Tom and Linda laughed and then the animals went their separate directions, so it was a getting to know and now they both knew where each pet stood. Time may change things, but either way they didn't kill one another which was the most important aspect. Things were going well for them and they were both happy with their blossoming romance.

Yet while the two new love birds were getting happier and happier, another person was becoming more and more uneasy and continuing to go out as often as he could to watch and check the skatepark for his missing daughter. He always took a few drinks, a live pistol, and an increasing anger at the entire situation. Blain Astel was not happy in the least, and his angst grew more so as the days wore on. His wife and him had heard nothing new about their missing daughter, and to him that was completely unacceptable. So every night he continued to survey and roam the area to see if he could catch someone or anyone that looked suspicious. He was willing to do what it took to get answers too, so he always had his pistol on hand and he always checked it to make sure it was loaded and ready to roll if he ever found the man who took his girl from them. He had watched, intently, quite a few vehicles as they appeared to pose a threat to the young ones skating and minding their own business, but every time he thought he had someone, it ended up being a parent or guardian picking up their child. It made him happy to know that parents were still getting involved, but it also frustrated him as he was seriously wanting to find the prick who may have taken his girl. He would down another beer after such an incident or malcontent thought, and quickly the beer cans piled up in the back of his truck. He was smart enough to put a recycling bin back there, and so after he polished off a few he would get out of his vehicle and put the cans in the receptacle, so that it looked less suspicious to any police, if he would be stopped. He would take that time to get out and smoke and take a walk around the area, to further investigate

132

anything that may be suspect. Of course he would carry his pistol in his belt, just in case, because one never knows when the need could arise. He knew this was hurting his marriage, but at this point he had no family without his daughter, so he would do and give anything up to have her back. Hopefully one day his wife would understand why he had to do what he was doing.

Nearly two weeks after he had started his reconnoiter outages at night, on one particular night, he was finally rewarded with something he questioned. He got one of his three normal spots, as he rotated to look less obvious as well, and as usual he started drinking two beers directly. He had been having a rough week at work, and so he was exhausted and tired of coming out here every night as well. He was starting to second guess his motives and his drive, as he had just guzzled the last beer, when a late model sedan type car pulled up. Oh great, he thought as he looked over, after the headlights went out after the vehicle parked. He reached back and pulled another cold beer out of an old styrofoam cooler, and of course the lid remained cockeyed, and so he had to practically turn and adjust it before he tackled his next beer. He turned back around after fixing the lid and watched the car. There was no movement at all and the windows were up, so he moved a little more to see if he could get a better view. But there was nothing going on in the car that he could see. A few other skaters and girls showed up, so there were at least ten kids down at the skatepark now. He didn't recognize them, that he could remember as he squinted to see if he actually did or not. Wait, there was that girl from the shaker shack, 'no, that's not it', he mumbled inaudibly. She worked at the sugar shack.... No that's not it either, the Steak and Bake, that's it, he exclaimed! She was a very pretty girl, and he didn't mean that in any sexual or interest way, just stating an obvious observation. The boys seemed to be trying to impress her, as they did tricks all around her and showed off their best combinations related to their passion of skating. The girls these days grow up so quickly, he thought to himself, as he opened the third can of beer. Then he thought of his darling girl Teresa and how much she had grown up, especially the last three years. He knew it wasn't possible to stop time and keep his 'little' girl little, but dammit, did it have to fly by all too quickly as it had. He lowered his head and was immediately ashamed of how he couldn't protect the one thing in this world that he promised he would always protect. He had truly and miserably failed his daughter, moreso now the more he thought of it, over and over again, and each night. How had he become so less of a man, he thought as he chugged his next beer. He drank not to actually get drunk, but to drown his sorrows and make him forget what a 'loser' of a father he inexplicably found himself to be. While trying to chug the beer, he ended up spilling more down his shirt than he had wanted to, as he definitely didn't wish to waste his brewsky in any way shape or form. Unfortunately he had, so he grabbed an old and dirty towel that stuffed down between his seats, and one that he commonly used as a napkin when he got his spicy chicken meal with onion rings at the local fast food joint. So the stench of the towel was not very pleasing, in any sense, but he still used it to mop up the wetness on his shirt and pants. 'What a complete asshole I am', he mumbled to himself in a slightly inebriated slur.

Just as he finished spot drying as much of his clothing as he could with the nasty towel, he looked up for some odd reason. He looked over at the car and still there was nothing out of the ordinary, but then again why should there be. He should go home, he thought to himself. Enough of this bullshit staying out. He had a loving wife at home who misses him, and that was all that mattered right now. They had to use each other to console one another in such horrific times. He had not only failed his daughter, but now he was failing his wife too. He could hardly stand himself anymore. He reached for his keys, but dropped them on the floor, and he bent over to try to find those pesky things. He reached around for over a minute, not finding them and cursing in the meantime at his freaking luck, when all of a sudden he heard the jingling of keys. He said, 'A-ha' and he found them under his boot. What a buffoon , he thought, as he grabbed them good enough to pull them up to his lap. Now his head was spinning after having his head lower than his heart and he needed a few minutes to 'righten up' his senses, before he would leave here for the night. Suddenly he saw movement to the right side of the vehicle and some bushes were moving, as if someone had just walked on by. He watched again, but didn't see anything else, and yet he still had an inkling to check out what was going on in that area. He grabbed his gun, opened his truck door and stumbled out of his vehicle. He nearly fell over as he was slightly inebriated, or at least enough to have his coordination not working cohesively with what he wanted it to do. He stumbled a little and then stopped, took a deep breath and started to walk a little straighter now, as he crossed the road. He made it across the road and headed in the direction of the movement in the bushes, but he still didn't see anything. So he unsteadily walked on, and then he looked over toward the skateboarding kids to see where they were, in

134

relation to where he was. He stopped and looked around again, but there was nothing, no movement, anywhere that he could see. Just when he was about to give up he turned and suddenly ran into someone.....or something. He fell backwards, nearly flat on his back and his arms flew to his side as he tried to catch himself. The other person , who wasn't impaired didn't lose their balance enough to fall, but just stumbled some. Blain spoke immediately, saying much louder than he had expected his words to come out, saying;

"Hey....watch.....out.............. Mister....." Blain said, slurring his words. The other person, who was a man, immediately put his hand out to help the downed man, saying;

"I am so sorry, friend, so sorry....I didn't even see you there." Blain glared at the man and grouchily asked him;

"Hey, what are you doing here........... anyway........ and.......... what's that in your hand?" The man looked down at his hand and he had forgotten the camera that he had been holding. He looked at the man who was on the ground, who was now trying to get up and scramble to his feet. The inebriated Blain made it to his knees, and then he remembered that he still had his pistol in his pants belt. He stood up finally (but not till after he received help from the stranger), and once more pointed at the unknown man and said;

"Hey...I asked...you...a question.........Did....... you ......hear..... me?" The man stopped and looked sadly at the staggering and obviously drunk man, responding to him saying;

"Sir, I am sorry I startled you, but I am just here for my daughter." There was a moment of silence as Blain tried to comprehend what had been said to him. Then out of nowhere, Blain sputtered;

"Ha, what daughter, I thinks.....you ...be lyin'..... Where's your proof, mister?" The man looked at him oddly, and was about to reach for his wallet, when Blain all of a sudden brandished his pistol and pointed it at the man. The man backpedaled once more, but this time with a disconcerting look in his eye. This was not going well at all, the stranger thought to himself as he backed up with his hands in the air. Blain spoke a few more slurred words, saying;

"Answer me.....you..... lily-livered chicken...shit...." He yelled pointing the pistol right at the strange man. The man could do nothing but hope that the drunk didn't fire at him, and so he continued keeping his hands up in the air and stopped moving backwards, at that point. It was not a good situation.

As it so happens, just as Blain had brandished his gun and started backing down the stranger, Deputy Tom Moors of the Sheriff's department pulled out of an alley and was in direct eyesight of what was about to occur. He didn't know why the one man was pointing his pistol at the man opposite of him, but he could see that in a few short minutes this may not end very well at all. He pulled his vehicle up behind the two men, and turned on his lights, but not his siren. The deputy didn't flip on his siren just in case it would startle the man and cause him to discharge his firearm. Fortunately, once the lights came on, Blain turned around to see what the fuss was and that is when Deputy Moors, who had already exited his car, stood there with his firearm out and pointing at the aggressor, saying;

"Sir... you need to drop your weapon now, or I will fire on you!" Blain looked dumbfounded, as all of a sudden the tables had turned and now he was being told to comply or else possibly die. He didn't want to die, so he looked down at his gun and then slowly dropped it in the grass. The deputy rushed forward and told Blain;

"Drop now, face down and arms behind your back! Do it, NOW!" Blain complied the best he could but his arms weren't working well, and he was unable to get them behind his back without assistance. So they were forced there by the deputy, which caused Blain severe discomfort. About that time at least two more police vehicles showed up, and two more officers scurried out and assisted the deputy who had Blain down. Of course now with all the lights and activities, the skaters had come over to the fence to see what was going on and investigate the reason so many cops were around. As soon as the deputy raised up the downed man, the Sheriff, Joe Jenkins, looked at the man and said;

"Blain? What the hell has gotten into you? Does Lori know you are out here? Tell me what is going on!" He looked sheepishly at the sheriff and slurred his words, but said:

"Sor....rry... Joe.... my daughter......Teresa....." It was at that very moment, he broke down and started crying profusely which was a surprise to those who stood around him. He cried hard for about a good five minutes, and that was when Sheriff Jenkins took charge of him and took him over to his deputies' vehicle and sat him down on the curb, to talk with the man. The stranger who Blain had raised his gun to was standing off to the side talking to one of the other officers about what had happened and how it all transpired. Sheriff Jenkins could smell the alcohol on Blain's breath and he said to him;

"Blain, my friend, what are you doing? I know you are distraught about your daughter, but man you can't go around serving vigilante justice to anyone that you don't know. You could have killed that man! Do you realize that?" Blain just lowered his head and started tearing up again. The Sheriff continued with; "This isn't you my friend, you wouldn't normally do this, but you know I gotta take you in." The sheriff sat down beside him and continued whispering and trying to get Blain to truly realize what the implications were, but the slobbering and ashamed man could do nothing but look away in an ashamed fashion. Once the deputy got a report from the stranger, whose name was Todd, he then asked the man;

"I imagine you want to press charges, and if so, you will have to come down to the station and fill out some paperwork, okay?" The man looked at Deputy Moors and then quietly asked him:

"What's wrong with the man and what did I do to trigger him off?"

"Oh, well, his daughter went missing, probably a runaway, but either way he has been in bad sorts since that had happened."

"I feel truly bad for the man, and I wish I could apologize for giving him the wrong vibes. I was just taping some footage for my daughter, Hilde, who is an avid skate enthusiast, and I heard about this park and figured why not since I was passing through the area tonight. (He showed a picture of his daughter to the deputy, which the deputy looked at and smiled at how cute the girl was). So, I stopped to get some footage and that was when he came up on me. It frightened me, that is for sure, but I was in the military before so I have had weapons pointed at me, in my previous life, if you know what I mean." The deputy shook his head in affirmation and then Todd spoke up again, saying;

"Honestly, if the man is hurting that much, I don't want to press charges and have him put away for a poor decision in the midst of such a stressful ordeal. If he wouldn't have drank so much, then maybe he wouldn't have done such an unceremonious type of deed. With that in mind, I decline to press charges, sir. I just want him to get the help he needs and hopefully he will find his daughter as well. It seems like the right thing to do for him."

"Well, you are an unusually honest but truly honorable man for not wishing to press charges against him. I will let the sheriff know and we have your contact information, so if we need anything else we can still get a hold of you."

"Yes, deputy, anytime. Just please see that he gets the help he needs and thank you."

"Thank you, Todd. Take care and you have our number. If you change your mind, you take care, sir." With that Todd was gone and the officers had to get Blain in the officer's car so that he could be transported downtown. Now that the situation was diffused, the skaters went about their tricks again, but after that odd police issue, Cheyenne decided it was time to leave and so she walked home alone, in the dark.

The Sheriff went back to patrolling while the deputy took Blain to the police station. There he filled out a report on what he saw happened and what he took down from the witness, Todd. As Deputy Moors was typing, he thought about the stranger not pressing charges and thought, wow, what a stand alone type of guy. It was nice to know that there are people out there who wish for someone to get help rather than lock them up. Because Todd wasn't pressing charges and Blain did have a license to carry, the only real charge they could give him was a misdemeanor charge at this time. Todd had talked extensively about not giving poor Blain a felony charge, and so he would knock it down to two misdemeanors and maybe the judge will let him serve it out in community service and fines, only. That would remain to be seen though, so until that time, Blain would sleep it off in the jail cell overnight and then be released on his own recognisance in the am, to his wife. Lori (Blain's wife) had already been called and she was livid, but she also sounded sad and defeated. So the deputy placed Blain in a cell and hopefully this will allow the defeated man to sleep it off, and think about his decisions that brought him to the low point in his life. It was not a good night for Blain Astel, and he figured neither will the next few weeks be any better. Not until he paid his penance for the crimes committed by his intoxication and his poor judgment. Only time will tell, Blaine thought to himself, as he laid his head down and fell soundly asleep.

Todd drove down the road slowly, away from the drama that unfolded back at the skatepark.Was he truly scared? No, not in the least. He wasn't worried at all that the drunk man, Teresa's father, as he learned now, was the one who had him hostage, or so to speak. He could have easily run off and not been caught by the drunken idiot, but he played the game and it actually helped to solidify his position not only to bystanders, but also to the police as well. That worked quite well, he thought as he smiled driving down the road. Then he stopped his vehicle and shut off the lights and waited. He waited to see who would come walking down the road, and low and behold within fifteen minutes, he was rewarded with a young girl walking toward his vehicle. She walked on up and right on by and he watched her go. Her sway of her hips was amazing, and her long black hair was perfect. She was his next prize that was for sure as he continued to watch her walk by. So now he confirmed her path that she went on her way home and now he had the upper advantage. One day, no not just one day but someday soon, he would confront her and have her as his own. He started to lay the groundwork for his plans on obtaining her, for his collection. This would be the last one in this area, the last one before he moved on to another area. He was taking a chance taking her lastly, but he was so delighted by her beauty and by her innocence. He had been watching her off and on for some time, and so he would soon be ready to complete his collection. Not yet but soon. This took preparation and besides he also had to prep his next area that he was going to move into, which was of utmost importance. He watched Cheyene disappear into the darkness and thought that she was the perfect triquetra for his last three. Suzie, Teresa, and now Cheyenne. He looked around to make sure that no one else was around and then he started his vehicle back up and slowly drove back down the road, toward his hideout. He had to do some things in preparation for his next girl. So he drove at a safe speed and in the constraints of the law, so as not to add any type of suspicion onto his already event-filled night. He looked at the road, but in his eyes, he was looking directly at Cheyenne's beautifully stunning eyes. He could imagine them, peering into them, and looking into them endlessly as she lay there unable to stop him from doing anything he wanted to, to her. He smiled a deep and sincere smile as he imagined what she would fetch in a stable market, if he had the connections. But he didn't so he didn't fuss himself with could of or would haves. He finally made it back to his compound, and he closed the gates at each location that he had to cross the gates to enter. He relocked the inside gate with his favorite old lock, and then he slowly pulled his vehicle around in the darkness and parked it right where he always did, right next to the house, and under the old carport overhang. He checked his car, wiped it down for fingerprints, and then he finally went inside for the night. He unlocked and entered his building, then relocked the

139

door, and went directly to his office. He had taken a really nice picture of Cheyenne's smile and he wanted to put it up on his wall, until she became his. He did this with all his girls, he would watch, take pictures, interact, and then they would give themselves to him, and be a permanent part of his collection. Within an hour, he had his rough plan and how he would implement it to the minutest detail. He had to be sure that this last one was done just right, and he would. He will continue to iron out everything until the day he is ready to make it happen. This was what he lived for, what he loved doing, and what he desired the most. All in a day's work, he thought whimsically. Then he started to whistle.

Chapter Twelve

The next morning, Blain awoke from his drunken slumber with a severe hangover and an awfully stubborn severe headache. It took him a few minutes before he realized where he was, and then after he got his senses back about him, he remembered what had happened. He was completely remorseful in every way imaginable and just hung his head low. He knew he did something wrong, but he didn't remember who he had wronged and why. Those were the points that he couldn't remember of , well at least not yet, but he knew he had done something stupid. Then he thought of his wife and what she would say to him. He knew he was in trouble and he knew he had hell to pay for whatever his actions had been. He asked for a drink of water when an officer walked by. Officer Scott obliged him and went to get him a foam cup of water, which he downed in nearly one gulp and then asked for another one. The officer gladly went over and retrieved another cup full, and handed it to Blain, which he downed once more. Blain expressed his appreciation to the officer for giving him that. Officer Scott then asked Blain;

"So how are you feeling, partner?" Not knowing fully how the man must have felt, but he knew it wasn't well.

"Well," (Blain said shaking his head) "I feel like I was dragged through a field, stepped on by some cows, and then hung out to dry in the intense heat of the sun.....but other than that I am fine!" He smirked weakly. "Do you happen to have an aspirin by the way?"

"No sir, I don't, sorry. We will let you out once your wife gets here. We called her and told her last night, but she didn't say when she would be here to pick you up. So hang tight and we will call her again. Are you hungry?"

"I am, but I am also nauseated even with the water, so I will hold off on eating anything, but thank you kindly."

"Well ok, But I'll be back in a bit. Let me know if you need anything." Blain just waved his hand to mean he understood, but then laid back down on the bench. Hopefully if he slept longer, the pounding headache would resolve itself, hopefully...!

Tom crawled out of bed that same morning and sat up on the edge of the bed. He yawned once and then stretched out his arms. At about that time another arm wrapped around his waist. He looked down and smiled at the person in bed with him, and he responded;

"Good morning, darling Linda."

"Good morning...to you...too, lover." She said as she smiled and even purred some at his nickname for her. He leaned back over and kissed her on the forehead, and then asked her what she wanted for breakfast. She rolled over and covered herself back up with the covers and said to him;

"Awwww, do we have to get up"..... She said as she put on her most pouty face that she could like she was having a temper tantrum. He smiled back at her, and said;

"Sorry, darling but duty calls." He laughed and stood up walking toward the bathroom to relieve himself. On the way there, she whistled at him as his bare butt shook and of course once she whistled, he exaggerated it even more, so much that now he had an absolutely ridiculous swagger. He laughed just as he reached the door and then closed it. She had already gotten up at the bedside and tossed a robe around her nude body. She traipsed down the hallway to the kitchen to see what she had to eat or make for themselves. Unfortunately, she hadn't made it to the store recently, so she had the bare minimum in her cupboards. Just about that time she was looking in her freezer, Tom came walking down the hallway wearing a floral robe of hers as well, not caring the least. He went over and once more greeted Linda with a kiss, but this time on her cheek. She gladly accepted the loving offer, but she had a frown on her face. He knew exactly what the issue was, just as she closed the freezer.

"Well, I guess we are eating out this morning. My Treat!"

"Okay!" She responded and hugged him lovingly. "Can we go to Bev's Breakfast Nook?"

"Sure, that would be fine by me." Tom responded just as his stomach let out a large growl, and he realized how hungry he just was. Tom put on some coffee in the time being, as they wished to get ready for work. She went to the shower and turned it on, then dropping her robe, she stepped into the walk-in shower. After Tom got their coffee cups ready, he walked into the bathroom as well and he got naked and then joined Linda in the hot shower. They rubbed each other's back with soap, embraced quite often, kissed a few more times, and then Tom got out to allow Linda to wash her hair as she normally does take longer with her gorgeous locks. He dried himself off and was already mostly dressed by the time Linda came into the bedroom, ready for herself to get dressed for their day. Tom kissed her once more and she smiled at him as he walked back down the hallway to check on the coffee. It was done so he poured them both a cup and he walked it down to the bedroom. Linda didn't dally much as she was nearly ready by the time he came into the room. Now her hair wasn't finished, but she was mostly clothed and about to head back to the bathroom to fix up her hair. She took the cup of freshly made coffee and sipped it, eliciting a 'hmmm' as the brew was the perfect taste, hotness, and flavor. She took her coffee and scurried into the bathroom, to finish up her morning ordeal.

Tom sat down on the side of the bed, after opening up the curtains, and looked outside. He was here with his new love, but his mind was elsewhere. Linda's puppy jumped up on the bed and sat next to him, cuddling up close as he continued looking outside. All he could do was think, think of how he was lost. He had extended all avenues of thoughts on where to look, who else to ask, and what else to do concerning the missing ladies. He had checked and rechecked everything and he still didn't know what else to do. Every direction seemed to be a dead end. What was he missing? He kept asking himself, at least on a daily basis. He just needed another solid clue, which he couldn't seem to materialize. This truly sucked and it was also completely disheartening, not only for him but the family of those missing as well. Still, he had no answers for them, none at all! He felt defeated, even with the wonderful new changes in his life and his new found love, Linda, he still felt like he had been a failure in his job recently. There are always cold cases, but he had never experienced one as of yet, well until now, that is. He looked out into the early morning sun, watching the sky becoming more brilliant little by little, over the mountains. He loved this view from Linda's house and he enjoyed it as often as he could. As he was lost in his thoughts, Linda had walked up behind him and saw that he was deep into a session of being lost in his thoughts. She looked lovingly at her man, not sure if she should interrupt him or not, in case he was thinking of something that would be advantageous to what he was working on. She took a chance and went over, sitting beside him, and slowly taking hold of his hand, placing it in hers. She watched his reaction as he went from being lost deep in his thoughts to looking lovingly at the amazing woman beside him. He brought her one hand up and kissed it, as she brought her other hand up and placed it on his other cheek. He mumbled to her;

"Sorry sweetheart, I was deep in thought."

"I know my dear. I didn't know whether to disturb you or not, but I didn't want you to linger too long there and feel lost. Hope it was ok to interrupt you?"

"Yes, sweetie, anytime. Thank you! I guess we have to get going here soon anyway." He said dejectedly, and got up. She stood up with him and embraced him, saying to him;

"I love you, Tom!"

"I love you too, Linda, so much!" And with that they left the bedroom, and headed toward the front door. Her little puppy followed them to the door, she kissed her pup, he patted the dog on the head, and then they left for the day. They were going to go in seperate vehicles, their own, just in case they had to do something or remain later than the other one, but then they changed their minds and just took one, his. They drove toward Bev's Nook for their breakfast meal, just as the sun started coming into view. It looked like it would be another glorious day in the mountain community they lived in. Within minutes they were able to get close enough to where they needed to go, they found a parking space, and exited the vehicle while walking hand in hand. They were the talk of the town, as everyone was always nosey and liked to interfere with each other's business. They arrived shortly at the nook and then they entered, with Tom holding the door for Linda. Bev was inside as she always is and looked up from doing her orders that were directly before her, to acknowledge who had entered her place of business. She saw 'her Tommy' and she exclaimed;

"Tommy, my boy, where have ya been?"

"Well, I have been busy, Bev. I can't be here all the time to enjoy your company." With those eloquent words said, she smirked and laughed heartily. But it was then that she looked harder and saw Linda by his side. She skeptically looked at Tom and then looked Linda over. Bev knew who she was and she had heard something of the such, but actually hadn't seen definitive proof of the two together. Yet here they were standing awfully close to one another, and that was when she went back to work on her orders that she was tending too. She didn't like sharing her Tommy, but she also knew how nice a person Linda was, so she may have to let this go for now. At least he chose the second nicest woman in this town, of course besides herself being number one, and that would be Linda. She looked at Tommy and said;

"Well, Tommy, it is good to see you and you also, Linda. I am happy for y'all." That response was nice for both of them to hear, and Linda squeezed Tom's hand gently, and he reciprocated the action. If they made it past Bev, then no one else would bother them about their new romance. They got up and placed the order for their breakfast sandwiches and waited till they were ready. Bev gave them each one free coffee for the new lovebirds, and then she went back to fulfill their orders. A few minutes later they had their sandwiches, and just as they were about to leave, Bev spoke up one more time, saying;

"Just remember Tommy, I am here if she breaks your heart." She said that while she coughed a laugh once. Tom turned around and smiled, laughing as he held the door open for Linda. Linda was also chuckling at the playful banter from Bev, as they went out the door together and onto the sidewalk area. Bev shook her head, saying to herself, 'what a lucky woman that Linda is, a real lucky woman, indeed'.

In the meantime on the other end of town, Lori Astel (Blain's wife) was already distraught with her daughter missing, and then to find out, from the Sheriff, that her husband nearly shot someone the previous night. This is just too much, too much for anyone to take, she cried as she leaned down to pick up her shoes to put on her feet. She couldn't believe the horror story her life had now turned into. She lamented on what direction her life would go now. She was saddened and also infuriated by her husband's actions. She wanted to punch him hard in the throat, but she also felt sad for what he was going through, as a father. She wanted to reach out and get him out of jail, but she also just wanted him to sober up and get his act together. There was no way she could continue to put up with his antics. He had been gone every evening and left her to fend for herself at home, which she could do, but he acted selfishly. He acted selfishly by doing what he thought was right without consulting her in the least. He was a horse's ass, and he will stay in jail till she feels like picking him up. She couldn't continue to deal with this by herself, so they were going to have to have a long talk. He may be on house arrest anyway, once he gets released from jail. Either way, she didn't wish to deal with this mess anymore. Her heart strings are pulled too taut already. She walked over to the closet and pulled down an old shoe box. She placed the shoe box on the dresser top, and then she slowly opened it up. Inside the box was a pink colored item, well pink and black to be exact. There was the main item, another item to the right of it, and then smaller items rolling around in the box itself. She picked up the smaller metallic items and slowly started putting them inside the next larger item. Once she used all the smaller items, she grabbed the pink and black pistol and slid the magazine into the pistol completing the combo. She looked at it, wondering if she was too scared to do it, but then again she couldn't take anymore of this life, not the way it was heading. She had been abused by her father for so many years, and had finally gotten over those ill-placed scars on her psyche and heart. She just wanted to move on and start her family right and see it through. Sadly, life had different ideas for her, as she kept hitting roadblock after roadblock in life. She had experienced two miscarriages prior to having Teresa, and even then she had to take multiple rounds of fertility drugs just to get pregnant again. Now here she was with her only child going missing, and she could do nothing about it. The cops seemed to know nothing more either, which was more or less complete hopelessness to her. She had had enough, and she would not be able to live a life without her Teresa, and with her husband being in jail. He could be sentenced, depending on the judge, and that was not a best case scenario, because the local judge was a hard ass, that was for sure. He could throw the book at him, and then she would have no one with her, especially if Teresa isn't found. That was something she just couldn't take. Even now, she was crying as her mind continued to wander and see if life was worth living. She turned the pink and black pistol her husband had purchased and given to her, over and over in her hand. Just then, the sun poked through her window, blinding her to everything for a moment. She sat there, on the edge of her bed, placed the gun barrel up underneath her chin, and then back to her temple, and sat there motionless as indecision wrecked her brain. She waxed and waned in her decision on what to do and before she knew it, she had cocked the gun, loading a bullet into the previously empty chamber. The sun was so brilliant today and it looked like it would be such a lovely day, but one never knows. She sat there, not making any decision on what to do with her life. She remained there as the sun continued to climb the morning sky, slowly. The outside grounds of the trailer were starting to come to life as the flowers, with fresh dew on them, leaned toward the warm sunshine. They yearned to capture the light as the new flowers waited to spring forth from their buds. The entire partly vacant trailer park was deathly quiet, except for somewhere down the road where a lone dog was barking, not once but three times loudly. All was familiarly quiet, when all of a sudden a single gunshot echoed through the silence, and the canine ceased its barking. As quick as it had occurred, then it became uneasily quiet once more. The morning sun continued to climb the beginning of the day's cloudless sky.

Chapter Twelve

        Suzie was miserable as she seemed to start having continual leg cramps; firstly, for being coped up in this god forsaken cage, and secondly for being malnourished and poor vitamin regime by her captor. She was always feeling nauseated and she knew she was getting weaker by the day. If she were ever going to make her move, she would have to do it sooner than later, that was for sure. She felt it and knew it was so, that she was becoming weaker and weaker every day. Her captor probably worked that into her diet, and that was making sure that she was not getting even anywhere near 1000 calories a day of food. She felt disgusting, she was sure she looked disgusting, and mentally she was disgusted with life and how she had gotten here. She did see an occasional girl, more the Teresa girl than any of the others, but once in a while she would see another one. Most of those had patches over their eyes as well. She hadn't seen her captor in so long, and wondered if he was ever going to come around at all again. It was disheartening, that was for sure, because she couldn't formulate a plan if she didn't know where he was or what he was doing. That was the struggle and the struggle was so very real for her. The only other person she saw everyday was Weasel. Weasel made herself known and as chance would have it, she actually started talking more normal and not so hateful toward the unsual woman, the henchperson of her captor. She didn't have a choice, that strange woman was becoming the only human interaction that she was able to converse with. She was lonely, and she wanted to be free, she screamed internally, as she shook the cage externally. The cage rattled hard and creaked with her effort. Within minutes of her tirade, she was exhausted and she had to sit down. Even though she couldn't see any other faees at this time, there were two sets of eyes looking back at her in fear. Those eyes belonged to two women who were severely worried that her tirade would cause them repercussions from their captor. Those two women cowered in their cages, trying to hide out of sight of any prying eyes that could be watching them. Fifteen minutes had passed and no one had come to correct the enraged woman, but they watched as the exhausted woman continued to lie on the floor of her cage, gasping and trying to catch her breath. Suzie's muscles ached and hurt from the effort and her lungs felt like they were being ripped from her chest. It took her a good thirty minutes before she finally was able to breathe easier and truly relax somewhat. She rolled on her side, after catching her breath, and curled up into a ball. She so wanted her life to end, in one way or another. She looked toward the roof and up into the unseen heavens, exclaiming for relief from her torture, from her misery, and from this hell on earth she was barely existing in. Finally she fell asleep again, in a state of mourning. A state of mourning and depression as she wanted her life to end. Hopelessness had now started to seep into her and was slowly starting to eat its way into her fragile psyche. This was only the beginning of the end, she thought.

Meanwhile back in town, it was now quickly becoming mid morning and Blain was restless in his jail cell as he tried to patiently wait for his wife. He called out for the officer again to see if they had truly called her. The officer present, Officer Lapard said to Blain;

"Blain, we called your wife earlier and an officer talked with her, telling her the entire situation. You are just going to have to wait for her. Maybe she is making you think about your actions, before coming for you. Don't you think so?"

"I don't know? It is not like her, not like her at all. Could you please send someone over to check on her. I really want to make sure she is ok!" Blain pleaded with the officer.

"Okay, I'll see if someone can stop by.... Hang in there. You hungry yet?"

"Yes, sir I would appreciate something to eat, if you will."

"Okay, I get ya something in a bit. Be back in a few." The officer said lastly as he walked out of the cell area. As soon as Officer Lapard walked out of the back area, he practically ran into Tom as the two stumbled into one another. They both apologized, and Tom asked him;

"How's Blain doing?"

"Not too bad, feeling better finally, but still waiting for the wife to come over and sign him out. Maybe she got hung up....Don't know though, since I wasn't the one that called."

"Hmmm, that doesn't seem like Lori. Maybe I'll run over that direction and see what is going on, make sure everything is ok. Sounds good to you?"

"Yes, sir. I would be thankful if you could, so I can get something done here. As soon as you know, radio it in and let me know and I will relate the information to Blain. Thanks a lot!" Tom nodded his head in affirmation and then he went out the back door.

The drive to the Astel's trailer was a nice little drive as the sun was out in full force early in the day and the heat would definitely bake them by the afternoon. He drove with the radio on low volume, the windows open, and he was donning a wide smile. He thought about Linda and him and how much he appreciated, cared, and even loved her. Their relationship was going quite well for the two of them, and that made it perfect in his mind, as they have shared so much of themselves in such a short time. To him, they just clicked, and he was amazed that he could find someone that he clicked with so easily, almost as easily as his late wife. He still had trouble believing that he could be so fortunate as to have such amazing love twice in his life. He was definitely one of the lucky ones, that was for sure. He made the last turn to head into the trailer park and then he slowed significantly as he went down the narrow road, being sure to maintain the slower speed limit as is posted in the area. He drove until he saw the familiar nice trailer that the Astel's lived in. He hadn't been here for a little while, but everything looked nice as always and was maintained so pristinely. They were folks who definitely took pride in how their place looked. He pulled up into the parking area and stopped his vehicle beside a small sedan that must have been Lori's, and he exited his vehicle. He heard a lone canine barking down the road, a little distance away. He walked up to the front door and knocked once, a mildly light knock. He waited patiently for a few minutes, before he started knocking a little harder. After a few minutes, there was still no response, so this time he knocked even harder and stated aloud;

"Lori, this is Detective Tom Royce again. I am checking to make sure you are alright! Are you here?" He repeated not once but two more times. Still there was no response from inside the trailer. He tried the doorknob and it turned, so he opened it up. It creaked from lack of recent lubing, and so his going inside would be heard by both his voice and the noisy door. He announced himself once more to anyone that could be inside the home. "Lori, this is Tom Royce. I am entering your home, please be aware that I am just here to check on you." He entered and slowly closed the door. He looked around the living room and it was quiet and peaceful as he heard the air conditioner running, keeping the home at a nice cool but not too cold temperature. He looked around but heard nothing, so he gingerly called out once more Lori's name, but still no response. He continued walking through the home, trying to see if he could find her, or maybe she walked to a close neighbor's house. He wasn't sure, but he still continued looking as he walked into everyroom checking it out. He came to the last room, and the door was partially closed, but it was a little open yet, so the door was slightly ajar. Then he knocked lightly and announced himself even louder, saying;

"Lori! Are you here, this is Tom Royce. I am here to do a wellness check on you and make sure you are okay. Please respond as I am about to enter the room." Still there was nothing and so he pushed the door open slowly. This door creaked also, as if the hinges needed lubed just a little, just like the front door. It still pushed open easily and he looked toward the inside of the master bedroom, obviously. He saw a red and white comforter on the bed and the bed was only partially made. He looked toward the bathroom door and started walking toward that door to check in there. He went up to the door and knocked again, announcing himself once more. After he waited and there was still no response, he opened the door and found nothing. He turned back around and went back toward the closet, which was on the other side of the bed. Just as he was about to round the corner, he heard a noise behind him and he turned quickly, but it was just a cat that had jumped up onto a bedside table. He stopped and then started toward the closet once more, with his head just turning when he kicked something that stopped him in his place. He looked down and there on the floor was the body of Lori, with a pink and black gun beside her. He bent down and quickly checked for a pulse, but he found none. She was truly gone, her eyes were still open, so he closed her eyes and he saw the gunshot wound against her temple. Now he saw the splatter remnants of the bullet as it exited her skull, and the puddle of blood that lay beside her. He touched her cheek and thought, such a shame. This was something he truly didn't expect from her, even with everything going on. Yet again, he didn't know that she had a troubled past also. He covered her body up with a folded sheet that was sitting on the edge of the one dresser and then he left the room. After he got outside, he made the call for assistance and to relate the bad news. Such a sad day, to find this tragedy in their town. Maybe someday he will find out more about her past or her gentle psyche. Such a sad day, indeed! He said aloud even though there was no one around him.

Back at the station, Officer Gus Lapard got the call from Tom and it was not the news he expected to hear. He hesitated on telling Blain and honestly went and got Linda to assist him with breaking the news to the man still recovering from his ill-fated actions the previous night. The two officers walked into the holding area, where Blain was and saw that he was sleeping. They hesitated for a moment, but at that exact time, Blain rolled back over and looked toward their direction and immediately sat up. He questioned them first, asking;

"Hey, is my wife here yet?" Both officers looked at him, and then Linda spoke up first, saying;

"Well that is why we are here, Blain." Blain sat up even more attentively. The officers opened up the cell and asked him to follow them. They were taking him to an interrogation room to talk more personally with him. Linda opened up the door and let Blain go inside.

"Please have a seat, Blain." Linda said to him. He cautiously took a seat and looked at the officers questioningly. He was about to say something like being sorry for what he had done the previous night. He wanted to confess that he was definitely not himself at that moment in time, but Linda held up her hand as if to indicate that wasn't why he was here. "Listen, Blain, we haven't heard from your wife, and you asked us to go check on her, ...so Tom volunteered to drive over there to make sure she was okay, to do a wellness check on her."

"And........?" Blain asked quickly and with a look of horror in his eyes.

"Well, Tom found your wife on the floor with a pink and black pistol by her side. It would appear that she had taken her life. Tom checked her over, but she had no pulse and had been down for some time. I am truly sorry, Blain, truly sorry." Blain sat there in utter silence, in shock and complete disbelief. He started to say something but then stopped, and then suddenly the water works spewed forth and he burst into tears. He put his face in his hands and let loose his sorrow. He couldn't believe this! How could have this happened? First his daughter goes missing and then probably because of that and because of his actions, his dear and loving wife had taken her life. What a buffoon he is, he thought dismally. If only he kept his anger in check and went home to be with his wife, she would still be around today. He was in complete and utter dismay. Why should he keep living? What was the point of living? He put his head up and just as Linda tried to console him by standing by his side and placing her hand on the shoulder blade area, he made a move and he went for her holstered gun.. There was a scramble as neither officer could believe that this distraught man would do such a thing, but then again he might have seen the darkness at the end of the tunnel. He grabbed her gun, but she grabbed his hands in the meantime, stopping him from having complete control of the firearm. Gus Lapard, the other officer in the room, lunged for Blain, in an attempt to subdue him while the struggle for the loose weapon continued. Blain was able to get enough control that he was about to be pointing the gun at himself, as Linda tried in vain to wrestle it back from him, which was proving to be most difficult for her. Yet what Blain didn't know was that Linda hadn't cocked her weapon, and therefore the chamber was empty and not loaded at this point. All of a sudden, he violently yanked it away from Linda, pointed it at his head, and he pulled the trigger(which was a double action trigger pull). So what he was expecting was that obvious sound of a gun going off and then the pain as the bullet entered his cranial cavity, but to his dismay all he heard was the resonating click. 'Shit', he thought and he quickly put his other hand up to cock the slide, hopefully now loading the chamber with a round, prepping it for another attempt, a real one this time. But before he could finish what he started, Gus had grabbed the distraught man's one arm and he was able to ultimately keep him from chambering the round. Linda, in the meantime, had pulled out her taser and so she went to tase the disheartened man, and she warned Gus immediately as she shot the taser at Blain's back. The points struck home, lodging themselves in his back, just as Gus rolled free with Linda's gun in his hand, and Blain convulsed uncontrollably as the electric shock coursed through his helpless body. Blain had also inadvertently soiled himself in the meantime, as the shock took its desired effect on him. The shock was delivered not once but twice, because after the first shock, he had enough strength in him to still lunge for Gus to try to grab the weapon back from him. Blain had a horrific pleading look in his eyes, as if to say, 'just shoot me, please.' Gus shook his head with a definitive 'no' and also with a saddened look on his face. Both officers worked to get the handcuffs on the incapacitated and prone man's arms to make sure he was secure and safe. The frazzled officers looked at each other in disbelief at what this man just tried to do, which was commit suicide right in front of them. Neither of them expected that at all, and by the time they finally had the prone man under control, the Captain came bursting into the room, after hearing the commotion from down the hallway. He exclaimed;

"What the hell just happened here?" Linda looked up and confessed immediately, saying;

"We had just found out that Blain's wife, Lori committed suicide, so we brought him in here to tell him the catastrophic news, and the man was distraught and suddenly he went for my gun."

"To shoot you officers?"

"No Cap't, he tried to shoot himself and end his life. Thankfully I hadn't loaded a round and so we got control again, I tasered him twice, and now he needs to go to the hospital for treatment. He needs to see a grief counselor and/or a psychiatrist, most likely. We will have to have him committed to the hospital and in their care, if that seems the right thing to do, sir?"

"But he wasn't intending on harming either of you, correct?" Gus looked at the Captain and said;

"That's correct sir, he just wanted to shoot himself."

"Okay, but you two get this cleaned up and I want that report by the end of the day!"

"Yes, sir." Both officers resonated their response simultaneously. Gus went out to call an ambulance and they would have to escort him over there as well, and finish up the paperwork to have him involuntarily committed for severe depression and attempted suicide.

In the meantime across town, Tom waited patiently for the ambulance and the coroner to show up to remove Lori's body from its final resting place in their home. This was not good, not good at all. He felt even more helpless now, that he had no real clues to what happened and now this. Just as he was still trying to figure all this out, he got a text from Linda. He read the text and couldn't believe what he just read that Blain tried to kill himself, right there in the interrogation room, when they had taken him there to relate and confess to him that his wife had killed herself. He kept reading what Linda had texted him, and wow, she had to tase him to get him under control. He responded immediately after he read it all the way through, saying: 'Are you okay?'. She texted back a resounding 'yes', but she did admit that it was scary, because she didn't know at first if he was going to try to kill Gus and her or not. She also confessed that she felt like a fool, letting someone get her firearm from her. He texted her back trying to play it off, as it can happen. You can't always expect the unexpected, he wrote to her and finished with a concerned emoji face. She sent back a frazzled face emoji, and then she asked how he was doing. He texted her that he was just waiting for the coroner to show up. 'Probably gonna be a long day', he texted her afterwards. Yes, indeed , she responded. Then she wrote, 'love you and miss you' and he responded back in similar fashion. About that time, the ambulance showed up at the scene just for support. It was about another hour before the coroner showed up, but by that time the ambulance crew had gone and got something to drink and snack on as they all waited patiently around. After the coroner showed up, he went in and did his work with Tom by his side. They snapped pictures and collected the gun, placing it in a plastic bag. Then with the help of the ambulance crew they loaded Lori's body up for transport. Once secured, the ambulance and the coroner left the scene, and Tom checked on the house again, not seeing anything else that needed taking care of. He picked up the soft and cuddly feline that was left in the house, found a front door key, and he locked the door. He also secured some police crime scene ribbon/tape on the front of the door. He kept the key for now so in case they would have to get in or if by chance Teresa would show up. He also wrote out a note, just in case , Teresa would show up, miraculously, so that she knows to contact him first. That done, he got back into his vehicle and he drove away from that sad debacle.

Tom had headed back to the station, but only after making a pit stop at the local shelter to surrender the cat and hold it until such time that someone could claim it again. He didn't need two cats, so he thought it best to surrender this poor alone animal. He arrived back at the station just as the ambulance and officer Lapard were getting ready to depart. The distraught and concerned Linda was standing outside, smoking a cigarette and trying to relax from the stressful events that had just occurred. Tom walked over and embraced Linda to try to ease her nerves and calm her down some. She embraced back with a firm grip, and then he looked down at her face and there were tears streaming down her face. He once again brought her close, essentially wiping her tears on his shirt, and placed his one hand behind her head, while his other one was around her back. There was nothing said for a few minutes, and then he finally whispered into her one ear, saying;

"Are you sure you are okay, sweetie?"

"That was so scary, I honestly didn't know if he was going to shoot Gus and me. It totally caught me by surprise, which it shouldn't have. I dunno……." She confessed with a shaky voice.

"Well, why don't you take the rest of the day off, my love. I will work it out with the Cap't." He tried to console her by saying.

"No, I can't, I have to do the report, since Gus is taking the distraught man to the hospital. I will be fine, I just need to smoke this partial cigarette before heading back inside. But thank you, darling for your support!" She said, looking up into his eyes and then kissing him with a gentle and loving kiss."

"Okay, but if there is anything I can do for you, please let me know, and I really mean that."

"Okay, and thank you." She said as she dropped her cig and squashed it on the ground, ultimately putting it out, half smoked. He let her go as she turned to leave, but they trailed touching hands as she went to walk back into the station to start her report. He had concern on his face for her as he watched her go back inside. She was a strong woman, that was for sure, but all it takes is one moment to truly rattle someone up enough, to cause a lasting impact. He heard thunder in the distance and he looked up into the sky as a group of angry looking clouds were rolling into this mountain community, as an impending rain shower was rearing its ugly head.He stood outside watching the clouds roll in and then it started to slowly rain, first a few drops and then he saw the downpour coming in the distance. He stepped inside the door of the station, to go work on his own report concerning Lori Astel and her unexpected and sad demise. Always the perpetual paper trail, he thought to himself as closed the door behind him.

Later that afternoon, Cheyenne was walking to work as she always does, but this time she had an umbrella covering her as the rain had come like a roaring lion and was saturating the community. She hurriedly walked around the puddles as she was heading to work early. Just as she was walking toward her destination, she was oblivious to something behind her. There was a vehicle driving slowly behind her and to the right. The roads had a lot of standing water, so when she finally did notice the vehicle, she blew it off as someone just taking it easy in this unexpected deluge. At present, there were no other vehicles on this stretch of road, and so the vehicle edged slightly closer to the walking young girl. It was at this time that Cheyenne stopped in her place, turned, and looked at the vehicle. She grabbed her small can of mace that she always carried, in her purse, with her free hand just in case she would need it. The vehicle's window rolled down and she looked from her distance inside the vehicle. She looked hard and saw the figure inside the vehicle and she recognized the person for who it was. The man inside spoke up firstly, saying;

"Hey, Cheyenne, how are you? It's me, Todd, from the restaurant. Sorry, I didn't mean to startle you, I just wasn't sure it was you at first. This rain is hideous. Would you like a ride to work?" She knew the man, as he had come in many times, especially during closing hours to snack and lightly drink. They, on many occasions, had sparked up a conversation, as she would divulge her desires and future aspects for her life. He was always kind and never tried anything, as he seemed to be a perfect gentleman. She did notice however that he had a little OCD as he would always straighten his table up, to be just right. Who doesn't have issues, she thought whimsically as she pondered what to do. Her shoes and, of course, her feet were soaked and so was the lower part of her work attire. She thought long and hard and then she said to him;

"I appreciate your kind gesture, but I will be okay. Thank you so much though." He waved at her and as if to say have a good day and then he started driving away. Around the corner, up ahead, a few cars slowly drove through the water and headed toward him, trying to navigate the standing water on the road. He couldn't do what he wanted to do today, and so he conceded that he would try another day, and he slowly drove off, already thinking of another time to catch up with her. Cheyenne continued to traipse through the falling rain, trying to remain as dry as she could. All she could think about was what a miserable day at work this was going to be tonight. Some day, someday soon, he will complete his collection and then he will leave this area, and move on to another new and exciting site with more prospects.

On the drive back to his compound, he thought about this area, this community and how he lived, breathed, and collected right under the nose of the police. He was meticulous, and that was his key. He didn't make mistakes, he didn't rush anything, and he kept his patience and wits about him. That was the key, to be invisible and yet right out in the open. He had perfected his routine to the point that he was rumored to be honored among the collectors who were out there in the world. He had fan mail, and he was always asked questions about certain aspects of collecting, which he answered when he could. He was careful because he knew the FBI was always roaming the internet for people such as him, trying to bust the men who lived for this type of life. That was why him being such a computer whiz helped him to stay out of the limelight and under wraps. He knew of a couple of his online meteors and proteges, that were busted by the fuzz, and he knew how to drop all sense of communication and cover his trail, when the need was pressingly evident. The drive was short, and he backtracked a few times, as he always did, so that no one could follow him without him noticing. He pulled into the front gate, he got out, opened the gate, and then drove through it. After stopping to reclose the gate, he drove slowly and quietly down the gravel road. He parked his vehicle near the old house and he did a few checks around the perimeter again. The rain hadn't reached his compound yet, but it would soon be here. He finished up outside and then he headed indoors to check on the status of things. He was thinking about how to dispose of the ones he had right now. He was going to start moving his collection along. He had only three girls at present, with Suzie being one of them. He wanted to make this fun, and so he was contemplating how to remove her in a pleasing and sport way. He needed to medicate her more, without her knowing and perform another surgery, to make sure that she was prepped for his fun games. She had lost considerable weight, but she still had her spirit and her wits about her, which would make her a fun target. Now that that was settled, he started working on his other girls and how to dispose of them. Now was a sad time for him, as he started thinking about cleaning up and moving on. He became attached to the areas that he visited, and he really enjoyed this area, but he had pushed his time here and so he had to move on and start anew in his next location. He grabbed a vial out of the metal cabinet that was in front of him, and he drew up 20 ml of a viscous white liquid, named Propofol . He would use this to sedate Suzie so that he could perform his next surgery on her. It was time to exact his penance on her for the unruliness that she had given him, since he had obtained her.

He was walking down the corridor and he came across Weasel, and he asked her a few questions, saying;

"So how are my girls?" Weasel looked sheepishly down at her feet, responding with;

"They are fine, master. What would you have me do?"

"I want you to inject Suzie with this med, just half of it for now, and then come back to me. Do you understand me?"

"Yes sir, half of the med and then come back to you."

"We will see how she responds, and then we are prepping for surgery. RemoveTeresa from that area, so she doesn't see what we will be doing. Do you have that?"

"Yes sir, I will do your bidding."

"Now go, get to it, and I will see you again in a few minutes." With that Weasel went about her tasks and did her masters' bidding as she was instructed to do. He would reward her with a better meal when she does as she is required to do. She remembered that one time he had given her a steak, a nice T-bone steak for a meal, which she enjoyed thoroughly and ate with such delightful gusto. She always did what she had to do, or she would end up like all the other girls, and that was something she didn't want. She was a survivor and she would do what she had to do to continue living, even if it meant hurting others. She had decided that long ago. She went over to the holding area, opened up a cell, quietly, and whispered to the girl inside. She said to her;

"Teresa, come hither child. I need you to come with me. Teresa was half out of it, as the continuous med infusion worked to keep her lightly sedated. She also had an eye patch on, and so Weasel led the exhausted, malnourished, and defeated Teresa out of her cell and led her down a corridor to another room. Once there, she placed her in another holding cage, and Teresa laid down on the small dog bed that was inside the cell. Weasel made sure she was good to go, and then she kissed her on the forehead and closed the door. She said to the fading Teresa;

"I'll be back soon, pet." Then she left that room, and headed toward Suzie's cell. She snuck up on the cell trying to keep quiet, and then through the IV infusion she added the milky white liquid. It mixed with the IV fluid somewhat, but it looked cool as the streaks of white fluid intermixed the entire length of the IV. Suzie opened her eyes and looked at Weasel, but the medication was already entering her veins, and so she closed her eyes again, because of the sedation. Weasel whispered to her,

"Sleep my darling, girl, sleep peacefully."

Maybe some two hours later, Suzie awoke to a groggy sense of uneasiness. She felt up at her face for her eye and she still had the bandage over one eye, but her other was still present. Thank God, she tried to say aloud, but there was nothing. She reached up toward her mouth and she felt an immediate discomfort in her oral cavity. So she opened up her mouth a little(since that was all she could muster with the pain) and tried to speak, which caused her severe pain. She tried to suffer through the pain, but she could not and so she immediately closed her mouth to decrease the pain. What the hell she thought to herself, and she then felt the gauze packing inside her mouth. She pulled some of it out and saw the gauze covered in blood. She wiped her chin as there were droplets of blood also trickling down her chin, because she removed some of the packing. What had the asshole done now, she thought as she tried in vain to feel for her tongue, but it was not there. That prick cut my tongue out, she thought, with a new scorn and hatred for the man that had abducted her. Why would he do such a thing as that? This is even more heinous than taking her eye. She was livid and sadly she finally came to the realization that she may truly perish in the horrific care of this sinister man. Her own life was not in her hands anymore, and she may never see her family, her sister again. Immediately her psyche took a hit and she slumped down in the cage. She soiled herself, not even caring if she did or not. Her spirit was broken as she lay there, completely helpless, and with no one to save her. How did it come to this? This free spirit of hers that she had always conveyed and with never a care in the world, but now she was caged up worse than a discarded, beaten, and malnourished dog. She looked around for the other girl, the one named Teresa, but she didn't see her. Had they removed her also, and done something with her as well. God, she hoped not. Weasel came back inside the area where she was, and she tended to some tasks. Normally, she would have responded to her, even chat with her to pass sometime, but now she couldn't even do that, sadly. She had no idea how her life would end, but she knew that sooner than later her captor would come up with a diabolical plan to snuff the life from her. She was in such a bad state physically, that she didn't even know if she had the strength, nay the willpower to resist. She just wished she could see her sister one more time and tell her how much she loves her. Oh, she could only imagine what prospects in life she would miss out on, what trails she would never hike, and what it would feel like to be free again. She started tapping the cage, the only sound she could make at present with her food bowl. It was the only noise she could make at present and she continued doing it, without a concern anymore what the repercussions would be. Honestly, who gives a shit anymore?! She sure as hell didn't. She still knew she would go down with whatever dignity she had left, and that was all that mattered anymore. She would not beg, grovel, or ask for special permission, no that would not do at all. She would go down as stubborn and as proud as she always was and had been. She promised herself that.

Weasel watched Suzie through a small hole in the wall from her room, trying to see how she was doing. She was concerned for her 'friend' but she had been given explicit orders not to go near her, except to deliver food only. Her master expressly said, and because of that she remained hidden and watched Suzie respond to what had been done to her. Her master would collect the girls, give them just enough food to make sure they lose weight and mass, keep them hooked on drugs, and then remove nonessential parts of their bodies for his collection. Yes, it was gory and gruesome work, but she did what she must. Besides, if she didn't do it, someone else would. She looked around her little room that she resided in. It was adorned with stuffed animals, little trinkets, and drawings that she did of some of the girls that she liked. The drawings weren't that good, or so she ridiculed herself, but it was all she had of girls past. She smiled as she looked from one picture to another, remembering all the times that she shared with each girl. She thought fondly of each one, some of the talks she had with some, some of the intimacy that she shared as well with a few select ones, and then she stared at one drawing in particular. It was the true love of hers, Jade, who she adored and loved. In a different life, she would have followed her or been with her through everything. Jade was her one true deep infatuation. She had cried many nights and many times over her loss of such a dear dear friend and love of hers. Even now she bowed her head in solemn respect for her Jade. A trickle of tears streamed down her pale cheek once more, and then she wiped them away as quickly as they had started. It was not the time for tears, not yet. She went to another wall and moved a slight piece aside to check onTeresa, who was alone in this room. She watched Teresa quietly, and she noticed how hopeless she was by now. She hadn't started off that way, that was all because of the master, and how he would decide how to break each woman's spirit to get what he wanted. This was what happened to all the master's favorites, he would collect them, break them down, save pieces of them, and then discard them, like they were roadkill. She almost hated herself for contributing to the success of his work, but what could she do but play along and do what she was told. Her own spirit had been broken long ago, so long ago, by the man she called her master. She had given up and conceded her fate was not her own and so she has been with him these last three locations to help him do his deeds and his biddings. She never knew when he would tire of her, because that was always a very high probability that he would one day discard her as well. Still he always promised that one day he would set her free and she would be rid of this tasking and crimes that she assists him in. She knew exactly what she would do also, when that time comes, and it would be to hide somewhere in a secluded cabin in the middle of the woods and not speak to anyone ever again. Or so she thought that was what she would do. Then again she would get lonely, because she did like talking to people, especially girls. So maybe she wouldn't be alone, but who knew at that point. She imagined herself living next to a fresh water supply, growing her own food, and living off the land as much as she could. That was her ultimate goal, to live off the grid and to be nonexistent, which funny enough is not much different than what she is now. Well, that is except for the fact that she is being used and abused in ways she never thought possible to her. And yet here she still was a survivor among survivors in life. She would see it though and she would be sure to make it out alive, no matter what. Hopefully her time would soon be up and she would be released for her good service, because he had promised her that and he always kept her promises. Promises are promises, he would say to her, and she believed him. Still, she had that little voice, that tiny little inkling in the back of her mind telling her you can't trust everyone, especially him. Sadly, she didn't listen and she kept blindly hoping for the best. Hope was her best friend as of now.

Chapter Thirteen

Tom was fed up with not finding anything of substance on the missing girl Teresa. Now that she lost one parent to suicide and mabye another one to the psychological aftermath of the first event, she would be all alone if she were found. He stared up at his makeshift white board of the women and girls who have disappeared in or around this area in the last year. There weren't that many, but it was enough to truly warrant high suspicion. Still, he had no remarkable leads at all to go on. If there was a person or persons abducting these girls, they were professionals at it, and they covered their tracks so well. He knew of the dark aspects of the internet where there are still predators looking for their next fix or get off, and so there were others who helped them with that by providing such stories, videos, and pictures. Those media would also include such horrific acts on innocent children as well, which is another heinous crime in itself. He wasn't shielded in this world, and he knew of it but he had never come across such or experienced it as of yet. He was desperately trying to think of how to get into the mindset of a predator. But for him that was proving to be difficult. Still, to catch a person as such he would need to stretch the limits of normality, and his comfort zone to see if he could come up with something that may just be an advantage to an opportunity. He needed to think to make some smart moves and investigate more in depth, putting it all into this or they just may lose another one, which was totally unacceptable on his watch. With Linda now in his life, he had got his passion back, his will to continue his service, and a new found look on life. So he can thank her for the rejuvenation of his spirit, heart, and soul. In doing that his drive and his desire were to reach beyond his past stagnation, which can happen to anyone in any type of job. Unfortunately, his stagnation could mean problems for others and the public not getting his best, which, sadly, could lead to people becoming injured or dying from his lack of dedication. That was not him and that was not why he took an oath of office to become a public servant. It is not for the glory, not for the pay, but for the desire to fix a wrong to make it right and protect the innocent from those with malicious intent. He grabbed his gear, looked at his cell phone, and decided to text Linda. He told her that he loved her but he had something he had to go do to look into the missing girl of Blain and the late Lori. He knew she was busy with her report or maybe even got pulled away to do something else. She politely responded back, saying: 'I get it, go get 'em tiger' with a heart emoji. With that he left the building not telling anyone else anything , and on his new mission to find out more. Come hell or high water, he was going to crack this case and have an answer for the missing persons.

He hopped into his vehicle, started it up and pulled out in a hurry, but still safely so as not to hit anyone or anything. He took off down the road at a fairly fast speed, and he knew where he was heading, which was the trailer of Blain and sadly the late Lori, the parents of missing Teresa. He was going to upend that trailer to see if could find anything at all that would lead him in any direction. He drove down the road, but ran into some typical traffic incident. He flashed his lights and sped down the road past the stopped vehicles as they waited to continue onto their work site or errand, wherever they were going this fine day. He made it to the incident spot, and was waved through by the young officer attending the traffic, and he waved back, continuing down the road and toward his destination. Eventually he made it there, but not before having to use his lights two more times for slower drivers that seemed to be out only for a Sunday drive. He pulled up into the parking space for the trailer, just as he had done twice now in the past. He got his flashlight, but instead put that back and removed a headlamp out of his backpack in the back of his vehicle. At least when he looked he could do handsfree looking, instead of carrying a bulky flashlight. He went over and detached the police tape yellow ribbon that adorned the front of the trailer, and opened up the trailer. The air conditioning was still on, thankfully, as he opened the door, but it did smell stagnant in there, that was for sure. He made his way into the kitchen, looked around and knew he wouldn't find anything here, and so he moved onto Teresa's room, which was the best place to find something. He opened up the door, and immediately noticed the cleanliness of the room. It was like her mom(Lori) was trying to keep it perfect for her, just in case her little girl came back home. It wasn't a bad way of thinking. Hope is always good, because hope can keep one from going crazy also with either regret or blame. He went into the room, working clockwise and moving everything he could to look for any clue, any freaking possible clue that could lead him in any direction. He started moving everything on the dresser, looking under everything, and even feeling inside the drawers. He didn't wish to pry , but he had to find something so he kept looking, going through every piece of clothing, no matter what it was. He found nothing in the dresser, and so he started next in the closet, which was the next area in his field of view. He looked thoroughly through all her hung up clothes and then next he started in on all the boxes on the floor, checking through them to see if there was anything he could relate to the case. He found lots of love notes, but by the writing, they all seemed to be written by a young boy, like junior high level or grade school, as the spelling and writing were both atrocious. Still he put those to the side, for just in case he came up with nothing else. After finishing off on the floor, he then started up on the upper shelf area. He pulled boxes down, some purses, and even a small plastic container. He looked all through this as well, everything was inspected and made sure not to have anything of importance. He did find a box full of pictures, of what looked like skater friends of hers and such, so he took all of those as well. He was still hoping for the grand prize, which is an actual diary. Nowadays, maybe young people don't do that as much, but he could only hope that maybe this young woman was different, which by all conversations so far, she was.

He ended up looking all over her room, everywhere, inside everything, and under every piece of furniture, which meant a lot of moving pieces out of the way as well. Still he found nothing to give him any solid evidence. He had a box full of pictures and old love notes from previous interested boys and that was all. This wasn't good enough, he thought to himself as he sat down on the chair that he pulled out from under her desk. He leaned back and looked up in the air, toward the ceiling and closed his eyes. He then slowly reopened his eyes after a few seconds, looking over the ceiling as well and then he saw something over in the corner of the room. He stood up and walked over toward the corner in the wall and looked up, but alas it was only a small old water stain. 'Shit!' He proclaimed out loud in frustration. He walked by an old rocker with a big stuffed animal in the chair and he grinned as he saw the gentle looking large bear sitting with a grin on its face. He laughed at himself and then he walked by it, smacking its foot, which unexpectedly caused it to lean forward and fall over. He tried to catch it but missed it as it fell and landed face first on the floor. He turned around, grabbed the bear by the butt and tossed it back into the chair, but oddly enough it sounded funny when it landed. There was a definite thunk, which was unusual since it was a large plush animal. He picked the animal back up until he found something. He felt what seemed like a hardcover of some sort. He kept searching until he found a zipper near the butt area of the bear and he unzipped it. It revealed a pocket for hiding something. Inside the pocket was in fact a book. He pulled the book out and opened it up to reveal a diary of sorts, which looked to have her thoughts, feelings, and even her accession of tricks on her skateboard. It was a thick book, so he knew this may take some time, but this was the best lead that they had so far, as of recent. He zipped the butt back up, placed the bear back where it belonged and then he patted the bear on its head before he left with the box of pics, notes, and the all important find, the book. It has taken him nearly two hours to find it, but he might have finally found something worth his while. He walked out of the trailer, closed the door, reapplied the police tape, and then got back into his vehicle. He pulled away with a new found happiness with what he had managed to find. He paused momentarily at a stop sign and quickly texted Linda to see how she was doing. Today was a good day for him, and even though tragedy had struck this family, he now had a glimmer of hope that maybe what he found may lead them to something concrete, in regards to the whereabouts of Teresa.

At the hospital across town, Blain Astel had sunk to the lowest point in his life. He didn't know how the hell his life had spiraled so, but by god it had done so in a matter of weeks. First his baby girl went missing which of course made him and his wife so distraught and uneasy. Then next was the fact that the police department didn't seem to have any answers , and so at that time he took it upon himself to start his own observation and dabble into vigilante justice. He never thought he would actually find anything, but he honestly hoped and wished he would. Still his doubts were there. Yet, the more time he spent out on observation, the more he became more uncaring and unfortunately more drunk. Until that fateful day that he was so drunk, he nearly shot a man and that was the start of the domino effect on his life. He was then subsequently arrested, charged, and then his wife had found out. His wife had already been troubled by the entire ordeal, and now that she knew her husband was in trouble, she decided to take her own life. He had completely let her down and he was unworthy of living anymore himself, he figured. So that was when he decided to take his own life and try to take the officer's sidearm. He desperately tried to end his life and be with his beloved Lori, one more time, but sadly his plan was thwarted and he now was where he was. He was admitted to the hospital, restrained to a bed, and given some intravenous cocktail for him to chill out with. Now he was barely awake and his mind was becoming fuzzier by the minute, but he still could remember how his life went from heaven to hell in a matter of no time at all. There was no coming back from this. Permanent changes in his life had occurred and in the throws of stupidy, insecureness, depression, and foolhardiness he had quickly been demoted to a reckless mental patient with suicidal ideologies. He just wished he could crawl up under a rock and just die! Die the worthless pondscum that he is and has become. He jeopardized what life he had for revenge, and it got him nowhere but utter misery, that was for sure. He jerked and tested the restraints, but whomever had put them on, had put them on quite well and so he knew he was stuck. He raised his head up and could see a figure outside his room, and it looked to be a security person of the hospital's. They were watching him via camera and with a person outside the room to cover him and make sure he remains safe, or so it seems. He was now a prisoner, a prisoner of life, a prisoner of his poor decisions, and a prisoner of his own stupidity! He turned his head away and looked

164

outside the small window in his room and it looked nice outside. He didn't know if he would ever see outside again, and it was then that he started to tear up. He started weeping, weeping for his daughter, weeping for his wife, and begging for his own life to end. He had no control any longer and that was that! He lay there weeping without the ability to wipe his own tears, and so they ran down his face and onto his white pillow case that he was lying on. His life had spiraled him so far down the rabbit hole, that there seemed to be no exit to this unsettling insanity. This was hell on earth, he finally imagined, a real dark omen.

Meanwhile back at the compound, 'Todd' had to take a break and leave the area for a few weeks. He knew when he was cutting it close and just too many things were trying to tell him that. It just seemed like opportunity was not on his side, with getting caught up with the father of Teresa, even though he managed to squeak himself out of that. Also the close call when trying to pick up Cheyenne with those cars coming the other way. He needed to leave the area, to disappear, one to set up his new camp and two to just lay a little low and let the coals simmer. Maybe he had pushed a little too hard in this small town, but he had made preparations and started implementing his plan. He was going to load nonessential things up in his rental moving box truck(which he had paid cash for and using another alias name), and he was going to store it in storage until his new site was ready. He had to leave the refrigerators behind, for now, but he moved a lot of his extra gear, some unused fridges, and some files that he kept on everything. After the box truck was packed up with all he could fit inside, he gave explicit instructions to Weasel and he left, not knowing when he would be back, at this point. It could be a few weeks, but he wasn't sure. Either way a few weeks or a month, it was time to make things happen. He walked his compound and saw that even taking nonessentials, he could see it was emptying out and he got that normal feeling of giddiness of moving onto another area. Some people hate moving their lives and uprooting everything to move closer to family, start a new job, or just because they needed a change in life. He, however, didn't look at moving as an uprooting, but in fact it was a rebirth. A new step to take that will expand one's horizons in life and another way to start anew, a refreshed self. He already planned on growing facial hair, changing his present hair color, and also he had been working on having an accent for his future self. Time for things to change! Besides that, it meant new opportunities for him. He was moving to a rural Pennsylvania town, another one in the foothills of the Appalachian mountains, but there was plenty of opportunity nearby in the surrounding communities. He had even seen some Amish buggies which was something he had never thought of before, and some more tempting choices. The Amish had a perfect scapegoat too, as all their kids had the choice to leave the order at a certain time in their lives, and given that maybe he could tempt some to leave, his way. He smiled as he thought about it, and his mind was already reeling with all the possibilities, which of course were endless for him. Right before leaving that night, he started a little fire and burned most of his old documents with the name that he affiliated this area with. He even burned his ID and he dug a deep hole and buried the ashes , but not before pouring acid on them as well, melting them into oblivion, before covering them up for good, with dirt and then stone. This is what he does and this is how he does it. Did he still want Cheyenne, yes, oh God yes he did, but did he know that he may not be able to get or have her, yes he did, sadly. This hadn't happened often, but it did happen once before, when he had to leave an area before his final prize. It upset him, but he had too much at stake to risk it all just for one girl. That was one of his cardinal rules for collecting, and begrudgingly he had to remind himself often of those rules, especially at times like this, but he knew what would happen if he broke his rules. Breaking rules meant the collapse of his empire, the end of his legacy, and the demise of his future. He already knew that he would never go to jail, because he would be raped and torn asunder in that atmosphere. For that reason, he always carried a small tin with him, that carried some cocaine and some cyanide powder mixed together, so he would snort the mixture and be in a euphoric state as he slowly dies. That was what he chose for his final ending, if that day should ever come. It was a way out, the only way out. It was all planned to a 'T' and he always dotted his 'I's' also, because that was who he was. He checked on his food stores and IV supplies, and he had enough to last anywhere from three to four weeks, so that was perfect. He took a little nap and left in the middle of the night, under the cover of darkness. It was how it was to be.

Weasel watched her master prepping and she knew what was coming, so she listened and did what she was told to make him happy. She knew what all this movement meant, because she had been through it before. She was excited and sad at the same time, because it meant the end of an era for the women that she took care of and loved here also. Yet that meant new girls to love and take care of though, and that was always good for her also. Still without her master present, she could have a little free time to herself, and her girls together. She could bond more but she still knew he would be watching remotely, so she had to be very careful also. Still he did allow her some freedoms, or that is what she called his slight leniencies. Still she would bide her time and see how it goes, because she still had a job to do and that came first, she reminded herself. She went about her jobs daily, and then one night when she had just fallen asleep, she heard a door lock and she ran to a small peep hole window that she had of the outside world, and she watched as she saw him get into the box van, turn it on, and then slowly drive away under the cover of darkness. He was leaving and now gone, she thought excitedly as she cuddled back up onto her little bed and snuggled one of her stuffed animals. She just so needed a good long break from him, just as she needed a good break from the daily routines. Now she could go about at her own pace, go outside and revisit nature, which she wasn't always allowed to do when he was there; it just depended on his mood usually. She was ecstatic to be a little free, so much that she had trouble falling asleep, which took her nearly two hours longer than normal. By the morning, after some restless sleep and numerous vivid dreams, she awoke groggily, not ready to get out of bed yet. She jumped up thinking he would be on her soon, but alas it was then that she remembered that he was gone for the time being, and she lay back down on her bed and fell back asleep for a little longer. Such a refreshing feeling as she woke back up about an hour after she had taken the nap, after lying back down. Now she felt better, so she made herself a meal with what she had, stale bread, scrambled eggs, and refried beans in a can. After that she kept herself hydrated by drinking enough, and then she went around doing her daily chores. She went about in a normal manner, like her master was present in the compound today. Once she was done with those chores and it was daylight, she did something she didn't always have time to or was allowed to and that was sit outside watching nature, enjoying the sights, the sounds, and the smells. The sun beat down on her pale pasty skin on her arms and then she decided to take a chance and she stripped off her clothes and put them down on the ground. She lay there before the sun god and soaked in the rays of what was bestowed upon her. She was in total heaven as she took it all in. she had to be careful though because of how pale she was, she knew she might burn in no time. Still, to her that was just something she didn't care too much about at this time. Her naked body was on display for anyone to see, and she honestly didn't care if anyone saw her. She was free, or at least she felt free for the first time in such a long time.

After some time she got too hot, so she walked over and found a hose where she put the nozzle on a cone type spray and she hosed herself down with the cold spring water. It was cold, but it felt refreshing after lying in the hot sun for longer than she should have, but who cares about such mundane worries. The spray of the water hose sprinkled heavenly droplets of refreshing liquid sunshine over her thin silhouette and pale skin, as she moved her body causing her to sway in the mist and she shook her head, like the actresses who pose for those glamorous pictures with water in those fashion magazines. She imagined that she was one of them, as she dipped her head, shook her unkempt hair, and just enjoyed every second of this delightful respite. Eventually when she was thoroughly refreshed and ready to dry off, she turned off the hose and went back over and lay back down to air dry herself. She hadn't had a day like this in so long, so she enjoyed every second of it. Then she had an idea. Yes, that would be fun, and she had to think about it some, but she was going to do it. She had another plan in her mind as she enjoyed the sun for a little longer. Yes, this would be fun.

        Back in town and at the office, Tom was on a reading frenzy, trying to find anything that would help him in Teresa's journal, but sadly no matter what he read, it seemed that nearly all of the entries were from her earlier years in life. Most were about cute boys she liked or girls tht she liked and didn't like. Once he finally finished reading every page, he came to the realization that Teresa had stopped writing some time ago, long before her present age, that was for sure. So again, he was back to square one and he had no idea where to go once again. Every lead was a dead end and every trail had gone cold. He was absolutely clueless! He wasn't giving up, but he had no idea what or where to go next. This case was just so full of nothing. This was insane! He wanted some damn answer, some clues, something that could help him and he was growing more frustrated with the effort and the lack of results. He left his office and went down the hallway to get another cup of coffee. He passed Linda's cubicle, but she wasn't there. He imagined that she was out on patrol at this time, since it was midday. He texted her to see where she was, maybe he could meet up with her and have some late lunch with her. He smiled as he saw the picture of the two of them on his phone (his background photo). She was such a lovely woman and he still had trouble believing how lucky he was to have the love of two amazing women in his life. He would count his blessings and be happy for the results, because he hadn't been this happy with his life since his late wife. He realized that he wasn't even living life as he had become a shell of a man living an existence just to exist, but not truly living life as it should be. He walked by Gus Lapard, who was busy catching up on some paperwork issues that he had let lag and now was trying to finish up this aspect of the job that they all hate. They (all the officers and himself) called it, cover your butt time. Ryan, who was standing beside Gus's cubicle, was talking to the sitting Gus about the 'Blain' issue and him trying to get Linda's gun from her. Then they got on the issue with Blain holding a guy at gunpoint, which made Tom stop. He had heard something about it but didn't truly listen to what had occurred that night too much, well because Blain was drunk, so he brushed it off as poor timing for the innocent man. Tom listened to the entire story as if was being retold as he stood behind the two men and didn't say a word. He heard the recantation and didn't intervene or question anything. He listened and started to wonder about the entire Blain issue. It was a crying shame that the entire incident happened, the heinous domino effect that started it all with Teresa going missing. He thought how controlled the man that Blain pointed his pistol at had been. Amazing nerves of steel, if he had ever heard of any. Luckily it didn't turn out as it could have, with a wrong turn, like Blain actually shooting the visiting man or even one of their own. That would have been a catastrophe in itself, but the end results would have been much different, sadly, with Blain probably being shot dead. He had to make this right again, bring back some semblance of order to the devastated Astel family. He knew how he could by finding Teresa again, but he didn't know how to get there. All he could continue to do was be diligent, pay attention, and be ready at a moment's notice if anything looked awry. About that time, he received a text back from his sweetie, saying: 'would luv to, where?' He texted back, 'Frank's Deli?' and then within a minute, she responded: 'Sure thing, darlin! See ya in ten.' Then he left the two talking officers and hastened his step to leave the building and meet up with his sweetheart. He got outside the building, looked at his vehicle and then looked down the street, and he decided to walk it. He walked at a little faster than leisurely pace, but he wasn't hustling it either. He should make it there in about seven or eight minutes, so he should be good.

He made good time getting to the deli of his old friend, because just as he was within eyesight of the little eatery, Linda had just come out of her police vehicle and she waited for him to finish walking up to her. He walked over to her with a big smile, embraced in a lover's clinch, and then kissed one another on the lips as well. Tom spoke up first, saying;

"Well, how are you, my love?"

"Oh sweetie, I am just fine. Just been busy today. A few B & E's, a hit and run on a vehicle, and some perv running around exposing himself to old ladies." She said the last one with an odd frown. "As if someone would wish to expose themselves to old women in their 70's and 80's. What's the point, too many have cataracts and such poor vision, it would be such a wasted effort." Tom laughed at her reasoning of why someone would do something to older people. She smiled at him and raised her hands as if to say, ' oh well'. They walked toward the door, and Tom held the door for his beloved and they walked inside. Frank was inside , of course, as always and he greeted them with an exuberant smile and then a cheesy grin, when he saw his friend holding hands with his new girlfriend. The people in town were talking about the two of them, saying how cute it was and how it was about time that both of them started over again. It was nice that they were starting over with each other as well. So, even though they weren't looking for any approval, most of the town's folks did approve it, well except Bev of course. Well she approved, but she wanted to be the woman that Tom liked, and not that 'nice but skinny broad Linda'. Fred looked at his old friend and smiled, because he had seen him down in the dumps and had been there through many conversations with him. Tom walked over and shook his friend's hand and then Frank said;

"It is great to see you, friend, well both of you....." As he smiled at Linda too, and whispered a thank you, a thank you for making his friend happy and alive again. Linda blushed some, but she squeezed Tom's arm a little more as if to respond that it was a mutual rejuvenation for both of them. Frank smiled at the small sign of affection but which carried a big meaning to them both. Frank spoke up, after washing his hands from shaking Tom's extended one, asking;

"So what will it be for the two lovebirds?" He said with a wink and a huge personal grin. Tom laughed at his friend for the comment, and Linda silently cooed after a smile. Tom ordered after Linda did, and they got their homemade (no self respecting southerner would sell and serve the fake instant kind, just as Frank doesn't either) iced teas and they went and sat down at one of the cozy little tables for two. They made some small talk and she asked him how his day was going. He lamented over what happened with the Astel family, and he confessed that he didn't know where to go from here. He also mentioned that it is so frustrating to see something, like the Blain and Lori event, unfold and not be able to do anything about it. Linda readily agreed as she had told her story to him a few times, just to see if she had done anything wrong or could have done something better, in such a situation. He had nothing to add because she had done everything right and it was totally unexpected of him to act in that fashion. He and she were just happy that she hadn't chambered a round yet, or it may have been a totally different outcome. Thank goodness for that he often said regarding that stroke of luck. They consumed their meal together talking about life and what each one wants out of it, in other words what their outlook on the future was. She would love to have a house or cabin by a lake so that they could boat and swim whenever they wished to. He was open to that, he just wanted to be sure they had a few acres so that he could enjoy being outside, experiencing nature in every aspect. He imagined two adirondack chairs before a fire pit, overlooking a pristine mountain lake. He couldn't imagine anything sweeter, and so they put that on their bucket list of future endeavors to experience and share as a couple. It was a delicious meal as always, especially here at Frank's. Frank used the best local offerings from the farmer's markets and even from local meat vendors as well. He took pride in what he offered his customers and he always said he wouldn't offer anything that he wouldn't give his family. And he was a devoted family man, that was for sure. He smiled as he looked over and watched his old friend move about and do his due diligence to not only keep his customers happy, but also because of his dutiful work ethic. He needed to hang out with his friend again, because he missed him and his lovely family. Maybe they could have a cookout or something, just to have a nice day together as friends. That sounded like a great plan, and he would mention it to him before they left today. Linda was asked a question by one of the other patrons sitting nearby about the Blain and Lori Astel incident, but Linda respectfully and smartly declined to comment on the situation. That decline didn't sit well with the nosey passersby, but you can't make everyone happy nowadays, can you, thought Tom to himself.

After they were done eating, they sat around a little longer, then Tom went up to get refills and some to go cups and Frank happily obliged. They chatted about getting together soon with promises to keep in touch and not just here at work. Tom and Linda left the deli then, with Tom holding the door for his beloved again to prove that chivalry was not dead, not in the least. They went outside in the overcast weather as the sun jutted behind some clouds once again, and they found a spot on a nearby park bench, enjoying one another's company. They lingered as long as they could, but they knew they had to, each one, get back to the grind and back to work. He walked Linda to her police vehicle and he opened her door for her, gave her a hug, and kissed her on her pouty lips, enjoying every second that they lip-locked together. She was an amazing and responsive kisser and he so enjoyed and loved that about her, well that was just one of the endless things she admired and loved about her. They promised to catch up later and then she backed out and drove off, down the road, waving to him as she left. He looked around and slowly started the walk back to the office, but decided to take the long way and just walk around town some to see what trouble he could get himself into.

Back at the compound, Weasel finished up outside, enjoying the afternoon sun as the clouds had rolled in and made it more an overcast now. So she gathered her clothes and belongings, but she didn't put her clothes back on as she shamelessly walked back inside the compound. She stashed her clothes near her room, and decided to walk completely naked into the holding area. She walked over to the cage that held Suzie and she slowly and quietly unlocked and opened the door. It opened with a little squeak, but it wasn't too bad so she slowly reclosed it as well. She walked over to where Suzie was lying, in a newish plush dog bed, as she begged for that for the ladies seeing how uncomfortable that they were on a daily basis. She walked over and snuggled right beside Suzie. Suzie woke up a little, glanced over and at this point said why not, and allowed Weasel to join her in a nap. It felt nice to Suzie to have a warm body next to hers, no matter who it was. She felt comforted and didn't even care that Weasel was nude and spooning her. She just enjoyed the company either way. Weasel enjoyed every bit of this and she felt free as her naked body snuggled closely with the one woman she respected and enjoyed the most. It wasn't before long that she fell asleep cuddling with Suzie and having vivid dreams of how the two would be outside of this situation. It was a marvelous dream at that and she slept, slept better than she had in quite some time. Suzie, however nice it felt to her, had ulterior plans and she allowed Weasel to lay with her until she fell asleep. This was perfect, she thought, a means to an end. After she heard Weasel's heavy breathing, she painstakingly and slowly inched her way out from underneath Weasels' arm, which had crossed overtop of her. She gently laid it back down, and Weasel still slept. That was when Suzie went over to the cage door precariously, and slowly opened it, but this time she made sure there was no squeak. Suzie had to take her good old time, because her legs were wobbly as she hadn't carried her own weight in some time. Her muscles had atrophied over time of non use, just as a sedentary person becomes less mobile the less they move. She left the door open and she clumsily walked around the holding area, holding onto everything she could to maintain her upright position. It felt so weird to finally walk again, when after all this time she had not moved as such. She was unsure where or what she was doing, at the moment other than to try to get her legs about her. She even smacked an overhead item not once, not twice, but three times as tried to maneuver now that she only had one available eye also. Her depth of vision was off and so it took her that long to acclimate a little better. She found another few cages, but no girls were in these at the time, and so she moved on. She continued to walk until she found a closed door. Thankfully though, Weasel hadn't locked this door and so she slowly and quietly opened that windowless door, but she only closed it a little, to make for an easier return. Her legs finally seemed to do better now, but she had no idea if the prick was here or not. He imagined not since Weasel had come into her cage naked, but she still didn't trust either of them as far as she could throw them. She hesitantly and gingerly moved about the corridor, ready to leave if she had to in a moment's notice. Luckily though, no one came out to stop her or chase her back to her cage. So maybe he was gone, but then again she had to be sure, so she continued to snoop around some. Each one she checked though, she found that all the doors were locked. Then she came to what looked like an outside door with a small window to it, but it was covered with a light covering. This door too was locked but she could move the covering and she could actually see outside and into part of the old barn that she had seen when she first arrived. She saw the house too, but it seemed so far away and she didn't know if the captor was in there or not at the moment. She better not press her luck ,she thought grimly. Now was not the time. This was a time to reconnoiter and get the lay of her escape route. At this point she had time and patience, and they would outlast anything else. She had seen enough on this trip and so she quietly and quickly as she could move, returned to her cell. She made sure to close all the doors behind her, that is until she made it back to the cell door. She went inside her cell, but left the door slightly ajar just as her admirer had upon entering her area. She then gently moved Weasel's arm to slowly crawl back into place, trying to be as stealthy as she could be. Just as she was about back in position, though, Weasel awoke with a start, and instead of giving her reason to question, Suzie made it look like she had just rolled over. Suzie rolled over and kissed Weasel on the forehead, not out of affection but for a reason to make sure that the girl was not questioning her motive. Suzie had a plan , she had a route, and now she just had to implement it. The fire was not gone in this woman yet, and the spark had just been brought back to life. Out of the darkness she will arise, she thought like on the wings of a phoenix and come out of the fire reborn and remade into an even more formidable woman. Weasel smiled at the kiss she gave her and Weasel responded back with a kiss on the lips. It was not at all what Suzie wanted, but again it was a means to an end, a means to an end. Sometimes, one has to do what one has to do in order to survive and her spirit was willing, that was for sure. She fell back asleep cuddled up with Weasel again, laying out her plans, her escape, her road to freedom!

Weasel had felt and seen Suzie on her little expedition, but she allowed her to do what she felt was an act of freedom. She hadn't been duped as Suzie thought she had been. Weasel knew that she had locked all the important doors, so her getting out was not a big deal. She watched quietly as Suzie tried to walk around and find the strength to keep her legs underneath her. She did however wince when Suzie hit her head a couple times on low items because her vision was off being only having one eye now. Still she watched her as she eventually left the room, thinking that she had gotten the best of her. That was not the case whatsoever. She gave her this freedom for her to open up more to her and hopefully form an even closer bond, maybe even a lover's bond of affection. She had a plan, just as Suzie was formulating a plan, and the plans were not the same in the least, but they both had their ulterior motives in what they were doing and wanted. Still Weasel couldn't help but wonder if she wanted Suzie to escape. Did she want her to have her freedom? Still giving her freedom, would probably mean her being locked up for contributing and helping her master for the crimes he had committed against these girls. So in essence, giving Suzie freedom, would doom her own existence. This was definitely a quandary she found herself to be in. No matter how much she loved 'the girls', she loved her own existence and the preservation of her life even moreso. But right now she didn't have to think about that as she lay there cuddled up naked with such a lovely woman. She reached down and touched Suzie's butt, which didn't elicit a response and so she found bare skin and touched it, enjoying and reveling in the softness of her skin. She dare not try more at this time, but even that little sinful delight was a sweet welcome for her. Maybe next time she will try more, she thought as she slowly fell asleep, this time for real.

Chapter Fourteen

It had been a little over a week now that had passed and nearly everyday Weasel went outside
to enjoy the sunshine, well except when it rained a lot. The heavy rain made her too cold if she were in it very long, but she did stay outside long enough to get a natural shower from mother nature. She frolicked in nature, enjoying the sunshine, the overcast skies, or whatever else should come, what may. She was in a whole other world being by herself. Her master had been gone at times, but he had never left her alone this long without returning. This was a new first for her, and she loved every minute of it. She still did all her chores, but she was able to have her own time to herself without being watched 24/7, which was the freedom aspect of it. She honestly didn't care if he was watching her or not, because she was enjoying this way too much. She even had longer and longer talks with both Teresa and with Suzie. She liked both girls, but Suzie was still her favorite, so she tended to spend more time with her than with Teresa. Teresa was sweet but completely docile and broken or so to speak. Still she started to take both girls out on a leash, but still bound. She first walked the lumbering Teresa outside in the sunlight one day, but not till after she got her legs back under her as well. Teresa tried to shield her eyes from the bright light as they were not accustomed to such brilliance, especially after being in the darkness for so long with only a dim red light to live by. After some time, though, Teresa started enjoying it more and more. It was then that Weasel had the girl strip down so she could give her a shower with the hose. At first Teresa denied the need to , but then Weasel got strict and told her that the master will punish her unless she does as instructed. That was one thing Teresa didn't want is her captor's menacing angst and the way he punished them and caused them pain. She never wanted to be hurt like that again, as she placed her hand up toward her missing eye. She now had a makeshift patch on that missing orbital region, and she still felt pain, whether it be phantom pain or not, it still ached her. She was able to lay outside on the grass, the

real outside grass for a little bit of time before Weasel told her it was time to head back in. Teresa did as she was told, and was led back inside by her leash to her cage once more. Still that night she dreamt of how amazing it was to be outside in nature again. It was one of those things that she always took for granted when she had been living in her past life, but now she respected, honored, and longed to be outside all the time again. She promised God that she would never take her life for granted again, if she were ever able to be free once more, she thought as she laid back down on her dog bed and curled up once more in the darkness and dim red light. This was her life now and there was no escaping it. She tried to fall asleep again, but her mind was back outside, as she smelled the fresh grasses, the delightful flowers, and all the lovely scents of nature. She wanted to be back in the world, back with her mom and dad, and back in the comfort level of the safety of her parent's home. Maybe one day it will come true, one day, hopefully.

Weasel was satisfied that she could see how happy Teresa was to be outside again. She knew that Teresa was a skater and loved being around obstacles to jump, but that was not possible at this time. So she allowed her what respite and freedom she could give her, and she could see how much she genuinely enjoyed it. So she planned on doing this more often, to give the poor demoralized girl some hope. Now Suzie, that was a totally different story, because she didn't trust her enough to bring her out yet. Maybe someday, but she wasn't ready to take that big of a step at this time. She also started to wonder about her master and how long he will be away. He had done this once before but she didn't recollect whether it had been this long or not, so she did start to wonder. What if he wasn't coming back? What would she do if he didn't? Was this part of his plan? Hopefully not, or at least she could only presume. Just as she was wondering that , she heard a vehicle come down the road. Her master had come back, and so she scrambled to catch up with her clothes as she was still naked and also what she had to do to satisfy him. As unexpected as it was, he was outside and in the adjacent house loading up more items again. He kept loading until he cleared out the house, or so he said when she asked him. He also removed a few of the extra generators, leaving only one running one behind, and one of the extra cans of fuel also. He unloaded one of the smaller fridges of its contents and he placed the items inside a cooler that was in the back of the box van. He looked at Weasel and asked her;

"Do you need anything from me, Weasel?"

"No sir, I am fine. I have this under control? But when will you be back again?"

"Not that it matters, but I will be a few more weeks. I am preparing for another wonderful spot that I have found. You should like it there, and a lot of new prospects for us…." He said winking at her. She smiled bashfully and looked down at her feet. "There , there Weasel, don't get all bashful. I will reward you as always, so don't fret. Maybe this time, I will give you a pet of your own." He smiled sinfully as he looked in her direction. Her eyes lit up at that possibility and she smiled a crooked grin, eliciting her not so great teeth to him. He finished with;

"Well I am off again, have a long drive ahead. Hold the fort down and you can always use your panic button, if you should need it, as he handed her a necklace with a button on it, in the shape of a green gem. "Just push down on that gem and I will take care of things, okay?"

"Yes master, I understand."

"Good, wish me luck, then. Bye Weasel!"

"Good-bye, master!" And then he got back into the box van and off he went, back down the gravel road and toward the exit of the property. It was becoming dark now as the sun was heading down. So she watched the sun fall down behind the clouds and the tree line for the night, thinking about the possibilities that she still has to entertain since her master is gone even longer now. She walked around and finished up what she had to do for this day. Once that was done, she walked back to the main holding area and stripped off her clothes once more and lay down beside Suzie, who welcomed her with open arms. This was perfect, thought Weasel to herself. Just plain perfection!

In the meantime back in town, Cheyenne walked her normal route after an early work day. Since it was slowly becoming dusk, she decided to walk home because she enjoyed that. She was in good spirits and happy as she had made some good tips from this late afternoon/early evening rush of people. A bus had gone through from the casino in one of the neighboring towns, and they stopped off there for an early supper. That was when she got so many of her tips and made some good bank. She had stopped on the way and even picked up one of her favorite lottery tickets to see if she could win some more dough for her future endeavors. She lightly strolled without a care in the world, when a car started moving up slowly behind her. She ignored it at first but it continued following her, so she took a glance behind to see that it was a dark blue rusty Camaro looking type of car. She was nervous and didn't like the looks of this vehicle at all. She picked up her pace a little and started moving in a hastened sense, as she was not in a good spot. There wasn't any cover around her for her to hide or get away from as the buildings were in some of the older parts and less inhabited parts of town, but it was the quickest way for her. She was becoming more worried as the car sped up, also moving faster and coming even closer. She saw a corner up ahead and it might have to be there that she makes a stand, but at least she would have her back to a wall. Or maybe she would be lucky and someone would be walking around town, but the chance of that on this night was very slim. Still, some hope was always better than none. The corner was less than forty feet away, but she already heard the car stop and someone getting out of the vehicle, she imagined the passenger side. She went into a full run now as she ran for her life and her well being. She ran hard as she heard footsteps behind her also pounding the pavement. This was her all or nothing chance, and just as she rounded the corner, she looked back and ran smack dab into someone, at full force. There was an 'umph' sound from her as her body impacted another person's body, and she found herself in someone's arms. She looked up and it was a scraggly unshaven mid twenties man, and he grabbed her wrists. She yelled and fought but he was much stronger than her, and then his buddy was upon them from behind and they both grabbed her and man-handled her, pulling her into a small alleyway. She kicked, screamed and clawed at the man, trying to fight for her life. One of the men grabbed an old shirt and stuffed it in her mouth, but not before he was bitten hard on the hand and suffered some damage. He swung his free hand, slapping her hard on the side of the cheek and making her see some stars. It was long enough to put the gag in her mouth and secure it with tape, taping her hair up as well. She still kicked but the other guy punched her in the stomach and knocked the wind out of her, and she nearly collapsed from the blow. The other guy kept the car running and sat at the entrance to the alley waiting for his buddies to finish up. The first one, whose hand was bitten, grabbed her shirt and ripped exposing her black sports bra and her upper chest area, as they were about to fondle her and grope her with their rough and calloused hands. She still squirmed but her strength had left her and she was feeling queasy and weaker by the minute. Just the thought of these disgusting punks violating her in any way, nauseated her beyond reason. The one down by her legs started to yank off her polyester pants that she wore to work, ripping them in the meantime, exposing her toned long legs of her lower body, her matching black lace panties, and her flat stomach. They all marveled at her sexy body for a second before getting back to what they were about to do. She kicked one more time and the guy at her legs reeled back and lost his balance falling backwards in the meantime, as he was attempting to pull down his pants and expose himself to her so that he could rape her. Then the driver got out of the car, but kept it running, and he went to help his down friend who had his pants around his ankles and had trouble getting up. Then the skanky one holding her upper body and touching her soft supple skin without her explicit permission, reeled back and cold cocked her across her temple, which was probably not where he meant to hit her, but it was effective as she nearly lost consciousness from that blow and then the world became a fuzzy haze. She realized that she had nothing left in her, no fight anymore, and she more or less surrendered to whatever her fate would be on this miserable and hopeless day. God, please save me, she prayed silently as she felt her clothes being completely ripped off her body and exposing her entire young body to these nasty vermin. She was completely at their will, now as the one dirtbag stood back up, the one with his pants down to get ready for his unlawful and non consensual penetration. She looked up at the sky, disappearing into the void of nothingness as she looked for some mental reprieve from the reality that had been thrust upon her this very moment. She knew at any minute there would be something done to her that she couldn't stop any longer, and so she just lay there, hopeless, helpless, and saddened beyond comparison. This is not how she wanted this to happen, she thought, as the guy moved closer into his final destination, which was to violate and rape her.

Tom walked down the pavement, heading down toward some of the less inhabited areas of town, to check on some of the folks who still lived down here. There were a few older couples who he enjoyed checking in on occasionally, and to his dismay he hadn't done that in some time. He walked along leisurely, but then heard something in the distance. It stopped as soon as it started to his dismay. It almost sounded like a stifled scream, but he had just passed an oversized air conditioning unit as well, which was drowning out any noises from a distance. Still he knew he had to check it out. He quickened his pace, trying to figure out where the noise (scream) had come from. He rounded a corner and up ahead in the distance, he saw a car sitting on the side of the road, near a building. Then suddenly the driver jumped out and ran into the alleyway and disappeared. This was strange behavior to say the least, and he immediately called it in and pulled out his firearm and advanced quickly on the alley that the man had disappeared into. When he was within 15 feet, he heard men talking, and one distinct voice saying to an unknown amount of people in the hidden alley;

"Hurry up and get in her, we all need to take a turn, so get your shit on and do her!" After hearing that, Tom advanced with his drawn weapon out in front of him and ready to stop whatever heinous activity these assholes were up to. He stopped just around the corner as he heard the men mumbling and that was when he spun around the corner and yelled;

"This is the police! Everyone down, now!" There was a mix of activity as the two had their backs to Tom stopped immediately, not sure who or what had interfered in their fun. Tom saw that they held a girl down and were about to commit rape upon this unfortunate soul, but he still couldn't see who it was that they were trying to violate. The one at Cheyenne's head stopped but glared at the person who interrupted them with hatred and malice. Tom saw that look immediately and continued with;

"Listen here scumbags, drop to the ground now, face down, and arms behind your backs. This won't be repeated, so…… DO IT NOW!" The two at the foot of the downed girl dropped and did as they were told, and it was at that moment when those two went to the ground, that Tom saw that it was Cheyenne, the innocent and lovely Cheyenne who these scum were trying to rape. In that split second of recognition, the man at Cheyenne's head, reached behind his back and pulled a pistol out, brandishing it as he swung it around to point it at him. Tom, even though he had a split second lapse, he was not that slow and he raised his own weapon upon seeing the unknown assailant reach and bring his own weapon to bear. Tom yelled at the man;

"Don't Do it!" but it was too late, in about another second he would fire on Tom, so Tom did what he had to do and shot twice at the man, with the first shot hitting him in the shoulder of the arm that held the pistol and the second one, square in the chest, knocking the assailant to the ground in a no time. The man grunted and started crying in pain, as a pool of blood started collecting underneath him.Tom spoke again as he ran to the side of the downed man, saying;

"Dammit, I said don't do it, you idiot!" He called for an ambulance on his radio immediately and about that time he heard sirens coming down the road. The other two men lying on the ground with their face in the pavement couldn't believe their eyes, as their friend had been fatally shot. Tom tried, in vain, to stop the bleeding by putting pressure on the man's chest with his bare hand, but the dying man was already gurgling on his own blood as it came rolling out of his mouth in bubbles, as he tried to say something. Unfortunately, all that came out though were garbled noises, and so Tom was unable to understand what was being said. He maintained pressure and would do so until the ambulance crew came. It was in his nature to try to help the best he could, even given the situation. Another police car showed up quickly and it was none other than his darling Linda. She saw Tom dealing with the shot man, so she went over to cover the other two men lying prone and harshly spoke commands to them, saying;

"Keep your heads down and place your arms behind your back, NOW!" They did as they were told as they could tell that she wasn't having any shenanigans, and then she immediately roughly handcuffed the first pants down one and then the second one who was the clothed driver. After they were secure, she cast her eyes over at the cowering Cheyenne, who was desperately trying to cover up her partially exposed young body with what remnants of clothing she was able to grab hold of. Linda, immediately, ran over to her police car, grabbed her jacket and a blanket, and made haste back to the cowering, shivering, and scared Cheyenne. Linda instinctively tried to comfort her, by saying to her;

"Sweetie, it's okay, you are safe now! I've got you! Here, here, cover up and protect yourself." She cuddled the shivering Cheyenne as the girl tried to curl up in a tiny fetal position to try to protect her young adult dignity yet. The thing was that she wasn't shaking because she was cold, but because of the intense fear that overwhelmed her, the vilenesss of her attempted rape, and the reality of knowing that this could have been her demise, the end of her young life as she knew it. She then started crying into Linda's chest as her arms encompassed the poor girl. Linda continued holding her, cradling her for security reasons, so that she felt somewhat safe. She whispered to the crying girl;

"Let it out, child, let it out." As she continued to embrace and cradle the emotional Cheyenne, then seconds later, another police car showed up and it was Officer Jeremy Pine, who immediately got out, surveyed the scene, and went to the prone men, first, who remained lying face down on the pavement. He then roughly picked up the two prone and already handcuffed men one at a time (but not till after helping to pull up the one man's pants so that he could walk and wasn't exposed any longer), placing both of them in the back of his squad car for transportation. Now that they were out of the way and secured, he went back to the scene and saw how Linda was attending to Cheyenne, therefore he went to help his friend out with the downed and injured criminal. Jeremy looked at the shot man and immediately placed his hand on Tom's shoulder, saying quietly to him;

"Tom, he is gone. There's nothing you can do for him." Tom looked at the man lying on his back in a pool of blood, and then he checked for a carotid pulse with his already bloodied hand and found nothing. So Jeremy was indeed right, the man was deceased. Tom slowly rolled onto his butt, as he had knelt down to try to help the man that he had shot, and sat there watching Linda hold Cheyenne. Cheyenne looked toward Tom with eyes wide and afraid, and Tom mouthed an, 'I'm sorry' to her. She looked squarely at him asking;

"Isss......he.....de...ad.........?"

"Yes, he is Cheyenne. He was judged for his crime."

"Goooood, I.... hope..... he.. rots... in... hell!" She said with explicit hate in her voice, even though it was still a little shaky. Her hatred toward him for violating her and her innocence was the straw that broke the camel's back. The tears continued to stream down her puffy face from the abuse that she had received at the hands of the now dead prick.

"Linda, can you take her away from here and back to the station, please. Are you sure you are okay to walk, Cheyenne?" Cheyenne shook her head in a resounding 'yes' gesture but as she stood up, she first turned toward the deceased man and walked over toward the supine body. She remained covered up the best she could, but for a second she let her long legs slip out from underneath the blanket. Linda followed her, unsure what she was doing, other than maybe getting a better look at him. Then out of nowhere, Cheyenne reared back and kicked the dead man as hard as she could, making his limp body jolt from her maximum effort. Not one single person present said a single word regarding her action. They just let her do what the girl needed to do, then Linda made sure she was covered completely again, and then she ushered her back to her vehicle to transport her to the station. Tom and Jeremy watched the strong and proud Cheyenne walk away, get into Linda's police car, and drive away safely. It was then that Jeremy spoke up, saying;

"Well, I didn't expect that."

"Neither did I friend, neither did I...." About that time the ambulance came rolling up and the medics jumped out to check on the shot man. They pronounced him dead at the scene and wrote down the time for their records. They got their gurney ready and all of them (the two ambulance crew and the two policemen) picked up the deceased man and put him on the gurney for transport to the local hospital morgue. The one medic gave Tom some sterile water, a large sterile towel, and some hand sanitizer to wash up his hands from the blood that was all over them. After washing up and cleansing his bloodied hands, Tom walked over and sat down on Jeremy's car hood, asking him;

"Well I guess we have to go get these idiots booked, are you ready?"

"Ready when you are boss. And by the way nice shot in taking down that armed perp and saving the girl. You are a true hero, my friend."

"I was just at the right place, at the right time! I sure don't feel like a hero, buddy." He said as he thought about Teresa and Suzie out there somewhere beyond his reach and his help with their situation at this time. He only hoped they could fight and hold out just as the lovely and innocent Cheyenne did when she had to, even when the odds were stacked against her. He could only hope for the best for them. They loaded up, drove back to the station to book these guilty deviants, and then properly booked them in jail for first degree sexual offense, attempted rape, assault, and accessory to a crime for the men. Tom just wanted to bury them for their part in the heinous act of savagery against the innocent Cheyenne, and he would make sure they got it also.

Back at the station, Cheyenne was in a separate room away from the assailants, while Linda called her parents' number to have them come get their daughter. Jeremy and Tom escorted the criminals inside as they started to book them, fingerprinted them, and placed them both in a holding cell for the time being. Both men would not look either officer in the eyes, and the officers were none too kind to them either, as they didn't deserve any rights for what they were a party to. The driver would get off the easiest, but the man who nearly violated Cheyenne will get the full charges for his vile act. Once they were locked up, Tom walked over to the office that Cheyenne was in, but he stopped in his tracks as her parents had shown up, so he took them to the side and to explain what had happened to their daughter. Their names were Harriet and Steven and he went over how exactly he found what he had come across, by starting off with;

"Well let me tell you first, Cheyenne is safe. I will take you to her in a second, I just wish to explain what happened to her." Harriet and Steven were on the edge of their seats as Tom paused for a second. He continued with the story, saying;

"Okay, I was as luck would have it, walking down Trace street, toward some of the less populated areas, when I heard a stifled scream. I quickened my pace, rounding a corner where I saw a car in the distance running, which seemed odd. I heard a shuffle noise and then the driver got out and ran toward an alley. So I advanced quickly and peeked around the corner, seeing that there were three men trying to assault someone. I ordered them to cease and desist, which the first two did and dropped to the ground, but the third one, by your daughter's head, decided he didn't want to listen. He pulled a gun on me and I shot him dead with two rounds. Another officer attended to your daughter, while I attended to the other criminals (he left out the part about trying to save the shot man's life because that was something they didn't need to hear or know). He paused for any questions, and he saw that Harriet was crying and Steven was fuming at hearing what had happened. Steven spoke up first, asking;

"Did my ....daughter...get violated....raped?"

"No, sir. I managed to bust up the scene before any act was done forcefully against her innocence. She is shook up, but she is in fairly good spirits considering. I just wanted to let you know what had happened to the full extent, so that you know and are able to understand the trauma that she had just experienced." Harriet stifled a sniffle and she thanked Tom for his help and for saving their daughter and then he stood up directing them out of the office and into the room where their daughter was. Tom knocked first on the office door, and then he walked in, with Cheyenne's parents following him in. Cheyenne was sitting in a chair, drinking some coffee with Linda as she was trying to get her nerves back about her. Upon seeing Tom, not immediately seeing her parents, but Tom first, she jumped up and ran to him, hugging the man who saved her life and her dignity. She buried her face in his chest as he stood there taking the embrace and then he returned the favor by lightly hugging her back, out of respect for the young girl. Linda's eyes welled up with the emotion that was displayed between her man and the young girl. Even her parents were also emotional as they saw how grateful their daughter was at Tom's actions. Then she saw her parents and she went and hugged both of them, and then the waterworks commenced by all three as her parents tried to console her as she just wanted to hug and be held by both her mom and her dad. It was a very touching moment considering how it could have ultimately ended for the young Cheyenne. After the initial loving embraces and words of endearing love by both parties, Steven asked;

"Is there anything else she needs to do, or us at this point?"

"No, sir, you are free to go home and all I ask is that you take care of this amazing and strong girl." He said to Cheyenne as he looked at her with such respect and admiration that one human being gives to another for how they respond to such a stressful time in one's life. Cheyenne beamed, and so did her parents at the kind words spoken by the detective. The parents ushered out their daughter, and Linda went over and hugged and kissed her man, the savior of the day. She didn't say those words to him as he would dispute them, so instead she showed her appreciation of him in loving actions instead of spoken words. She was so proud of the man she loved with all her heart! He was truly a man of action and someone she never would have expected to have such a relationship with. She was both thankful and proud of the man in her arms. Tom on the other hand was thinking the same thing about Linda. He embraced and kissed her and saw how responsive she was to the distressed Cheyenne, and how she went from police officer to motherly caretaker in seconds as she tried to comfort and help the young girl in her time of need. He still couldn't believe how lucky he was to be able to have someone as amazing and wonderful as Linda in his life. He whispered sweet nothings in her ear and then he passionately kissed her one more time, before he had to go start on his report of the entire situation and how it unfolded. She graciously accepted the loving smooch and she knew he had reports to follow up on, so she left him to do his work as she blew him a kiss as she left the room. He stood there, in the office, for a moment amazed at how lucky he had been to have been walking just at the right time and at the right place to thwart the crime, and right before it occurred. He thanked his lucky stars that Cheyenne was the strong woman she was and put up a fight to keep the punks from doing their wishes upon her. Another five minutes later and it would have been a totally different story and scenario, that was for sure. He thought his luck was not about him, since he didn't seem to have any luck trying to figure out the missing persons issues, but after this he wasn't so sure that his luck wasn't turning around, now. He poured himself a fresh cup of coffee and took a long drag, taking the hot liquid in his mouth as it slightly stung from the heat of it, but the flavor was so perfect that he took the mild pain for the instant delicious taste of the brew. He poured a little more and then he left the office to go start on his report of the situation, having to relive it in his mind again as he made sure he got everything right for the upcoming arraignment of the two young men. Their time will come and they will soon have to answer for their distasteful deeds and associative actions. He would make sure of that.

        A week had passed since the incident with Cheyenne and Tom had heard from her parents when he did a follow up call with them, to make sure their daughter and themselves were doing okay since that fateful day. He learned then that Cheyenne had been doing fair, considering, but she had some bad nightmares over the last week which had affected her psyche. So in an effort to alleviate any connection to the trauma, she was seeking some counseling and just yesterday her parents decided to send her away to their parents, her grandparents for a period of time. A respite to get away from the stressors of life and live with the farm life for a little. The counselor thought that was a great idea as well. He was thankful that she was getting help and seeking refuge from that fateful day. He just happened to ask where the grandparents lived and the parents responded in rural Ohio, close to the Pennsylvania state line. They both thanked him again for his instrumental part in foiling the plan that the deviants had for their daughter. He respectfully thanked them for their kind words, but he also added that if they or Cheyenne needed anything at all, at any time, just let him know and he will make it happen. He confessed that he had the utmost respect for their daughter and how she handled herself in such a situation. He wished her a speedy recovery and return to her normalcy so that she could continue on in her life. They thanked him graciously once again, and then that was the end of the conversation. The remaining men who had assisted in the brutal acts upon Cheyenne were arraigned and were sentenced to remain in jail, without bond, until their trial date. Per the judge, those men were a menace and a high risk of flight considering their crime and deviance. So that went smoothly, thankfully, and things got a little back to the norm for their community, except for the missing girl issue that still plagued Tom to this day. Either he was missing the obvious and it was just chance, or there was a true and professional deviant out there abducting girls and keeping them somewhere, for whatever reason and to what end. Neither of which he still knew yet, as there weren't any bodies or any other signs of such a person doing such a crime. It was all so very perplexing, frustrating, and mind boggling, to say the least. He just kept doing what he could and hopefully looking for any signs. He at first thought maybe it was the derelicts that he busted were doing something, but he found out they didn't have the intelligence or the drive to do such. They were just stupid horny young men going about everything the wrong way. Well that and they were strung out on drugs, as their drugs tests came back to demonstrate that. He was able to properly interrogate the men, but now that their ringleader was gone, they seemed to fold to whatever plea deal they could to save their own butts, now that they were firmly in a tight sling. So he had to continue to look elsewhere for his answers with the missing girls, and that was all he could do. He did contact the State Police also, but they seemed to have no answers after going over all he had on everything and so they were in a holding pattern as well, until something broke in the case. He promised to keep them informed (and them as well with him) if anything changes and so he did all that he could do, to this point. He was just hoping and begging for a break, wishing it would be sooner than later.

Just as another week passed since the Cheyenne incident, another week had also lazily passed back at the compound. Weasel took Teresa outside daily and then one day she even made an attempt to take Suzie out, for a special treat. She had been sleeping with Suzie everyday now and she loved being next to her, touching her, and being loved by her. She could tell Suzie liked her more now, as she seemed to welcome everything she did now with and for her, which was totally different from the past tumultuous experiences between them. So the one day after she had taken Teresa out and her master still hadn't come back from his excursion, she decided to take a gamble and take Suzie outside, but on a leash of course because she didn't trust her that much. It was an overcast day, that day that she took Suzie outside, but it was still warm and felt amazing. Of course Weasel went out maked, frolicking in the water from the hose and also just soaking up the hidden rays of sun. Her thin and frail looking body was now overly tanned, which was a stark contrast from the redness that she had experienced in the first week of her naked body being exposed to the sunshine. She actually didn't look that bad, considering how thin she was, with her tanned / bronzed skin. She attached Suzie to a runner line, meaning she had a rope tied between the two buildings, and she hooked the leash onto that so that Suzie could move up and down the length of the rope. Yes, it was dehumanizing in a way, but she was allowing her outside, something her master never allowed her to do. Weasel did her things, dancing in the grasses as they had now become tall enough to cover up to her knees. She swayed back and forth, hoping that she was turning on Suzie some with her actions and her dances. She wanted to impress her, that was for sure at how nimble and agile she was/had become. She had been outside dancing at least once a day until she thought that she started to get some rhythm about her and show improvement. Suzie sat down on a log, not sure what to think, but then she removed her button down linen covering so that her buxom bodice could be exposed to the elements, as she used to do, in her previous life (before her captivity). She enjoyed that immensely as the sun escaped the clouds and shone down on her body, wishing she was elsewhere and in another situation. Of course now with her being topless, Weasel was definitely paying more attention to her now, but then again that was her long term plan. She had her plan and she would do whatever it took to implement it. She leaned back and enjoyed the length of the leash she had, until she reached its limit and it pulled at her neck, so she had to sit back up some. Weasel came over and kissed her on the forehead as she danced right in front of her. Suzie entertained the thin woman dancing before her with light touches of approval and smiles, just to appease her. Weasel groped her breast completely and unexpectedly, but Suzie put her hand up to slow her down and whispered to her, 'not now, pet'. Weasel appeared defeated for a second, but then she went back to her dancing, and it was at that time that Suzie looked around to see the lay of the land before her, since this was the first time she had been outside. She was looking around, fingering through her matted hair while she secretly looked all around to find the best way of escape. She could go down the road, but that was too much exposure and too easy to be seen. She looked to her right, over toward the house, but she was afraid that way may not be good either, so she looked to her left, where there were lots of woods and trees to conceal her. That would be her best avenue of escape she thought as she messed with her hair again, so that she looked inconspicuous. Yes that was the route, now she just had to find out when she should do it. She knew she had to do it soon, while Weasel seemed to be the only one here, and since she didn't know when her captor was coming back from wherever he had gone to. Yes, she thought as Weasel came over again and touched her body once more, but this time she didn't deny the woman for fear of turning her away too much may cause speculation or trust issues. So she allowed her to play with her body some, not that it didn't feel good in a small way, but she had to do what she had to get the hell out of dodge. She must do whatever it takes, she kept telling herself. Everything she did nowadays was a means to an end, a means to an end.

It had been a few days since the first time that Weasel took her outside to experience nature again. Yet after this one particular day, where she was out in the direct sunlight and sweltering heat with Weasel, she decided that later in the day she would make her break for it. She wanted to use the cover of darkness, therefore it would be more difficult to see and find her for the pursuant. She also didn't want to wait too long, because she didn't know when her captor was coming back. Therefore being too cautious and waiting was a huge risk in her end. She won't be able to get this kind of chance again, so she had to move when it seemed best to. She had to commit completely though or her plan wouldn't work. So this particular day seemed like the perfect day. Weasel was out dancing a lot in the heat, bronzing her thin body even more, but that also meant it took a toll on her and she would sleep more deeply when the time came. They spent most of the afternoon outside and then finally just after early evening, Weasel escorted Suzie back inside. Suzie, though, was being smart and so just as they reached the door, she pointed back behind them to show that she had left her top behind, as she was still walking around topless. Weasel told her to stay there and she ran back to get it. In the meantime, Suzie had picked up a decent sized rock to wedge into the door so that it wouldn't lock behind them. She bent down, placed the rock where it should work and then she stood back up, brushing her legs off as if something had gotten on them to cover her movements and actions. Weasel turned around with her shirt in hand just as Suzie was brushing her legs and looked at her with a weird look. Suzie immediately looked down and made a spider gesture with one hand on top of her other hand, and brushed her legs again. Weasel shivered as she seemed to get the hint and didn't question her anymore about it. Perfect, thought Suzie, just perfect. Just as they went inside after Suzie put her shirt back on, Weasel went to close the door, to secure it, but Suzie fell down on the floor like she tripped over something and rolled on her back, grabbing her lower leg. Weasel immediately left the door and rushed to her girl's side. She asked her what was wrong, and Suzie just pointed to her ankle area and then tried to get up but couldn't, or at least she was feigning it well enough to elicit the correct response from Weasel. Weasel had forgotten all about the door and she assisted the limping Suzie back into the cell area. This was perfect, Suzie thought happily, but she tried to keep her excitement to minimal so as not to set off any alarms. Weasel assisted her to her cage, and she left her there as she went to retrieve an ice pack for her ailing friend. Suzie just waited and counted her blessings that her plan was coming together, just as she had hoped it would. She had to be perfect with her set up, that was for sure.

After the evening meal of the day, in which Weasel actually gave both Suzie and Teresa a little extra food, Weasel went about her daily chores, checking things and making sure they were settled in for the night. Suzie in the meantime ate most of her food and waited patiently for her 'friend' to show up for the night. She was both excited and scared, because she still had no idea where a road was or which direction was the best, but either way she had to try and make an effort to escape. This could be her one and only chance, that was for sure. She waited for the weary Weasel to come into her area and then her cell. Like she had done in the past, Weasel didn't close or lock the door the entire way and therefore it remained slightly ajar. Suzie lay there acting like she was sleeping, breathing heavily and moving ever so slightly as Weasel cuddled up next to her, snuggling as if they were intimate lovers. Suzie moved ever so slightly to feign deep sleeping and then Weasel moved in even closer, putting her arm around her body. Some time later, when Suzie was still awake but patiently waiting, she could tell that Weasel was in a deep sleep. She tested it by picking her arm up slightly and then lowering it back down. There was no response at all from the snoring Weasel, so she moved ever so slightly, inching her way away from the woman cuddled up behind her. Slowly, ever so slowly, she shimmied her body out from underneath Weasel's arm. She even curled up the dog bed slightly so that her arm didn't drop down in an odd position which could awaken the sleeping woman. She then moved gingerly around the sleeping woman, and again there was no change in the sleeping patterns. She even waited a few minutes, but again she was rewarded with no change in Weasel sleeping. The long day out in the sun must have really worn her out, thankfully. She slowly went to the door, and opened it as gently as she could, without making a sound. She slipped out of the door and once more slowly closed the door, but she couldn't lock it because of the noise it would make, therefore she closed it as much as she could. She moved through the large room but used the walls for concealment, only banging her head lightly once on an overhead piece. She made it to the door and she stopped for about a minute, still watching the barely moving body of Weasel, rising and falling. Now was her chance, but still she balked just a few seconds longer, barely able to move for some reason. Maybe it was the unsureness of how this will all end, but then again, maybe it was just her being scared that she didn't know what would happen if she were caught trying to escape. Either way there was at least two full minutes of her standing steadfast in her spot, unsure and unable to move. Then finally with all the resolve she could muster, she took the first step and reached for the closed door. Thankfully it wasn't locked and she slowly opened the door with deliberate hesitancy, for fear of making a noise. Luckily the door didn't make a noise and she was able to get on the other side of it, before slowly closing it, which caused a very soft click. She waited again for about ten more seconds before once again moving down the hallway, toward the outside door. She clung to the wall again as she stealthily moved in an attempt to be as silent and secretive in her movements as possible. She made it down the long corridor without an issue and she knew she was right near the outside door. She slowly reached blindly for the door handle and then she gently pulled on the door, after turning the handle. It was all because of the rock that she had placed in the track earlier in the day that she was able to easily pull open the door. Once the door was open, she immediately smelled the nighttime scents of the outdoors. It was so refreshing as she moved on the other side of the door and very slowly and deliberately eased the door shut again, with the rock still in place. She couldn't believe it but she had made it outside. What a relief it was. Thank God for the simple things in life. She took a second and let her vision adjust to the surroundings and then she looked up seeing a fairly clear sky with oodles of stars lighting the darkness up. She started in the direction she thought that she had to go and she committed her life to it. Off into the darkness she moved, hopefully leading her to her freedom.

Not long after Suzie had slipped out the main entrance door, Weasel awoke with a start. She was groggy as she must have slept heavily from her antics earlier in the day. She found herself lying on her opposite side, away from her Suzie, so she turned back toward her darling girl. There was no gauging how surprised she was when she turned and 'her' Suzie wasn't there. She panicked for a few seconds, as she sat up looking all around the cage and finding no one but her inside there, alone! She was livid as she quickly searched the entire area that the cell was in and still she saw nothing, or no one! She sprang out of the cell and ran toward the unlocked door. She was scared to death that one of her master's girls had escaped. She let Suzie escape, was all she could think of. Her master would punish her to no end, so she ran through the door and used her key to open a hidden cabinet. Inside that cabinet was a crossbow and a quiver of arrows for the crossbow. This was her master's sporting crossbow, but she didn't care as it was the only weapon that was available to her and so she grabbed it. She ran toward the front door (the outside door) and tried to unlock it. But as she found out while pulling on it, the door opened unexpectedly. She surprisingly looked all around the door, knowing that she always locks this door, because it was the door to the outside, to the freedom they all desired. Then she thought back from earlier in the day when Suzie had supposedly forgotten her shirt and made her run back for it. Then she remembered that she had leaned down, so Weasel stooped down and felt around the door frame and that was when she felt the rock that kept the door partially open, and therefore unable to lock. She cursed Suzie for making her a fool, deliberately deceiving her. She was enraged and she loaded and cocked an arrow back in the crossbow. She ran out the front door, looking all around to see if she could find or track her whereabouts. Where had she gone, she fumed and she even yelled out loud, saying;

"How dare you, I trusted you, you traitor!" She stopped and listened but didn't hear anything at first so she ran to her left first, toward the quarry just to see if she had gone that way. She would find her and drag her back like a dog, by her hair for embarrassing her as such and humiliating her before her master. She would make Suzie pay dearly for her deceitfulness. Her face was beat red, her body was only half clothed (as she didn't care anymore about that), and her internal anger was boiling over from the way she was treated. She would never trust another girl again, that was it. She ran to the edge of the woodline, and stopped listening. Thankfully, the only other sounds out there were crickets chirping, frogs croaking , and the occasional owl hooting. She listened until she heard something, and then she heard something else coming from in front of her. She knew the approximate direction that Suzie was heading in and she would head her off and catch up with her to deal with her treachery. There was no forgiveness left in her now, and off she ran with the loaded crossbow swinging wildly in front of her.

Suzie started off moving fast but not running, and still she managed to hit tree limb after tree limb because of her one eye missing. Her spatial distancing was off for sure and she was paying dearly for it. She had been wacked by wayward low lying branches, jutting limbs from the ground, encapsulating and twisted vines, and raised tree roots. Every branch she hit hurt her as it not only tapped her head or body but actually thwacked it hard. She was going to be nursing some bruises when this was all said and done, she thought whimsically, like that really mattered in the grand scheme of things. She stopped suddenly when she heard something, and heard a distant voice yell out in the darkness. She panicked and started to pick up her pace, running even faster, which also put her at a better chance to trip over obstacles as she became desperate to get away. She knew now that she was being chased and it sounded like it was Weasel who was chasing her so diligently. She had double-crossed her and she was sure that Weasel wouldn't take that lightly, so she ran now with all her might and as fast her tired body would take her. She ran recklessly through the woods, tripping and falling countless times, but each time getting right back up and running again. She didn't have a flashlight and so she was seriously running blindly to her hope in freedom from her prison. It was then that she decided that she didn't want to go back no matter what and so she ran even faster with a firm resolve. She seemed to be making good distance when she turned to look back to see if she could see anyone chasing her, but in doing so she took her only good eye out of the equation and, therefore, by the time she turned around it was already too late. She ran smack into a low lying thick branch and it not only knocked her off her feet but also knocked the wind right out of her frail body. She couldn't yell or scream but the air left her lungs quicker than she could imagine and with such a high intensity. For at least two minutes, she lay there writhing around on the ground trying to get her air and her wits back about her. Her head was spinning from the lack of oxygen and also from the impact of her hitting the ground. She was dehydrated beyond compare, and also because she was relegated to eating hardly any food(easily less than 1000 calories a day), which didn't help either. The last aspect was the fact that she was so out of shape, because of her lack of physical activity for so long now. All this combined made it so hard for her to get back up again. She fought desperately as she rolled to her side and tried to rise up again, but only to fall down. She lay there without a clue on how to get her own body to listen to her again and cooperate so that she could get away. Then in the darkness she heard footsteps fast approaching and she even saw a small light from something in front of the person. She remained still as she could as she melded into the ground and became one with the foliage and the cover around her. She dared not move as the figure stopped some fifteen feet away from her, but luckily there were trees between her and the person chasing her, which was none other than Weasel. She could hear

193

Weasel's laborious breathing as she tried to catch her breath as well from the running that she did in pursuit, It was deathly quiet, save for Weasel's strained breathing, and then after looking around she darted off to her right, away from where Suzie was hiding, thankfully. Suzie waited another minute and then slowly got up, quietly listened, and then headed to her left, in the opposite direction that Weasel went. She made better time now as she covered ground easier and seemed to get her distance down with her one good eye. Her legs were still aching from the activity, but she willed past that discomfort to keep going. Unfortunately, she came to a spot where there was a drop off into a ravine, and so she had to deviate from her path. She didn't want to go back toward the compound again, so she headed right this time skirting the drop into the ravine and heading toward somewhere that she had no idea of. She kept running until she came to another drop off. This drop off looked like it ended in a body of water, like a quarry of some sort. She had nowhere else to go so she was thinking she would head back toward the compound and maybe down the gravel road to get to hopefully the main road. That was the plan and just as she stood up to run, she stopped dead in her tracks.

Standing directly in front of her was none other than the exhausted and pissed off Weasel. Weasel glared at her with a look of defiance, hatred, and stark lunacy. She didn't realize that she even had it in her to look as thus, but by god, she was facing that person now. Weasel had a crossbow in her hands and she was heaving heavily from the effort put in with chasing her around. Suzie looked at Weasel and smiled, but there was no smile back, there was only a look of angst and vexation. She may have pushed her luck too far, but she had to try. There was only do or die, she thought as the stand-off continued without Weasel saying a single word to her. Yet the way Weasel looked, it might be her time to die. Weasel suddenly raised the crossbow at Suzie and then Suzie got down on her knees with the body language of pleading not to pull the trigger. She then raised her hands in front of her and she was practically begging not to be shot, pleading one last time with all her effort. She raised her hands, placing them together as if praying for forgiveness. Weasel kept her in her line of sight on the pleading woman, for minutes, trying to decide whether to shoot her or not. It was a very tense few minutes, until finally after her better judgment, Weasel lowered the crossbow down. Suzie knelt there before the armed woman, not a few feet away unsure whether she should try to run again or just face the music of what she did. Either way she looked at it, it didn't bode well regarding a good ending, but she also didn't want to be tortured anymore, either. Still, she figured that this may be her only chance, but she was at a standstill as to what to do. The deathly quietness was overwhelming as Suzie was debating what to do and Weasel was waiting to see what Suzie's reaction was, as to what she will do next. It was a quandary both women found themselves in, that is until Weasel finally spoke up, after she also slowed her breathing down from gasping for air. Weasel said plainly and quite definitively;

"You used me! How dare you! I treated you with nothing but love and respect and this is how you repay me, you little deceitful wench! You...USED....me!" Weasel shook her head in disbelief and anger. Suzie just looked at her and cocked her head as if to say, well that's how the cookie crumbles. Weasel dropped the crossbow further down but still out in front of her. She started to walk toward the kneeling Suzie to reprimand her not just verbally but physically as well. Suzie knelt there prepared to take whatever it is that this frail woman would do to her. She was not afraid, not anymore! Weasel took two steps and then she stumbled on a raised root and incidentally started to fall. In the meantime, her fingers naturally squeezed the crossbow to keep a grip on it, but unfortunately she pulled the trigger and the nocked arrow released with a thunk and then there was a thud. After falling down, Weasel looked up toward Suzie, and what she saw made her immediately start crying. There kneeling before the fallen Weasel was Suzie, but with an arrow sticking out of her chest. Suzie looked at Weasel in disbelief before falling backwards and landing in a horrible contortionist position. Weasel started to run to her lover, to her friend because she wanted to hug her immediately for comfort. She dropped the crossbow like it was on fire, and then knelt down holding her friend's head in her arms, saying;

"No, no ,no, no, no, please NOOOOOO!" She screamed in agony at what had just happened. She had literally shot Suzie, her friend and her lover! She hadn't meant to do such, but that stupid tree root caused her to do it, she confessed aloud. She looked down upon the dying Suzie with tears in her eyes, and she wept like she never wept before.

Suzie had knelt down before the crossbow wielding Weasel, with a look of you got me in her eyes, but still a look of defiance as well. She had done her best and she was caught, that much was true, but she just didn't ever want to go back to that compound. She knelt before Weasel not in a show of mercy to keep her from killing her, but actually in a display and desire to actually kill her instead of letting her live. Weasel seemed to misunderstand what her intentions were, especially since she couldn't voice her thoughts anymore, with her tongue gone. She pleaded for Weasel to kill her and end her miserable life, because her life wasn't worth living any longer. She just wanted to die, die right here and right now! She watched the armed woman across from her lower her weapon with disappointment. Then just as Weasel took two steps, she stumbled unexpectedly and then there was a different metallic noise and Suzie looked down at her chest, just as a searing pain ripped into her. She gazed blankly at the crossbow bolt sticking out of her chest and then she looked up in amazement that what she truly wanted had actually happened. Weasel had shot her, square in the chest! Then she lost all control and fell backwards, contorting her body in an awkward position, not that she could change that any longer. Slowly her life started to drift away from her as Weasel ran over and tried to comfort her and apologize profusely for shooting her. Suzie looked up at her, right in her eyes and smiled. She was free, she was finally free! Then she left this world in the cover of darkness to end her misery.

She couldn't believe that she killed her friend. Suzie had finally stopped breathing, was deathly still, and slowly becoming colder with every passing minute. Weasel was in a world of shit now, with her master, she dismally thought. Still she cried over Suzie's body, completely devastated that this catastrophe had even occurred to such a woman she cared so much for. She never wished to end or snatch her life from her, she only wanted to scare her and then take her back where she belonged. This was not in her plan at all as she lay sprawled across the slain woman's body weeping uncontrollably. She couldn't believe how this had all transpired as it had unfolded this very night. Yes, she was mad at her, and yes she wanted to punish her, but she didn't want her gone from this world. What was she supposed to do now? She had no idea, no idea at all. It took her some ten minutes to figure out what she was going to do to rid herself of the body. She wouldn't be able to carry the dead Suzie back the entire distance to the compound and dispose of her the normal way her master does. And so she looked around, not sure what she was looking for at first, but then she thought of an idea that just may work. She left her flashlight and the crossbow near the deceased body and ran back to the compound for some tape and rope. Within a half hour she returned, and was able to find the body in the darkness because of the flashlight she had left on, beside the body. She now had a long length of rope and some duct tape to secure and use on the lifeless body. She quickly grabbed some larger rocks nearby, rolling them toward the edge of the drop off. After she had what she needed in rocks, she then rolled Suzie's dead body over beside the larger rocks and right near the edge. She first used the rope and tied each leg with a good sized boulder to it and then taped each one heavily, as well, so that it was secure as she could make it. Then she used one more slightly larger boulder, after sitting the body up some, around Suzie's belly and once again tied it securely. Of course, she finished with using the entire roll of duct tape around Suzie's midsection as well, so that the rock was completely covered and secure as all get out. Then once the body was completely weighted down, she painstakingly and slowly rolled Suzie's body over to the ledge and there she paused to catch her breath and also to whisper a little prayer of sorrow and hope that she was indeed in a better place now. After her little makeshift funeral service, she pushed the body over the ledge and it dropped twenty plus feet, splashing into the dark gloomy water that filled the old quarry. Within seconds the weight of the rocks pulled the body down from the surface and into the deep murky cesspool of water that filled this abandoned place.

She remained kneeling and said another little lover's wish for Suzie to be at peace. Once that was complete, she came to the true realization that Suzie no longer existed in this world and now her body was officially gone as well. Weasel then stood up after her exhaustive effort and wept another thirty some minutes or longer, before finally turning around, picking up her gear, and heading back to the compound, her home. This was not a good night at all, she thought as she tiredly lumbered back to her own room to sleep by herself once again. Her womanly lover was gone from this earth, and she was not happy about her actions that contributed to the untimely demise of Suzie. She lay there in her bed trying to get comfortable, but she couldn't because she had gotten so used to snuggling up to Suzie that being alone was now just not good enough. She tossed and turned as she tried to conjure up what to tell her master, about the late Suzie, when he did finally return. Her own life was now in limbo as she contemplated what may happen to her now. She had never interfered with her master's agenda with his collection, and now that is what just had occurred, to her melancholia. She had no easy answers for quite some time and she had no excuse other than she loved Suzie so much that she wanted to make her happy with the last days of her life, by giving her some leeway and some sunshine. She knew that her master had his own agenda (as always), but Suzie would be put down soon regardless, and that was the honest truth of the matter. She just had to try and convince her master that she was the victim and maybe explain how Suzie had taken advantage of her and hurt her so that she could finally escape, and then she had to ultimately kill her for that treasonous act. Yes, that was it! That was her reasoning! She just had to explain it in a fashion that made her not look like an idiot and a dolt, but as an innocent victim and then, of course, a very resourceful henchwoman.

Chapter Fifteen

Daily life continued on the compound and Weasel remained doing what she must to keep things afloat and she continued to take Teresa outside for some sunshine or rain or whatever, just to experience life again. She was still sad everyday about the loss of Suzie. At least once every other day, she would go back to the site where she had committed Suzie's body to the water and to revisit her, in a sense. She would sit there and talk with her like she was still around, like she was sitting right in front of her. She contemplated whether she was losing her mind over this but she didn't care at this point, so she kept doing what she thought was the right thing to do and also what felt right. She grieved and lamented daily for her lost friend, her missed lover, and her snuggle buddy. One of the days, after everything was done, she nearly went to the sleeping Teresa and she had the desire to cuddle up to her, but in a moment's notice she changed her mind. At that moment, she decided that she didn't want to cheapen what she had with Suzie and therefore she remained loyal to her memory, deciding not to convolute it in any way. Because of that decision, she continued to mope around with her chores and every night she wound up sleeping all alone, much to her chagrin. She had an idea that her master might be watching her and even the entire debacle, but she still had her story straight and she made sure she would stick to it, when the time would come for him to confront her about the incident. One particular day, one of the refrigerators broke down and stopped working, she found out when she checked the temperature of it. She carefully removed the plastic cartons that were still in this unit and she moved them to a different unit. She was careful not to upset, drop, or ruin them in any way. She knew that these items were his pride and joy and she would not do anything to upset that aspect of her job. Once that was done, she tried to move the old broken down fridge, but she could not, even with a dolly. It was too cumbersome for her, so she just closed it and labeled it with tape that it was broken. Then she went about packing some not needed items as he had instructed her before he had left for his trip. She had put it off, but she knew she had to get it down before he got back. She found herself dreaming excessively since Suzie was gone, now. Sadly, she remembered those horrible dreams also and she kept reliving over and over again the events that fateful night, that fateful night that Suzie left this world. She woke up many times either in a cold sweat or screaming from the night terrors. Many times in her dreams, the events played out differently, and with her dying instead of Suzie. So those nightmares that arose with that subject matter usually left her wide awake the remainder of the night. She was sleeping less and less and she was becoming more of a zombie as the days wore on. Eventually one day she didn't even have the strength to get out of her bed, until much later in the day. She had to kick this funk, but she just couldn't. She still took care of Teresa, but her heart wasn't in it anymore and soon, she stopped taking her outside for the daily breaks from her cell. Time was starting to stand still for Weasel as she started to sink into a deep depression. The meals she was giving Teresa were minimalistic at best, and becoming less and less. Teresa tried to engage her, but she waved her off and instead continued down her deep spiral of chaotic self-absorbed depression.

This behavior continued for about a week, until one day her master showed back up again to continue his work in this area a little longer. He came back and saw the disarray and deplorable conditions that Weasel had let the place go to, and he went off on her immediately. He pulled her aside and started yelling at her as soon as he got a quick look around, saying to her;

"Seriously? Was this so hard for you? You are a complete oaf and a worthless sham of a person! Why did I ever think you could do this job, without me here? You obviously can't! You will be punished for this …. This behavior and slothfulness that you have brought upon my treasures!" He ushered someone inside and put them in a holding cell cage, just outside his room, that was locked away from her. She assumed that he had brought someone home with him from around the new area that he would use for his next location. He didn't tell her anything and instead went about doing what he had to do. He checked everything, not once but twice, from top to bottom, fixing things as he went and trying to figure out what needed to be done first. Finally, after he took the first few days and a half to fix everything to his standards, he started to take a tour of the cages and see how his ladies were doing. He visited Teresa first and saw how much weight she had lost, so he gave her nutritional drinks to supplement her meals, since his henchwoman had done such a horrible job in his absence. Finally, he walked into the room that housed Suzie's cage and he didn't see her. He stood there not being able to speak and he was furious. Had she escaped? Had Weasel let her go? What the hell happened here???? Again he went to find Weasel, as he was beyond furious and he found her lamenting in her room, curled up in a ball, like a canine that knows it did something wrong and trying to cower away from verbal or physical punishment. He looked at her, wriggled his finger at her, telling her;

"What did you do? Where is Suzie?" Weasel had the story ready to go for weeks, but now that this time was here, she couldn't say a word. Her tongue was tied and she had severe cottonmouth, so she could do nothing but look down.He asked again;

"What did you do with her? Did she escape? Speak for yourself or so help me God, I will end your life in two seconds!! Speak, wench, speak to me!!" He verbally screamed at her. She finally started to say something, but she still kept her eyes in a downward cast, not daring to look him in the face. She responded with;

"Sh..ee..... Escaped, got....aw...ay...fro....mm me......" she paused for a moment and then continued with her original story. "She used me, tricked me, and ultimately she paid for her foolishness. I killed her." Those last words shocked him immensely, because he didn't think that Weasel had it in her. Maybe she would be a good one eventually, considering her cleanliness downfall issues. Well, now that made sense why she let things go, she was both embarrassed and humiliated that she had to do such an act, obviously, from her behavior. She even regretted it, but she did what she had to do to protect him, to protect them both. He eased his angst toward her but he quickly retorted, saying;

"Well what did you do with the body, if you really killed her? Could it be found or traced back to us? Do I have to follow up or is it truly taken care of?" Weasel just looked up and walked out of the room and she curled her finger , relaying him to follow her. She walked out of the compound and she kept walking into the woods, toward the quarry. He grabbed his knife and his gun out of his vehicle and he quickly caught up to her, following her to where she disposed of Suzie's body. They walked through the woods and to a spot where there was a ledge, one he knew quite well from coming here himself at times. She stopped at the edge of the drop off and she pointed down, down into the cold murky water. He looked over the ledge and then asked her;

"Is this where you disposed of her body?" Weasel shook her dejected head in a downward motion, not looking her master in his eyes. "Did it bother you that you killed her?" She also shook her head again in the same motion. "Did you love her?" She also shook her head in a yes motion, but only after a slight hesitation for about twenty seconds. "Thank you for disposing of her body, but there will be repercussions for not following my guidelines and rules. Do you understand that?" She absently shook her head once more and then she dejectedly started walking back to the compound. He stood there a little longer, hoping that the body will not come up to the surface anytime soon, at least not till after they are out of the area, for good. He would come up with a punishment for Weasel, for her insolence and her actions, which could have caused him to get caught by the police. She will pay for her behavior, he thought to himself as he started walking back to the compound, following her at a distance. There was always a penance for bad behavior, no matter who it is, he said aloud but to himself.

Meanwhile back in town, the police department was very busy. Yes, they still hadn't found any of the missing girls, but they were busy with a bad crime spree. Some out-of-towners came into the community and started breaking and entering not only unlocked cars(which wasn't uncommon in this small town), but also some homes as well, especially unoccupied vacation homes. All in all, they arrested some 6 juveniles (three being female gender), two adults, and even one senior adult. Odd as it was, the senior ended up being the driver most of the time and pointed out which places were the best ones to steal from. It was a big to-do in this small community, but they were able to successfully shut the crime circuit down and recover most of the stolen goods. There was some jewelry that still remained missing and at large, but overall it was a successful collaboration and coordination of both sections of the town, joint task force from across state lines, from both adjoining towns. The romance between Linda and Tom still remained intact and was growing in strength, as they even talked about the possibility of living together full time, which was a big step for both of them. At the end of the week, Tom's daughter made a quasi surprise visit to town to see her father. She came and brought with her, her current girlfriend and sweetheart Dahlia. Even she could see the positive changes that Linda and their relationship had on her father. He was laughing more than he had in years, smiling everyday now, and just had such a lighter heart. On one such outing where Tom, Linda, his daughter, and Dahlia went out together, for something to eat, Karly (his daughter) gave Linda a big hug and a kiss on the cheek, whispering to her;

"Thank you for bringing my father back to the land of the living!"

"Sweetheart, we saved each other. We were both in a funk in our lives and this relationship is an attestation of the suffering we had both endured over time. I thank your father daily for his love and for his addition to my life." Karly smiled immediately with that response, and then Linda asked her;

"So tell me about you and Dahlia? Is it pretty serious?" Karly beamed at Linda and shook her head yes. "So wonderful and happy for the both of you. You both seem happy together, and that is all that matters!" At about that time Dahlia came over and kissed Karly on the cheek with a little embrace. Linda smiled at the love in the room. They had gotten a table, as Tom had waited for it, while the girls were talking. They were escorted to their table by the manager of the Steak and Bake Grill. Once seated they scoured the menu looking for a good selection of food for the evening meal. Dahlia was a vegetarian, but the nice thing about the Steak and Bake is that they had vegetarian selections as well, so she paroosed those choices while everyone else was looking for their selection of meat choice. Tom and Linda ordered the filet mignon steak, the baked potato, and a side of seasoned vegetables, and a small salad for a starter also. Karly ordered the chicken parmesan, with a double portion of the medley of vegetables, and a small salad to start as well. Dahlia ordered the eggplant parmesan and followed with the order of vegetables and salad like her sweetheart ordered. Tom then ordered a bottle of wine to go around, while the girls (Karly and Dahlia) got a fruity cocktail to start. The talk was nice and flowed easily, as well as the laughter and the smiles also. They had a marvelous evening together in the enjoyment of food and with the genuine company also. They even ordered a shared dessert for all of them to enjoy which was a warm peach cobbler with some ice cream on the side. Once they finished their meal, they were all filled enough to stop eating but not overly full that they had to open up their top button on their pants. As they were leaving, Tom overheard a customer ask a waitress about Cheyenne. He listened lightly as they were standing up to leave, and he took his time as he heard the conversation go like this;

"Where is the ever bubbly Cheyenne, I haven't seen her here tonight?" The male customer asked casually to his waitress serving him.

"Well Cheyenne went to stay with her grams and pappa's in Ohio, I think, after the incident."

"The incident? Oh no what happened to her? I hope she is okay?" The wide eyed customer asked casually.

"Yes, she is doing okay, I just talked to her the other day. She is in good spirits, since the attempted rape."

"Oh no, I am so sorry to hear that. She is such a sweet girl. What a shame! What is this world coming to, I tell you."

"I agree, and I will let her know you asked about her. What will you have then to eat?"

"Well thank you, tell her my prayers are with her. I think I will have the medium rare T bone steak, mashed potatoes, and then some shrimp and grits as well, on the side. Oh and a sweet tea. Thank you, Evelyn." He said as he flashed his smile at her. She smiled back and went to place his order. Tom had since walked away, and as he walked he stopped Evelyn who was walking in the same direction, asking her;

"Who is that man who asked about Cheyenne? Sorry I am Detective Tom Royce, by the way."

"Well he is a regular, usually comes in here once a week, but I hadn't seen him in awhile. A really nice and generous man, always tips nicely and is pleasant as can be. I can't remember his name, but Cheyenne always talked about how nice he was to her." she said with a questioning look at Tom. Tom looked back at the man, who had glanced his way, and so he broke it off with Evelyn, saying to her;

"Okay, thank you, I appreciate it. Just wondering as I think I have seen him before, but … oh nevermind. Thank you, have a good night." With that he left but made a mental note of the stranger that he wasn't aware of. At this point he was suspicious of anyone whom he didn't know concerning the missing girls. Then again, it could just be as Evelyn said, a nice man who just enjoys a night out alone. He walked out with Linda and the girls, and then they drove closer to downtown and then decided to walk downtown a little as it was such a nice evening. Karly and Dahlia went their way and Tom and Linda went their way, each spending time alone with their loved one, walking, snuggling, and sharing a nice personal moment for the ending of a perfect evening.

The next few days were amazing and a whirlwind of activity as Tom was able to spend some quality time with his daughter and her significant other, sharing and just being together, which was the first time in quite some time. Even Tom could see how happy his daughter was with the new rejuvenated side of him that she hadn't seen since her mom was around. He drove the girls around showing them some of the sights of the area that one, Karly didn't remember about and two, that Dahlia hadn't seen. It was a wonderful few days, but as usual it went too fast and soon the girls had to head back to their apartment that they shared together near their university. That day was a sad day for Tom and Linda as it was time for the girls to leave. He hugged his daughter for a long period of time, saying to her;

"Hey kiddo, you take care of yourself and of course take care of Dahlia, she is a wonderful woman and so happy you have found love in each other. I love you!"

" I love you too, dad! And let me tell you, you and Linda are perfect together, so don't mess this up!" She said the last part with a crooked smile and a little laugh.

"I promise I won't! She is an amazing woman and I love her dearly!" Those last words made Karly's eyes tear up some and she hugged her father one more time before leaving. Tom also hugged Dahlia, saying to her;

"Thank you for taking care of my daughter and you are welcome here anytime. You are an amazing woman and I am honored to meet you." Dahlia hugged Tom like it was her own father, which she didn't have around anymore due to his untimely death some five years ago. At the same time Karly was embracing Linda with a mother/daughter type hug. There were tears in both women's eyes when they broke off. With that the two girls got back into their vehicle and headed off down the road. They waved as they left down the road, Tom and Linda were holding one another in a lover's embrace and waving at the disappearing car. Later in the vehicle, Dahlia looked over at Karly and said to her;

"Sweetheart, I just love your dad! He is the best! You are so lucky." Karly smiled at the nice words about her father and she agreed. He was back and Linda was the reason. They seemed perfect together and she so wanted this to work, for both of them. She held her girlfriend's hand as they settled in for the long drive back to their home.

That night, that fateful night when 'Todd' went to the Steak and Bake Grill, he enquired about Cheyenne and that was when he found out the horrible news. The news that someone, some group of guys tried to rape his girl that he wanted for his collection. He remained calm on the outside, but deep inside all he could think of was that if he had grabbed her, then that incident wouldn't have happened. She would be safe and secure with him, which was much better than being raped, or so he believed. He just couldn't believe that someone would do that to his girl! This world was truly insane. Have people not have any decency, he thought dismally to himself. The only thing he did notice that night was the Detective paying him notice. He knew of the Detective and he usually was pretty good at discerning other's intentions, but when the Detective asked his waitress, Evelyn, about him, or so he assumed in his best way of telling. He was also a lip reader, and so the Detective was not very good at hiding his intentions, his questions or his mouth so he was able to discern pretty much what he was asking the girl. Somehow he had gotten on the Detectvie's radar when he asked about Cheyenne, and in doing so he had to tread carefully and be attentive not to cross any lines. He usually was good at blending in, but now he was sticking out a little which was not good for his plan, his needs, and his long term goals. So he left the restaurant, and drove off, but backtracked not once, not twice, but three times so that he made sure he wasn't followed before heading back to the compound. Finally he was able to drive back and he parked his vehicle, and went inside to attend and check on things. He went into the side room first and watched the girl that he had in a smaller cage in a small anteroom off his main quarters. There inside the cage was a shy and quite timid girl in plain clothes, very plain clothes. When he was checking out his new area, on the way back down south to his present place, he found a girl walking alongside the road. He picked her up, but not till there was some convincing on his part. This girl's name was Rebekah, and she had just had a disagreement with her parents and she wanted to run away from home. So she was walking down the road, in her simple dress, her bonnet, and her plain and bulky shoes. Rebekah was an Amish girl and that was something he was looking for for his next collection. He couldn't believe his luck, perfect timing, perfect place, and in the perfect conditions. He had promised to drive her to her secular friend's house, just outside of town, but soon she realized that wasn't happening. She threatened to jump out of the vehicle, but he was too fast, as he had already a drawn up syringe and he got her in the neck, just as she struggled to get away. He expertly hit the external jugular with the needle and injected the white liquid. Not long after, she was down for the count. He loosely tied her up and placed a blanket over her to mimic her sleeping in case anyone looked in his vehicle when he had to stop for gas. He drove like that and injected her some more when she started to stir, but not too much as he didn't want to over sedate her or kill her with too much medication. So now he had his little Amish girl and she was a true gem. Here he lost Suzie and he gained someone even better: someone that wasn't as stubborn, difficult, and headstrong as Suzie. This girl was meek and easy to control because of her upbringing. So she did exactly what she was told, much to his happiness. She was one he wouldn't have to torture and try to get control of. That was a nice unexpected blessing for sure. He gave up on the girl Cheyenne now, as she was well out of reach and her name was bringing him to light. So he gave up on her and started to think how to get out of here in a timely manner so as not to be caught or get someone after him. He also decided that if he needed to get groceries or supplies that he would go a few hours away in another town to get them instead of taking a chance with this town anymore. He would have to speed up his timeline, just because of the Detective's wandering eyes and over-stimulated thinking mind. One always had to be safe, that was for sure. And besides he now had his Teresa and his Rebekah, two lovely specimens with their own beauty in their own perspective. He was happy and he was content with his collection. He did rounds around the compound to make sure all was okay and he stopped at one of his fridges and opened it up, revealing egg cartons inside, amongst other things in jars. Still he was there for the egg cartons, and so he pulled one out and opened it up, revealing the contents inside. He smiled at his collection and he enjoyed the very aspect of looking at his handi-work with so many girls. He inspected each specimen and happily placed it back down again. He closed it back up and continued checking every carton that he had in there. Then he checked the jars as well, and was content that all looked good. He smiled as he closed the fridge door and was content with what he had. He went back to his control room and checked on things before finally crawling into his bed in one of the adjoining rooms, and fell asleep. It has been a long few weeks and he needed some good sleep, because the upcoming months were going to be busy, very busy.

That night Tom tossed and turned in bed as he slept beside Linda. Eventually he got up and walked outside on the porch, so that he didn't wake up his sweetheart with his poor sleep that night. He stood outside listening to the crickets chirp and the cicada's hum their respective noises as his mind was deep in thought. He drank some water from a glass, and he was present in body, but his mind was a million miles away. He stood there not paying attention to anything around him, as even the insect noises cleared his mechanism as he focused on what he was thinking. He was so caught up in his thoughts as the gears in his mind were churning that he didn't even hear Linda come up behind him. She walked up and hugged him from behind, which startled him out of his mental barrage of thoughts, and he jumped a second. Linda looked at her lover with concern as he was that far into thought he jumped at her touch, which made her a little concerned. She spoke to him saying;

"I am sorry I startled you, sweetheart. I just woke up and noticed you weren't in bed any longer and so I came to find you and make sure you were okay?" Tom looked at her with apologetic eyes, and he responded with;

"I am sorry too. I just couldn't sleep and I didn't wish to wake you up, so I came out here to think, is all. I didn't mean to jump either but my mind was a million miles away, you know work and all....."

"I understand, darling. How about I sit up with you a little bit and let's enjoy the night time and the stars together." He looked up and did truly see the stars now, as he hadn't seen them when he first came outside because of how deep in thought his mind was. He was amazed as the stars were so brilliant and beautiful that night as there was hardly a cloud in the sky. They pulled reclining chairs up, setting them as close as they could be, and together they sat down in the recliner to start their star gazing. They held hands as they watched the early morning sky. They even saw quite a few shooting stars, but she definitely saw more than he did. He always seemed to be looking in the wrong direction when they shot across the sky. She saw twice as many as he did, but they had done this before and it yielded the same results. He was just happy to spend even these types of sleepless nights with his sweetie. Eventually she fell asleep in the chair and he went and got a blanket and covered them both up as they remained outside for a little longer. He watched Linda sleep a little and then his mind wandered again, back to the case at hand. His mind was churning ideas, until he finally fell asleep from exhaustion some hour and a half after his beloved had fallen asleep. He had to crack this case, and that was that.

Back at the compound that same night, 'Todd' was making 'Todd' disappear. He riffled through his identifications and pulled out a George, George Misken. His new identity would be that since that night at the restaurant, and so he was afraid that he was going to have to ramp up his timeline on his departure date. Too many things had occurred and he seemed to be over-extending his stay here, so he had to do what was best for his way of life. Weasel had done a cardinal sin and so he was going to have to replace her too and he may even possibly make her a scapegoat, which would be a way for him to keep his nose out of trouble. If he planned it right, he may be able to swing that. But in the meantime he was shredding all his documents of 'Todd', and opening up new accounts with George's identity, in the form of online bank accounts, and pertinent documents. Those documents would include shell companies which have no source, but one that exists as a separate entity on paper/ online without ever really meeting the true owner of it. He would set up secondary shell companies as well, which again would lead to nowhere but even have federal tax ID numbers. Geroge had darker hair and a beard, so since he hadn't shaved in a few days, he was working on the beard. He just had to dye his hair now as well. This was all part of the 'act' and to play another part with his new identity. He knew the game and he knew how to play the game to get the final result that he so desired. This was all part of the intricacies of his collective world and he knew all the ins and outs by this time, and he knew what mistakes not to make. He had seen his cronies go down in a blaze of glory because of small infractions or issues with minor details, but he would never make those mistakes, as that would mean the end of his life as he knew it. So he worked diligently at making an empty nest of falsehoods that he stood behind, but stood behind his invisible shield so as not to be pinned to something that he had done. He had seen other collectors be glory hounds and end up being foolish in their acts and foolhardy in their behaviors, causing them to be caught and prosecuted for their crimes. He vowed never to make such boastful statements nor act in such a manner. To do so, is actually foolhardy and being a dolt. He knew his limitations and he paid attention to all things, so that he wouldn't find himself in such a predicament. He has been doing this for such an extended period of time, and he is also seasoned, which makes surviving even easier, or so he thought. He made sure his escape routes were indeed routes of freedom and not of being cornered or trapped. That is the only reason he had made it this long successfully, and he wasn't about to change his game plan now. After he shredded all the old documents concerning 'Todd', he would then burn them in a small stove he had, that gets hotter than most and would incinerate paper to nothing but tiny ash particles. He cleaned hard drives off of secondary and tertiary computers, and absolved everything he didn't need. He started to make a pile to load things up that he may need yet, but it wasn't half the size that the burn pile was. He knew his move was coming soon and he was nearly ready to depart from this area, for good!

He continued to go about doing what he had to, and then he thought of his new girl, Rebekah. He really saw some potential in her and he wanted to explore that possibility to see if she would be as he thought and hoped she would be. First, though, he had to prepare her for being his next accomplice, caretaker of his girls, and mentor. She was meek but she was also steadfast. She was timid but she seemed to have a fierceness about her that was just dormant. He believed that she would definitely do what she was told, because of her upbringing in that religious order and how they listen to their men without question. She would have to get used to using such amenities as electricity, lights, a computer, and such forth to be able to do many of the aspects of the job that he required of his henchwomen. She may be slow to start, because of her lack of knowledge in some areas, especially with technology, but he knew she could get there with the right guidance and the right person to lead her, such as he. He would teach her all about Weasel's job without letting Weasel know, just as he had kept her out of the loop of his new place and what he had in store for this new and fresh girl. He had used Weasel about as much as he could but she had made dear mistakes and he wouldn't tolerate that. For that reason, he would now work on moving her onto her next task, which is party to the deceased, or so he quipped thinking about it. After some time, he finally finished destroying everything that he could to this point, and he kept his new identity in the portfolio called, 'New Beginnings. He did that so when he went to his next place with his new identity, his new compound, his new henchwoman, and his new selection of women, this entire new area would open for his choosing! It was a win-win situation no matter how he looked at it. A new area was a new life and that was another chance at the continuation of his dream, his collecting dream.

Chapter Sixteen

After such a busy work week, Tom was finally able to think about the missing persons case. He hadn't been previously since one of the officers was on a vacation, so they were short staffed. He had to pick up evening calls, make daily rounds, and attend to other issues outside his normal detective work. Then to add to the complications of that issue, another officer was out for a small injury for a few days, so they were two people down for nearly a week. So, unfortunately, because of that he had to put his duties and tasks on the back burner for the better good. Eventually he did get back to his work as one day he sat there staring at his whiteboard, the tacks, the pictures, and the strings which had a question mark at the end of each one, because he had no legitimate answers. He stared at the board longer and longer, until he started getting a headache and so he grabbed some tylenol out of his drawer and walked to get some more coffee. After grabbing a fresh cup from the new pot, he walked back and sat back down, sitting and looking into oblivion as he tried to answer questions he didn't know yet. Then he thought to himself, he needs to start to try to think like a predator. What if the person was stalking these girls long before even he or anyone else could think it possible? What if the person or persons was living close by whether a nearby town or reclusive spot, taking these girls? What if he lived right under their nose, in his town? What if it was someone that he knew on a day to day basis? What if he was collecting for the sake of collecting? He figured the last one was a stretch, but it could happen anywhere, nowadays! What if it was a member of this community? Then he started thinking about everyone that he knew of, the ones that stood out as odd or peculiar, and already he had a list of at least five to ten names. There were so many unknowns, so many questions, but he really needed to start to move, instead of waiting for something to fall in his lap. He was honestly hoping that the person or persons who were taking these girls would trip up and make a mistake, but at this point he needed to force it to see if he could cause the person to make a mistake. He always remembered a favorite quote of his grandfather's back when he was a child. He didn't get it back then, but when he got older it clicked. His grandfather used to say, 'that chance favors the prepared mind'. Well by god, he was going to get prepared and start pushing the envelope and maybe, just maybe, chance will be on their side.

He was going to start with all the local motels and hotels seeing if they had seen anything odd or suspicious in the hopes that something may break. From there he would start looking into more secluded areas, that could be a possible start site for an abducting crime spree. He knew eventually that if he kept poking, he would cause a ripple and causing a ripple would lead to an even bigger ripple and then something may rear its ugly face in his direction. Time to rock that boat, he said with renewed interest and desire. He finished up making a list of possible places to investigate, starting off with hotels and motels, and he even looked across the state lines at the neighboring sister town of theirs, listing ones from there as well.He would contact the department over there and have them start to look for possible subjects or places as well. Now that he had his plan, he only had to implement it, and have the time to, given their current staffing issues.

Meanwhile back at the compound, 'George' was moving objects from one refrigerator unit to another to consolidate his prizes. He also started putting small incendiary charges on some of the appliances and units that he didn't use anymore so that when the time came, he would start a fire and burn this place down to the ground, wiping out most or all of the evidence. He also went over to some of the main and alternate electrical panels and started placing small devices there as well to accelerate the torching of the compound. He did this all under the nose of Weasel so that she didn't get wind of what was happening, because who knows what that insane girl would do if she knew the truth. He decided to dump the car, by going around to the other end of the quarry and driving it into that side, letting it sink to the bottom. Yet, he would do so only after he thoroughly cleaned and removed all traceable fingerprints that were on or in it, removing license plates and even removing the VIN plate and identification stickers on the vehicle. In doing so, he completely sterilized the vehicle of it being related or matched up with him. He also went into another town some 100 miles away and sold the box van, replacing it with an older camper style van, which of course he paid the difference with cash. He did what he had to do to cover his tracks and start to move things along, as he felt it was right to do.

Her master made Weasel stay in Suzie's old cell a few nights for her transgression and negligence that led to Suzie's early demise. He just wanted her to know that all misdeeds or offenses are still punishable, no matter who you were. She took it with a grain of sand and accepted the punishment with a happy heart. She actually enjoyed being in the same bed as Suzie had been in because she was able to take in her scent, her smell on the bedding and just the presence of her being there. This is where her lover slept, her lover cried, and her lover made her devious escape. She really did miss her and she regretted the catastrophic events that led to her untimely demise. She, herself, wept while she lie in the cell thinking of all the wonderful times that they spent together cuddling and sharing one another. She even swore she could feel the slight roughness of her dry supple lips on her forehead, when she had kissed her before. She didn't care about that because she imagined what they felt like moist and on her own lips. She traced her finger over her own lips, as it it was Suzie's lips touching them, and not her own finger. She remembered how amazing Suzie's body felt, when her own naked body nestled up to it, keeping them both warm and comfy. She also dreamed of what it felt like to touch her at other spots as well, most intimate spots that she yearned to touch, but never got the chance to, sadly. She just wasn't brave enough to try and take a chance, for fear that she would have been swatted away or punched from the effort. She regretted not taking that chance to feel her soft skin next to her own as they embraced in a lover's twisted clinch. She could imagine touching her toned leg, her svelte waist, and her slender but strong arms as they would engulf her and she would do whatever Suzie had wanted her to do. That was what she wanted, to be at her beck and call and do whatever Suzie would desire of her to do. She wanted that, wanted that more than anything and now she will never have it, unfortunately. No matter what, she would have made Suzie happy, doing for her anything and everything and she would be whatever, whomever, and dress however she wanted of her. It would have been perfect! She would have loved her intimately until her last breath, and would have loved her till death do them part. Yet even then, she truly believed in the afterlife, she would have been with her loves. She would be holding hands with Jade and with Suzie. They had both crossed over to the afterlife and now someday it will be her turn, and when it is she will accept it with open arms, an open heart, and a willing spirit. She couldn't wait for that day to be new to those who are the nearest and dearest to her in this shamble of a life. 'One day soon', she said aloud as she cuddled up sniffing the bedding and enjoying every smell she could find of her beloved. One day soon, Suzie and Jade, one day soon!

One particular evening, Tom was winding down and enjoying a meal that he reheated that was left in the fridge by his sweetheart, Linda. Linda was working the evening shift and so they were unable to eat together tonight, so he instead enjoyed the delicious meal that she had made and prepped for him. Just as he pulled out the warmed up meal, poured himself a small glass of wine, and grabbed his utensils, his phone rang. He ignored it at first as he was so hungry, but then just as he got up to answer it, it stopped ringing. He looked at it and didn't recognize the number, so he figured it was a spam call and he walked back over to his still warm meal. He grabbed his fork, and took one bite of the appetizing linguini dish, and then his phone rang again. He looked once and then back down at his meal and decided to go grab the call. He reached his phone and answered, by saying;

"Hello, this is Tom, How can I help ya?"

"Tom, is this Tom? This is Dahlia…." She said with anguish in her voice. Tom quickly responded back, saying;

"Dahlia? What is it? Are you ok? Is Karly okay? Please speak freely." Dahlia stopped momentarily to clear her throat and try to speak more coherently so he could discern what she had to say. She responded with;

"Sorry I am calling…so …late… but …there …has…… been …an ……accident….." She stopped another second to pause for clarity and then continued. "We were in Karly's vehicle and a truck ran a red light, anyway….. Karly is in the Intensive Care unit and being monitored for a brain bleed. She has some injuries, but at this point she is in critical condition. I am sorry! " She stated with obvious and true sadness in her voice. He waited a few seconds to make sure she was done at the moment and then he asked her;

"Are you okay?"

"Yes I am, I just have some scrapes and minor superficial injuries, but overall I am okay, thank you."

"Okay, listen please. Will you stay with her tonight and I will be leaving here shortly to come to you. Which hospital is she at? I will drive overnight to come to both of you. Is there anything I can bring to you or for you?"

"Yes, I will stay with her, there is no question about that. We are at the Triad University Hospital, fourth floor, ICU, room 6. No, I am good for now, thank you kindly for asking. Thank you so much for coming up, we both need you here." After hearing those words, he knew he had to go.

"I'll text you when I am close to arriving. Will see you soon, and thank you again Dahlia for being there for Karly." She hung up the phone after that and he went about getting a bag ready for his travels. He quickly texted Linda and she was concerned for Karly and Dahlia. He wanted her to go with him, but if he left there would be even fewer officers, so he knew he would have to go it alone, this trip. She asked him if they could meet on the edge of town so that she could give him a proper send off. He was happy with that and so decided to meet at the Rapid Fill-N-Go gas station on the way out of town. He took two quick bites of her meal and then put the rest in the fridge, not bothering to even waste the time to cover it up at this point. He finished packing his bag, grabbed everything else he needed and then he left the house, to start his journey north.

He rushed down the road toward the gas station where Linda and he were to meet and in the distance he already saw her patrol car sitting there waiting for him. He pulled in and as soon as he exited his vehicle, they embraced. She started asking questions, some of which he didn't know the answer to at this point. He told her what he knew and that was the best for now. She understood and just asked that he keep her updated. She apologized profusely for not being able to go with him, just as much as he asked her to forgive him for not taking her. They both knew the circumstances were out of their control, so they left it at that. She hugged and kissed him passionately, but she also pushed him away so as not to get too comfy with their embrace and desire more. She wanted him to get going since it was such a long drive and it would be a sleepless night for him. She gave him a large fresh cup of coffee for his drive, and she blew him a kiss and told him to go, go to his daughter because she needed him. He smiled and thanked her for the wonderful woman that she was and then he got into his vehicle to head out of town. She waved at him as he drove away and down the dark lonely road he went. He drove the long drive, feeling tired at times, but thankfully he kept himself tanked off with fresh coffee. He had to stop for gas once and stop another time for a bathroom break and a refill on his coffee, but overall he was making some great time. The hours went by and by dawn he was in the same city as the university was where his daughter and Dahlia attended. He used his phone to locate where the hospital was and within twenty minutes he arrived, exhausted, sleepy, and still ready to see his dear daughter. He changed his shirt and attended to himself a little before going inside. In that time span he texted Dahlia to let her know that he had in fact arrived. She texted back saying she would meet him outside the ICU, at the waiting room. He responded that he would see her in a few minutes. He walked in, followed the directions and signs to where he needed to go and before long he was on the fourth floor and in front of the ICU doors. He heard a click and the doors opened, and out walked Dahlia. She immediately ran to him and hugged him in a daughterly embrace, like she had never hugged a man before. She was shaking as he could tell as he held her, and she wept on his shoulder. He did the best he could to comfort her, but overall he just allowed her to go through her emotions and let it out, which she did. He whispered to her;

"I am so ecstatic that you are ok and at least not in a hospital bed as well." After she let herself wet his shoulder from tears, she shakingly spoke up, saying;

"I was so scared to call you, at first, ...thinking you would..... be..... Angry......."

"No, not a chance, I am just thankful you did call and I am grateful that you are both still alive, and thank you so much for looking after our girl! She is lucky to have someone love her as you do!" He hugged her again and she accepted the show of love toward her with open arms. She looked at him and said;

"Karly is so lucky to have a father such as you. I am just as lucky to know you for who you are, a real man." Now, it was Tom's turn for his eyes suddenly teared up at the kind words Dahlia had said to him. He smiled and kissed her on the forehead. She smiled back, gave him a prepared nametag that she got from the nurses station and stuck it on his chest, right above the pocket of his shirt. She said to him;

"Now get in there and check on your daughter."

He smiled at her and the automatic doors opened to reveal a large twenty bed unit in a circular fashion. It seemed busy as ever as the nurses were walking by at a fast pace and off to do their tasks of taking care of their critically sick patients. He walked around the unit until he found bed 6 and he stopped at the doorway, looking inside at his daughter and what she had going on with her and what she was hooked up to. He immediately saw the scratches and bruises to her face, saw that she had a cast on the left arm, and then her left leg was up in the air with a metal apparatus around it. A nurse was walking by and he stopped her briefly, saying to her;

"I am sorry to bother you, Miss, but what is on my daughter's lower leg?"

"Well sir, no bother at all. What she has is called an external fixator, or an ex-fix as we call it. It is placed usually on a leg but over any area that has a severe break where the bones are crushed into smaller pieces. It stabilizes the leg and the area so that the bones can heal once more."

"Are there good results, recovering from such injuries, like prognosis?"

Yes sir, We have seen complete recovery in many patients. Sorry but I have to go, but I will send her nurse in to speak further with you. Good day, sir." And the nurse was off to attend to her own patient(s).

He walked inside the room and looked at his daughter. She definitely looked rough, but she was still breathing and he glanced up at the monitor in her room. He was relieved to see that her vital signs looked good, as he bent down and kissed her on her forehead. Then he sat down beside her in one of the available chairs and held her right hand in his. Her poor face had some bruises and cuts from glass, most likely from the windshield. He even picked a few stray pieces out of her hair that the staff hadn't gotten out yet. He looked at her arm in the fiberglass cast, winced at how painful it must be and then he looked down at her leg. The large metal piece around her lower leg had a spiral look and pins coming into her skin , probably attached to the viable bone. He was sure it was painful and he hoped that it wasn't too bad for her. He saw the many scratches and bruises that she obtained from the accident, but was so grateful that she still was alive. It could have been a lot worse. After a short period of time, a nurse walked in by the name of Amy and he asked her about his daughter and how she was fairing. Amy informed him that they were worried about a brain bleed from the impact on the glass, even though she did have a slight concussion from the impact as well. They did perform a Cat Scan on arrival and it was negative, but they were doing another one later today to make sure that she was in the clear. If the next one was negative and she was alert, she would move out to the floor and out of ICU. He smiled and thanked her for her time and the explanations. She left the room again after checking on Karly's leg and cast. Tom sat back down and held his daughter's hand for about an hour, and it was then that he decided that he needed something to eat in his system, since he really hadn't eaten anything since last night. He kissed his daughter's forehead once more before leaving the room and then he left the ICU. He found Dahlia sleeping peacefully and sitting up in a chair. He went over and gently shook her shoulder and she looked at him with hazy and sleepy eyes, as she was not fully awake yet. He said to her;

"How about we go to the cafeteria and grab something to eat?" He flashed his smile and she smiled as well and she started to say something, but he interrupted her, finishing off with;

"Young lady, that wasn't a request…" He smiled again and she got the hint. He helped her up and together they walked down to the cafeteria to rejuvenate their spirits and their depleted bodily stores.

They took the elevator downstairs and found the cafeteria only after two wrong turns and a little help from a passing phlebotomist. Once there, they grabbed their trays and stood in line until their turn so that they could get some good smelling and looking grub. Everything looked so delicious to their hungry eyes and famished stomachs, but they each got their own desires, and they even had vegetarian meat substitute for Dahlia, which was a nice plus. Once their plates were full, they grabbed some utensils, a drink, and a small pastry to finish up their breakfast tray to their delight. Tom paid per his desire too, and once again Dahlia thanked him for such a kind gesture. They sat down across from one another and immediately dug into their meal with renewed gusto. After they had consumed most of their meal, Tom decided he wished to know more about the accident and so he asked Dahlia what and how it had happened. She seemed like she didn't want to start or bring it back up, but he quickly added, to confront her, only if she wished to recant the events. She started off relating how it occurred and he listened intently, to every detail. They had enjoyed a nice day together and they had gone to a new coffee house, and then to do some light shopping , when they came up to an intersection. They had a green light so they continued driving forward to their destination, when out of nowhere, a jacked up truck ran a red light and caught them, with their vehicle going underneath it and getting crushed on the driver's side, more or less. The truck actually took off after it had hit them, and she had heard that they had caught the teenagers who were drunk, and were taken into custody. He was happy to hear that at least. She said she was terrified as it was a horrific scene and when she looked over and saw Karly, she honestly thought she was dead. Thankfully she wasn't and it did take the fire crew quite some time to cut her out of the vehicle, but eventually they did. She finished the recantation of her story with tears in her eyes, and so he got up from his seat and walked over and gave her another fatherly and supportive hug. She happily accepted and hugged him harder back. When she composed herself again, he collected their trays and disposed of the trash in the appropriate receptacles and then they went back upstairs again. She then confessed to him;

"I have to get to class and then I have an appointment to chat with Karly's advisor since she is in the hospital about her work and what to do. I must go for part of the day, but thank you so much for everything and for being the best dad and supportive person ever. I'll be back later this afternoon. She kissed him once more on the cheek and then she left the floor via elevator. He watched her go, amazed at how lucky his daughter was at having her in her life. He turned and went back inside the ICU to his daughter's room.

Once inside her room, he sat in the chair and before long, he fell asleep. He had been awake well over 28 hours at that point, and so it was inevitable. He slept soundly for quite some time and even the nurse brought a warm blanket for him, which only made him cozier than he already was. He slept until they came to take her down for the CT of her head, and then he quickly fell back asleep once she was gone. She came back to her bed and still he slept soundly after she had returned. It wasn't till Dahlia came back to visit that he woke up. She had brought him a fresh large cup of coffee, which once she stuck the cup under his nose, the aroma woke him up instantly. He smiled at her and thanked her for the kind and much needed gesture. Karly's eyes were still shut and it was then that he felt a vibration on his butt. 'Oh shit', he exclaimed aloud and he had totally forgotten about his phone and calling Linda. He excused himself and walked out of the ICU leaving Karly in the capable hands of her gf, Dahlia. Once he exited the ICU, he called Linda back, as he saw that he had three missed calls, and four unanswered texts(unanswered on his part). He called and the phone rang, within seconds, Linda answered, saying;

"Oh my goodness darling, is everything alright? I didn't hear from you, thought something was wrong, you gave me quite the fright. Is everything ok?"

" I am so sorry, my love. My brain is foggy today, and then I fell asleep in her room this afternoon. I am so sorry for not getting back to you. It was a complete oversight considering my tiredness this am. Yes everything is ok, so far."

"Well I am happy to hear that and I forgive you and understand what stresses you have been in. Is she awake yet?"

"No, she was sedated for a follow-up CT of her head to make sure that there is not a definitive bleed. Still waiting to hear back from that, but her vitals look good. She has a cast on her left arm and an external fixator on her left lower leg. So hopefully she will be okay. Dahlia is here and we have been taking shifts to be with her. I miss you, and I promise to keep you informed. Again I am sorry sweetie! I love you!"

"I love you too and no need to apologize any longer. Just keep me in the loop please and tell Dahlia she is loved and thought of, as well as Karly when she wakes up. Talk to you soon sweetie!"

"Yes, dearest, talk to you again soon." With that they hung up the phone and he went back inside the ICU, but before he entered the room, he saw a doctor leaving his daughter's room. He quickly stopped her, asking her for an update. She responded with;

"Well your daughter is doing wonderfully, and thankfully the CT scan came back negative so she just suffered a mild concussion with no subdural hematoma. We will continue to monitor her, but she will probably be moved to progressive care unit now as she is not as critical."

"Thank you for the update and the great news, but when will she wake up Doctor?" The doctor smiled and looked back inside the room and there was Karly with Dahlia, smiling and looking in his direction. He left the doctor's side without an additional thank you, and rushed into his daughter's room and gave her a gentle hug, and kissed her on her forehead. Karly smiled and thanked her dad for the attention and the love, but she was also a little overwhelmed at the attention. She smiled and thanked him for being there, and she looked past him for Linda, saying;

"Dad, where is Linda? Could she not make it?"

"Sorry, pipsqueak, but no we had staffing issues and she was unable to get away, but she was so upset that she couldn't be here with us and for you. Maybe we can video chat her later, she would appreciate that. If you feel up to it that is." She rolled her eyes at the nickname he used to call her when she was a little tike, but she took it in stride. He then pulled another chair up to her side as Dahlia was on the other side. He could see Karly was still tired so he didn't press any conversation. He just wanted to be there beside her, and that was more important than trivial talking. So they remained by her side as she fell asleep off and on throughout the day. Eventually it started to get late and he decided he needed to go crash at a proper place, like a hotel room. So he called around and found an extended stay hotel just ten minutes away from the hospital. He booked the room and gave Karly a last hug for the night, and also Dahlia who was only going to stay just a little longer before she had to leave as well. He left explicit instructions with the nurse to call him if anything changes, no matter what the time. She promised to as they were about to move her to her new room anyway which was on the same floor, just at the other end. He thanked nurse Amy for taking such good care of her, and he left to head toward the hotel.

The drive to the hotel was short and uneventful. He took his meager belongings with him and checked into his room. The front desk clerk checked him in and informed him of the indoor pool, the workout room, the balcony with his room, and the free breakfast. He thanked her kindly and dragged his weary body to his room. He stopped at the ice machine on the way to make sure it worked, which thankfully it did and then he went to his room, used his key card, and entered a luxurious room. The bathroom wax to the immediate right, with a kitchenette to the left as he entered. There was a mini fridge, some pots and pans, and even a small dishwasher for his use. He walked further in where he had a nice king sized bed and a large office area also. He didn't care too much about the television, but then again he wasn't the one to fall asleep in a quiet room, so he often kept it on for background noise. He went to the door and opened the balcony and it was a very nice view. He enjoyed that as it looked like there was a small park and a stream the hotel overlooked, which made the view worthwhile. He heard the sounds of the birds and the running water as he stood there, mesmerized by the melodious tones of nature. He eventually walked back inside the room, and went back to the bathroom to turn on the shower so he could refresh himself some. He turned the hot water on and got it to the perfect temperature that would feel wonderful for his worn out body, then he unclothed himself, and jumped into the refreshing shower. He took the longest shower he had taken in quite some time, enjoying every second of the water. Once he was finished washing himself, he just stood there, letting the water run over him without a care. The rejuvenating shower was just what he needed, and he even thought about visiting the pool, but he was too weary for that this evening,so maybe another day, he thought. Once done, he turned the television on low volume and he picked up his phone and checked in with Linda. He just texted her to see how she was doing. She mentioned that she was near exhaustion as well as it had been a long day at work. She had eaten previously and was already lying in bed, nearly to the point of falling asleep. They texted lightly and he informed her of the great news with Karly, and she was ecstatic that she was doing better and technically out of harm's way. She asked him if there was anything she could do for him, work related also. He thought for a second and then asked if she had the time to check all the outlying smaller motels and hotels to see if they had seen any weird activity from any of the customers. He was going out on a limb and he didn't know why, but he wanted to check those places first and foremost, and then go from there. She mentioned that she would start looking into it, and then there was a long pause. He figured she fell asleep on him, so he texted her a 'goodnight with love' and he left it at that. He saw a familiar cop movie that he hadn't seen in years and so he lay on the bed watching that before he fell asleep for the night. He rested peacefully and with minimal disturbances, which is some of the best sleep, in a bed, that he had experienced in quite some time.

The next six days were a whirlwind for Tom as he attended to his daughter, enjoyed time with Dahlia, and just took care of basic things that were needed of him. He went with Dahlia to find them a decent affordable used vehicle for them till the insurance figures out what they were going to do with their demolished car. They went to many used dealerships, but with no luck and then they went to a new car dealership that had certified pre-owned vehicles and they found something that was a decent price and both Dahlia and Karly liked. They were able to real time video their experience and went over the car's details and aspects as Karly still remained in the hospital. She was tickled they found a gorgeous car for the price they did and so Tom cosigned the loan with Dahlia, after he put a considerable amount down to help get the payments down. By the end of the week the girls were set and Karly was discharged from the hospital and sent home with visiting nurses to help her out with taking care of the ex-fix on her leg. Tom assisted them and made sure she was set and that was when he had to confess that he had to head out of town and back to his job, for now. Karly understood and she was sure that he desperately missed Linda as well, which he did but he didn't confess that aspect to her, she just knew. He gave hugs to both the girls and again told them to call him if anything else comes up. They both agreed, but he knew that Karly was in the capable hands of her girlfriend, Dahlia, and that they would be just fine. On the way out of town, he stopped by and checked out of the hotel and then he started the long trip back home to his sweetie and his ongoing investigation. The long drive was a good way for him to think everything over and start moving furiously on the case. He had to come through for these girls, their families, and for his community.

Chapter Seventeen

221

'George' was working on his plan and things were going perfectly. He didn't make any trips to town, and only used less traveled roads when heading out of town to run errands. He had essentially excommunicated himself from the town already, and he just had to finish up his moving some additional items and then he would decide what to do with the reminder of this compound and how and when to end his time here, officially. Rebekah was doing wonderfully and her meekness was a great plus with him requesting her to do things. He had shown her some of his prize possessions from previous girls, so she knew that he was not joking in any sense of the manner, and that loyalty, duty, and diligence were his main expectations of her. She was going to be so much better than Weasel, especially in the long run. He kept at his work to clean up this place and get it ready for its destruction. His new place was nearly ready too, so he just had to take care of a few more loose ends and then he would be ready. He didn't know what was happening in town and really didn't care, as long as his own timeline was on par, he would be gone before anyone should come looking for the girls. He was just hoping that his timeline and the cop in town weren't going to coincide or clash, as he didn't want them to truly search hard for him. He had to admit, he might have pushed it, a little, but he still had wanted to collect Cheyenne, yet. She is like the white buffalo, the one that got away. Still now that he learned she was up in Ohio, he still had a faint hope that he might be able to eventually meet up with her again. But if that did happen, he would have to scout her out and snatch her, because the chance that he would be in the same area with her would raise suspicion on her part, that was for sure. So she would be a snatch and grab, but then again if he continued to nab some distant Amish or Mennonite girls, that would be a nice collection to compensate for him not getting Cheyenne. He had to admit he had fallen for her young and gorgeous eyes the first time he had met Cheyenne, and since that first day he wanted to add hers to his collection. Who knows what the future holds, as he was breaking down a console and placing it in the hole he dug to pour acid on the items to destroy and reduce the items to nothing that could be traced back to him. The acid had worked great for him for years, and so he stood by it. A little bit goes a long way too, especially if he lines the holes with rocks and gravel and then heavy pool liner plastic, it helps a little with keeping the volatile liquid where it needs to be and long enough to do its job. He knew what worked by now and he stuck with it, and that was one reason why he still remained uninhibited and free to do what he wanted to. He kept working on his duties to finish them up. It takes just as long to set up as it does to destroy things and tear down. He must stay diligent and finish it up soon, to limit his chances of being noticed. Time was essential and he didn't have any to waste, so he kept doing what he had to do.

One day, he had decided to move Weasel and Teresa to a building on the back end of the quarry, which was between where Suzie met her demise and where he had sunk his car. He did that for them to remain there for now, while he prepped for the destruction of his current location. There was a back road near the old structure he housed them in but he didn't concern himself with that as it was barely used. To be safe, he kept both of them in cages made of seasoned wood now, not as solid as the metal ones, but there was a reason why he didn't bring the metal ones here. The girls could easily get splinters and get prodded by the rough wood, but he didn't care about what unpleasantries his last two girls had. Such is life, he said regarding them. That was his plan and his plan was what was of the utmost importance. He was still somewhat punishing Weasel for her actions with the demise of Suzie, and it wasn't that she had killed her but it was the fact that it could have caused him to be caught, if she had gotten out onto the main road to get help. Thankfully that didn't occur, but still it was another blemish on Weasel's record. Weasel assumed and thought that his punishment was a little severe and rather lengthy, but she wasn't at all worried that she might have gone too far with the Suzie debacle. She took care of the problem as he would have expected her to, even though it was something she wished she hadn't had to do. So she just waited until his anger subsided and then he will need and use her again as he always does and had in the past, which she figured will be sooner than later especially since he was planning a move soon. Weasel understood what he meant, she had helped him before, and even though he seemed content on not needing her, which was a first, it didn't bother her too much as she was in another world, mentally. Especially since the death of Suzie at her own hands, as she looked down and lamented at her weak and thin fingers that now had blood on them. She wasn't worried about the new girl either, the one he thought that he was hiding from her, because she didn't know anything compared to her. She was irreplaceable, she knew that and that knowledge was on her side. She almost wished now that she had cuddled up with Teresa after Suzie's death, but because she wanted to stay true to her love, she didn't. Still having a rebound person was always nice too, but now that she was locked up, she wouldn't be able to do that again. Still at least he didn't have tons of cameras in here, and actually as she looked around, he didn't have any cameras in this location which was odd to her. Still she reasoned just because he was so busy doing everything by himself was why. Or maybe he was using the new girl. Maybe he was going to replace her?! There was no way, she thought to herself, but not without a little fear in her mind. Maybe this was her last hooray, that was always a possibility, but one she still refused to admit or accept it at this point. There was always a chance for her to weasel her way out of this, as she has now become known as. She had her sweet and sincere ways to make her plea and enforce the importance of her worth to her master. She would do so to keep surviving, to stay alive, and to keep her position in his hierarchy. That was how she rolled, how she made it this far with him. Still she knew she had tripped up twice now and third time's the charm, or so she had remembered hearing long ago, in another lifetime when things were simpler and she was in more control of her life. She snuggled up again once more, but sadly the bedding that Suzie had used did not smell like Suzie anymore, but only like herself. So even that sweet remembrance was leaving her, and still she was starting to question more and more what her next step will be. Will she move on with her master or will she be reunited with her dear loves, Jade and Suzie. Either way, she would accept what is. This is all she had time for was to think, so that is what she did, over and over again almost to the point of driving herself insane with the constant barrage of thoughts. Eventually she wound down and fell asleep, with nothing better to do but to wait for her master to come get her again. Maybe tomorrow, she thought as she drifted off to sleep.

Meanwhile in the wooden cage across from Weasel, was none other than the tired, extremely thin, and weakened Teresa. She was not like herself in the days gone by, as she had lost so much weight from undernourishment that she didn't even look like herself, or so she imagined. She likened herself to a ghast or equivalent, barely existing but still able to function, for the most part. She watched Weasel across the room, as this building that she was now in was not the same one as before. There was no darkness, no minimal red lights, and no dingy smell. This place smelled musty, but because there were gaps and holes in the walls and it was without great insulation, if any that she could see. She sensed a change in the 'captor' recently, and especially now that he locked up Weasel in the same cage as Suzie had been in. She was afraid that this might be the end for her as she sat in her cage, unsure what the future would hold for her. She wondered how her parents were. She missed her mom, and hoped she wasn't too worried sick about her. She often wondered if they really missed her, since she had become more distant over the last few years from them. She almost regretted being that way toward both her mother and father, but then again her father never seemed to understand her over the last few years. So sadly her father and her haven't been close in quite some time. She just wished only for their safety and even yet, she still managed to have a sliver of hope that she may see them again. But she also knew reality, and she also knew that things were not looking good for her, or for Weasel. She sadly admitted to herself some time ago that she just wanted this to end, one way or the other. She couldn't imagine living like this until someday her captor decided to dispose of her for whatever reason. She would rather it be sooner than later. Her life was a shell of what it used to be, just like her body. She looked down at herself, and furrowed her eyebrows at what she looked like now. Her pale skin was thin, easy to bruise, and wrinkly at best. Where once she was developing some nice shapely breasts, she now just had small bumps as she had lost nearly all her fat tissue that was normally there. Her normally flat and toned stomach from skateboarding was actually now slightly protruded from her malnourishment as well. It was abnormally bulging and yet it rebounded easily, oddly enough. She was so malnourished that she hadn't had her menstrual cycle in so long, and she felt so dirty that she hadn't truly been cleaned in such a long time. Her hair had started falling out at lengths also, and as she felt it , it was splotchy at best. She missed her long locks which she prided herself in and she remembered how many times she spent a long time brushing and maintaining her hair, to tease the local boys. That is until she met the older man, named Todd. She had fallen for the story about the man's daughter, if he even had a daughter, which she doubted by now, because he had said she wanted to learn how to skate well. It was such a simple ploy and she had fallen hook, line, and sinker for it, like an idiot. Then the last thing she remembered was when he was walking her to his car to meet his so-called daughter, and then it happened. That was when she felt the needle enter her skin and then she lost all control after that. If only she could turn back time, and change that entire day. Yet, sadly that wasn't possible and this is now the life she was forced to live. In due course, she ultimately fell asleep, because there was literally nothing else to do besides sleep.

Tom had made good time coming back into town, but he was still exhausted from the trip and the long week. He wanted to surprise Linda, by coming home early in the morning, and not telling her when. Funny enough as soon as he pulled into her driveway, she came running out with nothing but a bathrobe on. It was almost like she already knew, and then he thought of Karly and her texting, which is probably what happened. She smothered him in hugs and kisses and he sheepishly enjoyed every minute of it, as he showered her back with return affection. They walked inside arm in arm, after he retrieved his bag. It was good to be home, he thought as they entered her abode that they have been living in. She had another late night last evening, so she wasn't going in first thing this morning, and so he was doing the same so they ended up crawling back into bed together and falling asleep in each other's arms. Eventually they woke up in the early afternoon, and they enjoyed a shower together, a meal together, and some more quality time together, and then another quick shower afterwards. Then they left the house, she had to go her way and he went his, to start checking out more hotels. She was able to scour some on his list but not many because of the high workload and the low number of officers to do such. So he started where she left off by checking all the hotels and motels within a fifty mile radius. He would stop by each one and see if there was anything , any strangers, or any shenanigans that would arise any questions. There had to be something or someone that one may have seen that aroused some suspicion, in some way, shape, or form. It was a blind chase, but he had to try to figure something out since there was nothing to go on. His time of inactivity on this was over and he was now committed to find something out, which would hopefully lead to anything tangible. He started closest to town, and would move outward from there.

He drove down the road, heading toward the first hotel, the Mandarin, a seedy little place, but people still lived there and obtained rooms there from time to time. He pulled up and parked his vehicle, got out, and walked around the hotel, the long way to get to the office. Once in front of the office, he opened the door and entered the building. There was a long desk and he started with asking the man at the desk;

"Excuse me sir, are you the owner?" The perturbed owner looked up from what he was doing and quickly asked;

"Why, are you a building inspector?"

"Uh, no. I am a detective...I am just looking for some missing girls." Immediately the man got defensive responding with;

"Listen, I run a reputable establishment, so don't go throwing accusations around..." Now Tom was getting pissed off and said to the man;

"Listen here jack-hole, I am asking only about some missing girls to see if you had seen them or anything funny. I don't care about your building and what you have going on here, yet. But if you keep with the half-cocked attitude, I will take an interest and make sure this place gets shut down, one way or another. Do you understand me? Now take a look at these pictures for me. Do you recognize any of these girls?". He pulled the pictures of Suzie, Teresa, and even Jade out for the man to look at. The man looked and then shook his head no, not uttering a single word otherwise, as he had already dug himself a hole with Tom. Tom finished up with the man saying;

"Thank you for your time and have a wonderful day...." And with that Tom walked out of the office, muttering words under his breath at how he was just treated. 'Damn', Tom thought, 'seriously what a freaking dick'. He will have to keep an eye on this place in the future. He went back to his vehicle and went to the next hotel, which wasn't that far away, but seemed just as seedy as the last one he just left. He got the same kind of reaction at first, but then it settled down some, but still the man and the woman behind the desk had not seen any of the girls in the pics. This was going to be a long day for sure, he thought grimly as he drove to the next one.

He spent the entire day going around and checking with each and every hotel on his list, save a few, and all reaped the same results, nothing at all. He was frustrated and it didn't help that a lot of the owners thought he was trying to cause trouble or find trouble. Actually it was the opposite, he needed their help, but it just seemed that in most places he only found animosity, except for a few mom and pop ones. There was even one particular hotel that offered him a full breakfast which was surprising, one that they offered and two that it was almost midday. He respectfully declined as he had so many places to check out. He kept going till he couldn't go any longer. Finally he called it a day well after six in the evening. He checked in with Linda a few times during the day, and even with Karly and Dahlia. Things were going good on Linda's end, she was just busy that day, but they planned on having supper together. Dahlia told him that Karly was doing great, even with the pain issues, she seemed to be in good spirits and getting stronger and more like herself everyday. He was thankful to hear that his daughter was doing well, and he missed her. Linda and he would have to go visit sometime soon, to be able to spend some more time and memories with her and Dahlia. He made his way back home, to Linda's place, where he was now living full-time. He had a little freetime left prior to Linda arriving home, hopefully she would make it home on time, but that was not always in the cards when dating an officer of the law. Therefore, he hopped in the shower and he grabbed something cold to drink also. It had been a long day and tonight he wanted a beer. He popped one open and sat outside on the back patio, thinking and looking up into the evening sky. He had checked all the local motels, hotels, and places that someone would pay to stay, and he had come up empty so far. So where was there now to check out? What other places could this person or persons be staying at to do their deeds and heinous acts of abduction. He started to think about abandoned houses, and he knew of at least a dozen in the area that would warrant a look at just to check. One never knows where some person may lay in hiding. He then thought of a few abandoned structures that weren't houses, and of course there was the old abandoned mine, on one end of town, but he couldn't remember if there were any structures there or not. Still that didn't matter, he would have to check that out as well. There was also the old quarry, just outside of town, but again he couldn't remember if any structures remain there or not. He wasn't sure if it was as nasty as the quarry he grew up around, but back in his childhood hometown, there was one where they would dare each other to jump into it. It was murky, disgusting, and probably full of horrific chemicals from over the years. Who knew what lied at the bottom of that childhood quarry. He had never been to this one, that was close to town, but he definitely would put it on his list of places to check out very soon. He had made another list and just about that time, he heard his sweetheart's vehicle come into the driveway. He heard the door open and slam close and then the side gate open, as she didn't even bother going through the front door, but immediately came back to the patio where she figured he would be. He stood up to go meet her and they embraced, after she dropped her bag she had with her. He kissed her passionately and she returned the kiss with just as much desire as he had given her. They kissed for a good two minutes, as their hands groped each other as well. Finally they broke it off, and he looked down and at the bag she had brought home, and asked;

"What ya got there, babe?"

"Well, I might just have some supper for us, in the form of sushi and some Chinese food as well. What do you think?"

"Sounds delicious, honey, but what about the other bag on top, the plastic wrapped one?"

"Well, darling (she purred), that is for after supper for me to wear for you!"

"Sweet!, now go get your buns in there and let's eat. We have a busy evening ahead of us." They went inside and got some dinnerware, utensils and some wine in a glass and took it outside to eat by the diminishing light. He lit some citronella candles to ward off the bugs, and then they ate at the table outside, with her little dog and his cat begging for scraps. They talked about work a little and then he talked about Karly and his desire for the two of them to go visit her sometime soon. She welcomed that idea, because she could use a little vacation.

"Yes, a vacation is in order", She said aloud. Then she brought up something else she remembered saying to him previously and jokingly, when he was away, which was; "I had to slave away working while you were out gallavanting around taking care of your daughter and enjoying yourself." With that comment, he gave her a, 'what you talking about look', and then smiled and laughed immediately after. That was their relationship as they were able to joke with one another and not take it personally, no matter what it was about. Shortly after they were done eating, he cleaned up the table and she went and got a shower, to freshen up some. Suddenly out of nowhere, while Linda was in the shower, there was a call on his cell phone and Linda's own phone rang a few seconds later as well. This was not good he thought as he walked over to his phone to check it out. It was one of the other officers, who was out doing late night rounds. The officer spoke immediately, saying to Tom;

"Hey buddy, sorry to bother you, but this is Ryan. I got a call from an old timer that lives a few miles away from the quarry, and he was out walking near the back end, off Buckle trail, and he heard some noises just before dark coming from the old storage building that sits there. He didn't know what to do and he didn't look into it, and sadly I am caught up with a big accident off route 401, so I am stuck here for now. Would you mind...... Do you mind checking it out for me?" He said with a higher pitched voice at the end of his request, that Tom immediately picked up on. Tom responded as he always does;

"Yeah, I can check it out. Thanks, buddy." Tom stated rather sarcastically and it was something Ryan didn't pick up on, thankfully. Tom heard the shower water turning off and Linda, with only a towel barely wrapped around her, peek out from the bedroom and asked him;

"Did I hear you talking to someone?"

"Yes you did, my dear, and guess what....." she rolled her eyes and said in response;

"Really, you have to be kidding me?!"

"I am so sorry, but Ryan is caught up at a big accident he is dealing with, and he needs someone to check out the back end of the quarry. Some old timer said he heard voices coming from an abandoned building, an old storage building. It is probably just some damn kids, but I have to do what I have to do. Sorry, love." But before he was finished talking, she had disappeared into the bedroom and he heard drawers opening. He quickly asked her, just as he finished up clearing the entire table;

"Um, excuse me, what are you doing in there?"

"Well.." she yelled from her bedroom as she was making noises. " I am going with you. It is our date night and if we can't enjoy it at home, at least we can enjoy it together, even if on duty." God, he loved this woman who he was dating. She was just a pistol and amazing in her own mannerisms. He started to say to her;

"I really don't think......." But she cut him off immediately, saying a few words, before popping her head out and smiling at him as she was nearly dressed and ready to go;

"Listen bub, you are stuck with me either way! So either suck it up and deal with it, or get your big boy pants on and try to stop me from coming along." He laughed hard and loud at her alliteration of words which she battered him with, and then smiled so eloquently afterwards. What a lucky man I am, he thought to himself, just as Linda came out wearing a pair of jeans, smart hiking boots, a dark tie dye t-shirt, a black hair band, pulling her hair back, and, of course, her holster with her gun on. He laughed again at her attire as she looked down and then back up at him, as if to say, 'what the hell is wrong with casual attire?' She threw a rolled up t-shirt at him, in a mock display of anger, and he just ducked and playfully avoided her innocent projectile. So after that he got his clothes back on and donned his gear and off they went out the door, to enjoy a romantic evening together, out investigating. They both got into his vehicle and off they went down the road to see what all the hub-bub was about.

Earlier that evening, when Tom had just arrived at his home, 'George' hiked it to the old dilapidated building that he had stored Teresa and Weasel in, for the time being. He had a combustible liquid with him and he had some matches. He also carried something for Weasel as well. She would be doing his bidding again tonight, for penance for what she did to Suzie. He took his time, to make sure he backtracked so that if anyone was around they wouldn't see him. He also wore a hooded sweatshirt, and all dark clothing. He needed to blend in as much as he could so that no one would see him come in and do what he had to do. He started first by pouring the volatile liquid around the outside of the small building, around the entire perimeter. He then walked around toward the door, leaving his nearly empty container behind as he entered the old creaky door. Inside the building, Teresa looked to be sleeping and Weasel seemed to be doing the same. That was going to change soon. He went over and smacked the wood cages with a wooden bat, waking up the two occupants immediately. They both startled awake and George kept hitting the cages, as both Teresa and Weasel covered their ears from the noise. He looked at Teresa, and said to her;

"You want to be free of me and your prison?" She slowly shook her head and then he continued with, "Well this is your time, my dear. However there is a catch…." He said as he glanced over at Weasel too. "Only one of you will live tonight and therefore you have to decide which one it will be. Should we draw straws? No that is just dumb. Should we do rock, paper, and scissors? No, that is too childish. Hmmm ……., what pray tell shall we do?" Then he dropped two metal old time scythes, one in front of each cage. Both girls looked at the metal tools and then looked back at George, as if to say 'What?'. He then said;

"This is your final test. You either have your freedom or you will die. Your fate is in your own hands. With that he walked away and out of the building, but not till after he unlocked the cages, leaving them slightly ajar. He left the building, but neither of the girls moved, as they were in shock, yet. Still even after five minutes, they didn't move. Finally they heard him say a little louder to them;

"You better decide soon, and make it fast!" Then they heard a distinct 'whooshing' and then they saw flames from inside the building. He had started a fire to the outside of the building that they were still trapped in. The fire started off slowly but then started to creep up the walls, and still for some odd reason, neither girl moved. Then finally Teresa had her wits about her enough to get out of her cage and run for an opening. But sadly enough the front door was already engulfed in flames, and so she saw a small break in the board on one wall where she may be able to wiggle through, safely. Just as she headed that way, though, Weasel interrupted her and knocked her off her feet. With a gasp of air being knocked out of her, Teresa tried to get to her side, to see what had happened. Then that is when she saw Weasel coming at her with one of the old scythes, held up high and ready to deal the strike of death to her. The look of pure evil, pure hatred on Weasel's face made her realize that she was coming to kill her. She knew that that crazed woman's instincts had kicked in and she was coming for the jugular, to get back in the good graces of her master. Teresa thought as she watched, nearly in slow motion as Weasel moved on her, that she looked like a frenzied troll or orc, as she used to read in her fantasy stories. The look on her face, the twisted grin of pleasure, and her fierce and evil eyes,.... oh those eyes were so hideous. It was then she had to decide what to do, and just as Weasel was about in striking range, she came up with the only idea she had. Thankfully, the way she was lying was perfect for her to rear her foot back and with all her meager strength she kicked up at Weasel just as she got within distance. Weasel was ready to block the kick to her belly, but she wasn't fast enough to stop the intended spot. Teresa's barefoot slammed hard into Weasel's lower jaw and in that instant the approaching woman was stopped dead in her tracks. Her forward momentum halted and with the force of the blow to her lower jaw, Weasel lost the grip on her weapon and she fell backwards in a hard thump on her rump, hitting the floor extra hard. She was writhing in pain, as she felt for her lower jaw and it felt like it had been broken in at least one place. She cursed Teresa harshly, not saying but slurring as her jaw wouldn't work right when she tried to move it;

"You... fre... aken... bit...ch... I...go..na.... Kil..lls...you...... de...ad!" That was all Teresa needed as she scrambled for the hole in the wall and tried to push herself through. Luckily there was no fire here at this wall, but all the other walls were being engulfed in flames rather quickly. She tried to get through the hole, but hung up on a nail that protruded out and caught her clothing. She ripped it away, but also in the meantime she fell onto the rusty old protruding nail, which caused a deep puncture in her side because of the sharpness of the object. She gasped for breath as the nail penetrated her skin and then she felt it go deep inside her, as she was so thin now. She looked back and still saw Weasel scrambling on the floor trying to fix her broken jaw with her hands, but nothing seemed to work, so she still had time to get away.

The fire continued to lick the walls of the building as it became more and more engulfed with heat, smoke, and flames. She wanted to laugh, laugh at her predicament and at Weasel but she had her own misfortune to deal with as well, and so she got back to getting out of there. She slowly pulled her impaled body off the nail as it eased out, but not without having blood oozing down her flank now. She quickly gazed at the wayward nail and it looked like it had some blood and hamburger on it, as it had penetrated deep into her. She managed to continue to wiggle until she was through the hole, but unfortunately not without a few more cuts, a splinter or two, and of course her impalement wound. She held her injured flank as she tore a piece of her nasty pants off, at the cuff, and she placed it against her wound, putting pressure there so that she didn't bleed out. She then started to walk toward the woods and she didn't even care where it led her, just as long as she was away from the burning building, the crazed Weasel, and hopefully toward her freedom.

Weasel, in the meantime, was trying to hold her jaw together as the pain was excruciating to her, and she couldn't get it to stop moving around, which caused even more severe pain. She finally grabbed part of her top and she ripped it off, exposing her left breast in the meantime, and started to twirl the fabric up. She got it fairly tight and then she wrapped it around her head and under her jaw, which seemed to help control the movement of the loose mandible. Finally with it stabilized the best she could do, she looked around and didn't see Teresa and cursed within herself. She reached around the burning and smoke filled building until she found the metal scythe and then she grabbed it. She was about to scramble for the same hole that Teresa had gotten through, when her hand touched something hot, something metal and that left hand of hers was burned instantly, and she cried in pain at the anguish of her sizzling skin as it melted some from the heat. Weasel got back to the whole after taking a few seconds to deal with the pain, and luckily she was still thinner than Teresa, so she was able to wiggle through much easier and without getting injured like Teresa had. Weasel stood there for a second collecting her bearings, as the smoke had entered her lungs and the flames had caused her eyes to water up and become puffy. She could hardly catch her breath or see for a near full minute. Finally she looked around through the smoky haze of her vision, and up ahead in the distance, with the help of the bright flame engulfed building behind her, she thought she saw a staggering figure traipsing off into the woodline. There she was, Weasel thought to herself, and then she looked down at her metal tool of death and she started walking fast after the escaping Teresa. She was going to be the one to live this ordeal, not that skinny skateboarding bitch who just broke her jaw. How dare she do such a thing to her, after all she had done for her, for so long. Taking care of her, taking her outside, feeding her, making sure she was taken care of like no one would do for her. That ungrateful and degenerate hag will get what she has coming to her, that is for sure, she thought to herself as she started getting closer to the escaping and wounded Teresa. Just when she was making good distance, she saw Teresa turn around and a look of horror crossed her face and that was when she started running at her, but Teresa ran as well, running for what life she had left in her. It was a foot chase now as the escapee tried to outrun the maniacal woman intent on killing her, as both searched for their own type of freedom. Teresa trying to get free to be with her parents again and live life once more, and Weasel to kill the woman in front of her to get back in the good graces of her master. Teresa ran as fast as she could, but she hit many limbs along the way as she was running with only one eye. She smacked so many low lying branches and debris on the ground that her one eye didn't pick up immediately, especially now that it was nighttime, as she tried to flee the crazed woman, chasing her. Thankfully, Weasel wasn't doing much better either though, as she was hitting the same branches, yet not because of her eye, but because they hit her jaw and she would stop in severe pain as her jaw moved awkwardly again. It was a slow and painful scramble for both of them, and they didn't make good distance or time, because of all their hindrances to moving expediently through the woods.

In the meantime, Tom and Linda were heading in the direction of the old building via the crappy old trail that they were driving down to get there. There was hardly any traffic out tonight, so they made great time getting closer to their destination. They were driving down the old unkempt road, when up ahead, they both saw the fire start licking and outlining a building, which was slowly becoming engulfed in flames.Linda immediately got on her phone and called the fire department and the ambulance, just in case there were injuries. The first thing Tom thought and said aloud to Linda was;

"Stupid local thugs out having a good time and now they set a building on fire. Shit, call for backup, we may need some help with this one," he asked Linda, perturbed that these kids would ruin their date night together. He tried to speed up

234

but the road was so bad, he had to slow down just as quickly as he sped up to navigate the potholes and elevated areas so that he didn't ruin his vehicle just getting to the scene. Eventually he got there, close enough that he could pull off the old gravel road, and he parked his vehicle, but left the lights on. The building was fully involved now, but still he ran up to it yelling for anyone to see if there was someone inside or not, in danger. He looked through the large openings, and thought he saw what looked like wooden cages, but he thought it might have been a smoky haze which made him see odd things. Linda looked around the other side of the building, as she was doing the same as he was, trying to reach anyone. He looked toward the woods, which is where he would have run if he were kids running away from the law, but he didn't see any movement immediately. He ran back to his vehicle and got his flashlight, and started heading in the direction of the woods, signaling Linda, who also was heading back to the vehicle to get more gear. They stopped momentarily to interact with one another. He asked her as he was itching to move quickly to hopefully catch up with someone fleeing the scene;

"Did you see anyone, babe?"

"No, I did not see anyone. It looked like there were wooden cages inside the building. That doesn't make sense, but who knows what kids were keeping in there." He nodded his affirmation at her and then he pointed at the woods, saying;

"I am heading into the woods, since they would most likely flee that way if they had any sense about them, ok!"

"Got ya, babe, I will be following shortly, but after I grab my flashlight and then call for more police help. I think we may need it!"

"Okay sweets, catch ya soon!" And he was off jogging into the night. The going was somewhat impeded by the unkept woods, as there were monkey vines hanging down from trees, the quite annoying thick kudzu vine, and low lying branches which kept slowing him down. He didn't see any lights up ahead, but still he yelled to no one in particular and into the darkness, saying;

"This is the Glen Fork's Police Department, halt your escape now and you will get leniency, but if you continue to flee, there will be worse trouble for y'all." He heard nothing at first and then up ahead, some distance ahead, he heard a scream, a terror filled scream yell from the darkness;

"Help me, she is trying to kill me!!!!" After hearing that he picked up the pace and ran even faster and as fast as he could to catch up with the voice, which seemed to be coming from in front of him, thankfully. He also didn't know where the quarry started, so he kept that in the back of his mind as he kept moving forward, to hopefully save whoever screamed for assistance!

Teresa was running for all she was worth, tripping over everything, but no matter what slowed her down she still got up and kept moving. She had to flee, to get away from this maniac of a woman that was trailing her. She just had to keep a few feet away from her, just so she couldn't swing or throw the metal scythe at her, with the intent to murder her. She was happy that she kicked her so hard and hopefully broke her jaw, because she deserved it a million times over for all the hateful deeds that she had done at her master's beck and call. There were always repercussions in life, she thought and it was about time the Weasel got hers. She kept running, having no idea where she was going or where her path was leading her, but it truly didn't matter to her as long as it was far away from the madman and the crazy henchwoman. That was all that mattered, but then in that second she got tripped up by a stiff vine of kudzu and fell flat on her face. She got twisted up and her hands slid under another vine and so she had trouble standing up. She looked back in fear but she couldn't see anyone in the dark night, and that was when she heard someone yell out in the darkness, well behind her, saying;

"This is the Glen Fork's Police Department, halt your escape now and you will get leniency, but if you continue to flee, there will be worse trouble for y'all!" All she could think was holy shit, someone is out here with them and it is the police, so she sat up and with all her might she yelled out, screaming to the top of her lungs, saying;

"Help me, she is trying to kill me!" There she had responded with everything she could bolster in her voice and hopefully the officer will reach her before Weasel does. Then she heard movement and she looked behind her, and barely ducked as something was thrown at her. The object thrown grazed her shoulder but ultimately missed her for the most part, and the part that grazed her shoulder was a wooden handle, thankfully. She fell to her side and then Weasel was on her. The two women fought in the foliage and vines and rolled around trying to get the upper hand on one another. Both were weak so their effort was only half as normal, but still Weasel had bloodlust in her eyes, and Teresa wanted to live, both high enough intensity to perform any act of strength in such circumstances. Weasel had gotten the upper hand and was putting her hands snuggly around Teresa's throat, trying to suffocate the life out of her. In a different moment this might have looked comical as the enraged and maniacal looking Weasel was trying to suffocate her, her lower jaw was dangling around some, with a stupid partial shirt fabric holding it up, and her one breast danlging out from the ripped shirt. It was not funny though as Teresa was fighting for her life. Just as Weasel, with surprising strength for the thin woman, grabbed her throat she scratched and fought to pull those grubby hands away from her own throat. Her breathing was becoming more labored as Weasel had a grip like a vise on her thin throat, trying to crush it with all her meager might. Unfortunately, it was working as Teresa was slowly starting to fade from the effort and lack of air into her lungs. In a last ditch effort, Teresa raised up her one hand and stuck her thumb right into Weasel's left orbital region, pushing hard and thrusting her thumb deep into the socket. Then there was a squish sound, as the eye popped and oozed disgusting fluid. Weasel yelled in pain and that was when she let up her grip on Teresa's throat, thankfully and none too soon. Teresa rolled over as Weasel fell on her back at the intense pain of having a thumb press into her eye socket, in essence ruining and crushing her eyeball. Teresa coughed and wheezed for breath as she struggled to get air back into her lungs, and then she slowly got up and ran as fast as she could away from the wiggling Weasel. She coughed and hacked and the going was even slower, but she kept moving ahead and that was all that mattered! One step after the other, keep moving in any direction besides backwards, she told herself over and over again as her throat hurt from nearly being crushed. She hurt all over, like she never hurt before, but she kept running, kept moving and kept hoping for someone to save her from this nightmare of a life she was existing in. she only hoped and now for the first time in her life, she even prayed for assistance. Hopefully someone was listening, she thought almost hopelessly. She heard someone moving behind her again and she knew that Weasel was probably back on the chase. All she knew is that she had to keep moving and keep distance between her until someone found them, which was hopefully soon as she was almost done, tired with exhaustion.

  Weasel had come up behind Teresa and pounced on her with the upper hand. She nearly had her, nearly choked the very life out of her and then that prick of a girl shoved her finger into her left eye socket and crushed her eye. The pain was so intense, almost worse than the jaw, she thought, but then her jaw moved and she thought differently almost immediately. She got up after a short period of writhing around and pain, and used her only good eye to try to find the scythe that she threw, which as luck would have it, she found quickly and then she started her pursuit, lumbering through the woods to try to catch up with Teresa once more and end it now for good! She heard the voice behind her, the cop, but she didn't care about that, as she wanted to make sure Teresa was dead and then she would be back in the good graces of her master once again and she would be back doing what she knew and had come to love over the years. She kept tripping, and pain nearly seized her body, as now her jaw and her eye hurt, but she had her adrenaline coursing through her body and she was given a mission and she would complete it, come hell or high water. She kept moving, kept pushing forward and soon she was right behind Teresa again as she tried to pick up the pace, but she fell again also, slamming her broken lower jaw into a tree limb, which caused her to wince and cry in pain. 'Dammit that hurt', she yelled deep within the recesses of her convoluted mind. She had to finish this and see it through, was the only thought she had, no matter how hurt she got, how mangled she looked, or if she died doing it. As long as she was able to complete what was expected of her. The darkness enveloped the two girls as they ran, one from the other through the dense woods, to an ending of unknown.

      Tom was moving as fast as he could, but he kept getting hung up, tripped up, or slowed by all the debris and foliage that he came across. It was pissing him off immensely, that was for sure. He knew someone up ahead needed his help but he couldn't get to them quick enough, which was frustrating and irritating all the same. There seemed to be no way around these cantankerous obstacles as he stopped to flash his flashlight around, so he just tried to do the best he could and follow the direction he last heard the voice scream out. Hopefully he wouldn't be too late. Then he wondered how Linda was fairing with this overgrown crap, hopefully better than him, but probably not. Then he heard a scream of pain and anguish, maybe some fifty or so feet in front of him, and he knew what that yell sounded like, so he immediately started running as fast as he could and trudged through the dense foliage. Finally he broke free of some of the denser obstacles, and then he ran harder in the direction of the scream, drawing his weapon out because it sounded like he was going to be needing it! Hopefully he wouldn't be too late and he could stop whatever was happening up ahead. He also hoped they have some reinforcements coming their way, as this might be a big can of worms they are opening. Who truly knew? Up ahead he heard some noises, like someone was also working on getting around the debris he was having trouble with, but he flashed his flashlight in that direction and still he saw nothing. They must be just out of range of the light, so he tried to pick up his pace the best he could. His legs were on fire too, as he hadn't run this long for quite some time, and it showed. He just had to keep moving in the hopes that he would save a life.

Teresa was nearly falling every few steps as her lungs were burning from lack of air that she felt like she could intake, her legs burned from the effort she was putting in, and her chest was heaving, almost like her heart was going to be ripped out of her chest. Still even with all these she kept rambling along, stumbling every few steps, but kept moving forward until..... 'Shit', she exclaimed to herself as she came to a ledge overlooking what looked to be a body of water, but with the moonlight she could see it looked like a large pond or quarry of some sort. The drop down into the water was like forty feet, and she looked to each side but it seemed like the ledge ran....... Wait there was a lower section to her left, so she ran that way now. She ran along the edge and slowly she was getting closer to the water's edge. She was only now probably twenty feet, but it looked like there was a possible area up ahead (as she could see by the moonlight somewhat) that touched down with the water. Suddenly she stopped in her tracks as she was now face to face with Weasel. Weasel looked pitiful now as they faced off one against the other. Weasel stood there, eye contents had leaked down her face, looking like she was grotesquely deranged, and then her jaw being slightly loose, made her look like a villain in one of Teresa's favorite horror movies! Teresa was done running as she couldn't run any longer, that was for sure. So she curled her fist up and was ready to fight it out with the stupid and ignorant Weasel. The only advantage Weasel had was the stupid scythe and she brandished it like she was ready to slice her up. Teresa finally spat out hateful words toward her nemesis, saying to her;

"I guess this is where it ends? Well, I am ready to go down with a fight, so bring it with the best you have!"

"You...r...gon...na....diiiee...hag!" Weasel managed to slur out between the shooting pains of her jaw. They stood there for a few seconds and then Weasel made her move, bringing the scythe up and swinging it in an arch motion as she tried to impale Teresa with the blade, right through her shoulder blade area, trying to cleave her. Teresa dodged that bullet and tried to push Weasel off balance, by feigning an uppercut. That move in itself made Weasel move to the side for fear of her getting hit in the jaw again. Weasel brought the metal death tool back to bear again, but this time when she looked up Teresa had a decent sized thick broken limb in her hand. Weasel smirked and swung again and this time Teresa lifted the limb up to block, and the scythe got stuck in the branch. So now the two were across from each other, in a sort of a standoff as neither one had the strength to pull the other one from their weapon. Weasel eventually pulled hard and Teresa let go of her limb and Weasel went flying backwards, hitting the ground hard and with a thump. Teresa reached down for a decent sized rock next to her, but one she could actually lift up, grabbed it, and went over to smash it on Weasel's head. She grabbed it with both hands, standing above her with the rock raised above her own head, and was about to drop it on Weasel's deranged looking head, when all of sudden she felt something enter her body. She looked down and saw that somehow Weasel had swung the scythe up, free of the branch now, and Teresa had inadvertently impaled herself onto the old rusty blade. She backed up off the blade, and dropped the rock, just shy of Weasel's bare feet. This time Weasel was up and standing above Teresa, who had dropped down to her knees, holding her stomach as she was bleeding out profusely from the new wound. Weasel looked down at the mesmerized and astonished Teresa, who was looking up at her with a pitiful and remorseful look. Weasel spoke up one last time, saying to her once friend, but now nemesis, saying to her;

"No..w…. y.oo..u… die……!" She raised up the scythe and was about to chop Teresa's head off, with a vivid and mangled smirk on her face and the devil in her eyes, when all of sudden there was a loud gunshot, out of nowhere.

Tom came out of the woods just in time to see a crime about to unfold. He didn't have time to yell, didn't have time to hesitate, and he just acted on pure instinct. All he saw was a thin nearly topless woman about to chop another woman's head off. The kneeling woman also looked to be injured by the way she was holding her stomach or flank area. The kneeling woman looked over in his direction, and that was all he needed as he saw her pleading face. He raised up his pistol and fired a single shot at the standing woman, which escaped the barrel just before the aggressive woman swung her lethal blow. His shot rang true and hit the woman in the shoulder, which spun her around, causing the woman to hit the ground in seconds. He was about to run up and help the injured kneeling woman, but then he saw the one he just dropped move again. She was still somehow managing to hold onto the weapon though, and she was starting to get up again. Her intentions didn't seem to be menacing toward him or so it seemed, but it looked as if she wanted to finish the job and kill the injured kneeling woman no matter what the cost. 'What the hell', he thought to himself as he quickly yelled at the crazed woman, saying;

"Don't....!". He did what he had to do to protect the other woman and so he took aim again, and fired off another round. This time he aimed for the head, not out of choice but out of necessity as her chest was not visible enough to hit her heart, so he did the next best thing feasible. Thankfully, he was a near perfect shot and he let off another round, this one also hitting its intended spot. The fired bullet went through the crazed woman's right side of her head and exploded out the left side, spilling brain remnants, blood, and bone out that side. In that very moment, Weasel ceased to exist, never finishing her job to please her master, but she had died trying. Hopefully, he will honor that with her was her last thought, as she passed from this world and into the next existence. Her body slumped down, dropping the scythe at her feet, and she lay motionless. He hated to do that but she had given him no choice, and he had to protect the innocence of the other girl. It was then that he quickly looked over at the other girl, but she wasn't there. He ran over to the ledge and looked down into the murky water of the quarry and he didn't see her, but he saw rippling waves from something falling into the normally still water. "Oh no!", he exclaimed out loud as he looked back from whence he came but didn't hear or see anything. He yelled out;

"Linda, I am over here, near the edge of the quarry!" He placed his flashlight down and leaned it up against the rock that Teresa was going to use to kill Weasel, and he had it facing back from where he came, hoping that Linda would see and track it. He took off his shoes and any extra clothing, leaving his t-shirt and linen boxers on and he did what he had to do, which was jump in.

Chapter Eighteen

Linda was also trying to run through the woods, when she heard the sirens coming behind her, so at least maybe one other officer was arriving and hopefully the fire department as well. She heard the gunshot from up ahead and she hastened her pace, trying to get through the quandary of foliage as quickly as she could. She was worried for her honey, and then she heard the second shot. 'Oh shit, this is serious' and she was scratched up, winded, and beat up from the foliage trying

241

to grab at her, but she kept pushing forward. She heard his voice and then she heard a splash and nearly at the same time, up ahead, she saw a flashlight beam pointing toward the easterly direction she was running. Finally she broke free of the woods and she got a better bearing on the light up ahead which was just to her left and about thirty feet directly in front of her now. She didn't see Tom, but she saw a body lying on the ground and she ran with reckless abandon, thinking it was her dear sweetheart who was down on the ground. She ran up on the downed body with her weapon drawn as she also looked around all over the perimeter to see if there was any other movement. As soon as she was close enough, she could see it wasn't Tom who was down, thankfully, but still she didn't see him. She looked down at the nearly topless and skinny woman lying there and she saw that the woman had been hit in the shoulder and also in the head, as the contents of her brain continued to leak out onto the ground. She checked for a pulse just to be sure and she was of course dead. She yelled out loud;

"Tom!!! Tom! Where are you?" She walked over to the ledge of the drop and she saw the quarry water below with her flashlight beaming down on the surface of the water, she saw some ripples yet as if someone had jumped into the water. Had Tom jumped in? But why? Maybe someone, another person, fell in and he jumped in to save that person. That was the only reason she could think of. She continued to use her flashlight and keep the beam on the water, as the water looks murky, dark, and full of algae. She wanted him to be able to have some way to come back up to the surface and the light would be the perfect beacon for him, she figured. She got on the radio and called for any and all help to get where to she was. She gave them the approx direction that they had traveled and she mentioned the flashlight which will lead them to their spot. She mentioned they were at the edge of the quarry and that Tom had jumped in to save someone. They would need EMTs or Paramedics once he comes back out, so she was trying to get him the back up he needed so that he could hopefully save the person who fell or was pushed in. She would do all she could for her honey, her new love, and the best man that she had ever known intimately. She was afraid for her sweetheart, but she also had to trust him and his instincts, so she did what she could do to support him. She kept the light on the water until his head popped up suddenly out of the water. 'Thank god', she thought, at least he was alive. He spat some directions at her and she did what he needed.

Then he dove back down again. "Find them Tom, darling, find them, please!" She said aloud to no one but herself and the stars above.

Tom had dove into the water to try and save the girl that had fallen in. As soon as he hit the water, he came back up to grab some air before diving down to find the now drowning girl, and he exclaimed out loud;

"Holy shit, this is freaking cold!" He mentioned with a shivering voice, already. He should have grabbed his flashlight because as soon as he dove in, he found out how disgusting, murky, and opaque this water truly was. Yet he needed to guide Linda to where he was, so he dove down and blindlessly tried to find the girl, just by touch, which was nearly impossible, obviously since this water was so nasty. He opened his eyes, but it burned every second they were open, but he didn't have a choice. Who knew what chemicals were in here, but at this point he didn't care as he had a life to save! He remained down as long as he could and then he had to come up for water. He actually got confused and wasn't sure which way was up, at this point and he almost started to panic, but then he saw a faint beam of light up above him. 'Aww, there you are', and he swam hard for the surface. He broke the surface gasping for air, and looking up at who the light belonged to, and he saw the concerned but happy face of his darling Linda. Thank gawd, again he thought as he waved at her. She yelled down at him;

"What do you need?"

"I could use a waterproof flashlight, ...and maybe a pair of goggles(he said sheepishly), if you have one..." He also uttered his request with an obviously shivering voice. "This water is ridiculously cold, sweetie, so don't come in. We don't need two victims here." She asked him if he was ready, to which he nodded yes, and she dropped her really good military grade tactical flashlight, that was weatherproof and supposedly waterproof. He waited for it and she dropped it right practically on top of him, hoping that he wouldn't drop it, hence losing it in the murkiness. Thankfully it was a spot on throw and he caught it perfectly, but nearly blinded himself in the moment of catching it. He took a few seconds, let his eyes adjust again as he knew she didn't have goggles on her, so he took a few deep breaths and he once again dove beneath the surface of the water. He swam down not knowing how deep this quarry was, and with no bottom in sight, he just kept shining his practically worthless flashlight as it was so cold and dark the further down he swam. Even with the top notch flashlight, he could see maybe a foot and a half in front of him and that was about it. He swam down and diligently searched, but he didn't see anything, well except for an old telephone pole sticking up, which he would use as a landmark for where he had come from. He kept shining the light and swimming around but he found nothing, absolutely nothing, but he knew she was down here, somewhere and he had hopes of finding her. He was nearly out of breath again and he had to resurface. He wasn't sure exactly where the surface was again, but then followed the pole until he saw two dim looking beams of light now shining down in a circular motion, as he came potentially closer to the surface. He broke through the surface of frigid water again, looked up, and there was none other than his buddy Jeremy standing beside the concerned Linda. He heard Jeremy call down;

"Any luck, my friend?"

"No, I can't see shit down here, even with the flashlight. Damn murky ass water. I am going down again!"

"Are you sure that is a smart move, my friend?"

"No, but I have to try!! I have to try!!!!"

"Okay buddy we will be here lighting your way out, be safe and best of luck." with that Tom took as deep as a breath he could after he tried to blow it all out of his lungs as much as he could. He dove down one more time to see if he could find the drowning girl. He didn't know how many more times he could do this without him getting too hypothermic. Still he knew he had to try, try to save a life, if it was in his power.

This time he dove down deeper and further than he had previously, going way down into the depths and kicking his way down into the deeper, darker, and even murkier water. He had grabbed a bountiful breathful so he was still good when all of sudden he dropped........dropped out of the water and directly into a room? He stood there, wet, tired, and utterly confused beyond anything he had ever experienced before. Then he looked down at himself, and he was still wearing his underclothes as he did when he jumped in, but somehow, he was in a dry room in an odd looking old house. Somehow,...... wait, how is this possible? What the sam-hill is going on here? This doesn't make any freaking sense, none whatsoever! He looked behind him, from where he had dropped in, and there was a shimmering wall there. He was thoroughly confused, but then he unexpectedly heard whimpering from a distance away from him, but he was unable to discern which direction it was coming from. So, he started checking out the entire room, as his instinctive investigative nature kicked in. However, this wasn't a normal room, but an old style room, like one you see in an old dilapidated house. The room was definitely musty, but dry and with multiple layers of dust everywhere. It had the creepy and eerie feel of a house that one would see in a horror movie of some type. Upon second glance he noticed that there were no visible windows on the walls. It was almost like it was an endless walled house. Odd, he thought, but then again, just look at where he found himself, now. It can't get much odder than this. There were broken windows lying around, small closets and cupboards with doors that were half off their hinges, miscellaneous wood and furniture piles everywhere, and even small nooks and areas that someone could hide in or behind. He observed a door at the far end of the room, but instead of being concerned about that, he went about checking every aspect of this room to see if he could find the nature of the voice. He moved as much wood as he had to, checked in every dark nook, and even looked behind anything and everything he could find that someone could hide behind, in, or near. This all made no sense to him as he stood there momentarily, not sure what to do next after searching so many spots. Oddly enough, he was still dripping wet, but the water dripping from him seemed to not even touch the floor or show signs that the water had even touched it. Even the layers of dust were untouched by his movement throughout the room. Was he even breathing? No, in fact he wasn't! It was all discernibly odd, quite odd as a matter of fact, and overwhelmingly bewildering to him as well. How was this even possible? He thought grimly. Was this the afterlife? Was this the end of all end, or maybe a purgatory between two worlds? Not that it really mattered because, one, he couldn't explain any of it, and, two, no one would believe him either way even if he could explain it. This entire room and whatever this was was nearly freaking him out, but he maintained his composure above all because he had a job to do first and foremost. Still, last he knew he was in the water of the quarry, but none of this made freaking sense, none at all!!!

He was quickly brought back out of his moment as he still heard some faint whimpering, and so he quickly moved into the next room, with his dim flashlight leading the way. The shadows played tricks with his eyes also as he continued to search all over this room, leaving no dark spot or hidden area unobserved, as she could be hiding in one of these areas. Then suddenly, he felt like he was getting weaker, and he started slowing down, that much he could feel. More and more, he felt like he wasn't hardly moving, and he had pressure in his chest, which was disconcerting to say the least. He looked down at his watch and it seemed as if time had stood still, ticking by in such slow milliseconds. All of a sudden, he felt woozy and then he realized that he was most likely running out of air, as the pressure in his chest was about to explode. He quickly ran back to where he came in, jumped up and at the wall, and then suddenly he was back in the water scrambling for the surface as his air was nearly out. He finally and exuberantly broke the water surface, gasping severely for air, trying to once again breathe as all human beings need to, to survive. He floundered in the water there for a few minutes, not daring to look up and deal with questions and answers as he still had none to what he had just experienced down there in the depths of the quarry. Then the concerned Linda said with a fearful voice, looking down;

"Sweetie, are you okay and what happened to you? You were down there so long. We weren't sure what happened! " He gasped for air some more but managed to respond with;

"Sorry ...love, (gasping) but.....words ....cannot ......describe....... what...(gasping)...... I ....just.... witnessed."

"Please stop, please stop.....my love. Whoever it is is gone and I don't want to lose you.......too" she said pleadingly. He looked up at her with a face of resolve and commitment, saying;

"I am so close, I have to try one more time, just one more time to find her. I promise, darling." He sort of pleaded for her to understand. She shook her head solemnly with an eerie feeling deep inside her, and then he did the same routine as he had done last time and he exhaled all he could and took a huge breath, and once more dropped below the surface of the mysterious and he dared to say, mystic water. She was afraid that at that very moment was the last time that she would see him alive. Just behind the two officers, some EMTs had arrived with bags and gear in hand and a few firemen as well with rope and some tools. Everyone waited for the detective to find the missing person so that they could do their job and hopefully bring them back to life. At least they had the equipment, just in case, Linda thought grimly as she looked back to see who came up behind them, and then she turned back to the dismal water as she watched, concerned deeply for her love, her man whom she held with so much respect in her life!

He swam down just as he had done before going deeper and into the darkness even further until once again he popped out in the roomy old house again.

246

He had landed at the same spot as he had done previously, not that he saw his tracks, which weren't there, but he recognized some of the same features he had seen with his previous excursion in this realm. Everything he had moved, previously, was back in its original place and position, like he had never looked through this room. Yet, he knew he had been through the first two rooms, so he hastened and moved quickly to pass these rooms and moved further and deeper into the old musty house. He didn't hear the faint whimpering as he had heard previously, but this time he heard actual conversations and voices talking amongst themselves. How was this even possible? This makes no damn sense, as he still picked up his pace following the noise instead of wasting time looking and not finding anything. Finally, after he went through maybe four large rooms, he saw a light shining up ahead in the next room. How the hell, he thought, but he was past asking questions anymore, and he just did what he had to do. Questions and answers would come later, maybe, after all was said and done. He didn't know how he knew, but he knew that who he was looking for was in that room. He burst into the well lit room with reckless abandon, and in this room there were five ladies talking amongst themselves: not one or two, but five. They wore nondescript pale white dresses, which had no design or pleasant look about them, just as this world had no color to it so did their attire. They conversed with one another like it was just a Sunday afternoon discussion over coffee. Four ladies were sitting down at a white oval shaped table, but there was one still standing. He immediately recognized the one who he saw standing, because she was the woman he saw kneeling before the other one that he shot. He looked at her, and strangely enough she had no wounds or injuries, and also she looked dry. This was freaking weird, he continued to think as he tried to figure out what he was going to do now. He looked quickly around the room surveying the lay of the land, as it was well lit but void of any decorations. The light was made even more brilliant by the reflection off the white walls, the white table, and the entire room being of a shade of white color. The table itself looked to be antique white in color, it had a small pale white vase of dead white flowers in it, and empty off-color white teacups and saucers was the setting that was on the table. None of the women touched the empty cups or saucers, it was almost like they were just there with no purpose. He continued looking at the girl standing up, as if he knew her. because he couldn't see her face when he was topside. Yes that is it, it was in fact the missing Teresa, the daughter of Blain and the late Lori Astel. Thank goodness it's her, she is the reason I am here, he exclaimed internally! Then he took a longer look around the table and he saw an intact and perfectly normal looking Suzie and another one he recognized also was none other than the missing Jade Freely. He didn't recognize the other two women by their names but he remembered seeing their pictures as ones that were missing also. How was this all possible? Why were these ladies here? What the hell was going on in this crazy limbo world, he had somehow come in contact with. Once again, he gave up on any answers at this point, and he just looked at the five women. They in turn looked up at him with a questioningly look, asking him;

"How did you get here?" The one named Suzie asked him quizzically.

"I dunno", he responded. "Are we still in the quarry?" With that question, all the ladies but Teresa laughed, and then Jade spoke up, with a nice and gentle voice, saying;

"No love, you are not in the quarry. You are where we are, in a purgatory, trapped here, somewhere between worlds. We could not be saved so we are all here in the afterlife limbo, sort of to speak, until our souls are set free, or so we assume." Teresa looked at him with a pleading look, and she burst out, saying;

"But, I don't want to die yet!"

"Neither did any of us dear, but it is the hand that the world had dealt us. Sorry love, but accept what and where you are for now." Tom looked at them and said to all of them;

"Well I am leaving here with all of you, and now!" Then the four girls at the table laughed again and Jade spoke up again saying;

"No, that is not possible, kind sir. You must go now or you will be here with us also and once you are here at our table, you can never go back. Come, and sit down, Teresa, make yourself at home. You are among friends!" Jade said, smiling to her, nicely and with all seemingly good intentions. Teresa looked at Tom and then nearly sat down at the table but Tom stepped in and firmly grabbed Teresa by the arm. He looked down at his watch and once again he saw time slow down as his life was starting to fail him. He looked at Teresa and said to her matter of factly;

"Listen Teresa, I don't know what this place is, and I don't know how I got here, but I am here and I know a way out. Follow me and live, or stay here with these unfortunate girls and remain in purgatory, until such a time. We are out of time, and you have to decide, NOW!" He saw the indecisive look on her face and so he quickly added, saying to her;

"Teresa (he said as he grabbed her lightly to get her attention), I am not leaving her without you, so if you stay, ...I stay!" She looked at him and then back at the table, one more time. Teresa hesitated another moment longer as she looked at all the smiling girls, and then back to Tom. It was then that she confessed to him (and the other ladies sitting and watching and waiting for her reaction);

"Please take me out of here, I wish to live, yet!" He then grabbed her hand roughly, pulling her away from the table, and off they ran with her following his steps and matching his stride back through the last room closest to the table full of women. It was then when he heard Suzie's call out to the two fleeing bodies;

"Don't worry Tom and Teresa, we will see you soon again, soon!"

"Not if I have anything to say about it!" He mumbled roughly under his voice.

He had started to slow down considerably now as his legs would not move as fast as he wanted them to move, and it was then that he knew he was slowly drowning. Still, somehow, and by some will of power deep within him, he still found the strength to pull Teresa along and into yet another room. He quickly realized that she couldn't come of her own accord or run ahead, as she was trapped there unless freed by someone, so she could only follow, those must be the rules of this plane of existence, not that either of them knew of such. They ran as fast as they could for their lives, for their souls, and for the sake of living another day in the world they knew and loved. Tom continued to slow every step he took, but he still dragged her along, but it also seemed like they were connected now. It was like she was tied to his soul or his destiny in such a way that they either both make it out or they die together, and end up at the table with the other ladies. He cursed this realm of existence as he kept trudging along through the dust filled rooms, until finally, he saw the room up ahead, the room that had contact with the living world. With whatever strength he had left, he grabbed Teresa's hand, holding firmly to her as to not lose her, and with his last ditch effort he dove upwards and into the shimmering wall. The next thing he knew they were back in the murky and disgusting water together, he was swimming for hope and she was a limpless heavy body weighing him down. He was about to take a breath instinctively which would not be a breath in fact, but an intake of water, drowning him in essence. He knew that Teresa wasn't breathing or alive at this point because of how long she had been underwater, and so with whatever strength he had left he slowly struggled to head toward the light, the light of the above world, the way to freedom. Sadly enough and to his dismay, he knew he wasn't going to make it as they both started to sink ever so slowly for every stroke he swam up. It was then that he knew what he had to do, and that was to make the ultimate sacrifice. Immediately he thought deep within his mind, 'I am sorry, Linda but I will always love you!' Instinctively and with what physical strength he had left in him, he pushed Teresa's limp body up and amazingly enough she started to slowly rise, heading toward the surface. Tom watched her rise toward her freedom, toward the land of the living, and to be saved and hopefully brought back to life once again. She had so much to live for, because he believed that no one should die that young, if it can be helped. She deserved to live more than he, and he gladly sacrificed his life for hers. He would now let go of this world as his strength had now failed him, and so in that moment, he finally took a breath, ultimately inhaled water, and jerked spasmodically over and over again. Slowly his physical body started to sink a little deeper into the gloominess of the depths of the quarry, as his lungs took in the foul water, essentially drowning him. Goodbye good world, I leave it now in the hands of the afterlife, was his last thought.

   The people up above couldn't see anything and those who saw Tom go down last, Linda and Jeremy knew exactly how long he had been down there. Finally, when they were close to giving up hope there was movement down below and all the lights they had were shining down at the water, and quite unexpectedly and miraculously a body, a female body, popped up out of the water. Jeremy had already taken most of his gear off and so the firefighters there, tied a rope around Jeremy and he immediately jumped into the frigid dank water. He grabbed the limp body of the girl and all the EMTS, firefighters, and Linda helped pull Jeremy down to the small embankment some fifteen feet away from the ledge they were at. Once there the EMTS pulled the cold, limp, and lifeless body of Teresa out of the water and started working on her right away, checking for a pulse and then starting CPR on her, trying to revive her and bring her back. Jeremy looked back at the water and didn't see Tom, and he looked up at Linda who had a pleading look in her eyes, and so he did what he knew he must and he dove in the murky water. He swam with all his strength and as fast as he could back to where Teresa had floated to the surface, he grabbed a large breath of air, and he kicked and swam down to try to find his dear friend. A few of the firefighters held onto the rope, giving him slack and seeing if he could find the missing detective down in the gloominess of the quarry. Hopes were definitely dismal, but they had to give it a try, because Tom wouldn't give up on

Teresa, so they wouldn't give up on him either. Jeremy came back up to the water's surface around two minutes later gasping for air, with concern on his face but he wouldn't give up and so he dove down again, after intaking another large amount of air into his lungs. By this time more people had shown up, more firefighters and paramedics, also to aid in the rescue activities of the downed and lifeless girl. The paramedics were working diligently on Teresa with the EMTS, and the firefighters not holding the rope were busy cracking, shaking and then throwing chemical light sticks into the water, to try to light up the obscurity with whatever light they could to try and help find the missing detective. Teresa was getting the best care they had in the county, as they worked hard to bring her back from death's door. They secured an airway, shocked her when it was indicated, but mostly did high quality compressions on her to get her heart to start working again. They would try until their last breath to honor the sacrifice that the detective gave, his own life, to bring this girl back to them. That was the least they could do.

   Tom had essentially drowned and was floating in the water, but that was merely his physical body, as his spirit was elsewhere. He looked around and suddenly the darkness was not so dark as a light started to penetrate and open up into a scene of unknown proportions. He looked around and suddenly he found himself in a field of flowers, a field of bountiful and beautiful yellow flowers with other colors thrown into the mix as well. It was funny there was no wind, but yet the flowers swayed and moved as if there was a breeze pushing them to and fro. He surveyed the entire area as he was mesmerized and awestruck by the incredible beauty and serenity of it all. How had he ended up in such a glorious place as this? He truly marveled at his luck. After the first minute of awe, he looked up, down and all around and couldn't believe his lucky stars, because he wasn't in some dusky old house, like those unfortunate girls, but he was here amongst nature and in the middle of natural perfection. He glanced around, looking uphill, he noticed the slight grade but it was not a steep uphill, just a gentle slope. Oddly enough there was someone standing at the top of the crest of the hill, standing amongst the slightly moving flowers. He waved and the person mimicked his wave back. Intrigued at this, he started walking through the field of flowers to meet up with that person, whoever it was. Strangely enough from the moment he arrived here, wherever here was, he felt an overwhelming feeling of genuine love, a true inner peace. It was if this place was pure serenity to his soul, as he gazed around trying to take everything in from his surroundings. He walked a little further, only stopping occasionally to smell some of the gorgeous flowers, the marigolds, French Marigolds to be exact, his late wife's favorite type of flower. Imagine that he thought, but then he looked up once more and he was finally able to discern who he was walking toward. The person who had waved at him and who he was moving slowly closer to, was in fact his late wife, Jeanine! He smiled at her, a smile of true happiness and she smiled back at him, but she also opened her arms for him to come to her. He walked on and with renewed energy that he was going to be with his wife again, the first love of his life, that he missed so dearly. She was gorgeous as ever as he gazed upon her, because she radiated natural and perfect beauty. She had her generous hair flowing freely and not pulled back as she would normally wear it, especially once she was afflicted with sickness. She stood there with her hair blowing out with a non-existent breeze, but oddly enough, it looked like she was almost in water, but that's not possible because we are in this glorious field, he thought. Again, she beckoned him with her arms and her gorgeous figure, as her sun dress was covering just enough skin to keep her concealed, but he knew what curves she had under her clothes. He also remembered how much he loved her spirit, her heart, and yes her child-like demeanor. She was the true epitome of perfect loveliness. The closer he got, the more excited he became and the more calm he became at the same time, strangely enough.

He continued on his path, to walk through the blooming flowers, with ease and when he was within maybe twenty feet of his wife, he ceased his forward momentum for some unknown reason. He didn't know why he had halted his advances on his late wife, but he felt something pulling at him. She was there, right in front of him and in plain sight, to be with and abide with for all eternity, and yet he balked for some unforeseen reason. It was then that he heard a peculiar noise, coming from behind him, the way he had just come. He swore he heard someone banging on something, from far behind him, and he didn't know what or why it was so he turned to see what the fuss was all about. There was indeed someone banging on a wall, a clear wall, which hadn't existed previously. He couldn't hear what the voice was saying but it was screaming at him, that was for sure. The person pounded the clear wall for all it was worth trying to get his attention, which it had, but still he looked back the other direction, toward his late wife. He smiled again and she reciprocated his smile too, but she didn't say a word, she just smiled and kept her arms open wide for him to come and rest his weary head on her bosom forever. He took one step more forward and then stopped again as the banging became louder from behind him. The person was definitely persistent, to say the least, and yet again his forward motion was stalled. He looked back at the person banging on the wall. He swore knew he knew the person, but he just couldn't remember the name of the person, the lady, who was frantically trying to reach him. It was almost like every step he took forward, he forgot more of the world he had just left behind. He honestly didn't even remember how he got here, now, in this field. What mind trickery is this, he thought? Why couldn't he remember anything, and yet the vision of his wife stood there waiting for him to embrace and go with her. He took one step back and then two, not out of disrespect for his late wife, but because for some reason his heart and mind told him to do so. After a few steps backwards, he started to remember, remember what had happened and how he truly got here to this in-between world. He had saved a girl from her untimely passing after she had drowned, but in the same instance he remembered that he had most likely drowned also. The other perplexing aspect is the further he got away from his wife, the more difficult it was to discern who she was, and who he was heading toward. Almost like she herself was an apparition and truly not his actual wife, but still her pull was strong on him, and he felt his heart strings want to go to her and please her.

He once more looked down and smelled the aroma from the flowers , as he stood there with indecision keeping him from moving. Before him, he could not only smell the flowers, but he even smelled his wife's scent on them as well. He remembered and loved her scent, her perfume, and her hair products which made her stand out. With those vivid memories in his mind, he took another step toward his wife, yet again. She, of course, came into view once again as she reopened her arms as if to say, come to me my dear and find the sanctuary that you seek. He so wanted peace, peace of mind, peace of spirit and peace of heart. And yes, he wanted her in his arms again to have and to hold, for as long as he could, however long that may be. However on the opposite end of the spectrum, he still heard the insistent banging on the clear invisible wall, and it was then that he heard a faint utterance, almost like a melodious voice rolling through his mind, saying to him;

"Please Tom, come back to me, I need you, I love you, I don't want to live in this world without you, my dear. Please come back to me and grow old with me! So fight Tom, fight,........ Tom, fight for me, fight for us!" Then just as suddenly as he heard the voice, he felt his chest and his chest ached immensely for some

253

inexplicable reason. 'Now who the hell is pounding on my chest', he thought in a stupified type of feeling of unsureness. He looked back toward the vision of his darling and loving wife and he said to her, not aloud but almost telekinetically;

"My darling Jeanine, I will always love you and that will never change. You will always have a part of me and I will always remember a part of you, forever. But I cannot come to you right now, I feel that it is just not my time to be wrapped in your arms. Please forgive me!" Almost instantaneously, he heard a low rumbling across the skyline above, almost like a growling or low voice. The rumbling spoke out, almost like thunder rolling across the sky and the words he thought he heard from above, said;

"Always a choice........"

He looked back at the woman screaming at him and he smiled as he slowly walked back down the hill away from his late wife. Eventually the lovely yellow flowers, the lush rolling hills, and his beautiful late wife had disappeared into the world of nothingness. Eventually the scene faded to black, a cold wet blackness, in fact. It was then that he found himself surprisingly back at the quarry again. He stood there looking down at his physical body as the paramedics, EMTs, firefighters and all involved worked hard on him to bring him back from the realm of the dead. He stood there, outside his body, like an ethereal spirit watching others work hard on the physical aspect of him. It was a zen type of feeling, watching this from outside his own body, but he still wasn't physically back as he was floating there and watching from above his cold lifeless body. After some time had passed, the first responders, and those involved in trying to bring him back, stopped and shook their heads in solemnity, admitting defeat and pronouncing Tom officially deceased. Linda looked at them with a horrified expression and then she wept, sprawling over her lover's body, completely in irreconcilable distress. Jeremy and all the others just watched, just as Tom himself did from outside his body, at the unfolding events and Linda's pitiful response. That wasn't good enough for her though, because all of the sudden she reared up and punched his chest, an old school precordial thump type of hit, screaming at him;

"Don't you die on me now, Tom! Don't you dare leave me now, darling! You have so much to live for!" She screamed at him, with all the air in her lungs and then she gave him another hard hit on his chest, followed by a desperate slap on his cold lifeless face. After she hit him in frustration, but not anger, just loving frustration, she immediately started doing compressions again, not giving up, in the least, on her man. As he watched from a short distance, his spirit body's chest started oddly hurting again from the abuse it had been taking from the responders and his beloved Linda. Still, he remained watching outside his body as Linda wouldn't give up on him. If he could shed a tear he would have because of her tenacity and stubbornness in not letting him go without a fight. Then the questions started barraging his thought process. Was he permanently stuck here watching in limbo, like the girls at the table in the old house under the water? Was this his perceived purgatory? Was this his punishment for his deeds in life? Was this all there was in the afterlife? All these questions came rolling over him and so many more. Yet, still he watched Linda compress his chest, and blow her breath into his physical body, trying to bring him back. Not thirty seconds later (after Linda had started CPR again), Jeremy took a step forward to try to have her stop this insanity, but the look she gave him said it all. She would not give up on this man that she loved so fiercely and with so much of her heart! She would not let him die! That was out of the question and so he decided to kneel down and help her do what she must do. Then shortly after he started again, the remaining ones not attending to Teresa also started working on Tom again, taking turns and trying to still bring him back, somehow. Even though most of the rescuers believed this was in fact a futile effort, they did it to appease the relentless and unyielding Linda.

Tom's spirit stood there, imagining that they were all wasting their time on him, but then again he felt a heavy pain deep within his ethereal chest. Then suddenly the responders checked the defibrillator and he actually had a shockable rhythm, much to their surprise. It was an ugly and erratic rhythm, but it was there, it was something, it was hope, and that was all they needed! Tom's ethereal body stood there motionless when they shocked him, but something unexplainable happened to him. He was suddenly pulled toward his physical body a few steps. He abruptly thought, 'what the hell was this', but then it happened again as they shocked him once more and he was pulled once more, even closer. What is going on here, his ethereal spirit wondered with amused perplexion and skeptical uncertainty. He thought his physical body was dead, he was gone. Then Linda unceremoniously slapped him across the face not once but twice before she resumed compressions, and she screamed at him;

"Get your ass back here, NOW!"

She said those harsh words to him as she pounded on his chest. It was at this moment, that his spirit saw a chasm of light appear, not out of nowhere, but coming from his deceased physical body. Without comprehension, his ethereal spirit was instantly sucked back into his physical body. His wayward soul had returned home. Suddenly, in a moment's notice, the monitor showed an actual rhythm, a discernible rhythm, even though it was abnormal, it was still a rhythm to show that he was once again alive. Linda instantly collapsed beside him, hugging his available arm and kissing him on the face. He wasn't awake or alert to them, but his heart had come back to this world and that was all that mattered to her! The medics hurried up and got ready to transport Tom and Teresa out of there. Both were still unconscious and still in very critical condition and they weren't even sure if they would make it back to the ambulance without running into problems. Still no matter what, they had managed to get both of them back from the land of the dead, somehow and beyond all normal or even expected comprehension. There was a small grass trail, found by two firefighters, that an arriving rescue squad was able to get down with their 4WD rescue truck. Once they navigated and got as close as they could to the group of responders, The responders gently carried the two victims to the vehicle, which was maybe only one hundred feet hike. The responders then loaded the two portable stretchers up on that piece to get them both out to the ambulance, which was closer to the road. They also had bagged up the deceased Weasel and they stowed her tiny body on the back of the vehicle. Linda was beside herself and crying uncontrollably at the thought of nearly losing her new found love. Jeremy comforted her, as a friend comforts someone who goes through such a traumatic experience. He consoled her by trying to say appropriate words of encouragement, but also being realistic as well, by saying;

"There, there you brought him back, Linda. We were ready to call it, but you wouldn't give up on him. You are one amazing woman and I know Tom is so lucky to have you in his life." She looked up at Jeremy and with such a serious and direct tone, said to him;

"I am the lucky one, Jeremy, I am the lucky one." she said between wiping her nose and clearing the tears from her eyes. "He is one man this world can't afford to lose or give up on!" After something that powerfully said, the two walked in silence, knowing all too well the gravity of the situation which they had just been through.

They walked back out following the rescue truck out and to the waiting ambulances. Yes they brought both of them back from the land of the dead, but they will probably have a long arduous road to recovery ahead of them, each of them. Teresa and Tom were in no way out of the danger zone yet, and that was a fact that wasn't lost on Linda and even all present who did all they could to revive the two drowned individuals. Still, the stubborn detective had saved the drowned girl beyond all odds, and brought her body back, and the detective, himself, was miraculously found and brought back after being dead for an undisclosed amount of time. The rescuers eventually left the quarry behind them as they headed back out to the gravel road and the now burned down building. Back in the water, the chemical lights had dropped deep down into the opaque and hideous water, but just as they continued to shine their minimal light upon the depths of the murkiness, there were four girl's spirits who watched with renewed interest the events above. Just the fact that the man had come down into their realm and still managed to save the girl, says something about that man's fortitude and resolve. They could still hardly believe as they whispered in hushed tones to one another, that both the girl and the man made it out and are in fact still alive in the physical world. Maybe, just maybe, that means that their spirits will someday be set free also, eventually. They could only hope as they lamented their purgatory, and slowly disappeared back into the unknown depths of the dark frigid water. Only time will tell, Suzie thought to herself.

Chapter Nineteen

After that fateful night, with all the activities going on, and the involvement of the cops, George packed up his remainder of items and took Rebekah with him, and off they went to Pennsylvania. That was way too close for comfort, he thought, as the officers were only a few miles away from him. He didn't burn the compound yet as he had planned, because of all the activity and besides he hadn't properly cleansed the area yet, either. He would wait until the high activity settled down and then he would burn it to the ground. He maintained a few of his outside perimeter cameras, just for that reason, to keep an eye on things going on. He would set the plan in motion, when the time was appropriate and besides even if there was an issue, he had white-washed the entire area, removing all fingerprints and cleaning everything with bleach to sanitize it all and keep it immaculate so that he couldn't be traced. He kept calm, he did what he had to do, and he maintained his composure. He did find out about the accident and Weasel's demise, but he lost no sleep over her. He had used her and she had served him to its extent, so it was all inevitable in the long haul. He did hear about Teresa living though, so he knew he wouldn't have been able to stick around anyway. Funny thing is, he heard about Teresa and the detective still alive after he moved away. He literally applauded the detective for saving the girl's life and being a formidable adversary. He toasted a wine glass for the detective, but he still had last read that both were in a coma for a long period of time, and who knew, maybe they wouldn't come out if it, after all. One never knows about such tricky aspects of the human body, so anything is possible. Without them alive, his secrets would remain intact and hidden, but if the girl lived she could disclose some of his secrets, that was for sure. That was why he would burn the compound soon, very soon, but still not yet. He would wait and see what develops. He loved the thrill of the chase and this little unexpected turn made it even more thrilling. Was he breaking some of his rules, NO. He was just bending them slightly to see what would develop and what he could control, as he did like controlling and managing all aspects of life. Still Rebekah was proving to be a worthy companion as she did exactly what was told of her, because, well, she had witnessed what he does to those who don't deliver or disobey him. He had taken a break from collecting, for now, and concentrated on getting his new compound up and running. The key was efficiency and routine, with those women that he collected. He managed to buy two old refrigerators for his new collection, off one of the well-known internet sales sites, and he wore a disguise to each meeting, plus he used a rental truck. He covered his tracks and he only went to any town when he had to and never to a town again where he 'picked' from. He had learned his lesson from being observed by the stubborn detective, so he chose not to make that mistake again. Live and learn he always said, but he also said a prepared mind is the best defense. So he continued doing what he was doing, to get ready for his first 'new' girl in his new area. This is going to be a lot of fun, he thought again. Still the nagging prospect of losing out on Cheyenne, still haunted him. It was her two dissimilarly colored eyes which drove him to want her and both of her eyes, since she was such a prize. Maybe he would find another gorgeous two eye colored girl near him, one never knew.

        The first week was a whirlwind of activity in the town of Glen Fork,after the ill fated incident. The news spread fast about the heroics of Tom, but both him and Teresa were still intubated and in a coma since their ordeal. When they arrived at the trauma center in a neighboring city via ambulance, Teresa and Tom were found to have a core temperature of 68 and 75 degrees fahrenheit respectively, which is well below the normal of hypothermic activity. Still even with their low temperature, they were not warmed right away, because of fear of brain injury and shock to the system which could cause instant death. They were warmed ever so gradually with slow intervals over a period of a week. Yes they were in a coma, but the doctors also wanted them to remain in coma, so using constant electroencephalography monitoring to make sure both of them remained in a coma state, until they deemed it appropriate to come out of such. They each had at least two bronchoscopies to clean and flush out their lungs of the putrid water that they had taken in when they drowned. Teresa's wounds were slowly healing with high doses of antibiotics, due to the nasty water that she was in, after her near fatal wounds by Weasel. The statuses of both Tom and Teresa were deemed critical the entire first week, as even though they were back from the dead, their status could turn at any moment. It was definitely a tough week, as Linda had to call Karly and let her know of the incident and what her father did to save a girl from the grips of death. Karly was beside herself and she made a trip down, with Dahlia, within a day of hearing the news. There was much crying and lamenting over Tom that day when his daughter, her girlfriend, and Linda were all alone in the room with him. They hugged him more than he could have imagined, but then again he couldn't respond because of his condition. His daughter remained at his bedside for two days with only trips to the bathroom and two times to visit the ailing Teresa as well. She wanted to see the young girl that her dad had saved from imminent death. She remained with Teresa at length during her visit, since she had found out her mother had committed suicide and her father was being treating for psycholoigcal issues, resulting from his wife's death. So she held her hand and remained with her to give her love and support as well. Linda did the same, at times she would visit Teresa as well, and show her support and kindness, by bringing her stuffed animals and little trinkets from her room in her house. Everyone wanted Teresa to live, because of the great lengths that Tom went to find and rescue her, those lengths which almost cost him his life, especially Linda. Karly and Dahlia remained as long as they could, but Karly had to get back for follow up appointments regarding her leg, as she still was sporting the ex-fix apparatus to her leg. She was hoping to get it removed in the coming weeks, if all looked good with the x-rays, that is. Karly hugged Linda over and over again as the news broke of this dedicated woman's heroics on not giving up on her father when everyone else had. Karly was truly touched by Linda's devotion, love, and steadfast tenacity, all of which secured the fact that her father was in a hospital bed, now, instead of a grave.

Those first seventy-two hours, Linda hardly left Tom's bedside, as she wanted to be there in case he woke up. She took a leave of absence from work and remained by her love's side, no matter what. She asked the doctors what the prognosis is for coma patients as she had no clue, and she was told by them that if a person does come around, it is always an unknown time period, meaning that it could be a week, three weeks, six months, or sometimes even never. The state of being in a coma was difficult to navigate and it still was a mysterious threshold, that no one had all the answers to, and also varied so much individually, case per case. It all depended on the body, the spirit, and the will to live for each person, and that was why the results varied so much in all the studies. They could only do so much and then the rest, as some would say, is in God's hands. She didn't relish that thought of him never waking, so she pushed that prospect out of her mind right away and just hoped for the best. She bathed him, fussed over him, and was found holding his hand all the time, even when she was napping with him. She would lay her head on the bed, not daring to let go. The attending nurses would often bring her warm blankets, a pillow and something to drink, whether it be hot coffee or a refreshing drink to help her make it through the day. Jeremy would often stop by and bring food for her from Frank's Deli, to replenish her own stores to keep her strength up as well. The ICU didn't allow many visitors at one time, but Tom had many visitors checking in on him, being his crime fighting fellow brothers, a few of the firefighters, and even Bev, from Bev's Breakfast Nook, stopped by one time, giving Linda a solid and reassuring embrace to keep up the fight for their 'Tommy boy'. It was a touching and unexpected gesture of kindness from that unusual woman. Linda even snuck Tom's cat in one time, not that the cat gave a damn about its owner, but she thought maybe a common feeling of the feline would help him somehow along the way.

Still no one knew anything about what truly happened that fateful night, as both of the people who had witnessed anything were both still in a coma, with an undecided future. No one truly knew why the two girls were even out there where they were, or why the building was burned to the ground. No one knew why there was one dead girl in the morgue and why she tried to kill anyone, or even how she tried to kill. Was it gang related? Was it some type of sick initiation of some sort? Was it more involved than what they knew? What did Tom see when he came back up the next to last time, when he said he couldn't explain what he saw? So many lingering questions and the only two who had any answers were beyond questioning at this point. No one knew any pertinent details, save the two in a resting coma, therefore, everything regarding the investigation was put on hold again, until one or both of them awoke from their ill fated induced slumber. Life went on in the small town for the next few weeks, as the stories spread of Tom's heroics and the mysterious girls that fateful night. They were able to ascertain the unknown girls' (Weasel's) true identity, but not by the usual fingerprints, since her one hand was slightly melted from the burns and the other, well, didn't have visible fingerprints. It was almost as if they were burned with acid, leaving her hand smooth as butter and with no distinct markings. They found out that the girl's true name was Jessica Oshe. She had gone missing some six years prior from Arizona. She had dropped off the map and she had since been considered a cold case now for three years. It was odd and unusual that she would show up here in their community. Had she been with a traveling band of gypsies or did she just hook up with the wrong group or man of ill repute and they were traveling through the area now. Still, the police were on alert and always checking license plates, licenses, and unknown strangers just to be sure. Not to harass them, but to be sure that someone wasn't present right under their noses, that is until the two sleeping victims could arouse from their slumber. It was all very mysterious and something that didn't sit well with any of them, so they had to keep themselves open to any unusual activity, even more so than usual. Still the case remained open until further notice.

The days went by ever so slowly, as Linda waited and hoped that her man would come back from the brink of death. She remained hopeful, but every day that passed and there were no changes, also slightly crushed her hopes that he would come out of this alive and hopefully unscathed, at best. She cried herself to sleep many times over the overwhelmingness of the entire situation, and the fear of losing that which she had newly found in love and holds so dear to her heart. She sat there with her love, wondering what all he had experienced when he was in the water looking for Teresa. She thought about if he was afraid for his own life, if he unexpectedly drowned, or if had sacrificed himself for the girl, which she honestly believed he had. Not that he didn't enjoy, like, and desire to live, but he was that kind of man, selfless and honorable. That was what she believed and that was why she couldn't and wouldn't give up on him, when she was trying to bring him back. He wouldn't give up on finding Teresa, and so it was her duty to not give up on him also. Everyone at the office called her a hero, but the real hero, she knew, lay there in the bed in front of her. That was the honest to God's truth in the matter. He had jumped into the unknown waters to save a girl he didn't even know. He took down a potential killer in the other girl, and when both Jeremy and her asked him to quit, he would not. He took one more dive, which unfortunately cost him dearly, but it also gave a chance to a young girl to live her life out, if she recovered from this. It was strangely odd the differing reports she got, as the report from the one doctor on his case said he showed positive improvement and he may turn around and come out of a coma sooner than expected. Yet on the other end of the spectrum, another doctor said that he was still in critical condition and his future was unknown, meaning not sure if he will ever come out of a coma, and whether the side effects from the trauma would have long term and lingering effects on his health and body. It was frustrating to her, but still she held the hope, held the hope for both of them that he would in fact turn around and come out with minimal side effects. She had asked for physical therapy to work with him as well to keep his muscles from atrophying and to keep his ligaments and tendons from tightening up from non use, which would cause a longer recovery time, for sure. She worked with him as well, as she was there more than anyone else. One new nurse tried to get her to leave, as she was stating the hospital guidelines say that non family members couldn't stay over in the ICU, but obviously that didn't go well for the nurse. Linda kept her cool and didn't explode on her, but she said to the nurse after a curt comment said to her, by saying;

"If you think I am going to leave my man's side just because I don't have a specific piece of paper naming us as spouses or married, you have another thing coming to you, missy. This is my man and I will remain at his side for as long as I damn well please, but thank you for your concern for my well being." She said sarcastically and with a definite hint of resiliency. That nurse was never assigned him as a patient again, per the nurse manager of the floor. She didn't want the nurse reprimanded, she just didn't think the nurse thought out her words before she spoke them to her. It was the way of life, we all live and learn and so she saw the same nurse later that week and she said hello and wished her a good day. She didn't try to hold grudges, as life was too short to worry or dwell on such aspects in life.

The next two weeks following (now three weeks since the unexpected events that befell the town of Glen Fork) were the same for the two in the state of coma, and for Linda as well. She continued to dote over Tom and make sure he was in as good condition as she could help him to be: talking to him, moving his muscles and joints, and even bringing in a masseuse to help his muscles remain loose and prevent more atrophy and tightness of his body. She was willing to do anything and everything it took to do what she could for her man, until that time when he could do for himself. That day couldn't come soon enough for her, and every new day was the day she was hoping he would come around, and back to her, to this world. She was not a religious woman, by far, but in times such as this she prayed for guidance and help to whomever was listening to her calls for help. All she cared about was having him back in her arms again, because her world and the world was a better place with him in it. It was times like these though that she also second guessed herself, saying what if she had jumped in and tried to help him, would they both be in the same state? Would she have given her life for the girl if the tables were switched? She would have hoped she would have said yes, but she wasn't absolutely sure, and that was why he was so special not just to her, but to this existing world. If someone was willing to give their life for someone they hardly knew, then this world needed more people like that in it, if we as a race, the human race, were to survive another thousand years. Times like these made her think about her career choice as well, but she still loved what she did and the help that she was able to give people in their time of need. Also to be out there and stop those who try to hurt the innocent, just like when Tom happened upon those scum trying to rape Cheyenne. If people like Tom weren't around, the act would have happened and the girl would have been traumatized for life, even if the scum would have let her live. So many questions she had running through her head about life, since all she had time to do was think as she sat beside her man, hoping for the next minute that he would wake up.

Linda would sit there in the hospital room and watch the days go by, but she did get to enjoy the fall leaves changing though. She was about to truly enjoy the full spectrum of colors that the leaves did when they turned from green to orange and yellow and then ultimately to the color brown, before dropping to the ground to finish the living cycle of the year. Yes, she saw the color changes every year, but this year since she wasn't working at the time, she truly got to visualize and take in the perfectness of it all as nature went through another one of its normal cycles, like the year before. It was just past the three and a half week mark, that both Teresa and Tom were brought in and still they remained in their coma state, with no idea when or if it would ever turn about. One lazy day where she was extremely tired, and it was raining outside, she decided to go grab a large cup of coffee from the cafeteria in the hospital, so she left her sweetheart's bed for just a few minutes. She walked through the nurses station, waving and saying hello to most of the staff since she knew them nearly all by name, by now. She got into the elevator and went down to the ground floor, to the cafeteria. She stood in line, got her coffee, and a sweet danish since it looked so temptingly delicious and she paid for her treats, then headed back upstairs. She got off the elevator and made the walk across the ICU, as she had done countless times before, and headed toward her honey's room. She saw a nurse she hadn't seen in a few days, so she waved at her with the half eaten danish, and then turned to go into Tom's room. Suddenly she stopped, froze, and even dropped her coffee on the floor as she was looking not just at Tom's resting face, but at his open eyes. She ran into the room, after a slight shriek, and wrapped her arms around her love. She started crying as emotion had overcome her at the sight of seeing a response such as this from her dear man. A few other nurses came running into the room, as they had to avoid the dropped and spilled coffee to see why Linda had shrieked and then they saw that Tom's eyes were open and trying to adjust, as he partially looked around the room. There was not a dry eye in the room, as tears were streaming down Linda's face from excited happiness, and tears were forming in the nurses' eyes from seeing a true miracle take place before them. The doctor was immediately called and within fifteen minutes, she arrived to check on her patient. She checked the pupils and their responsiveness, asked him to nod if he understood, which he slowly did, and then she proceeded to tell him about being intubated and in a coma for the past three weeks. He looked marveled at what she said, but listened nevertheless. She said to him;

"If everything looks okay, we can extubate you later today. But since this is your first positive response of being out of coma, we will wait to see how it goes." He nodded his understanding at the precautions of it all. The doctor turned and smiled at Linda, touching her hand to Linda's shoulder and said to her;

"Such a happy day, such a happy day indeed."Linda smiled and nodded her head in agreement as well. Linda looked back and she saw housekeeping was already working on cleaning up the spilled coffee, which she sheepishly apologized for dropping it, instinctively when she saw Tom. The housekeeper shrugged it off as he too knew about Tom's heroics, and said calmly;

"All in a day's work, ma'am, all in a day's work." He reiterated smiling at her and her happiness at seeing her man back from the state he was in. She didn't ask her man any questions, she just held his hand and was with him as he tried to acclimate himself once more to everything. He had enough to think about, besides she will wait till he is extubated before she starts filling him in some, when he can talk again.

Later that afternoon, the doctor came back around and they did a weaning trial on Tom and he passed successfully, so they were able to extubate him and remove the endotracheal tube from his throat. Once that was out, the first thing he asked for was water. They gave him a few ice chips to start, to make sure he would aspirate on anything, which would cause an immediate nothing by mouth status and a speech consult. Thankfully, he took the ice well and Linda sat him up some as he tried to get his beings about him. His throat was a little raspy, so the doctor told him to take it easy with talking for a day or so and see if it improves with time. He respectfully listened to the doctor's advice and kept trying to chat to minimal. They brought him a board to write with so that he could communicate, but even that was difficult since he hadn't written anything in over three weeks. His writing when he first wrote something looked like a small child's handwriting, but Linda was able to figure out what he was trying to ask her. He had written down one simple sentence and that was: 'What happened?' It was then that Linda started telling him all that had occurred up to the part when he went into the water after the girl. She told him of the fact that he saved her and that Jeremy pulled his body out of the water as well. She also related to him the entire events (of her knowledge) that fateful night. She also told him that Karly and Dahlia had come to stay with him as long as they could, but she was right by his side, just as he had been for her. He smiled weakly at hearing those words of his daughter and her girlfriend. He listened intently but didn't say anything or write anything as he tried to soak it all in. He just listened as his mind tried to place the events into the respective area, but still he had a nudging feeling that that wasn't everything pertaining to the obscure night. Then finally after some consideration he was able to write something down, which was an important question for him to know and that was: "Is the girl alive?" She confirmed that she was but that she was still in a state of coma and they didn't know her definitive prognosis, so he took that fact all in stride as well. He looked off into the void for a few seconds and then turned back around and wrote one more thing, which was: 'I love u!' It was then that she leaned in and kissed his sweet lips, not caring how his breath was or when he brushed his teeth last, because she loved him too. She kissed him once on the cheek as well as she whispered to him, saying;

"I love you too, my darling!" Then she added; "But you need to rest darling, we have a big day scheduled for you tomorrow and we are going to help you get your strength back. He smiled weakly at her, turned his head and closed his eyes and she maintained a loving hold on his hand, as she turned and watched the funny comedy television show that was on at the moment.

The next day was in fact a whirlwind of activity as PT pushed him harder and harder to get his body to remember what it was supposed to do. He lay there exhausted after the first day, but content on how well he did considering what he had been through. In fact, the next few days were the same and they beat his body left and right, but he accepted the good aches and pains and responded each time positively as he was already showing marked improvement. His voice slowly came back as well, and even though it started out raspy and tight, by the end of the few days he was talking in short choppy sentences. The doctors and Linda, both, were happy with his progress and his physical recovery from the traumatic ordeal, and also with the memory side from the transient amnesia as well. Still he wanted to push himself more and he did so by continuing to work when they said he could stop. Because of his tenacity, he was recovering by leaps and bounds, so much that he had to take extra pain meds at night just so he could rest and sleep. It was a means to an end, that was for sure. Shortly he was using a walker to get around and Linda couldn't keep him down, so she went with him everywhere to make sure he was safe on his travels around the circular unit. Still, though, his memories were not coming back as fast as he would have hoped to. He remembered shooting the crazed girl and even seeing the other girl missing, but he couldn't remember anything after jumping into the water, sadly. The doctors still remained with hope that it would all return in due time, but Tom wasn't so sure about that. Still he had his life, he had his daughter, and he had his darling love. That would just have to do for now, which it definitely did to him.

Chapter Twenty

Meanwhile back at the old compound, 'George' had come back into town to finish up what he had started. He stayed away for some time, not wanting to make his presence known, until he had to. He had heard of the heroics of that pesky detective, who questioned his actions so long ago at the Steak and Bake Grill. He knew that man would be a threat and he had proven to be thus by far. He had also read in one of the local papers about the detective saving the girl from death and drowning. He also picked up that there was a crazed girl (Weasel) who had been shot and killed during the incident. He thought, well, she finally got hers and he left it at that. Besides he had an even better and more competent girl with him now. He came back into town to set his infrared trip sensors, meaning that if someone would pass the line, it would set off the charges in the compound and in essence incinerating everything that could be used against him. So he parked a distance away, so as not to be seen by driving in and he hiked it to the old compound. He set the infrared detonators near the gate, up closer to the compound, one near the house and the other from the woodline. He set them so that anyone crossing them would trigger them. It was the best way for him to torch the place and not be here. He was afraid if he did it now, someone would have more of a chance of tracking him. He wanted to make sure that he was in another area and a completely different state, If he wasn't around then the less chance of him being caught. He had done this before and it had worked like a charm, and he was the poster child of a regimented routine. He set a sensor at the gated entrance, halfway down the road to the compound, one by the woods, or the back way into the compound, and one by the house in case someone would come that way too. Once he was done, he stood there admiring his work and his dedication at doing what he set out to do. After he had set all that he needed to and everything to his heart's desire, he bid one last farewell and then he backtracked with his original steps in to make sure that he couldn't be tracked. He also performed his normal circle back also to confuse and railroad any potential followers. Finally, after he made it back to his vehicle he got into the vehicle and left this place, this county, and this state behind. Good riddance, he thought, with mild regret. He had achieved what he wanted to, but his white buffalo had gotten away, meaning Cheyenne. He still regretted not having her in his collection, but it worked out the way it did. Maybe someday, he will cross paths with her again.

Back at the hospital, Tom was getting stronger every single passing day and he was now walking with a walker, just for safety reasons, and he was able to talk and write much clearer too. He had made progress because of the assistance of the doctors, the nurses, the PT staff, and, of course, his dear Linda. Still, his memory remained boggled and incomplete from the time he jumped into the water, including up until he became alert again in the hospital. Still he felt not himself without his memory, and so one day he wanted to see the still asleep Teresa. He asked Linda to go with him and she agreed to it, and she also hoped that it would help jar his memory some, which would be of help to him. He walked down the ICU using his walker with Linda following him with the wheelchair, as they had done so many times before. This time, though, he made a pit stop to a room that he had never visited yet. He walked his aching body to the entrance, and looked in to see the sleeping and calm Teresa. He hobbled in and stood beside her bed as Linda moved the wheelchair in place so that he could sit down safely. He thanked Linda for her help, and she kissed him on the cheek, for good measure. He now surveyed the sleeping-like figure of Teresa, wondering just how she was doing with her recovery, even though he knew she wasn't awake yet, he was still concerned. He looked at her with genuine hopefulness and then took her one hand in his own hand, and he started to speak to her, saying;

"Teresa, dear Teresa, please don't give up. You have so much to live for, child, and so much ahead of you in life. You have people here who love you and want you to return to us. Don't give up yet! You have your entire life to live! Don't give into the light yet, it is not your time And for goodness sake, don't sit down at the table.........."
As soon as he said those words, his memories started pouring back into him like a cascading waterfall, dropping them one at a time back from the deep recesses of his mind. He suddenly remembered being in the water, diving down for Teresa a few times, until that fateful time he landed in that odd musty house. The memories continued to flow in one at a time, about him searching the old room filled house, and

then finding the ladies at the table with Teresa standing beside them. His memories resembled filling a mold with a thick viscous liquid, like with epoxy. As it is first poured into a mold , it is poured by starting slowly and then eventually takes over the entire area, filling it till there are no empty spaces left. He looked up in amazement at Linda, as he was remembering every single detail, and she knew by the look on his face, as she gazed back at him, that his memories were finally coming back to him. She could see it with the expression on his face, even without him saying a single word. He looked back at the resting body of Teresa, but he knew her soul was tormented and she was probably watching them from the ethereal-type plane of existence that he had watched in his body from when they were trying to bring him back to life. She was stuck in that limbo and she needed a reason to commit back to this world. So with that thought in mind, he finished what he was saying to her, by stating;

"Don't listen to those seated ladies, because you have so much to live for! We all are rooting for you and we love you dearly, Teresa! So fight, FIGHT with all your life and fight for your right to live another day! You are not alone!" As oddly as it sounds, but as soon as he said those words, her monitor started alarming loudly and two nurses came running in to check on her status. Linda moved Tom away from the bed, backing the wheelchair up, to let the nurses do their job and work on Teresa. The nurses popped down the bed rail and checked for a pulse, and the girl had one so they didn't start compressions, and then suddenly out of nowhere Teresa's entire body convulsed. One of the doctors(the intensivist) came into the room, just at that moment, and called for 'valium IV stat', and seconds later it was given intravenously, into Teresa's venous access. The convulsions stopped shortly after and her body settled back down into a more relaxed position, with only some mild twitching from her hands from post-ictal activity. The nurses rechecked her vitals and the intensivist remained at the bedside a little longer to make sure she was still ok. He ordered phenobarbitol to be given intravenously to minimize the seizure-like activity, and then he went back on his way to the next problem in the unit. Tom remained in the room the entire time, and it was only after he was about to leave the room, wheeling himself toward the entrance to the room, when one of the nurses gave a startled gasp of surprise. She immediately looked from Teresa, over to the back of the seated Tom (who was at the door), and then to the astonished Linda. Linda stood there awestruck in seeing what she was seeing, just the same as the speechless

269

nurse at the bedside. And then Tom finally turned his wheelchair around to see what the gasping was all about, but instinctively he knew. What he saw he sort of expected to see, which was none other than Teresa with her one eye open and looking directly at him. He winked and smiled at her, but he knew, he truly knew what she had just been through in coming back. She had made her choice, just like she made her choice at the oval table before the ladies. Like the booming voice said to him, ' Always a choice'. She had made it out alive, not unscathed, but alive! She had wanted to survive, and her waking up was proof that she wanted to live.....

"Good for you, Teresa, good for you." He said smiling as he turned again and wheeled himself out of the room, for now.

It was touch and go for Teresa as she slowly made her recovery. She ran into more issues, as even though she was awake, she wasn't responding as well as the doctors had hoped for. They tried a weaning trial the day after she opened her eyes at Tom, but sadly she failed. Therefore she remained intubated for another few days, but each day brought a new weaning trial, and sadly each day was another failure for the young girl. Still she was waking up more and more and so they left her off any type of sedation so that she would be sure to come around soon enough. Eventually they were able to wean her off and eventually she was on her way to a full recovery, to a point. She ended up having some stress induced selective amnesia as well. So her memory was even shorter and the only thing she asked(in writing on the board) about was her parents. There was no answer for her for that one, and at first the question was not answered, until one day she got so upset, she kept hitting her board, until someone would tell her. So not that the staff asked, but Tom volunteered to break the horrific news to her. He went into her room, with Linda at his side, and one of the nurses. When Teresa saw Tom enter, her eyes lit up, like she had known him from a previous life, but she didn;t know from where. He walked into her room and sat down on a chair, where he took her hand in his own. She enjoyed the caring interaction that he was showing her. She wrote something slowly on the board and he looked at what she wrote, and the one question was, 'what happened to my eye?' He looked at her and spoke steadily and coherently, responding with;

"Well dear, we are not exactly sure. You are the only one who would know that, but because of your amnesia, you have yet to fully remember those events. It will all come back to you in due time, so don't fret, child." she nodded her head lazily as he had given her the best answer that he could, at that time. She then pointed back to a question regarding her parents. He sighed once, and then he started to relate the truth, knowing that this might make this worse, but she had a right to know. So he started off saying;

"Well sweetie, after you disappeared and we were looking for you, it was a traumatic event for your parents. Something happened with your father and he made some silly mistakes, and was committed to a psych unit because of his actions. Meanwhile your mother, well when she found out what had happened with your father, she ended her life in a fit of despair. I am sorry, it must have been she thought that she lost you, and then the incident with your father, must have pushed her over the threshold. I am so sorry, Teresa to give you this horrific news." He watched Teresa, and she had gently gripped his hand a little firmer when he had confessed what had happened to her parents, but she didn't let go of his hand. He saw the tears start to well up in her one eye, and she must have been internally sobbing. He stood up and hugged her, and once he broke away from her, Linda also hugged the grieving Teresa as well. It was a hard period of time, but even though she found out the truth, she was still loved by those who continued to be around her. She had loss, felt loss, but she also gained love from others where she would have never expected to receive love from. She would continue to get better, one day at a time, but still her memory waned in its return to her. Tom patiently waited, hoping that it would, but as of now she was the only one that knew why the girls were there in the first place. She was the only living one who knew the answers. They would still have to wait for any further answers in the entire catastrophe.

One mid afternoon day, about four and a half weeks after that fateful traumatic night, Tom walked out of the hospital of his own volition, and with no extra support. He walked out with a nurse pushing a wheelchair behind him, just in case of unexpected weakness, but he hadn't needed it, thankfully. He had been transported to the local hospital in their community where he continued rehab, since he wasn't in that critical condition any more to warrant staying at the trauma center, where he had been for so long. Of course as he walked out, he had his dear Linda by his one side, and his daughter Karly at the other side. Karly was now walking with crutches and she had on an immobilizing knee type brace to help her leg heal a little more without putting undue stress on it yet. It was much better than the heavy ex-fix she had sported previously, and so much easier to take care of as well. Of course right at her side was the lovely and always supportive Dahlia. He walked outside to the cool brisk air, and breathed in nature again, knowing that he finally had his freedom from the trauma of the ordeal. It was an unusually brisk day because of the cold front that had unexpectedly moved into the area. His darling Linda gave him a jacket, covering him up with it to keep him warm, as the coldness made him shiver slightly. He was supported by his loved ones, his immediate family, and he was genuinely happy to be alive. He felt strong, considering the length of the recovery time. He knew he should be going home, but this was not him. He figured he had slept long enough, and so he asked Linda if he would be taken to the scene of the crime. She wasn't sure at first but if they got one of the police SUVs they could make it down the trail that the rescue squad vehicle had made it down. He thanked her for offering that option, and they would meet up with Karly and Dahlia for dinner later in the early evening, all four of them. But first, he wanted to revisit the scene where he and Teresa had nearly perished. It was a type of closure for him as he waited for Linda to pull up in her vehicle, to take him to his destination. His daughter kissed him on the cheek and he smiled and hugged her back. Dahlia did likewise and it felt like he had two daughters in his life now, both loving and kind individuals. They promised to see Linda and him in a few hours and then he got into the vehicle and they drove toward the site of that unusual night.

Linda drove Tom down the road toward the site, and all Tom had was mixed emotions. He just felt like he needed to go back, as he was drawn to the area for some reason, since so much had happened to him at that point in time. They drove down the bumpy gravel road at first and came upon the ash filled remains of what once used to be a building. He wasn't going to get out, but after a while he did, and all on his own he slowly traversed the short distance to the outline of the remains. He found a stick nearby and he used that to prod the well charred remnants, not finding anything worthwhile. He found some old nails, some hinges, some screws, and some miscellaneous metal pieces, but nothing substantial to him. Still, he searched for answers and still he wondered what had occured here that night in that building. Everything that may have been of importance was burned to the ground by the fire. Still he wasn't a fire marshall, but he knew enough about crime scenes that this wasn't just a typical fire. This one had to have some type of accelerant to make this old building become that involved, so quickly. That was the only thing that made sense to him. Oddly enough there was one thing that didn't burn as he kicked something metallic in nature, and that was when he saw another scythe, like the one the crazed girl had tried to use on Teresa. He looked at Linda and she looked up at him and then down to where he pointed. She exclaimed to him;

"No way, what is that?"

"It looks to be the metal curved blade of a scythe, like the one that the crazy girl used on Teresa that night. This is just too coincidental to have two girls and two scythes. Hmmm..... Do you have an evidence bag that we could drop it in, because I wish to compare it with the other one that is probably in the evidence room."

"You betcha, babe. I will be right back." And she went back to the vehicle for a pair of gloves and an evidence plastic bag. Once back, she carefully picked up what was left of the tool and placed it carefully inside the bag, closing it up to secure it. She then took it back and placed it in the back of the SUV. He walked back and got into the vehicle, and he said to her, rather whimsically;

"Mush on girl, mush on." She looked at him with her look of you must be crazy and then she laughed hard at him trying to be silly. She had sorely missed him when he was in the hospital, not that she wasn't by his side, but she missed his slapstick humor, his sweet and warm smile, and his genuine laughter, which she fell in love with since the beginning. Soon she had backed out and found the little used trail that took them down by the quarry. It was a rough trail and extremely bumpy, but finally they made it to the spot that Teresa and he were pulled out. He got out slowly and went to the water's edge, looking into the water with a fondness and sadness as well for what he had experienced. He stood there and then he asked Linda;

"Do you remember when I came up that one time from diving for Teresa, and you asked me what I saw? I believe I said something along the line of, I had no words to describe what I witnessed..."

"Yes my love, what is it that you saw?"

"Well let me tell you, what I had witnessed, experienced, and been through. It may not make sense to most, but just hear me out and try to be open with what you hear, if you would please."

"Of course my love, always.." And so it was then that he started to recant the entirety of the story, the complete dramatic events that occured that odd and enlightening evening. She listened quietly as he retold everything he saw, everything he came across, and everything he even questioned. She listened with a facial expression of both awe and amazement with what he had seen and gone through during that traumatic experience. He hesitated for a few seconds, not sure that he wished to relate what he had to say next, for fear of disillusionment. But then he decided it was best to keep their communication open and he also felt that he could say it without feeling any remorse or envy from her. She truly gets him, he felt. So then he started delving into and related to her about seeing his late wife in the abundant field of flowers. He continued to relate that part of his experience completely. He confessed about his indecision at first and that seeing his late wife was refreshing and also quite unexpected. Yet it was the fact that she was banging on the clear wall of division that separates the ethereal world and the real world. Still he made sure that she understood that it was her tenacity and her unwillingness to give up that made him turn and choose her, because she had been banging so hard on the wall to get his attention. Her eyes teared up at the last confession of what he said and why he did what he had done, in choosing her over his late wife, and choosing to live instead of die, and remain to enjoy life with her. It was not only a testimony to how much he loved life, but it was a direct relation in how much he loved her and wished to be with her. She broke down and fell to the cool ground as she lost her composure as he related the entire story to her. She gazed up at him and he reached down to console her and comfort her in finding out all this information. It was right then and there, that she confessed, to him;

" I honestly thought that I lost you that night. Everyone else had stopped after trying so long to bring you back, but I would not give up on you, dearest Tom. I was selfish and I wanted you back with me! I confessed to you, right then and there, that I wished to grow old with you. Maybe it was only pipe dreams at the time, but the heart wants what the heart wants, and I can attest to the fact that I want you." He looked at her with such deep admiration, and after a minute of staring into her eyes, he also confessed that he actually was standing over his body, at that time in a spirit state. She looked at him with utter confusion in her eyes at first, but while she was actively fighting for his life to bring him back, he related that he had heard everything that she had said. He continued saying to her;

"All these events I cannot explain, nor would I believe them if they hadn't happened to me, but they did and I now remember everything exactly as it had happened that night. So against my lack of any other way to explain what occurred, I acknowledge and accept that I had an ethereal or spiritual occurrence that night, that was for sure. It was both surreal and frightening at the same time. I don't believe it was a dream, but a spiritual awakening or so to speak. That is all I know." He held her close as they looked out over the murky water of the quarry, looking out into the beyond. They had both had their traumatic experiences, one on each end of the spectrum, but either way they had survived, one fighting for the other and both not giving up. He turned to her that moment and said her, plainly and directly;

"Linda, you are one of the most amazing women I have ever known and I dearly love you with all my heart. I am sorry I am technically unprepared for this, but if you would excuse my lack of preparedness, I would like to ask you something of utmost importance." He hesitated briefly and she looked at him quizzically, unsure of what he was up to. "Sweetheart, I would be honored if you would share life's journey with me, and entertain the aspect of growing old together: loving, laughing, and experiencing all that life has to offer. I don't know much, but I know this much, and that is that I desire you in every way, just as you are, and I hope that you would accept my proposal and be my wife." Linda sat there on the cool ground with absolutely nothing to say. She was completely speechless, as she had not expected this, his proposal, at all. She couldn't say anything for at least half a minute, as she was both in awe and surprised at his in-promptu proposal for marriage. She was not disappointed at all, to say the least, and finally after he waited patiently for her to respond, she finally broke the silence and said to him, looking deep in his eyes;

"Darling Tom (as she took her hand and touched it to his face), I am truly honored with your words and your commitment to me. Yes, I will happily marry you and spend the rest of the days of your life annoying the shit out of you!" She said those last words with a brief smirk and then a snide smile. He couldn't hold back and he laughed his hearty and well developed laugh, which made her laugh in response. Then they embraced one another and kissed lovingly, both happy about how the events of the day had unfolded thus far. After some time of hugging and sharing together at the quarry's edge, they stood back up, and Tom looked out over the water one more time. He was thinking suddenly about Suzie and Jade, and where they are right now, other than in the abyss of the murky water. He hated to admit it, but they were going to have to get out there with divers and see if the ladies' bodies were out there in the quarry somewhere. There was no other way to do it, but he had to know where their bodies were. It would cost some money, would take a lot of tedious time, but it was all inevitable, and the only way to truly discern the fate of the missing women. He walked back hand in hand with his love, his wife-to-be, and suddenly it started to flurry, like in a winter wonderland. What a bizarre change in weather, as

275

they don't normally have snow this early, especially in the month of November, in this area. However, for right now he would enjoy the time with his new fiancee and he would have dinner with his daughter and Dahlia. Such a wondrous day, he thought to himself as he felt Linda squeeze his hand in happiness. What a wondrous day to be alive he thought, as he took one last glance back at the still water of the quarry.

Tom and Linda drove back to their house to change clothes as he was looking forward to taking a refreshing hot shower in their home, instead of at the hospital. Karly and Dahlia had already left the house to check some local shops for fun shopping, as Linda had quietly given them some money to spend, to buy anything of their choosing. Tom got into the shower first (per Linda's kind demand) after getting back to the house, and it felt divine. He enjoyed letting the water roll over his recovering body, and a shower at home just feels so much better than anywhere else. Linda in the meantime, cleaned up around the house, and then she took a quick shower as well after her darling man was done. He dried off quickly, as it was a little cool in the house, since they had this cold spell moving in, and dressed in some nice presentable clothes. He had lost a little weight while he had been hospitalized, so he was definitely a little leaner, and he wanted to remain that way. He liked his newer look. He let his hair grow out some, but Linda did help to keep it from getting too scraggly, per his request. Before long, they were both ready to head to the restaurant they were supposed to be meeting up at. They pulled up looking a little astonished that the place was packed already. The two lovebirds walked up to the door, and there they met Karly and Dahlia, who gave a side wink to Linda, which was unobserved by Tom. They opened the door and walked inside to a dimly lit room, then all of a sudden, once they were all inside a few feet, the lights flashed on and all sorts of people jumped out from their hiding spot exclaiming in unison;

"Surprise Tom! Welcome home!" He looked around stupefied and a little embarrassed with all the attention from everyone. But it was all with good intentions as he received warm welcomes and kind hearted gestures from people of the community, attending to show their support, concern, and friendship for him. He felt truly blessed, as he started shaking hands with the well-wishers, friends, and coworkers. There was a banner overhead and streamers adorning the restaurant throughout. He didn;t like being the center of attention, but he accepted it for now. He was talking to some of the locals who came to show him support, when he looked over at Linda, Karly, and Dahlia, they were all giggling and hugging one another. 'Oh no', he thought his secret was out for sure. He smiled as they looked his way and Karly gave him the thumbs-up, but she also pointed at Linda's ring finger, which he quickly mouthed, 'I know, I know!' They laughed at him, pressuring him already, even after he just got out of the hospital. He was able to chat with his buddy Fred, Jeremy, and even Bev stopped in for a quick hug and congratulations for making it out, and looking none the worse. She did say to him that he had to fatten up again, though, which made him laugh. Then she mentioned kindly, in her own gruff mannerisms;

"Don't be getten' too skinny now, Tommy-Boy!" she said, smirking and slapping him gently on the shoulder. She was a tough love type of woman, and he took it all in stride as he always did. He turned to say hello to someone else behind him, and he swore he saw Suzie's face back in the crowd. He stopped and looked harder but then she wasn't there anymore. Odd, he thought but then maybe he just pushed himself too much today. He kept chatting with so many people, even having a light drink, but of course against the doctor's wishes, however it was only a small one. He turned again saying hello and to thank them for coming to another town local, when suddenly back behind the man, he swore he saw Jade Freely's face. Now once could be a coincidence, but seeing two possibly deceased women, was more of an omen than anything, he started to ponder quietly to himself, and wondering what it meant. He cleared his vision and looked back at the same spot, but he didn't see her there, but some other woman. He already knew he had to have the quarry checked, but what if it was more than that, he started to contemplate. What if what he had witnessed, what he had gone through, was only the tip of the iceberg? Before long, he found himself not paying attention to those around him, as he was in his own little world, pondering what to make of it all. He really needed to know what Teresa knew, but her mind was not ready to relinquish that pertinent information yet, and so they had to wait for the time that she was ready to receive her memories again. Still he couldn't wait, as he was seemingly being haunted by those that he had shared a moment in time with, somewhere between the afterlife and a purgatory state, he assumed. He wasn't sure what to call it, but either way he had come in contact with those in another realm, and they seemed to wish to make sure that he didn't forget about them. Why did they choose him, he wondered? What did they want of him? What was he not getting? He thought with renewed concern. Across the room, Linda saw the change in his demeanor and his facial expressions, as if he might have been lost in his thoughts again, as he seemed to not be paying attention to those around him any longer. She wondered if maybe this was just too much for him, so she went over and rescued him from those surrounding him, asking him questions, and trying to engage with him and she took him outside for a brief break from it all. After he made it outside and breathed in the fresh cool air, he came back out of his wandering thoughts. She looked at him and asked him;

"Where were you? Where did you just go? I saw the change in your facial expression, and so that is why I removed you from the mob."

"I am sorry, sweetheart. I was talking to people and having a good time enjoying seeing those I hadn't seen in such a long time, but then over in one of the corners I thought I saw………." He paused, not sure if he wanted to continue.

"You thought you saw what or whom, sweetheart? Please tell me….."

"I thought I saw Suzie and then Jade Freely in the mix of people. I know they weren't there but I saw their faces, like they were right there, in the room. It was weird and disheartening as well. I don't know what else to say, but then I started thinking all about the case, the quarry, and the unfortunate missing women. We are missing something, I feel it, we are missing something big." He told her with a steady tone and a stoic face.

"Well what do you propose then?" She asked him, even though she already knew part of his plan.

"As you know, I think we need to have divers check the quarry, and maybe even use boats and sonar if possible to see if something more is down there. Last but not the least, we can dredge it, if we have to. We need and have to get to the bottom of this, sweetie. It feels like I have been given a second chance in life, and I won't let any of those ladies or Teresa down." He paused again and she spoke up, quietly and with a steadfast tone;

"I understand my love, and I am with you. I am with you through whatever it is you must do or have been led to do. So, I will stand by whatever you think is right."

"Thank you, dear sweetheart. I appreciate it. There is or was something going on here, in this area, and we will and must find out what it is!" She moved close to him, hugged him and kissed his cheek to show her full support of him. He took her hand and kissed it, and they stood outside a little longer, before she got too chilly, enjoying the stars in the sky.

That very next day, after Tom had gotten up, and Linda went into work to see when she could get back on the schedule for rounds and shifts, Tom unexpectedly got a phone call from the hospital. He answered it, and it happened to be one of the nurses that had taken care of Teresa. This was odd he thought, but he answered and listened to what she said;

"Hello, this is Amy, and I have taken care of Teresa off and on for the past few weeks in the ICU. I know she doesn't have any family available to her and I was there when you sort of got her to come back to us, so I wanted to relate something to you. You are the closest person to her as of late, and of course a detective also. Well, I came in early one morning about a week ago, to cover another nurse's shift and I walked in and found Teresa talking in her sleep. It was odd, because her voice was mumbly but it sounded clearer than previously. I was about to wake her, but then thought it best not to. I listened and she kept talking about a girl named Suzie, another girl named…. Weasel or something like that, and also someone called 'matter' or 'the master', sorry but not sure which it was though."

"Holy, shit, really, what did she say about them?" Tom asked excitedly.

"Well she mumbled a lot of it, but it sounded like they were trapped, like they were captives or prisoners somewhere. It was like there were a few of them from what it sounded like. Sorry not sure if this is making any sense to you, or this was all just a dream for her, but it sounded pretty real. That was all I heard and then the intercom went off and she woke up. I didn't know who else to tell, and figured well, you are a detective, so I called you. I hope this helps out some?"

"Thank you so much Amy, so…. so much. This could shed some light on a rather hazy topic. I appreciate it, and if you hear of anything else, you or any other nurses, let me know. I'll look into it, " He told her with a determined voice. Seriously, there has to be something to all this. There is no way all of this is coincidence. He looked outside and saw it was an oddly cold day and once again there was snow falling. He started going over everything, including Suzie and Jade sightings that he had, them being trapped in limbo in the water, and now something about a possible master. He had to go check out the quarry again, or around the quarry. That place had been closed for longer than he knew, and it was gated and locked, supposedly to keep people out. Over the years there had been some drownings out there, but the fact that there are four known missing ladies and their spirits existing around the quarry could not be by coincidence. It seemed too exact to be that, so the only other reasoning is that it was by design. He texted Linda to see if she could ascertain a warrant to investigate the quarry, because he wasn't sure if they had any guards there or someone looking after it. He didn't want to go in there guns ablazing and then be caught with his pants down, because they didn't have a warrant or legal right to be on the property. Which would normally not be a big deal, but if it is a crime scene, it does truly matter. If they didn't do it by the book, then a criminal could easily be set free by a sleazy lawyer, and he wasn't about to let that happen. Linda had been on her way back, but she texted him saying that, 'I am on it!' The snow started falling heavily, suddenly, and what was just a mild inclement weather cycle coming through the area, was now turning out to be a full fledged blizzard. He started hearing reports of accidents and issues within an hour of the heavy snow falling, on his police radio. He received another text from Linda, this one stating that, 'the judge was not available today, but they would be able to have it tomorrow, when he gets back in town.' He didn't like it, but he figured tomorrow was better than never. Linda then called him to tell him something, and she said to him;

"Hey babe, I am sorry but the other officers are running like chickens with their heads cut off. The station is getting calls left and right, so I am going to hang around and help out for a while. I'll let you know when I am on my way home. I'll check in with Karly and Dahlia to make sure they are okay. Love you and talk to you soon."

"Okay sweetie, I understand. Thank you for checking on the girls and for letting me know. I'll see ya later, then. Be safe out there." After hanging up with Linda, he decided he wanted to go see Teresa at the hospital, so he got dressed and left the house.

The drive would normally be short to the hospital as they had also moved Teresa from the larger trauma center to their smaller local hospital, since she was doing so well, but with this odd adverse weather it was slow and tedious, by far. Eventually he made it there, and checked in with the front desk to see what room she was in. He walked up to the room, after getting some flowers and a stuffed animal bear for her from the gift shop, to surprise her. After finding the room, he knocked on the door of her room, and he found her looking out the window with the television on for background noise. She turned immediately and she smiled a huge and happy smile towards him. He then walked into the room, gave her a fatherly hug and she reciprocated the embrace, and then he placed the flowers and bear down on her bedside table. He looked at her, brushed her hair back with his one hand, and said to her;

"My, my, Teresa, you are looking great. Happy to see you smile and also looking so healthy." She bashfully smiled and dipped her head at his pleasant compliment. Then she responded with;

"Well, detective…. I am happy to see… you around…. so well…. also" She said with a raspy voice, which was most likely still from the trauma she had endured, he thought. He knew she was technically deceased much longer than him, so he imagined her recovery would be twice as long.

"Please dear Teresa, we have been through too much together, just call me Tom, please."

"Okay, Tom…thank you …for visiting….. me cuz, you know…. it gets…..lonely…here by…..myself…"

"It is my pleasure and I enjoy checking up on you. You feel like my daughter, and what we had both been through, binds us in so many ways. But let me ask you, are you haunted by your dreams, as I am? Or should I say haunted by the experiences, not truly dreams as some would call them." She shook her head as if not wanting to go there, and then she looked out the window at the falling snow. He patiently waited for her to turn back, for her to be ready…., but then he continued, hesitantly, with;

"Only you know the truth, Teresa. Only you know what you had to endure in your time as a captive prisoner….." She looked up at him immediately, as if to say, 'how do you know about that?' "Listen you are the only one that can break this horrid cycle, this torturous hell that you and the other girls had to put up with for so long. I know these are not easy questions to ask of you, but I really need you to think and remember what you know and can bring back to light. It is that important, and I wouldn't ask you if I didn't honestly have to, but we have nothing else to go on. So in other words, if you can't help us. all those women would have died in vain, and with no way to get out from their captive purgatory." Those last words cut deep as Teresa slowly lowered her head and started slowly weeping. She knew the truth, even though she didn't want to admit it to herself. She also knew that she would have to entertain going back into the dark recesses of her mind, to find those repressed memories sooner or later, but here she was being asked to do it sooner than later. She wept for a few minutes, and Tom watched and waited, patiently sitting with her, holding her hand, because he couldn't imagine fathoming all that she had been through. She lifted her free hand and felt up at her missing eye, as now there was a nice custom eye patch there that the staff had arranged for her. Eventually, she stopped her weeping and sat there with a firm resolve on her face. Tom grabbed a tissue and wiped the tears from her intact eye, and she thanked him for that with a slight nod. She then suddenly asked him;

"Why are you so good to me? What did I do to deserve this treatment?" He looked at her mildly stupefied that she would even ask this, but she was questioning her worth amongst the severity of events that had happened to her. She was reaching for a reason, a reason to go on in life and he had to give it to her, that much he knew. He looked at her, moved his hand to her downcast face, and cupped her cheek to bring it to bear so he could truly look at her, without her looking away from him. He then said plainly and with a compassionate and caring voice;

"Teresa, YOU are worthy, YOU are amazing, YOU are loved, and YOU are worth every effort to save. If I had to repeat that night over again no matter what the outcome, I would do it all over again to help save you. Please don't second guess your worthiness, sweetie, just because of what has happened to you. You are not the sum of the events that were done to you and you have gone through. You are so much more than that! You are alive because of the fight in you and you are here because you desire to live another day. I am and will always be here for you, no matter what, come hell or high water!" She wept uncontrollably now as she leaned over and embraced him like a daughter embraces a father, burying her face in his chest for comfort. She didn't let go of him and neither did he of her, until she was ready to break away. No matter what she had been through, he is and would be there for her, is the one main statement out of all of that that she heard. She so wished that Tom was her dad, now more than ever as she finally pulled away from him, and he again wiped away her tears with a tissue. She laid back casually into her bed, relaxing into the pillows and he saw that she may be ready to bring the events back up. So he reached into his pocket for the small portable recorder that he carried with him so that he can do his follow up paperwork easier, and replay the tape to better remember certain aspects of what he needed to put in each report. Yes he may be old school, but his reports were thorough, that was for sure. He looked at her and when she was ready, she nodded at him. He pressed the record button on the recorder, ready for her to expel her deepest and dark secrets from inner recesses of her suppressed mind. She started off with how her day went, that fateful day that she was supposed to meet 'Todd' with his supposed daughter. The dissertation went on, long into the afternoon and into the evening with her not wishing to stop. She only had to take a few breaks to go to the restroom, and he also went and got her something to drink as well as himself something, from the cafeteria, before they closed for the night. When he was in the cafeteria, he texted Linda and informed her of where he was and what he was learning about the entire ordeal, from a victim's standpoint. She couldn't believe that he was getting what he was from her, but she was also happy as it was probably a relief as well to her, to get it out there in the open, finally. He told her he would let her know when he left and he had to get back. She understood and she would wait up for him. When he made it back to the room, she had a smile on her face and she was eating a solid dinner. Her spirit just seemed to be lifted now that she was getting all of this off her chest and expunging all of the convoluted memories. She kept relating the story as she remembered it, including all the aspects about Weasel, the crazed girl that tried to kill her. He at least had a name for the maniacal woman who wouldn't stop even with his explicit warning to her before he had to kill her. She continued until she recited everything she knew of, could think of, and could remember at this time. He stopped the recording, as there was barely any tape left to record any more. He then stood up and hugged her, as it looked as if she needed it, after the long confession session of events. She looked at peace and there was obvious relief on her facial expressions also. Her body language also indicated such, as she was laying more relaxed and she even had a smile on her face more so than earlier in the day. .She also didn't look as lost and she didn't seem as tightly wound, anymore. Still, she had the inner demons to deal with, and that may take up to a lifetime to come to terms with, but she was able to rid herself of any anger and abolish any regret that she had in divulging what she knew. He remained a little longer by her side, and then around 8:30 in the evening, he confessed that he had to leave and so he told her goodnight and hugged her one more time, before bidding her farewell for the evening. However, before he left, she confessed to him, saying;

"Thank you for your love and concern, and of course your wife's also. Sometimes, I feel like an orphan since my devastating family issues. However, with people such as you in my life, it is not quite as daunting. Thank you for accepting me and loving me like a daughter. It takes a special person to give out so much love to one, such as me….."

"Please don't say such harsh things, you know how I, we, feel about you. I would be honored to call you my daughter, and I already feel like you are my step daughter, if you don't mind me saying that.." She smiled at him with such a happy and content smile. After those delightful words, she finished up with;

"Thank you and I would love to call you step dad also, if it doesn't bother you, regardless of if it's true or not. Thank you for who you are, Tom. I love you and Linda! Thank you so much!"

"Goodnight sweet Teresa, and I will see you very soon." He said as he left the room to head home for the night.

Chapter Twenty-One

The next few days were a blur of activity as they got their resources together, got the warrant from the judge, and then implemented a plan to check out the area. They were able to ascertain by Teresa's testimony that she had been confined to the barn, thanks to the times that Weasel took her outside. They were able to figure out where the girls were kept, without going in blindly. The weather hadn't cooperated sadly, as it had snowed off and on for the last two days and the temps were dipping down into the thirties during the day and an unexpected low twenties/high teens at night. Finally they were ready to head out one fateful early morning to raid the area and see what truly they were dealing with, and also hoping to capture the mastermind behind it all as well, would be a definite plus. All the officers were involved, the fire crews were ready, and the ambulances were lined up also. They were able to attain some assistance from their neighboring town's police force as well as their own Sheriff's department. They left before sunrise and under the cover of the hazy mountain morning. No one really knew how big this would be so they planned for the worst and dearly hoped for the best. They started the drive, lining up in order of arrival and importance. The officers were decked out in full gear, ready for the worst, with their assault weapons ready to respond on a dime's drop. As they drove down the road, bystanders probably thought there was some kind of parade going on, but sadly they were not enjoying this moment, no way at all in regards to their mission. They drove down the road and arrived parallel to the property, but down the road a little ways, they stopped to make sure they were all ready and to have a few officers look at the map and head out into the woods, hitting it from another angle as well. This part of the woods wasn't as overgrown as the other side that Tom and Linda had navigated that night over a month ago, now. Tom didn't want to be the one that entered from the front gate, so he threw on a vest and geared up a little and went with the group of three officers who were going to observe from the woods first. The ones who traversed the woods were officers Gus Lapard, Linda, Tom, and sheriff's deputy Tom Moors. Jeremy would enter from the front gate and lead that charge at the entrance. Once inside and secured they would have fire and ambulance come in as they expected to find casualties. The three officers and Tom started to slowly traverse the woods and make their way closer to the buildings that were supposed to be there. They didn't know the condition of the buildings, but there was supposed to be a house and an old barn, as the only structures on this side of the quarry. The four slowly worked their way through the snow covered ground and brisk morning as the sun had not made its way into through the clouds quite yet. They moved stealthily as they could, keeping themselves undercover as much as possible. They found their way easy enough using the map and a few checks with their binoculars, but using the spy glasses weren't easy, because of the morning haze, yet. So they mostly used their map and eventually they were still hidden behind the trees and ready to move in on a moment's notice. They radioed back that they were all set, and the main raiding party was just finishing up readying everyone. They gave a five minute start time, after syncing their watches and so they would come through the front gate then.

Tom knelt there in the snow, not liking how chilly it was this early morning. They even had gloves on to combat the cold and keep their hands warm enough so that they wouldn't have cold and stiff trigger fingers. He looked over at deputy Moors, who appeared to be locked, stocked and ready to go. He looked over at his darling sweetheart, as she was looking nice all decked out in her gear too, but she was all business as she watched the buildings in front of her. Then he glanced over at Gus and he was the furthest away from him, but he could see that he was ready to roll as well, as he looked down at his watch again to check the time. Then out of the corner of his eye, he saw something odd. In amongst the blanket of white snow, this object stood out and definitely was something placed there, by someone. It was far enough away from him that he had trouble discerning what it was, so suddenly he moved forward in a movement that got him within five feet of the object. The other officers watched him, wondering what he was doing as they were concerned he may make them be observed from inside the house or barn. Still he didn't cross the object, but he did get a much better look at it now, and he saw it for what it was, which was a trip sensor with an infrared line that if someone crossed, would cause a response of some sort. He looked down at his watch and it was thirty seconds past the breech time of the front gate. He already heard the vehicles and then they heard the gate drop as they were able to take it off its hinges, so now they must be heading down the road toward the structures. He got on the radio, yelling frantically;

"Abort! Abort! Mission Abort!" He yelled across the horn with all intensity. Still the other officers around him hadn't seen what he had, until he looked back and motioned for them to get down. He and the other officers flattened themselves for an unknown response, and it was about that time that the first vehicle entering tripped the first infrared sensor and suddenly all hell broke loose.

There were a number of loud explosions and part of the house went up in an explosion, and so did the barn as set charges went off as they were supposed to, obviously. Once the initial explosions went off, he got back on the radio calling for the fire department 'to move their asses up there, now', to save any evidence that could be engulfed now in flames. Then all four of them stood up and started running toward the barn first and foremost since it was the closest structure and the one that Teresa said she came out of. The barn was engulfed in flames, but that didn't matter to Tom as he ran to the first entrance to see if there was anything that he could save or rescue, with his weapon at the ready. The door was locked, but Gus found an old ax along the outside of the barn, and so he chopped at the door, and after three hits it splintered and they were able to get inside. Once inside he saw a long corridor that had already started to lick flames along the walls of it. He saw some refrigerators lining the wall, two intact and two blown open from blasts, and some large plastic barrels along the same side of the corridor, but a little further down. He pointed up ahead to some doors on the right, then another door on the left, and then one at the far end of the corridor. They all hurried along the corridor checking each room quickly before this place was completely engulfed in flames. Linda checked one side room, which was a small room, and not that she knew but it happened to be Weasel's old room. There were all kinds of knickknacks, bedding and tidbits but no people in here, so she closed the door and moved on. Gus and deputy Moors went for the room on the right, and as soon as they got to that room, Gus grabbed the doorknob and even through his gloves it felt hot, so he did not open that door for fear of backdraft and causing another explosion. He shook his head 'no' at Tom not to enter that one and so they ran down the hall and towards the main cell area. Linda by that time had checked the other door on the right, and she also felt intense heat when touching the doorknob of that room also, so she balked and didn't go in that one either. They heard voices behind them as others were arriving and then the fire trucks' sirens as they were present trying to unload their gear to extinguish the fires. Tom shouldered the door at the end of the corridor, not giving a shit about explosions at this point and he burst easily into the main compound area that houses cages to hold people. He asked someone to take a few quick pictures, in case it goes up in flames and Linda did so instinctively as the other three checked the entire room for anyone living. Sadly and to their great dismay they found no bodies or anyone living in the cages. This was definitely disheartening to all of them as they truly hoped to find at least one girl. Still they kept searching the entire area, finding another side room, which again had another cage, but it was full of smoke so they did not dare enter it at the time. Still they searched all they could until they were all choking on smoke and gasping for air in that main room. They had to leave for fear of toxic smoke inhalation and the fact that the flames were decidedly licking the walls , engulfing this area completely in fire.

In the meantime, the fire crew was working on the outside trying to douse and extinguish the flames to prevent the buildings (both the barn and the house) from burning entirely down. Their main focus was the barn and they had to call for an additional tanker for more water. At the same time some of the other officers checked outside for anything of suspicion, and even parts of the partially intact house that they could enter or see into. However, inside the barn, it was on the way back that Tom stopped because he noticed that one of the blown up refrigerators was leaking some type of liquid mixture down onto the floor. There was also some shattered glass on the floor from glass containers falling out the fridge as well. It was a clear liquid intermingled with an odd looking more viscous fluid , and so he bent down to check it out, but being careful because of the shards of glass all over the place, and put his glove into the liquid to scoop some of the unknown liquid up. He looked at it and was about to even put it up to his nose to smell it, to distinguish what exactly it was. That was when one of the cartons inside suddenly dropped out and it opened up revealing its contents. To his great surprise and disbelief, what was in the heavy duty plastic egg storage carton was none other than two sets of detached or should he say intact eyeballs and their optic stem inside a clear fluid in plastic bags. He nearly retched as he had put his glove in the melting eyeball residue to see what it was. Linda had come up behind him and saw exactly what he was doing and what he saw, and immediately she retched and vomited a little off to the side. Tom looked up at Gus, who also had come into view and he was white as a ghost. Tom told more than asked, but he said;

"Gus, you and Linda get out of here, NOW!" They both nodded their heads in acknowledgment and then they started walking down the hall again, toward the exit. There was an explosion from behind them which knocked both of them off their feet as they were walking out. They looked back and saw the Deputy Moors was safe as he had just left the main room when it exploded, maybe from a late charge that didn't blow up previously. Tom grabbed the fridge door and remained kneeling. Unfortunately with that explosion, a few of the barrels tipped over, right near Deputy Moors. The lids fell off and fluid came pouring out of the plastic barrels, covering the floor. Still it wasn't the liquid that was the frightening part, but it was in fact the partially decomposed body that fell out of the barrel along with the liquid. Deputy Moors retched at the gruesome sight, then recovered, and started running for the front door, as now the stench and an overpowering odor, like a gas being emitted, overtook the far end of the corridor. He grabbed Tom, who quickly grabbed the only intact plastic container with the hideous contents for evidence, but leaving behind some sealed glass containers and other questionable items still inside the fridge. They ran as fast as they could for the entrance, right behind the fleeing Linda and Gus. They made it out just as the rancid smell of the decomposing bodies, fluid which was most likely acid, and the smoke from the fire overtook them. They were all coughing, gagging, and vomiting to their own degree of sickness from what they saw, what they smelled, and what they just witnessed. Tom's legs nearly gave out and he felt the weight of the world on his shoulders looking down at the snow covered ground. He had instinctively dropped the plastic container on the ground behind him, ripped off his gloves as they were tainted with eyeball fluid, and tossed them to the side. He stood there looking at his weathered, and tired hands, when suddenly he dropped to his knees. He retched and heaved part of this morning's breakfast sandwich that Linda had made for him just a few hours ago. He could see the definitive pieces of bacon and eggs that he had devoured with gusto earlier. He knelt there and retched until he could vomit no longer. EMT's came running over to make sure they were all okay but this was nothing they could fix. This was just an instinctive reaction of what they had seen and come across inside the building, and not just a reaction from what they had eaten previously. Questions were running rampant through his mind, as he knelt there, and he was just saddened that he hadn't been able to stop this before it had all happened. He felt a complete failure from his actions at this end of the spectrum. Yes he had saved Teresa, but how many countless others were there, he questioned without a definitive answer, because he honestly had no idea.

One of the young officers from the neighboring town picked up the plastic egg storage containers that Tom had dropped on his way out of the building, and this officer unfortunately made the mistake of looking inside. The grisly contents caused him to retch and vomit as well, nearly dropping the container from what he had unfortunately and just unexpectedly witnessed. There was nothing that could protect oneself from seeing something as sickening as human eyeballs in a bag of fluid, in a storage carton. Tom looked around as he heard the young recruit, but he had nothing to give him to help him through this awful experience and so he left him to deal with it on his own. Tom remained kneeling as his hands and knees and started getting colder by the minute, and so with reservation he stood up and walked toward one of the police vehicles. He sat down right on the hood of the car not caring if he marked it or not. He was beyond worrying about such meaningless aspects as that. He just had to support his wobbly legs, as he had to remember he was still somewhat recovering yet, and then hiking through the woods, then finding what they found, he knew he had pushed himself too much. So he rested there on the still warm hood of the vehicle. There was an awful stench that was coming from the felled barrels that was coming out of the building. It was horrific as it just stunk to high heaven, when the fluid intermixed with the flames. The only ones who were not having issues with the smell were the firefighters trying to extinguish the fire because of the gear that they were wearing, the self contained breathing apparatus(SCBA). Some of the EMT's nearby and nearly all the other officers were dry heaving or retching too, unless they had placed something over the face to cover the smell. They had to get further away from this building, he thought to himself as he remained resting on the car hood, taking his little break. He glanced around looking for his beloved Linda, and then he saw Linda coming toward him, pale faced and with the look of about to implode. He quickly told to her plainly bur with an empathetic voice;

"Linda....... Breathe, dear, please take a breath!" Instantly she looked at him and then she realized that she had, in fact, been holding her breath for way too long. Finally she inhaled some air, and miraculously was able to breathe, but not until after she was left gasping for a period of time. Her color eventually came back to her face as well, thankfully, and he knew that he just needed to distract her to get the horrific images out of her mind. He kindly asked her to contact the coroner's office, because it looked like he was going to be a busy man today, sadly. First, she stopped and got into her pack and pulled out her lucky cigarette container. She tapped the back of the container and one cigarette dropped out, but she had also taken her gloves off and her trembling fingers didn't grab it in time, and so it fell harmlessly to the ground. Again she tried with her visibly trembling hands, as she tapped another one out but, thankfully enough, this one she was able to maintain her hold on, so she put the cig up to her lips and then tried to light it. She was unable to get the lighter to work with her cold and shaking hands, so Tom, seeing her distress, removed himself from the warm hood and he walked over to help her out. He took the lighter from her, and held it close to her, as she leaned in taking a puff or two as the flame hit the parchment paper, lighting the cigarette up for her. She smoked a few puffs of her cig with fervent vigor as she tried to wipe the images of what she saw out of her mind. She then slowed down and enjoyed the taste of the smoke, smiled at him, and nodded her head in thanking him for helping her. He kissed her on the forehead once and then asked if he could have one. He hadn't touched a cigarette in some time, but at this point, Tom desperately needed and wanted one. She dropped one out of her pack and then he lit his own cig up, lighting it and enjoying a long drag from an old nearly forgotten friend. It was a sinful pleasure, but considering all he had been through, he thought at least he deserved one for old time's sake. He looked at his darling Linda, trying a weak and reassuring smile, but saying to her, quietly;

"Linda, I am so sorry this...... all happened....well.....the way it did, but I promise you we will get through this and hopefully catch this menace to society!" She nodded her head solemnly, trying to believe in the words that he had just said to her. Still even though he was trying to be positive and supportive, nothing he could do, nor anyone could do or say would make this day any less bleak. Tom continued to puff on his cigarette, now standing alone, after Linda went to sit down in the one running vehicle to try to get warm, but not till after a reassuring hug from him. It was just then that Tom noticed that the sun was out and beating warm sun down on them. Again questions of all directions clouded and clogged his active mind, wondering how all this could happen in their town. These heinous deeds were done and he couldn't turn back time to fix or stop them. All he knew was that people had died, grotesque crimes had been committed, and innocence was not just only lost, but had been completely obliterated! Still they only had limited answers and nothing that could truly lead them to who had actually committed these crimes. This type of incident, they might have to have grief counselors, and that was something he would have to talk to their captain about that aspect since he knew there would be some lingering effects with this ordeal. Any normal person would experience grief, disbelief, and sympathy toward not only the victims but the victim's families as well. Well that is if and when they obtain recognition from what remains they have between the containers in the fridges and the barrels. So many possible victims, so much carnage, and also so much blatant disregard for life! Those dreadful images would not leave his mind and instinctively he wiped his hand, that he had touched the eyeball goo with, when he had his glove on. There was nothing on his hand, but it still felt like his hand had someone's eye contents on it, instinctively. This place just elicited a pure and egregious evil about it, not that he was religious, but it just felt so dreadful in so many ways.

       Some time later, he had calmly and patiently watched as the fire crew finally managed to get the fire under control, but still there seemed to be gasses emitting from inside the building. The fire Chief brought up the possibility of hydrofluoric acid being inside the barrels after he had heard that there were decomposing bodies in them. That fire chief had worked in big cities and many industrial fires so he had a nose for such chemicals and their released by-products. As they remained a good distance away, the fire chief and Tom went back and forth about the need to enter the barn to collect evidence. The conversation went back and forth for a little, until the chief conceded that only he may enter, but only if he had some of his own men go with him. As Tom reluctantly agreed to that fire chief's stipulation, he dropped the nub of his cigarette in the snow and aquashed it making sure it was out, before he got ready to go inside. Linda came walking back over to him and they hugged as they watched the fire crew check to see if the structure was even safe enough to investigate, for at least the persistent Tom, for now. He placed his cold hands in Linda's jacket pockets to try to keep them warm until he was able to grab another pair of gloves. Besides his hands, Linda's own hands were in there as well, and they both tried to keep their hands comfy, holding one another's hands in the meantime. It was then he started to brainstorm about what they might need to wrap this investigation up. This was going to be a long day indeed, the more he thought about what they would need to safely and correctly investigate these buildings and the entire area. They would most likely need some tents/ shelters, heaters, extra lights, and definitely some food and drink for everyone who would be here helping. They would have to make sure that all the major fires were out and that only small hot spots were all that remained. The problem was that if the building was deemed completely unsafe, then they would have to wait, which would be torture, for the officers, in so many ways. No one wishes to tell an officer of the law that he cannot do his job, but that may be the case, if the structure is found to be too dangerous. What a quandary of a dilemma this would put them in. This could easily be a logistical nightmare, but he and his fellow officers would somehow make it happen and work, however long it took. Then his mind wandered back to all the cases he had witnessed in his lifetime, and this has to be one of the worst case scenarios, he surmised, as he looked inside one of the vehicles to get another pair of gloves to keep his cold hands warm. The sun was doing minimal damage to the cold feeling in the air, and now that the fire was out and everything was saturated in water, it got even colder.

After a few more minutes, he got a quick go-ahead by the fire chief to enter, but he knew it was entirely at his own risk. He knew that sometimes things have to be done, regardless of risks (just like saving Teresa, he thought). So, he grabbed some extra firefighter turnout gear, a breathing apparatus, evidence collection bags, and a small bag of tools from one of the firefighters nearby, and he started to put on the heavy gear. He had to have some firemen help him put it on correctly, then immediately before he donned his mask, he leaned over and kissed his sweetheart, Linda, one more time. Just at that moment, he got the go-ahead to enter the barn but he would be accompanied by two other firefighters, for safety and liability reasons. The last thought that entered his mind, just as he headed toward the entrance was; 'We have to get this criminal, and peg him to a wall for the atrocities that he has committed. We have to get him!' Then the three of them walked up to the entrance of the barn, hesitated briefly, and then headed inside the smoldering building, to start collecting any evidence he could find.

The End, for now......